Banana Shout

A Novel of Negril Jamaica WI

by
Mark Conklin

Fusion Press
A publishing service of Authorlink

Published by Fusion Press
A publishing service of Authorlink
(http://www.authorlink.com)
3720 Millswood Dr.
Irving, Texas 75062, USA

First published by Fusion Press
A publishing service of Authorlink
First Printing, February, 2000

Printed in the United States of America

ISBN 1 928704 73 5

Dedication

With all my love to Ilene, Eri, and Evan.

Special Thanks

To Debra Hill whose encouragement
and support motivated me.

To my editors Denise Wedderburn and Elena Oumano
for their kind words and helpful suggestions.

To Robert Graves and Roy Rodden of Negril.com
for their faith in me.

To my computer guru, Linus Aruliah,
for his wisdom, patience and compassionate guidance
in opening the door of cyberspace for me.

And to Jamaica and her wonderful people
who have enriched my life beyond my dreams;
they are my real inspiration.

Author's Notes

This is a work of fiction. All the names, characters, organizations, and events portrayed in this book are either the product of the author's imagination or are used fictitiously for verisimilitude. Any other resemblance to any organization, event, or actual person, living or dead, is unintended and entirely coincidental.

Foreword

The time frame for this story roughly spans 1969 to 1973. While the Vietnam War raged in Southeast Asia; back home in the US, it was being fought in the streets and on college campuses.

Although not involved in any way in this conflict, Jamaica was enduring its own troubles—the growing pains associated with its recent liberation from hundreds of years of colonial rule.

This fictional story brings together those parallel moments in modern history, as related to me from the viewpoint of an American draft evader, Tavo Gripps. All characters, other than historical figures, as well as dialogue and action are fictional. However, most of the places in this story do exist, as anyone who has been to Negril, Jamaica, can testify.

1

"Ooo-wee, oo-wee, ooo-wee baby,
Won't you let me take you
on a sea cruise?"

Frankie Ford
From the song
Won't You Let Me Take You
On A Sea Cruise?

Tavo Gripps woke in the morning with a rock-splitting headache, but that wasn't the worst of it. He was on a roller-coaster ride, his stomach rising up into his esophagus. The nightmare didn't stop there. Overpowering diesel fumes flooded his olfactory nerves, along with the nauseating stench of rotting meat.

He forced open his crusted eyelids and was disgusted by the sight of two huge flat feet planted soundly on his chest. Their jam-laden toes brushing his nose. He peered around cautiously and saw that he was lying on a short cot in a room the size of a broom closet. As the room came into focus, he realized the filthy feet belonged to Striker, who was squashed up beside him, head to toe, snoring like an old out of tune Evinrude out board motor. The ceiling was no more than a foot above his head, and was papered with some type of maps Tavo had never seen before, diagramming what looked like numerous islands in a field of blue green.

Before he had time to ponder this bazaar cage, his stomach began to churn like a blender. He shoved Strikers feet off his chest and stumbled for a small door behind the bunk. Reaching out touching both sides of the cage to steady himself against the rolling floor, and knocking his head on the doorsill he plunged into blinding sunlight and heaved his guts out, not onto dirt or the side walk, or grass or the road, which should have been there. Oh, no. He retched into a blue, white-capped ocean that stretched endlessly in all directions, as he hung with all his might onto a rail to keep his balance and stop him from falling overboard. His upchucking had woken Striker, who gazed with glassy bloodshot eyes at his agony from the cabin door. Looking as innocent as a deformed cherub, he said, "Mornin' matey, rough night last night?"

Tavo craved explanations, but his brain couldn't synchronize his mouth to verbalize. All he managed to say was "Where am I?"

Striker ambled up onto the rocking deck like it was his back yard, opened a long necked Budweiser with his teeth, spit the cap out, and drained the amber liquid down his gullet in one gulp and tossed the empty into the choppy sea. He belched loudly speaking through his burp, "Care for an eye opener, matey? Hair o the Dog?" He thrust a Bud into Tavo's heaving chest. Tavo pushed the beer away with one hand while gripping the rail with the other, swaying back and forth attempting to keep his balance. It looked like he was doing an out of step dance, not his usual good footing. He tried to talk, but almost passed out, falling onto the deck and slamming his head against some type of rusty pulley. Striker picked him up and carried him back below deck and laid him on the bunk. Then he slowly related the night before events to a green Tavo.

The two of them had spent all night in Sloppy Joe's Bar. Striker ordered more and more tequila until closing time. By then, Tavo was too drunk to stand, had passed out cold. While Striker knew the owner of the bar, he confessed, it was only because he'd been thrown out of there numerous times for drunk and disorderly behavior. He'd told the waitress that Tavo was "shouting" for the booze, and when he discovered that Tavo only had a couple of bucks in his pocket, he thought he'd better make a hasty retreat. So he threw Tavo and his backpack over his shoulders like a dead Mackerel, and made a dash for his boat, anchored with all the rest at the end of Duvall Street. He tossed Tavo below, fired up the engine, then navigated past reefs and small keys until they reached open ocean. Then he put the boat on automatic pilot, climbed below and joined him for a few winks.

"Blimey, matey," Striker shouted looking real compassionate. "Ain't one o' them blokes deserts a friend in distress! He cupped Tavo's woozy head in his hand forced him to look him in the eyes and said, "Anyways, you was mumblin all night bout that little hippie gal and leavin the country, so's I reckoned you must be down on your luck… maybe runnin from the law...what!"

Tavo sat up, pushed Strikers hands away, and held his throbbing head in his own hands, he dry heaved. "You'll soon feels better matey," Striker assured. "We're headed for Jamaica. They got ganja, rum, Red Stripe Beer, and native snatch that'll turn you inside out… You ain't never gonna wanna leave!"

Jamaica?—Why the hell was he going to Jamaica with this whacked out Australian? For that matter, what was he even doing in Key West getting plastered out a his mind at Sloppy Joe's Bar?—Shit! He was from Detroit, never been out a Michigan before.

Then it began to come back to him with a horrifying clarity that turned his stomach more, made his head throb worse—made him wish he couldn't remember, made him wish he could forget all about it instead, repress it.

It had all started months before when his clock radio alarm blasted CCRs "Bad Moon Rising" and jolted him awake. Rubbing sleep from his eyes and cursing the day he was born he forced himself from his warm bed on that frigid Motor City dull gray morning. Snow was lightly falling outside, mixing with factory pollution. It cast a dirty blackish brown blanket rather than a winter wonderland.

Today would be the worst day of his twenty-three year old life and he was terrified. He fumbled with the hot water in the shower and scalded himself, finally found the right combination, and hurriedly showered. There was no time to blow dry his shoulder length hair. He'd have to go outside with it wet, tied in a ponytail.

He knew his life was over with. His death certificate was signed, sealed, and delivered with Uncle Sam's draft induction notice summoning him into the Vietnam War. Nam, that'd be the end of him. At 130 pounds, he'd hardly be able to lift an eighty-pound pack, let alone hike all day through sweltering jungles humpin it. He also knew in his gut that there was a bullet somewhere over there with his name on it. He'd never come back alive. He had some options, like fleeing to Windsor, Canada. Just a short hop through the tunnel or over the Ambassador Bridge. But he knew no one over there, had no where to hide there. He'd refuse to go, burn his draft card, opt. for jail. But, figured he'd fare no better in the slammer than in Nam. Draft dodgers were labeled cowards no better than child molesters. How about become a conscientious objector—seek sanctuary in the church? But they were extremely religious guys. Just his bum luck, his parents had raised him an atheist, wasn't even baptized. A little late to get religion and impossible to connive the army he had.

He threw on a worn pair of brown corduroy Levis, an old tattered Beta Theta Pi fraternity sweatshirt, and a pair of suede motorcycle boots, finishing off his outfit with a string of Indian beads tossed over his head. Then he headed out the door into the deep freeze of the worst Michigan winter he could remember. He almost forgot his beaten up leather Air Force jacket and slipped into it right before exiting his flophouse Cass Corridor apartment.

He thought of one desperation loop hole, as his battered Chevy Corvair convertible slid and skidded over frozen Woodwand Avenue on those final miles to the Fort Wayne Induction Center. A battle cry, Tim Leary's: "Tune In, Turn On, and Drop Out."

Two capsules of LSD manufactured in his Alma Mater's Michigan State University chemical lab and snuck out by one of his buddies a chem major were wrapped in tissue paper in his Bomber jacket pocket. His buddy warned him the acid was supposed to be used for research by the Psychology Department it was extremely pure and super potent. Together the capsules packed one thousand micrograms of synapses-altering mind-blow.

As he pulled into the Fort's old front gate and read the posted sign, YOU ARE NOW THE PROPERTY OF THE UNITED STATES GOVERNMENT, he fumbled to get them out of his jacket pocket steering with one hand, then swallowed both.

Being a Psychology graduate himself, he knew that taken under stress acid could induce bad trips like schizophrenia, so he'd never messed with it. He'd fooled around with some mild psycilocibin magic mushroom, but never the strong stuff. He figured with this mega-dose the army would judge him a mental turnip, too crazy for induction, dumb as a post. As a backup he was armed with letters from various doctors who'd treated him for knee injuries inflicted throughout his college years. So what if he'd sustained those injuries dancing at beer hall fraternity blasts. Dancing was his only sport, he could leap into the air and come down into a perfect split like James Brown, and gyrate his hips all night Mick Jagger style. Anyway, these letters testified that his legs had been in casts numerous times making his knee ligaments loose as rubber bands.

More confident now, seeing at least a flicker of hope, he pulled into the Fort's crowded parking lot and found a parking space between a souped up 57 Chevy and an old flat black De Soto ablaze with red and yellow flames. Exiting his car, shivering now in the sub-zero temperature he made himself stand up straight military style and joined the flood of young guys entering the induction building. He fleetingly took note that they personified a melting pot of America's finest. Greasers with slicked back ducktails and cascading waterfall pompadours. Dudes high stepping in pegged black skin-tight pants, needle pointed shoes and white T-shirts, with Camels or Luckies folded tight into their sleeves. Scowling black brothers in bright orange or green banlons with waist-high sharkskin pants and two-tone shoes. But they all looked like they had one thing in common. They didn't want to be there.

There was also a large contingent of freaks like him, made him feel more at home wearing their long straggly hair, bellbottom jeans and fry boots like merit badges. One spaced out cadet standing on the steps of the old Revolutionary Fort's entrance stood out from the others, and caught his eye. At least seven feet tall and weighing three hundred pounds, with not an ounce of fat on him. Instead, he rippled with bulging muscle. His shoulder-length hair was sandy blonde, but his lips were painted bright red and he wore eye shadow. Around his bullish neck hung a sign that announced to all, I'M QUEER. He was bent over nose to nose with a nasty looking Sergeant wearing full dress fatigues. The fruit showed no fear, "I love ya Sarge!" he shouted "Marry me! I'm gonna fuck everyone in basic training! Ain't gonna kill Charley, I'm gonna love him!"

Tavo stopped dead in his tracks gapping at them not knowing whether to move on into the Fort or try to pull the bulking faggot away before the Sergeant belted the guy one, maybe court marshaled him. Then, shaking his head doing a double take, he recognized the hulking fairy. His old high school buddy, Manistoe Lowellen III, first strings quarterback for the Redford Huskies. Man, they use to cruise *Daily's Drive In*—down beers together—best of buddies. Hadn't seen him for years. But shit! Back in high school Manistoe had all the Husky cheerleaders lined up waiting to drop their drawers. What happened to him?

Suddenly the Sargent ripped Manistoes sign off his neck, tore it to shreds, and threw the tattered remains in his face, then stomped away in disgust mumbling curses about the fucked-up numbed-nuts he was supposed to make an army outta.

Tavo watched as Manistoe pulled a compact and lipstick out of his purse and re-applied make up as he rotated his hips suggestively at the departing Sergeant. Hesitantly, he approached him tapping him lightly on the back. Manistoe spun around and looked down at him, recognition causing his ruby lips to form a shit-eating grin. He lifted him off of his feet pulling him to him in a mighty bear hug and whispered conspiratorially in his ear "Gripps, don't let on man. This is my way outta Nam! They won't take you if they think you're queer. You know I ain't no fruit!" He put him down and smacked a sloppy kiss on his forehead leaving gooey lipstick marks.

Tavo tried to wipe the lipstick off, but only managed to smear it around causing his forehead to look like it was smashed with a ripe tomato. He gave Manistoe a worried look, and said "Ya, but won't it go on your record you're queer? That'll follow you for the rest of your life!" Manistoe shrugged his shoulders like he could care less and whispered, "So what, man! Anyone wants to believe that about me, let 'em! …beats being killed in some stinking jungle. Listen, I ain't no coward. I can kick ass! But who the hell knows what the fuck we're even fighting for?"

Manistoe paused, pulled another queer sign out of his purse and hung it around his thick neck. He looked real scared:

"Remember Ronnie Hamilton?" he said, "I just downed a few brews with him the other night. Man the horror stories he told knocked me on my ass! He came back from Nam with shrapnel lodged next ta his spine. If they operate he's a quadriplegic. So he carries those pieces o' metal around in him, suffers constant pain, whacked on painkillers! Call me queer any day man but call me alive!"

He was about to ask Manistoe for Ronnie's address, he should visit him, maybe cheer him up, if that was possible, when a loud buzzer jarred them, vibrating the marrow in their bones. A barking order sounded over the P.A., it directed the mumbling grumping motley grew into the old Fort, and then into a room filled with desks like a high school classroom. A sign read TESTING hung on one peeling, dingy, gray-green wall. A Sergeant pounded on an old chipped black board, and yelled for everyone to shut the fuck up. Then scowling he warned, "Any noise, act of rebellion, protest, or insubordination from this point on will be regarded as an act of treason, resulting in instant Court Marshall and years of hard labor at Leavenworth." His proclamation silenced everyone. Even Manistoe's enthusiastic endorsements of anal intercourse trailed off into oblivion.

Tavo reluctantly took a seat with everyone else, as privates passed out testing booklets. Then the Sergeant told the subdued group that they should all act like bananas, be just one of the bunch, try their hardest on the intelligence test. Those who did well would receive officer training, even if they hadn't gone "to some pussy eating college." On the other hand, low scores would result in private status and a front line battle station. They had two hours to complete the test and were to start immediately.

As he turned to the first page and filled in his name and social security number, a frightening sensation raced through his body. He forgot about Manistoe, Ronnie, the dour-faced Sargent at the front of the room, even forgot he was at the induction center. He thought he was on a forty-story elevator that free fell to the basement, with that tingly sensation in his groin and head magnified a thousand times. Then, his mind split from his body. His brain floated away on a breeze and soared around the room, looking down at himself, sitting there like a stump with the other inductees. He attempted from afar to wrest his mental faculties back into his body and grasp the number two pencil, but it turned to rubber and melted into his hand. The words on the test were indiscernible. The printing broke apart into molecules, atoms, and electrons. He stared in awe at the microscopic universe unfolding before his chemically altered vision. Nuclei flowed and pulsated in plasmatic primeval matter on the page.

An hour and a half passed by. To him it happened in an instant. Time possessed the same degree of reality as the dour-faced sergeant, who transformed—took on the face of Donald Duck, jumping up and down now; he quacked hysterically, "Ten more minutes left on the test. Ten more minutes left on the test."

He hadn't blackened a single multiple choice square, but summoned a shred of sanity as the acid eased up for a moment and filled in squares at random. Then Privates collected the booklets and ordered the broken brotherhood down a long hallway to the physical examination rooms.

He marched in line with them through corridors that vibrated like green silly putty to a room where they drew blood and took urine samples. As he entered the large glowing room staffed by white coated doctors, a blood-curdling, primeval scream echoed, piercing his ear drums, so horrifying and bone chilling it could have marked early man's first encounter with Mastodons. He not only felt and heard its terror, he saw the sound's vibration they looked like ripples on a pond. He could touch them, feel them. He reached out waving his arms and tried, then smacked the back of his skull with his fist attempting to bring the room into focus. He strained to see where the hideous noise came from, and spotted a tall, skinny black guy stripped down to his soiled jockey shorts. Somewhere along the line everyone had been stripped down to their skivvies, but he couldn't remember how, when, or why. But forget that, he was now completely horrified to see the black dude being held down by three military police wearing white helmets. A doctor stood over him with a large needle and was attempting to hold his arm still so he could draw blood. The youth struggled, fought, he screamed, "Hey man, I ain't no junkie! Get dat needle away from me, man! Get it away! I's a feared! I's a feared!" Spittle and sweat flew everywhere as he fought for his life. After repeated jabs, the doctor finally struck an artery in the guy's puncture filled arm. Blood dripped in a dark pool around his shaking, kicking feet.

Tavo's cognition had turned to mush. He wondered why beings from outer space were tormenting one of the ancient Earth tribes. The acid made him hallucinate he was on a space ship, abducted by aliens. It was the only explanation that made any sense to his freaked out perceptions. But he couldn't come up with a rational explanation for the alien's strange behavior, unless the African dude was an object for study by these extraterrestrials. That had to be it. Then he felt a prick in his own arm, and despite being mortally terrified, he attempted to keep calm hoping to minimize any damage to himself. He summoned up his courage and meekly stammered, "We earthlings wish no confrontation with an advanced race from outer space. That African boy is from a tribal society; he probably never even read Ray Bradbury. He's a stranger in a strange land, leave him alone."

The irritated doctor shoved a specimen jar at him, and shouted, "Shut the fuck up, asshole. Go piss in this," and pushed him towards the urinal. He stumbled to the john clutching the jar in his trembling hand and was surprised to find all the guys pissing in jars just like the one he held. But what really confused him was how these space beings could communicate so easily in America slang, and how could they have captured so many of his compatriots and make the inside of their spacecraft look just like a men's high school lavatory? But he had no time to ponder this semi rational thought. An unusual event was taking place here. A boy who looked like an American Indian was waving his arms excitedly, "I've got jaundice" he shouted. "I'll piss in anyone's jar for a hundred bucks! Line up girls!"

To his amazement, several guys pulled rolled-up hundred-dollar bills from their rectums, and handed them to the Indian, who pissed a radiant dark orange fluid into their jars. Maybe the aliens would let the jaundiced ones go, he thought. Maybe the healthy ones were destined for some interplanetary zoo. He suspected the aliens had drugged them all, he couldn't concentrate, could hardly walk, and his will to flee was zero. Anyway, when he probed his ass he came up with zilch. So he pissed a yellow stream into his jar and obediently handed it on his way out to one of the stone-faced spacemen who eyed him suspiciously, causing his hands to sweat profusely.

Next, the aliens ushered them into yet another room, and told them to wait in a long line, where a fat ruddy-faced ET resembling a pig was placing what looked like stereo headphones on the boy in front of the line. He inched slowly along hugging himself, trembling from the cold of the room, but most of all his fear. One by one, everyone in the line received the head phone treatment until it was his turn. He wondered if this could be a communication with their leader. Now maybe he'd find out what fate laid in store for them. Then pig-face looked him squarely in the eye with a coal black stare; his gaze seemed to pierce his gray matter, as if trying to determine his genetic make-up. He or it pointed to a bench where two greasers with tattoos decorating their arms and torsos sat. "See those numb nuts sitting there?" He snarled, "Well, they didn't hear nothin' when I put these headphones on em." He poked Tavo soundly in the chest to make sure he had his attention then went on. “Those fuckers are gonna sit there ‘til they do hear somethin’ or hell freezes over. You wanna join ‘em or do you hear the buzzer?” He shook the headphones for emphasis in front of Tavo’s sweating face. Despite the cold room, he was now perspiring all over from head to toe.

He wiped the sweat from his eyes stared at the greasers who looked bored and pissed off. They slouched down trying to be cool. One picked absently at his nose, wiping it distractedly on the guy next to him.

Not wanting to aggravate these strange creatures anymore and, despite his testicles having shot up to his stomach, he pulled himself up to his full five foot nine inch height and prayed he’d say the right thing, “We wish in no way to aggravate our interplanetary brothers.” He said as calmly as he could “We’ll cooperate and hope you will go back to your planet and report we earthlings are a peaceful lot.” He forced himself to grin from ear to ear friendly like, and maintain a shaky eye contact with the alien. Show him they were non-violent. But the alien went wild and almost pulled the headphones apart with his trembling hands, enraged he growled, “I’m gonna take that as a yes ta hearing the buzzer, turkey—you passed the test! Now get the fuck outta here, and he shoved him out the door.

He found himself in the hallway where the walls still pulsated an eerie glowing green. Aliens and his brothers milled about aimlessly. He was dumbfounded. Couldn’t remember how he’d been captured, how he’d been taken here or where the hell in the universe he was. Then he noticed an especially ugly greaser leaning up against a green throbbing wall. The guy was covered with red oozing boils and pimples that glowed, and throbbed iridescent red, needle tracks punctured his emaciated arms. He pulled a crumpled pack of Luckys from his jockeys, struck a match against the pulsating wall as if this were an every day occurrence, and lit up. He contently blew smoke rings that formed flying saucers; they danced around his oily hair. Then out of no where a big eyed alien with a white helmet rushed up to him, slapped the cigarette out of his mouth and grounded it out with his foot shouting, "No smoking dip shit." Then the alien stormed off and the grease ball flashed him the bird.

Tavo scratched his head in disbelief, breaking the rubberband that held his ponytail in place, causing his hair to tumble down around his shoulders. Then he started to understand. Get what was happening. Most of the abductees didn't want to pass the aliens' tests, and some were openly defying them, but this seemed only to piss em off more.

He walked as casually as he could over to the greaser, but his feet felt encased in cement, and he moved in slow motion. He looked around cautiously to make sure no alien was within hearing distance and reached out, shook the greaser's dirty bicep. The greaser wheeled around eyeballed him gave him an evil look. "Ya, waddya want?" He spat. Tavo glanced around again then whispered, "Look pal, I don't think it's a good idea to defy these extraterrestrials. They have us in their power; they're much more advanced than we are you know!"

The greaser shoved Tavo knocking him off balance and yelled, "Get the fuck away from me psycho!" Paused, then grinned slyly nodding his head and said, "Ya, I digit man. You're trying ta pull a mental on em—go for it, slick!" He walked away chuckling.

Tavo had no idea what he was getting at, he felt lost, completely out of it. Should he attempt to join his fellow captors and try to fail one of their tests? He wondered how to respond, as he was led into another large room, where the aliens told their khaki-clad sentries to line the earthlings up facing the front at attention. Then the head abductor ordered them all to do deep knee bends. Ah ha! He thought with a burst of clarity, remembering the doctor's letters stuffed into his briefs.

"Head being! Head being!" he shouted at the top of his lungs, causing everyone to stop and stare at him. "Here! See here!" he screamed, this was his chance. "You can't take me as a specimen to your far-off world!" Frantic now waving the letters in the air. "Read the words of my earthling physician. See for yourself. My injured knees would never permit such a long space journey!" He smiled hopefully as the inductees broke up in laughter.

But the white-coated monster in charge didn't share in their mirth. He turned various shades of blue, purple, and red that lit up the room. His eyes bugged two feet out of his head, and his mouth opened into a hideously enormous maw. He rushed at Tavo and snatched his doctors' letter out of his hand, ripped them to shreds, and threw them on the floor. Then he hopped up and down on their tattered remains. Gripping Tavo by the band of his jockey shorts, breaking the elastic he lifted him off the ground giving him a painful wedgie. He pushed his grotesque face that looked like the ass end of a mandrake monkey into Tavo's. "YOU PASSED, FRUITCAKE!" he roared and threw him out the door like a sack of potatoes.

He landed with a thump against an undulating wall more solid than it looked and pain shot up his spinal cord to his cortex. Red stars flashed before his eyes. Then, just as he was giving up all hope of remaining on planet earth, a loud announcement boomed over the P.A. system: "Tavo Gripps, Tavo Gripps—report to the psychiatrist Captain Rosenthal immediately!"

Hearing his name shouted over the PA shook him up sharply, he became more focused on his surroundings.

He was coming down.

This wasn't a flying saucer! This was the fucking army induction center! At least the spacecraft offered hope for survival. The army was sure death!

After getting lost several times, with plenty of cursing and pushing from angry soldiers who pointed him in the general direction, Tavo finally located the shrink's office. Naked, except for his stretched out jockeys, which he attempted to hold up with one hand and still somewhat transcendent, he was ushered into its inner sanctum by a sour-looking private.

Hidden behind a stack of government papers sat a clean-cut officious soldier dressed in a crisply starched captain's uniform. His hair was sheared to the bone, and his scowl, as he peered at Tavo through the coke-bottle glasses chilled him to the bone.

Then it all came flooding back to him. Those painful memories he thought he had repressed. He struggled to repress them again, but the LSD wouldn't allow for that. His recent past assaulted him, depression laden, and catapulted across his synopsis in the flash of a second. Tears rolled down his face.

2

"For it's one, two, three, four
What are we fighting for..."

—Country Joe McDonald

"Jesus Christ Matty, what a yer crying about" Striker was shaking him.

"I told ya were going to Jamaica mon, I thought you'd be happy, now you're bawling like a baby."

Tavo stood up on shaky feet, the boat swayed and rocked underneath him.

"Just leave me alone for a while okay," he said, "I'm trying to remember how I got here! But the more I remember the shittier I feel."

"Fuck it then," said Striker "open yourself a brew and forget, it's all the sames ta me."

"I can't forget unless I'm dead drunk and I can't stay plastered the rest of my life!"

"I don't know bout that Matty, I does a pretty good job at it and ya never sees me crying!"

"I'm sick as hell, I gotta make some sense of things—it's starting to come back to me now, I gotta lay down, stop the rocking—" And he crawled down below.

"I got everything top sides under control," Striker shouted, "just remember you's liable to get sicker down below you know! Better to stay top side in the fresh air."

"You got any aspirin?" Tavo yelled.

"Hell no! I only believes in the hair a the dog… gots some tamater juice and some hot sauce though, mix it with some beer, that'll do the trick!"

Tavo dry heaved and scrunched himself up into a ball. Striker shouted at him again, "If you's gotta blow lunch again aim for an empty beer case, but I don't think you's got much left in ya!"

Tavo tossed and turned trying to stop the motion of the boat. He thought he dreamed, but he was too wide-awake for a dream. No, this was real, all too real, and then he remembered the worst of it.

It had all came crashing down when his true love, Irene Goldberg, said her final good-byes. Her parents absolutely refused to allow Tavo into their clan. It was bad enough that he wasn't Jewish; but his shaggy hair, outlandish dress, pot smoking and incessant and hopeless dreaming drove Mr and especially Mrs Goldberg mashaguna!

He couldn't care less about their successful wholesale restaurant supply business unless it was to organize a union for their workers. What a drag! There business couldn't compare to his fantasies about South Sea islands, homesteading, getting back to nature on a deserted beach paradise, that one day would transform into a Aldous Huxley Island Utopia. That was were it was at!

His father had helped plant this bizarre notion in his head at an early impressionable age, and it was later spurred into maturity by one of his far out psychology professor. His father would obsessively rattle on at the dinner table or any chance he got about an opportunity he once had to oversee a coconut copra farm in the US Virgin Islands during the Second World War. Copra was being used to make bombs. Had he jumped at this rather than opting for security with the Michigan Gas Company, he would now be a millionaire. At the close of the war the foresighted man who did become the overseer, received ten acres of prime beachfront real estate as a thank you from the government for his war efforts.

Although Tavo abhorred anything to do with war, the part about Tropical Paradise captured his soul. He never stopped thinking about white sand beaches and waving palm trees, especially during Frigid Michigan winters.

But his love Irene was less adventuresome. She'd finally been beaten down, though not without substantial protests and succumbed to her parent's threats of disownment. After all, Tavo had no land in paradise and the Army had long since stopped using copra for bombs. In Vietnam, only synthetics were used.

With reluctance and pragmatism, Irene was now the intended of a Jewish psychiatrist, and would settle down to a safe, secure comfortable upper class life style in Bloomfield Hills, Michigan.

Tavo remembered more but wished he could forget. It had all come to a head in the living room of Irene's family's home in Southfield, Michigan, a suburb of Detroit.
Her mother had glared at him using the Detroit Free Press newspaper as a shield. Only her nose, blue frosted hair and hate-filled eyes were visible as she peered over the paper, and wined at him sounding like sand paper shredding "You're dreck Tavo Gripps…. Look at you… with that long hair and schemata for clothes."

He looked down at his shuffling dirty worn out boots and tattered jeans and stammered…. "I got a college degree Mrs Goldberg. I'll… I'll… " but she cut him off, rolled the newspaper up, snarling her lips, exposing her false teeth and shook the paper at him like a club. Made him feel that it was his neck that she was wringing and shaking furiously. She shrieked at him, "I'll sit Shiva you Goy! Your nothing but a dreamer!" He looked longingly to Irene for support, but finding only a blank stare he pleaded, "Come on Irene, tell your Mom how you feel about me!"

To his hurt and dismay, Irene turned her back to him, silent, embarrassed for him, for her, for them. Mrs Goldberg had had enough of this song and dance. Spitting hate she ripped the paper in two and shouted, "Get out of my house Shagitz! Stay away from my Irene or I'll call the police!" To emphasize her point she grabbed a nearby flower vase and threw it at him, he barely managed to duck as it whizzed by his temple and smashed into the wall spraying him with chunks of glass, water, and withered flowers. When she reached behind her for the fire place poker he put his hands up in surrender and backed out of the front door. Mrs Goldberg charged after him onto the front porch, poker waving in the air. She shouted with glee, shouted words capable of doing more damage than her poker. "Irene's marrying a nice Jewish boy! Harlen Rosenthal! A doctor! A Psychiatrist! So there!"

Tears started to form in his eyes and he looked to Irene for a denouncement of her mother's curse, pleading he said, "Your Mom's kidding… right? About Rosenthal?"

Despite her mother's wailing and poker brandishing Irene ran to him. Tears were rolling down her face now, running her mod make-up down her cheeks. She hugged onto him, then pushed him away. She looked up at him; her streaked eyes begged him to understand. "You know I love you," she sobbed. "I only saw Harlen to pacify Mom. This was the ray of hope he needed and he clutched at it like a drowning man grabs for a log and said "Great! So you're not gonna marry him then." But instead of the nod of affirmation he expected, this time she shoved him away angrily and blew up at him. "You don't get it… do you? Can't you see? You're DRAFTED!" She punctuated DRAFTED by pounding her fists on his chest. "What'll you do? What'll I do? You could get killed… crippled… maimed for life. What am I supposed to do… wait two years, four years? For you to come back? I'll go crazy with worry. You just don't get it. You're not thinking of me!"

He lunged for her, tried to hold on to her, make her understand. But she pushed him away, stomped her feet in frustration and cried, "No, don't touch me. I can't live with uncertainty. I need a husband. A LIVE husband who's going to be there for me."

His tears were blurring his vision. All hope fading. He made a desperate grasp for her, but she sidestepped his arms and he hugged only air, he moaned, "So you love that guy more than me?" Irene at first went to him, hugged him, wiped away his tears with her small hand then pushed him away with all her strength, wailed away once again with her fists on his chest, screaming at him now. "You're so dense! ...a jerk... haven't heard a word I've said. I do love you... but I can't! I won't love you!"

Her final words.

All she wrote.

She ran into her house, slamming the door leaving him shivering in the cold, tears freezing on his chapped face.

Now here he was, groggy, spaced on acid, confronted by none other than Irene's fiancé, Harlen Rosenthal, US Army Captain, Psychiatrist. But he shouldn't be so surprised it really wasn't a coincidence. He knew Rosenthal was stationed state side at the Fort Wayne Induction Center for his four years of easy service. Irene had told him as much at their final goodbye.

Now, Harlen stared at him through filmy coke bottle glasses with an expression of disgust and contempt, not even asking him to sit down in the only chair in his sparsely furnished office, making him stand there clutching at his falling down drawers. The ones stretched out by the alien or rather by the Army doctor. He finally spoke breaking a deadly silence dripping spiteful sarcasm, "Well Gripps, we meet at last. Don't need any introductions, do we?" then he finally motioned absently waving his pen for Tavo to sit down.

"You know who I am," he continued pompously. "I'm the guy Irene dumped your sorry ass for! In fact, were getting married next week. Tough luck pal. But you could never give her what she deserves. You don't want her to marry outside of her faith now do you?"

Tavo said nothing the blood was rushing to his head. His face was reddening but he couldn't form words, talk, or speak. "Enough said," Rosenthal barked ignoring Tavo's silence, distractingly shuffling a stack of his papers. "Let's get to the business at hand. I'm a US Army Captain, as well as a prominent psychiatrist. And you, Gripps, were sent to me for reasons that have nothing to do with Irene or our personal lives. I'll be completely objective and professional with you: not allow our past to infringe on the present. I'll utilize my advanced training and education to deal with you. In fact, I may actually be of help to you and humanity, regarding your army career path."

Tavo fumed but couldn't speak, Harlen prattled on about his attributes, his unselfish service to the war effort in his clinical overwrought jargon, and then a final rocket-propelled acid burst sent shock waves through his tortured skull. Suddenly Harlen's glasses began to dissolve like green flowing Coca-Cola bottle glass down his face. Where his eyes had been, dark holes appeared and his bland emotionless face contorted into a grinning skull. Fire shot from his eye sockets, and a pronged serpent's tongue lashed the air as he ranted on. His voice sounded like it was in an echo chamber.

"You see, Gripps, you can't fool an expert professional with your shenanigans. I'm a renowned scholar. I know my field. I also know about you. You have a master's degree in Industrial Psychology; yet, you scored the lowest of anyone ever taking the Army's Intelligence test. According to your score, you possess the IQ of a chickpea. I know you couldn't advance that far in college being that stupid. You intentionally scammed the test, thinking in your warped mind that you wouldn't be inducted and sent to Vietnam."

Tavo rubbed his eyes violently, trying to rid them of Harlen's horrifying image. Sweat poured down his brow, he attempted to reply but only a "Humph, oomph" dribbled out of his quivering jaw. Harlen's features were metamorphisizing in flashes. First, he changed into a hairy werewolf, then a zombie. Next he turned into a yellow skull, and finally settled into a red-faced devil with horns. Tavo stared at him, with white knuckled terror gripping the seat of his chair, his fingernails almost snapped.

"Oh no, Gripps. You're not bamboozling me into an easy out," he said. "No my friend! I'm resubmitting your test with a new form depicting you as above average intelligence. Thus, you will be slated for officers training" He tapped the new I.Q. test with his gold pen to let this sink in. A spit bubble appeared at the corner of Tavo's mouth then drooled down his chin in response.

"The Army needs psychologists, even those of your questionable character," Rosenthal continued ignoring his shock, or probably just not detecting it. "As for your duties as an officer psychologist you will counsel… do therapy on your fellow cowards, malingerers, deserters, etc., who fake mental breakdowns… pretend to go crazy under battle conditions… you will deal with those wimps who attempt to affect combat stress disorders, and send them all back into battle!"

Harlen folded his arms across his chest leaned back in his chair grinning at Tavo proud of his dissertation. "But don't think for one minute you can give those fakers a ticket home to recuperate," he added emphasizing this by pounding his desk with his boney hairy fist. "No way in hell will any one in Vietnam be allowed any type of mental deferment. You'll send each and every one back into battle to honor their country… to die a glorious death defending it.

Rosenthal rubbed his chin, it looked like the devils goatee to Tavo, he thought for a minute fanned mock concern then said, “Of course, give those weaklings a good hour of talk therapy first. Make them think the Army really cares about them. Then give them the old pep talk bola bola, you know the game, and send them all back to the front!”

Tavo leaned over and threw up on the floor. Everything inside him spewed out. Harlen jumped up cursing yelling. “If you refuse to do your duty, I’ll personally see that your ass gets assigned to pointman on a foot patrol… the first to get spiked by a punji stick!”

Harlen smartly snapped to parade attention saluted him and with finality stated flatly, “That’s all, Gripps! Dismissed! Report for duty at officers’ training school, Fort Benning, Georgia! Serve your country proud!” Harlen’s devils face settled back to his usual stone-faced, sweat sock look as the LSD bid his shell-shocked brain its final goodbye. He left the office juggling the papers instructing him to report for officers training. Harlen shouted orders to his private to bring bucket and mop to clean up Tavo’s swill.

He stood in the hallway dejected, banging his tripped out head against the wall moaning, “Shit! Shit! He’s no alien monster. He’s a real prick, Rosenthal! A doctor, a real doctor!”

Abruptly, out of nowhere a shrill “Quack! Quack! Quack!” exploded in his fried brain. He spun around wondering what tricks his mind was playing on him now.

Standing in front of him was an emaciated freak, naked, not even wearing stretched out underwear. His cock dangled limply. He had a long braided ponytail with a North Vietnamese Flag tied to it’s end, and was leading a large white duck, tethered to a leash. The duck wore love beads.

Tavo looked down at it mesmerized and it flapped its wings, attempted to nip him on the shin. Stepping back, shaking his head trying to clear the cobwebs he mumbled, “Waa… Wha didja say?” The freak chuckled, reached down and rubbed the duck's head and said, "Maybe he ain't a doctor! Just a Quack!" He broke up with laughter at his joke—or the duck's joke, whatever.

Tavo rubbed his eyes. There was something oddly familiar about this dude. "Say, don't I know you from somewhere." he finally managed to say.

The hippie picked up Tavos limp hand and smacked it a high five, "Ya man, John. John Curtis… from Art Class… Redford High. Class o' 63 man." Ya sure, now he remembered him vaguely, but he was too absorbed by the duck on the rope, and to stoned to reminisce over old times. "What's with the duck, man?" He asked, the duck was getting him all spaced out again.

John grinned, reached down and scratched its head again, "They think you're crazy, they won't take ya!" Tavo looked at him pityingly, shook his head. "Ya, sure, go for it. But that shrink in there is a real ball buster… doubt if he'd say the Mad Hatter was nuts!"

A devilish smirk cracked John's face. He grabbed his penis with his fist and started to jack off, stroking it like a piston. "Well, we'll just have to see if this nut can crack him," and he charged into Rosenthal's office his dick and the duck leading the way.

Tavo was about to shout good luck when he was lifted off his feet from behind and held in the air by Manistoe, his shorts slipped and fell around his shaking ankles. Manistoe turned him around to look him in the face and belly laughed "Tavo, my main man! I ain't going! I ain't gonna have ta go! I'm too fucking tall. Anyone over six-feet nine, they can't fit into a uniform. Don't make 'em that large. Hail the bureaucracy. Don't even have ta be a faggot. No records, Natta! Outta sight, Man!"

Manistoe set him down; he managed to say, "Great, man" and pulled up his shorts over his naked ass.

Noticing Tavo's funk, sympathetic now Manistoe said, "Guess it didn't go to well, huh? Sorry, man!" Tavo shook his head in the negative and tried to tie a large knot in his underwear to hold them up.

Manistoe watched him struggling with his shorts then slapped him on the back trying to cheer him up he said. "Come on man, let's party. For old times sake. We'll get some babes, some primo pot. Get loaded. Whatya say? Come on man, it might not be so bad. Ya might get stationed state side... maybe even Europe. Not everyone goes to Nam, you know!"

Tavo just shook his head no, looked at his bare feet, and shuffled away down the corridor that was almost deserted now, wondering where he could find his clothes. He thought he heard Manistoe calling to him in the distance but was too bummed out to respond. Harlen had sealed his fate. An agonizing fate worse than death; a mental death. He knew Vietnam had to drive some guys crazy, it had to. Intense combat stress? Not everyone could take that. Stand up under the horrors of that war. Never mind, that wasn't an issue for the Army. They were all considered cannon fodder and shared the same destiny meted out by the Great War machine that even presidents couldn't stop.

Somewhere in the background or maybe it was just in his mind he heard a, "Quack, Quack, Quack" as he searched empty classrooms for his clothes. And then he knew for certain that he wasn't going to sit at a desk, do sham therapy, send his brothers back into battle if they cracked up, couldn't take it. And he sure as hell wasn't going to be point man. Get the short end of a punji stick.

3

"Look over yanders wall--
hand me down my walkin' cane."

J. Clark
From *Look over Yanders Wall*
Blues song recorded by
The Paul Butterfield Blues Band

Ya, that's how it had all started, he remembered. …remembered every last horrible detail now as he rolled around doubled up gripping his churning stomach on Striker's filthy bunk. But how did he wind up in Key West at Sloppy Joe's Bar and how the fuck did he meet Striker and end up here on this rolling ocean in the middle of nowhere heading for Jamaica. Then it came back to him the rest of it. Jet engines purring in his ears, the plane's steady vibrations lulling him, he was headed for Miami, then to Key West, and then somewhere—anywhere hot, sweltering, steaming, and tropical—but not Vietnam.

He deserted, became one of thousands of young men forever labeled "Draft Dodger." If he wasn't to be caught, he had to flee the United States, never return again. He'd never see Irene again, but that was a mute point. By this time, she'd have already married Harlen, and was probably arranging throw pillows in their Bloomfield Hills mansion. He couldn't fathom how she could break his heart in a million pieces and marry that shmuck. Didn't she give all the outward appearances of loving him? He guessed he just didn't understand women.

Why, she could be right by his side now heading for adventure! Didn't she know he couldn't be security motivated with the Vietnam War looking down his neck? The future wasn't a guarantee for him. He was no "Senators son, no fortunate one." Wasn't born with a silver spoon in his mouth. Come on! His parents were lower middle class; then, mom and dad had died within a month of each other during his last year of post graduate studies.

They were both elderly and he was born late in their lives. He often wondered: worried if he was a mistake, but they had truly loved him and even occasionally helped him with his college expenses even though it was hard on them with his dads meager salary from the gas company. If only Irene had given him a chance. If only Uncle Sam had, he could've worked his way through another four years of college bussing tables and cleaning dormitories. Could've gotten a Doctorate Degree like Rosenthal.

But he was completely alone now. An only child no living relatives. The final Gripps, the ignominious end of a family that had come over on the boat after the Mayflower. He guessed his ancestors must've been colonialist misfit criminals who'd been expelled from England, ordered to choose between prison or settling a new hostile land. He never empathized with em more than he did right now.

Anyway he thought he wouldn't be missed much other than by Uncle Sam who still wanted his pound of flesh. Now he consoled himself it was probably for the best, that he had few ties, and fewer material possessions. Although his parent had willed him their small house in Redford Michigan just outside of Detroit, which he'd quickly sold for ten thousand dollars. He now had that cash stitched safely inside an old Boy Scout backpack, securely stuffed under the plane seat in front of him.

He gave the beat-up Corvair convertible to his best friend, Rich Bercherer, asked him to get what he could for it. Send him the money when he got somewhere, when he was settled.

It was Rich who advised him to leave America right away, warning the government would send agents to search him out, arrest him as soon as he didn't show up in Georgia for training. He cautioned him not to fly with a commercial airline to a foreign country; they probably had his name on a computer and would arrest him on the spot. If he was set on a warm sanctuary, Rich suggested going to Key West, then hitching a ride on a shrimp boat to one of the islands in the Caribbean or the Bahamas. Sure many boats left the Florida Keys daily to fish in and around all those islands Rich claimed. This made perfect sense to him, especially because it paralleled his South Seas fantasies. No way would Rich steer him wrong, he was his best buddy, a real smooth operator. He had an aunt who worked in the Detroit draft board office who conveniently misplaced Rich's induction notice. Rich knew the score. He painted a glorious picture of these guys called Conches, who would jump at the opportunity to smuggle a draft dodger out of the country, telling him Conches were a wild liberal bunch of rebels who opposed the Vietnam War and all the US Government stood for. Rich didn't even think they considered themselves Americans. Being the original inhabitants of the Keys, they wanted to be declared a separate country. Thought there was a good chance the Conches would hide him on one of their boats and he could live the life of a carefree fisherman right there, just so he didn't go ashore.

Armed with Rich's sound council, his old Boy Scout backpack that contained cut-offs, T-shirts, sandals, and the ten thousand bucks, he landed with a bounce and a jerk at the Miami Airport. He felt deep excitement stirring within him as he walked through the crowded terminal with everybody speaking different languages and airlines from every country flying to destinations all over the world.

This must have been like how his ancestors, great great great grandpa and grandma Gripps, felt so many years before when they set sail for America. He wasn't so unlike them.

They'd left England cause they couldn't take it's oppression and unjust laws. It was a rationalization that worked for him anyway, and he was pumped up to meet some real Conches. He needed some understanding friends now. Guys, who'd know where he was coming from, who'd help him out.

Not wanting to spend any of his money, knowing he'd need it for a rainy day—to start a new life—he walked through a warm tropical downpour outside the airport, to the entrance ramp of the expressway leading to the southernmost outpost in America, Key West. He stuck his wet thumb out. After standing an hour in the heavy rain, which no longer felt warm, but now chilled him, made him shiver, an old 1953 Cadillac screeched, and fish tailed to a skidding halt on the easement. He bottled for it almost forgetting his backpack. As he reached to open the rear door, a witch's ancient, withered face popped out of the passenger's window, it screeched, "Hey shit for brains! Got's any gas money?"

The car crawled forward slowly, wrenching the door handle from his hand as the old crone waited for an answer, not wanting to let him in if he wasn't gonna fork over some cash. He trotted beside the car shouting, "Ya! I got a few bucks." The Caddie slammed to a stop and he jumped into the back seat before she had second thoughts.

Looking around the back seat, ringing the water out of his head band, he noticed a large shopping bag—also he saw the driver now, a grossly obese woman weighing at least four hundred pounds. Large rolls of fat hung over her back headrest. "Gimmie five bucks, peace creep," she squawked in a thick southern drawl, "and don't touch nothin' back there! Don't get nothing wet!" Shaking from his cold dampness, he fumbled through his jeans for some bills, and handed them over to her blubbery mitt that snapped its fingers impatiently, inches in front of his nose.

Snatching up the money, Fatty half turned to him taking her eyes off the road and reluctantly said, "We're goin' ta Key

West. I's Beulah and dis old buzzard nexta me is me ma," she chuckled then said, "but I calls her Crinkles 'cause she's as wrinkled as an old road apple. Heh Heh Heh!"

Crinkles shot a withered claw across her daughter's bloated face with a resounding smack. "Screw you Beulah, that ain't no way to talk 'bout your poor old ma!"

"Shaw ma," Beulah whimpered rubbing her swelling red cheek. "I ain't mean no disrespect!" Scowling now teary eyed she turned on Tavo. "Hey pinko, see dat grocery bag sittin' next ta ya? It be filled with head cheese sandished… keep passin' 'em up ta me. I can't drives… keep my strengths up if'n I don't et… and don't get no ider bout snatchin' any youself. I's only packed nuff for me en ma."

She punctuated her warning with a horrendous mud-slapping fart that shook the car and permeated it with the stench of an over-flowing septic tank.

Tavo gasped for breath, pinched his nose shut between his finger and his thumb, rolled the back window down and blew his airplane breakfast into the following traffic. Pieces of half digested pancake splattered on the windshield of a red sporty MGB driven by a pissed off businessman in a Sear Sucker suit.

Crinkles spun around in her seat, hooked her beak-like nose over it and peered at him with the hate filled eyes of a demented vulture. "What's da matter, draft dodger. Can't take a little gas," she cackled. "You pansy peacenik, little fagwad."

Looking around paranoid, as the M.G.B. passed them, the business man shooting them the bird, he hastily said, "Listen, I'm no draft dodger! Just going to Key West for Spring Break you know, from college."

Crinkles shook with anger, hacked up a rubbery green and brown tobacco chawed glob and spat it squarely into his lap. "Bull sheet, ain't even spring," she snapped wiping spittle from her pointed shriveled chin. "Do what Nixon says, loves it or leaves it—that's me en Beulah's motto! Ain't dat right Beulah? All thems peace creeps needs ta learns in college is ta loves it or leaves it." She balled up her scrawny fist, shook it in front of his face for emphasis. "But oh no, what's theys learns is ta be bums—learns ta smoke Mary Jewana and takes a pant load 'o dope!"

She took a swing at him but he dodged it by scrunching up tight against the back seat. Cursing her near miss she turned her attention to her daughter. "They're all a bunch of nigger lovers Beulah! What 'bout them learnin' that free love crap? They's fuck in the open at dem lovins' like dogs in heat!"

Crinkles ranted on as Beulah nodded and belched confirmations through mouthfuls of headcheese sandwiches. Tavo tried to make himself disappear, scrunching down further in the back seat. But Crinkles kept up her attack talking indirectly at him through Beulah. "What 'bout them Beatles. That sheet ain't music!"

He said nothing and stared out the window, praying Crinkles would tire, shut the fuck up. But she was just warming up. "Why them Beatles is nothin' but white niggers, screamin' and shakin' like jungle bunnies! Nixon should ship them hippies 'long with the niggers back to Africa!"

He was about to inform Crinkles the Beatles were from England they didn't need to be shipped anywhere, but she wouldn't stop the roll she was on.

"Hot damn," she exclaimed as if she had the perfect insight to the problem and slapped her knee, "I believe Nixon's too soft. Sure hopes George Wallace gets lected president. He's one good ole boy'd turn the Klan on the pack of 'em!" She spun around once more glaring at him, tobacco juice dribbling down her chin. "What you think a dat hippie?"

He tried to hide behind his Boy Scout pack, hoping its wholesomeness would shield him from her wrath. No such luck. Crinkles was fired up with the spirit, she shouted to the heavens, "Old George would shave you head and tar and feather yo ass! Halleluya! And don't forgetts bouts Lester Madox! He'd teach them fairies a gott damn lesson. Shove a ax handle up they asses! He would! Well hippie, what you gotta say ta dat?" not taking her hateful stare off of him, daring him to respond.

Figuring any reply would be wrong, he said, "I think all we have here is a generation gap," and smiled benevolently hoping to defuse the tension. No way! Crinkles trembled and sputtered. Tobacco juice shot out of her mouth, flew through the air. "Gap my ass!" she roared "I loves Elvis Presley. He a fine young man. Sheet! He know ta love and honor his country. Ain't no fuckin' draft dodger. Served proud he did!"

He squirmed in the back seat, passed a sandwich up to Beulah, hopping to distract Crinkles. Figured he had about as much chance of her understanding him as convincing Eldridge Cleaver to be J. Edgar Hoover's butler.

But he was also getting pissed off. He'd been abused, pushed around by everyone he had come in contact with lately. Now a hitched ride to Key West had turned into a chamber of horrors. Before he could stop himself, he said the first thing that popped into his mind: "To quote Bob Dylan, I like Fidel Castro and his beard." And knew it was a gigantic mistake before he even had it out of his mouth. Crinkles jumped like an M-80 had exploded under her. She struggled to crawl over the front seat and tear him apart with her claws. She screamed with raw hatred, "Stop da car, Beulah! I'm a gonna rip his head off and shit down his neck!"

Beulah grabbed Crinkles and tried to restrain her with her ham-like arm struggling with her other hand to keep the car from swerving off the road or into oncoming traffic. She gulped down a sandwich, which was dangling, from her mouth in one swallow.

"Ah Ma!" she said in a half-asssed attempt to pacify. "Leave da poor bastard alone. He been passin' me saniches right regular like. Sides, he kina cute, too! May even let him pork me if he ain't too stinky. Ya knows they never wash! Say boy, how'd ya like ta pork old Beulah, huh?" She gave him a wink through the rear view mirror. "Yes sir," she said, "I'd grab hold ya twixt my ass cheeks 'n suck yas up my honey hole! Ha! Ha! Hee!"

Tavo sat silent, stunned. A sick look on his face as he contemplated the disgusting prospect of being Beulah's love slave.

"Aw shaw, Beulah," Crinkles snapped, shed' calmed down somewhat but was still struggling against the weight of her daughter's arm. "He ain't man 'nuff ta get a bone up unless it'd be ta plug a baboon up da ass!"

To make her point, she spat another gob of tobacco juice out her window, which blew right back in the rear open window splattering on his T-shirt producing an ugly brown stain. Par for the course so far. He figured they must still be about an hour's drive to Key West. So he searched his mind for a way to change these emotionally laden topics, the hostile atmosphere, while trying to wipe her tobacco juice off his shirt. Then he remembered from his psychology that people liked to talk about themselves, so as a way to steer Crinkles in a safer direction, he asked as sincerely and genuinely as possible," Say why are you ladies going to Key West?" Seemed to him an unlikely place for these two right wing red necks.

"Why, we's Conchs, Asswipe!" Crinkles answered curtly.. "Lives der. Sure as sheet don't preciate yo kind comin' down stinkin' the place up neither…."

He couldn't believe his ears, he must have heard wrong and swallowed the lump that was rising in his throat, worried now, he asked, "You two fish for conch?"

"Course we don't, poop-for-brains," Beulah said and laughed. "Pa and the boys fished 'em all out long ago's. We's shrimpers now… plenty o' dem critters all over de ocean!"

He fidgeted now, rubbed his hands together nervously, "So you drive boats to the Caribbean then? Fish for shrimp around the Islands?" How could these two be the rebellious liberal Conches Bercherer had told him about?

"Sheet fire and save matches," Crinkles bellowed. "Dis ass breath don't know crap from shinola! Beulah—what's I say? See… day don't learns him nuttin' at dat got damn college! Don't know one go to no nigger islands for shrimps! Shrimps lives right next ta shore." Crinkles now looked at him the same way Rosenthal had when he'd transformed into the Devil, "Say boy, why you so interested in dem islands? You ain't plannin' on cheaten Uncle Sam outta his dues, are ya?"

Sweat broke out on his forehead. How had she pegged him so easily as a draft evader? It must be written all over his face. Maybe he should cut his hair, take the look of a preppie or a red neck down here.

He told her once more he was on a vacation from college and was exhausted. Told her he needed to rest and curled up into a ball pretending to sleep. The rain had stopped and small islands and dense mangrove swamps of the Keys whizzed by under an endless blue skyway. The air was filled with the sweet smell of life. Life he still wished to live even if Irene had broken his heart

But he couldn't sleep. He cursed himself for being so gullible. Conchs weren't anything like Becherer described. It looked like Crinkles might turn him in or worse, butterfly him like a shrimp, not rescue him… give him sanctuary. He prayed these two monsters were exceptions… abnormalities, misfits from their own culture. He'd search the docks of Key West for the real Conches after his arrival

Rather than be consoled by his last thought, a flood of emotions swept over him from out of the blue, tears weld up under his tightly closed eyelids and rolled down his face. He was hit square between the eyes with the realization that in all probability he was nothing more than a coward. Yeah, sure, he marched in anti-war protests, confident then that the war was morally wrong, but that was when he was with hundreds of others who'd given him their moral support—strength because of their numbers. Now alone he didn't feel that strength. The protests became a facade in his mind and he was afraid. Afraid to go to Vietnam and die. Afraid to be all alone, on his own, not knowing what to do, where to go. Not knowing how to survive.

Then there was that Fiasco with Irene. He hadn't the guts to stand up to her mother—no backbone to fight for someone he loved—the only love of his life. Let Rosenthal walk all over him too. Rather than confront that pompous jerk, he'd turned his mind into a weak blob of Jell-O, escaped inside a drug. When life got rough, tough decisions had to be made, challenges had to be faced, and he took the easy way out. Ran drugged his mind into oblivion. Now he was blubbering out loud, crying, not able to conceal his hurt, his self-loathing any longer. Not even from these twisted hate-filled women in the Caddie.

Crinkles sure as hell took notice of his weakened state. She jumped over the back seat before Beulah could restrain her this time, she yelled in his ear, "End a da line, asshole!" She braced her back against the rear door and kicked him out of the other door that Beulah had opened into Duvall Street—Key West's main thoroughfare. "Aw' shucks, Beulah," she cackled reveling in his tears, "I musta' hurt the little peckers feelings." Then she thrust her scrawny fist out the window and flipped him the bird. The Caddie took off with a hollow backfire into his face and Crinkles hollered out of the departing wreck, "Sorry, peace creep. Gonna have ta report ya ass ta the Draft Board. Ha! Ha! Ha!"

He sat in the gutter, amid litter, broken wine and beer bottles, old crumpled McDonald's burger wrappers and milk shake containers. He forced himself to stand up, brushed himself off, tried to wipe his tears away and smeared the soot of the backfire over his pathetic face, so that now he really looked like the dirty bum he felt like. Not knowing anything else to do he put one foot in front of the other and headed for the boat docks Bercherer had told him were at the end of

Duvall Street, passing by bars and restaurants filled with partying tourists having a great time. He only had to walk a few blocks to find the boat marinas and then his heart sank to his sandals. A sickening sight greeted him: Macho male versions of Crinkles and Beulah. Rough, ugly, mean looking fishermen milling around beat up old boats of all shapes and sizes. The fishermen wore crewcuts or grease filled hair. Tattoos stood out on their brawny tanned arms. Their boats flew the rebel flag, and bore slogans slapped on with stickers sold in novelty stores, that proclaimed, "KILL A HIPPY, MAKE MY DAY," "THE ONLY PEACE I WANT IS A PIECE OF ASS," "WHITE POWER," and "GEORGE WALLACE FOR PRESIDENT."

The fishermen sneered at him; one threw a beer can, barely missing his head. Another shouted, "Get a hair cut faggot!" He made a quick exit, running, and headed back up Duvall. He slowed down to a trot, then stopped when he herd "Street Fighting Man" by the Stones blare out a more beckoning welcome. It came from an open-air bar, right in front of him right there on the corner, called Sloppy Joes. He entered and squeezed his way through the drunken tourists to the wrap around oval old wooden bar, dug into the pocket of his cutoffs for some money, and ordered a cold beer from the overworked bartender. He gulped half of its icy froth in one swallow, hadn't realized how dry his throat was. Things looked a little better here than the docks, but his hopes for escape, a sanctuary were shattered. He leaned against the old wooden bar, finished his beer, ordered another and sipped this one slowly. He contemplated reporting for officer's training school in Georgia. Ya, he could catch a Greyhound, fabricate an excuse for being late, like his car broke down in Tennessee… made him late… that might work. If he remained in Key West, it wouldn't be long before the Conch's pegged him for a "trouble-making hippie draft dodger." Crinkles sure had, and so had those fascist fishermen soon as they saw him.

All around him tourists and even a few freaks were partying up a storm. The jukebox now boomed out the Stones "Let's Spend the Night Together." But he was oblivious to the merriment. Lost in horrible ruminations depicting himself as Rosenthal's patient in a snake pit mental institution. Then he felt a gentle tap-tap-tap on his arm. Startled out of his daytime nightmare he turned and standing there huddled up close to him was this gorgeous little pixie, with wild frizzed-out hair. She looked up at him dreamily, with the deepest soft wide blue eyes. Her skin-tight jeans showed off her shapely figure. Her bra-less breasts stretched a Che Guererra T-shirt, their hard nipples making Che's eyes to bug out, demanding revolution for the people. Her sensual smile she flashed at him lit the bars dark interior. She shouted "Hi!" over Jaggers wails. "What's your sign?"

Someone played Street Fighting Man once again on the jukebox. This time it seemed even louder than before, coaxing all to take to the streets join the fight—"What could poor boys do?" He struggled to communicate with her over Mick's raspy voice and Keith's blasting guitar licks.

He managed to shout in her cute ear, cupping his hand over it, that he was a Leo. But there was something stirring tingly in his crotch. Something he thought was dead after Irene. She shouted something about what his scene was, or what his trip was, something like that, into his ear. Then suddenly the crescendo of the jukebox ended to rack up another selection, and he yelled at the top of his lungs for all the bar patrons to hear, "I'M DODGING THE DRAFT!"

Most of the drunk tourists looked at him, frowning angrily, but the few freaks gave him the peace sign. She put her finger to her luscious lips to shush him, winked at him and threw her arms around his neck, squeezing Che's beard, and her squishy breasts against his pounding chest. She planted a passionate kiss on his lips probing his mouth with her wiggly tongue, pinning him up against the bar by grinding her pelvis into his bulging crotch.

"I'm Donna" she screamed above the music that now exploded with Jimmy Hendrix's *Wild Thing*. She rubbed her sex up and down his leg letting her head roll back looking up at him as if in orgasm. His erection nearly popped his zipper. With her eyes out of focus, and a wet spot starting to ooze through her jeans, she shouted in his ear that she knew an underground group in the Key's, an Anti-War group. They'd help him! Spend the night with her—that is if he wanted to—she'd make introductions in the morning.

He felt what it must be like to be Manic Depressive, cause he was riding a manic magic carpet ride now to the galaxy, after being in death valleys depression for so long. Time to order more beer, maybe even the jukebox had Steppin Wolfs *Magic Carpet Ride* on it. He'd play that now! What a high, a natural high. No drugs, except for a couple of beers. As he shouted for the bar tender to bring more beers, a ships bell hanging over the bar clanged like a hurricane just hit. He and Donna looked up startled by this new sound, and saw a Neanderthal looking man, naked except for a dirty pair of clam diggers covering his privates and a red patterned pirates bandana tied around his ugly misshapen head. He was swinging by one arm from the bells rope, back and forth he sailed over the bar ringing the bell with hellish furry. All the bar patrons cheered and ordered more drinks. He was gripping a quart bottle of Colt 45 in his huge greasy hand, swigging from it—the suds dripped out of his ugly mouth and ran down his hairy chest. The bartender didn't seem to mind, just cheered him on like all the rest. This must be some nightly ritual, Tavo thought.

Without warning the brute dropped like a bowling ball smack dab between them knocking him on his ass, onto the bar floor's slop and muck. He watched in horror as this ape grabbed hold of Donna's luscious breasts, and twisted them like two rusty doorknobs. He bellowed like a mad bull, "Let's fuck sweetcakes! Or at least give me a blow job!" He just stood there grinning at her lecherously. She let loose a terrified shriek that overpowered Hendrix's screaming guitar, and ran out of the bar before he could stand up and stop her. He couldn't stand; kept slipping and sliding on the ooze of the bar's floor. Looking down at him still grinning his lecherous grin this Cro-Magnon daemon thrust out a hand and pulled him to his feet. "Tough luck, matey," he slurred in a drunken garbled Australian accent. "There's plenty fish in them thar seas," and draped a powerful arm over Tavo's shoulder, hugging him. Drunkenly he slurred, "Me mates calls me Striker." Yes, he remembered all too well now, that's how they had met—that son of a bitch. He pulled him, shoved him to the back of the bar, rudely pushing patrons away with one hand to clear a path. Then tossed him into an empty chair at a deserted table, sat down beside him, gave him a teeth-rattling backslap and pronounced with drunken optimism, "Ah, don't take it so hard matey! Key West is full a pussy. We'll both get laid fore the night's over!"

Tavo glared at this grinning idiot he wanted to kill him, but all he could do was whine, "You don't understand shit! That girl was my savior!"

Striker pityingly shook his head and said, "No matey, it's you who don't understands. No skirt can save yas. Yous gotta saves thems." He hunched his chair closer to Tavo's, put his arm around him, hugging him up, blew his stinking beer breath in his face, "You's got it all wrong. You's gotta save thems, that's what they likes—big, strong blokes! Yessiree! That little piece of ass you was with was too skittish. A real cock teaser, lucky I chased her away… she'd end up giving ya the blue balls." He slapped the table with his fists howling laughter at his whit. Then noticed Tavo sitting there pouting, not sharing his obnoxious joke. "Ah, don't look so glum," Striker said. "Let me shout for a few rounds." He looked Tavo up and down slyly, scrutinizing him and whispered, "I knows the owner of this dive, we can drinks all night long on the house. Me en him are best mateys! What ho!"

He grabbed him in a headlock and gave him a painful Dutch rub thinking that would cheer him up, and yelled for the waitress to bring them a quart of Colt 45 and a bottle of Jose Cuervo Tequila for a chaser.

So that was it. That's how he had ended up on this stinking smelling rusted out steel hulk of a boat with this demented drunken Australian oaf.

But there was more much more. He had at least five days and nights on this stomach turning, bouncing ocean before he reached Jamaica.

But Striker enjoyed his company, welcomed the opportunity of a captive audience and spilled his whole story after realizing Tavo was a draft dodger and wouldn't ever be returning to the States, posed no threat to him. He was a real modern-day pirate all right. Prior to operating between America and the Caribbean, he'd spent years sailing in and around Papua, New Guinea, and Australia, smuggling shrunken heads, decapitated by fierce headhunters. Even though head hunting was strictly forbidden by the New Guinea government, it was a cherished custom that the locals just couldn't seem to break. Rich Australian eccentrics would pay up to five thousand Australian dollars for a head, which only cost him a few beads and trinkets. But he'd finally saturated the market. There were few weirdo's left who coveted a head, so he picked up stakes and headed his old diesel burning scow for the USA. Now he was engaged in yet another smuggling operation. Marijuana. Smiling an innocent smile, he feigned the K Sara Sara attitude of a loveable sociopath. Claimed he was just the boatman, just paid a standard fee per dope run. Only helping out some rich kids who operated their drug ring out of Negril, Jamaica.

He boasted he had a foolproof way of guaranteeing the safety of the pots entry into the US After loading up in Negril, he'd stop not off at one of the numerous Keys off the South, Shore of Cuba and pickup a couple of Cubans. Usually they were criminals escaping from one of Fidel's prison, anxious to partake of the riches and good life of America. He'd then head for Miami engines full blast, with the Cubans on board, along with the thousand pounds of compressed grass under the floorboards. Reaching US waters, he'd radio The Brothers Fraternal, a right wing, anti-Castro Cuban group in Miami, and announce he'd rescued some of their fellow countrymen from Castro's grasp. When he docked in Miami, he'd be greeted by flocks of Cubans waving American Flags. The news media and even the CIA and FBI came out to applaud his feats of bravery. He'd then get stinking drunk, and be given declarations of honor and praise by all the patriots. The next day hungover, but feeling like a hero, he'd ferry his real cargo down one of the intercostal waterways, to some huge mansion's private jetty off Star Island, where the dealers were anxiously awaiting the pot. Striker claimed this was a lot safer and much more profitable than smuggling the heads. Never knew when you'd run into a factie witch doctor. One with a wild hair up his arse who may see a trophy in you.

Days past and the fresh salty sea air gradually calmed the throbbing blood vessels surrounding Tavo's cranium; he slowly adjusted to this vast new oceanic world. But with seafaring adjustment came fear, paranoia that he was not only a fugitive from the US Army, an international drug smuggler… part of the crew.

Shanghaied!

His principals compromised. Sure, he smoked some reefer with his buddies in college. Groovy! Thumb your nose at the authorities. But he'd always put his foot down to selling… from profiting from drugs. That was copping-out to capitalistic establishment values. You shouldn't make money off of drugs;

at least that's what he always thought. Drugs were for spirituality, mind expansion. He wanted no part of Strikers scam.

But his dissonance was overshadowed. He was headed in the right direction. The one he had started out for. A safe haven from the War, he was filled with hope, exhilaration, and anticipation. He wondered? could this be his island paradise, like the one his father longed for? Like the one he dreamed of?

4

"There is no hiding place
among the kingdoms Of Jah"

Bob Marley
From the song *One Love*

The five-day journey to Jamaica was more than eventful for him. The only boats he'd been on before were rickety old rowboats on small inland lakes in Michigan. Striker's old, steel-hulled, thirty-eight foot tub looked like it had been through World War I, and the Caribbean was no Lake Huron.

The old scow became a floating home to him. Like a cozy Recreational vehicle that chugged along faithfully over a vast blue ocean highway, unencumbered by annoying traffic or other distractions. His warm sheltering womb delivering him to a safe rebirth.

He asked Striker incessantly what Negril, Jamaica, was like, what he would find there. But Striker only laughed at his obsessive questioning, repeated his manta about booze and broads and drugs, "Sames as all the other dumps in the world," he'd grumble after a while, annoyed by Tavos pestering.

The only food Striker had bothered to pack aboard were jaw-breaking crackers he called hard-tack, and some moldy smelly cheese. For all his other gross habits he was confirmed vegetarian. There were ten cases of Budweiser but only enough ice to last the first day. He informed Tavo, nonchalantly, that all they had to do was troll a line behind the old tug with a large feathered jig head. They'd catch all the fresh fish they wanted. He'd fry em up on his trusty propane stove. No problem mon! The sea would provide, and Striker didn't care if his beer was warm, just so it ain't *Near Beer*.

Tavo lost himself in the exciting task of procuring fish for their dinner and to his delight caught all kinds of multi-colored species that he'd never seen before. As Striker navigated and chug-a-lugged beer all day, He pulled in skipjacks, kingfish, small tunas and dolphins. All went back to the sea to live and fight another day except one fish each evening for supper.

The tropical sun beat down and burnt him to a deep reddish bronze. He'd never been this tan before, and his hair bleached streaky blond. He even shed the few ounces of baby fat he always carried, and now an out line of hard muscle peeked out on his darkened frame. He felt strong, healthy, free.

There was only one downside when he tried to cook the fish and discovered that Striker had neglected to put in a supply of propane, the stove was useless. Striker was unfazed. "Don't fret, matey, ain't you ever et sushi?" He joked, then foraged amongst the mass of empty beer bottles piling up below deck and came up with a rancid jar of French's yellow mustard. Their meals of fresh raw fish liberally doused with mustard and washed down with warm bubbly Budweiser, really wasn't bad, and Striker had a stash of Vitamin C tablets that they ate for dessert, his only concern about their high-protein alcohol diet was the threat of scurvy. Anyway it beat green-covered cheese and moldy, hard biscuits.

His mood elevated with each passing day at sea. The endless expanse of blue azure sky dotted by slow floating wisps of cumulus clouds and mirrored by the gentle rolling ocean gradually faded into starlit nights where it felt time had stopped and he could reach up and touch the stars. He'd never known such peace before, especially those nights, when shooting stars showered the heavens and the seas became as calm as bath tub water. And he didn't feel as alone anymore; he was at one with the planet, though he had not seen land for days. Even Striker's earthquake snores, breaking the quiet nights, didn't bother him. He was on an adventure, a challenge. Most of all, he felt hope for a new day rising in his chest, and his spirits soared.

On their fifth day out at sea, after their warm beer and raw fish breakfast, Striker let loose an ear splitting wail, "Land Ho! Land Ho!" Tavo shaded his eyes with his hand and squinted in the direction he was pointing. Over the horizon he could barely glimpse the green tops of mountains. White Sea birds hovered above the boat, and a school of porpoises leapt over the bow as Striker headed for shore. Positive omens, he hopped, for what was to come.

As they drew closer to Jamaica, the water changed from deep navy blue to crystal-clear emerald green, and the distant mountaintops loomed lushly with tropical rain forest splendor. Then to his delight, and astonishment, there appeared the most pristine, white-sand beach he'd ever imagined, stretching endlessly for miles, surrounded by a teaming coral reef.

He gazed open-mouthed at this scene that had surely been created by an almighty power, it seemed untouched by human hands. At last, a paradise of infinite splendor. He felt he was having a religious experience. Some god or force beyond himself was communicating with him, telling him this place was created for his soul's survival, what a way for an atheist to feel. Beauty, peace, and tranquility still existed in the world, and he was part of it! Every cell in his body tingled. He sensed stillness, clarity, a mingling of natural colors more mind-blowing than any LSD trip. As Striker eased his old scow of a boat through the pink, purple, and golden coral heads, fish leaped out of the waters and soared with wings over the mirror-like ocean. Other schools of rainbow-colored fish played below the bow, as visible as if he was seeing them through an aquarium glass. Striker moored the boat against a concrete dock on the shore of an Amazon-like river that appeared from nowhere. It seemed to run from the jungle mountains beyond, and dump its brownish peat-colored fresh water into the sea at one end of the beach.

Across from this dock was a dilapidated cement block structure, peeling white paint, with a corrugated rusted zinc roof. The name ***Wharf Club, Willie's disciplined bar, Negril, Jamaica,*** and a sailfish were painted in fading red and blue paint on its front. A pulsating beat throbbed through open front doors, breaking the stillness of the hot, sweltering day. The Wharf Club stood out on the exquisite landscape like a festering zit on the nose of a Miss America contestant. Not even the palm trees, they're rustling fronds framing either side of this shack, made up for its ugliness.

He had no idea then, that this *disciplined* bar was anything but disciplined. It sure looked wilder than the saloons of Dodge City.

By now, Striker was more than ready to abandon his human cargo for another, much more profitable one. When all was said, Striker was a jolly sort of rough modern-day pirate, who'd been pretty kind to him. But more than that he'd delivered him unwittingly from a death sentence. In a round about way he ended up just where he wanted to be.

Striker told Tavo that a few fishing and goat-farming families lived on the beach and in the red hills behind the Wharf Club. He could find a place to sleep on one of their shack floors for about fifty cents a night. He suggested the Albert family on the beach or the Conwells on the cliffs, then said so-long, he was on his own now.

He set out on foot immediately to explore his new home with an enthusiasm he'd never experienced in his life, while Striker made straight for the bar and an iced cold Red Stripe beer.

He walked around a circular path surrounding Willie's, and found a paved two-lane road in surprisingly good condition. It seemed to have been built rather recently. The road led to a bridge that traversed the peat-laden river, and cut its way along the white sand beach. On the other side of this road was a great expanse of palm covered morass with white egrets and buzzards soaring above it that reminded him of the Everglades. Interspersed along the road at fifty-yard intervals were thirty-foot metal railroad tracks sunk in the ground. He was puzzled by them… why would anyone want to stick ugly hunks of metal into this newly built straight roadway? They looked like rusted old telephone poles without the wires… strange.

So this was Negril! The last outpost on Jamaica's West End. Visions of cowboys and Indians, pirates and pioneers, rampaged through his head. Conquistadors, pilgrims and swashbucklers competed to be included in his fantasies. This was the most profound experience in his twenty-three years of life. If somebody had asked him about Vietnam at that moment, he'd have been totally dumbfounded. All thoughts of that god-forsaken country, and its killing fields were completely forgotten—at least for the time being as he took in all the wonderment around him. He was on the up-swing rush, on a gargantuan manic ride. All he wanted was to wallow in the moment, leave himself open to anything and everything around him—let it all happen and unfold—he wanted to do nothing more than experience. This was the place of his dreams. Even he never really thought he'd actually find a place like this. Deserted island paradise on earth, they were his daydreams, just distractions for him. Something to take his mind off his problems. Help him forget about those freezing Michigan winters.

He walked along the seven-mile beach road and saw that the handful of fishing families living alongside seemed to eke out an existence that hadn't changed since their ancestors were emancipated from slavery. Then he found the Albert family's cluster of shacks about one mile from Willie's and negotiated for an old sleeping bag to bed down on their sagging floor boards, amongst a dozen or so bright-eyed children aged six months to fourteen years.

To his delight and astonishment, the family welcomed him like a long-lost relative into their humble home nestled in a palm grove on that beautiful beach. The children sat on his lap, playing with his long straight bleached hair and love beads. He tickled their ribs, and they screamed with glee, but everyone became quiet when Mr Albert, over a few white overproof rums, told a tale about Negril's history. They listened with pricked ears as the ageless head of the family spun the tale of Calico Jack the pirate. The only other sounds were the ocean breeze gently rustling the coconut palm fronds, and crickets and tree frogs chirping their accompaniment.

According to Mr Albert, Calico Jack who's real name was Jack Rackham, got his nickname from his fondness for wearing calico underwear. His mistress was Ann Bonny, and his sidekick Mary Reed or "Bloody Mary," was brought up as a boy and served with Marlborough's Army at Flanders. She was considered more ruthless and bloodthirsty than any man.

The trio and their henchmen had pillaged, plundered, murdered and wallowed in the gore of British ships, wielding dripping blood red cutlasses. Their grotesque behavior went on for three years along Jamaica's north coast, and these rascals had made their home on Negril's beaches and coral cliffs. That is until Captain Barnet, in an armed British sloop, found them at a rum punch beach party in Negril, and captured them. They were all tried in Spanish Town and sentenced to death. Ann Bonny and Bloody Mary were both pregnant and begged for mercy from the court, and were given life sentences. Mary later died in jail of fever, and Jack was hung from an iron gibbet on a small sand key outside Kingston Harbor now called Rackham Key. The small harbor on Negril's Eastern Shore is now known as Bloody Bay in honor of Bloody Mary.

Tavo was bone tired, but he forced himself to keep awake to hear every bit of this tale. It was better than any of his fantasies. The Alberts had fed him a huge meal of stewed kingfish with fiery peppers, and delicious coconut rice and red peas. The Albert children had snuggled up against him, as he finally drifted off to a dreamland filled with pirates, crystal seas, and an African race that showed no prejudice or mistrust, did no name calling, and asked no questions, that displayed unconditional acceptance even to total strangers. These were a people different from the ones he'd left behind. He dreamed sweet dreams of new possibilities, of hopes for communion, understanding, and maybe even love. This sure beat being poked in the eye with a sharp punji stick any day!

5

"You think it's the end.
But it's just the beginning."

By Bob Marley
From the song *Want More*

He awoke early the next morning, alone in the Albert's small clapboard shack. Mr Albert had set out for sea before dawn in a dugout canoe and had already returned with a boatload of fish from his traps. Mrs Albert was cleaning the fish at the ocean's edge, surrounded by a gathering of women dressed in brightly patterned dresses and head bandannas arguing amiably over the price of the catch. The Albert children were busily sweeping up the yard and mending fishing nets some just frolicked naked in the azure blue sea.

He was fired up! Eager to start exploring his new home. Ray Albert, the oldest of the children, told him other hippies lived up the West End Road, so he decided to walk there first in hopes of meeting them, might be some other draft dodgers… he'd find out how they were coping, and surviving.

The West End road was a narrow, two-rut dirt trail, more suited to the cows and goats that grazed alongside. He followed it as it lazily wound upward along cliffs that overlooked the sea. They ranged from a height of one foot to as tall as forty feet as they wound their way three miles up the rugged coastline.

These cliffs were the part of Negril known among locals as The Wild West End. Rayed told him a few hippies had erected some small hut encampments along the here, and he was really curious. Where had they come from? Why were they in Negril? Were they draft-dodgers like him? Striker said there was a group involved in pot smuggling; what would they be like? Marijuana had been sold in small amounts under guarded secrecy at Michigan State but he had only passing acquaintance with a couple of daring dealers there.

Mr Albert claimed hippies were the only white people he'd ever seen come to Negril, and asked him if all Americans were like them with long hair, beards, beads and a love of ganja. He attempted to explain the political, and cultural factors that had shaped them, but Mr Albert soon lost interest, he could care less about what took place in America. It had no impact on his day to day task of surviving off the land. To him, hippies were like the few rastafarians who lived among them. He'd occasionally "make a money" by renting the "Hippie Mon" a floor to sleep on and providing a meal.

Tavo was astounded by all he had seen, and experienced so far. Could he find a home here? Was the land for sale? Could he create a new life here? Was he safe from the draft now? Safe from prison, from Vietnam?

As he walked, he was dumbstruck by the natural wonder of this stretch of coastline. Ocean caves thirty feet high meandered into limestone rock walls that undercut the dirt path. At their feet, coral reefs teeming with exotic sea life dotted crystal clear waters tinged every shade from blue to green. The cliff edges blazed with fiery red poinsettias and yellow-green coconut trees. The rich spectrum of colors produced a rainbow for his eyes.

Every half mile or so, he saw a local family's board shack or a seven feet by seven feet bamboo store that sold Red Stripe beer, canned goods, rice, and rum nestled in a palm grove. But they barely disturbed the natural beauty of the place. No cars or other vehicles passed him; the trail was too rough and where would they be going? There was nothing here. It looked like it would take a car more than twenty minutes to travel the three miles; there were so many deep ruts and holes along the way. He walked the entire length of the West End kicking up dust but found no compatriots or expatriates, no hippies, so he turned around and headed back.

A few locals walked or bicycled to the roundabout circle that marked the midpoint between the cliffs and the beach but they seemed shy, and didn't stop to talk to or show any special interest in him. His initial thought that Willie's Bar was the center of town was correct and in fact Willie's *was* town, so he headed for there thinking maybe it was a focal point might offer some personal contact. Willie also owned a grocery store directly across the street that sold the same dry goods and spirits as the little shacks, only in greater quantities and at somewhat reduced prices. The rest of the inventory consisted primarily of ketchup, tinned meat, sardines, salt mackerel, rice, and flour. The West End road separated these establishments. When it was dry, the dirt road sent up great puffs of dust, when the torrential rains fell, it turned to oozing mud. When he reached the Wharf Club, he decided that even Ernest Hemingway wouldn't go in there, even if he were dying of thirst. But he was boiling hot, sweaty and thirsty, so he peeked inside saw that the interior was not as bad as its faded front and went in. The inside of Willie's bar was surprisingly dark and cool compared to the heat and glare of the day outside. The bar was a bamboo counter fifteen feet long behind which was stacked an assortment of cheap vodkas, rums, and garishly colored liquors. Hand-printed misspelled signs behind the bar amongst the clutter of liquor bottles read: NO BAD LANGAGE, NO SPITTING, NO IDDLERS, NO FITEING, NO CREDIT.

A carved mahogany African head three feet high sat on a raised round table in the center of the floor that appeared to have once been cement but was now mostly dirt. At the back was a beaten-up nineteen-fifty vintage jukebox with steel mesh bolted over its front. He walked over for a closer look, and noticed that the selections consisted of popular reggae tunes of the day by unknown stars to him like Big Youth, Toots and the Maytals, The Heptones. But there were some soul classics by Jerry Butler, Al Green, and the Impressions that he use to grove on. This was the place! Negril's electric power supply stopped here at Willie's jukebox. Negril's town: Willie's end-o-the-road gathering spot.

He'd also passed, on his walks, an old stone-cut Anglican Church, and a cement block primary school; both seemed empty. Willies looked like the sum total of civilization in Negril.

He began to spend his days at the bar, hoping to establish friendships or meet some comrades from back home, hoping to find out what expats could do here. How could they survive? Could they own land, was any available for sale? Was it expensive? Could he be extradited back to the US to face trial, court marshal? Anyway this was where his Jamaican odyssey began, and he now felt soulfully at home there. Willie also served food: fresh conch chowder, fried tuna fish, curry goat, and the traditional Jamaican coconut rice and red peas. The food was cheap, surprisingly good, and the portions large. However, he was seldom able to relish Willies' culinary arts without incident. The bar was also the town meeting place for drunks, rude boys flashing ratchet knives (a menacing gravity knife with a ring at one end that made a click-clack-click sound when flicked open by twirling it around one's finger), and goats. *El Presidente*—known to locals as the figurehead honcho of Negril—could be found there every day, at almost any hour. He was a three and a half foot midget, coal black with a scarred, distorted face, who guzzled overproof white rum nonstop… when he had money. These Herculean drinking bouts usually wound up with *El Presidente* vomiting on the barroom floor and cursing the patrons, the bartender, and Willie in Jamaican patois. His favorites were “bumbo claat” and “rass claat”—which Tavo finally figured had something to do with an old rag shoved up your ass. If a woman happened to pass by, the *Presidente* would demand to eat her pussy. As this spectacle unwound nightly, pigs, chickens, and goats meandered in and out of the bar, pissing and defecating on the floor. Some disciplined bar!

After he’d been sharing the Alberts’ simple paradise lifestyle and open, warm hospitality for more than a week, he knew he couldn’t continue this relationship forever. Not that he minded sharing their kind hospitality, but he wanted a place of his own. If he was going to spend the rest of his life here, he had to put down his own roots, he told himself, although he had no idea what those roots could be. So far, Negril had fulfilled his tropical fantasies and then some. The big, looming question was where and how did he fit in paradise? He was no fisherman… but maybe he could learn. With some help, he could probably hollow out a cottonwood tree, then, maybe, he could buy some woven bamboo fish traps made by the fishermen, learn how to set them, and haul them around the great barrier reef that helped to form the seven-mile beach, like Mr Albert did.

So far he’d spotted neither hippies nor any other Americans. Most of the locals were closed mouthed about their whereabouts, and even when someone spoke to him, he found it almost impossible to understand them because of the confusing patois they spoke. Syllables came out in a jumble of singsong words that held no meaning to his ears, although he enjoyed sitting for hours at the bar and be lulled by its hypnotic sound. On one occasion when he’d mentioned his difficulty in understanding the language to Ray Albert, he was informed in a modified patois “nobody inna Negril goin twis up dem jawbone so dat you can understan dem, you must learn de patois”.

Ruminations of companionship, communication with the outside world, wafted through his mind like butterflies on a breeze one afternoon, as he nursed a Red Stripe beer at Willie's bamboo bar, and watched a ram goat crap on the floor. Then the door swung open and out of the blazing sun walked a white man in his early twenties. As he peered through the dark haze of the bar, the figure became clearer. He was short, about five-foot-seven—and fat—at least two hundred pounds. He was clean-shaven and with shoulder-length hair, and wore a faded blue Izod shirt, khaki shorts, and brown topsiders. One eye squinted half-closed as he frowned, gestured passionately, and shouted in rapid-fire patois to a stoned local fisherman.

Suddenly, his focus sharpened, and to his astonishment, he realized that he knew the guy. He was Leonard "Buddy" Stern, from Michigan State.

Buddy had been a college drug dealer who everyone whispered was backed by the Mafia. He was extremely bright IQ-wise, ingested his product—LSD—daily, and even without dealing, he was rich—born rich. Tavo had heard that he'd dropped out of the dope scene and was living peacefully on some tropical island, but never really believed it.

Excitedly, he ran up to him and shouted over the reggae "Hey Buddy! Tavo Gripps! What're you doing here?" Buddy grinned warily, looked him up and down coldly with that one eye half-closed cockeyed like; "Hey, man, like I'm tripping on acid," he said, then shook his head in disgust, and looked out the bar towards the Negril river. "My cabin cruiser's sinkin in the ocean. Shit! Catch ya latter", and he charged out of the bar, heading for the beach.

Tavo waited, excited with anticipation for over an hour while Buddy and four barflies hauled his boat up the Negril River to a spot where it could be patched. Here was his first chance to find out about Negril from an American's perspective. Find out what was 'happening' where he might fit in… was he safe here… safe from the draft board? Hell Buddy would know! He out foxed informers, narks, and campus police.

When Buddy returned, he walked right up to him. “Hey man, no one calls me ‘Buddy’ anymore,” he stated coldly. “It’s Leonard or Len if we’re friends. See?”

Tavo took a step back, surprised by his unfriendly remark, even though he hadn’t been close to him, “Sure Len,” he managed to say, “Whatever you say. But what are you doing here, ducking the draft?”

Len looked him up and down once more, taking him all in through that squinted eye “Never mind what I’m doing here.” he said “What the fuck are you doing here?”

“I was gonna get drafted, sent to Nam, it’s a long story man but I ended up here… you see it all happened when….” Len cut him off.

“Ya, ya, ya I heard it all before, don’t bother. Anyways I might as well get it over with seeing it looks like you’ll be here for a while. Find out anyway…. I live down the West End”

“No kidding,” said Tavo “You rent a house there? What’s the story?”

“Man you ask enough fucking questions.” Len said.

“It’s just that you’re the first American I’ve seen… even knew from the States!” said Tavo not able to contain the excitement in his voice or act cool.

Len stared hard at him, looking annoyed, then reluctantly shrugging his shoulders and said “Hop in my car outside I’ll show you my place, get it over with, you’ll find out anyways.”

Tavo beamed; here was his connection, a guy who knew what was happening. “Sure” he said, and they left the bar and hopped into his car, a white Ford Escort.

But Len was quiet, didn’t say a word, ignored all Tavo’s questions as he tore up the West End Road smashing into pot holes, shaking the car’s front end, winding up the old cliff road like a race car driver.

About two miles up the road he slammed on the breaks and the Escort fishtailed to a stop. He pointed to five acres of land with over a thousand feet of ocean-cliff frontage that plummeted down into the turquoise ocean. The property, Len begrudgedly told him, had been given to him by a local Negril marijuana farmer who he'd bailed out of jail and paid his fine. Shit! Ganja was no big deal in Jamaica the fine for growing acres of it was only a couple hundred bucks. Tough luck if the farmer was broke and Len was loaded—tough luck for the farmer that is. He had paid locals to clear about an acre of jungle on the cliff edge overlooking the sea and plant it with coconuts, exotic-looking flowers, and bananas. He'd had some other homeboys build a thatched roofed, two-bedroom bungalow smack on the cliff edge. It boasted a generator-operated stereophonic sound system, a semi-modern octagonal bamboo kitchen with propane refrigerator and oven. Hammocks, wicker furniture, and kerosene lanterns adorned the spacious mahogany-floored open porch.

Len pointed out to him his sixty-year-old housekeeper, Miss Ira, and his two gardeners, Garth and Aubrey, who cared for the yard and his beautiful flowers. Tavo was awe struck that Len had achieved the most idyllic fantasy anyone had ever imagined. He remembered the money still stashed securely in his knapsack, and asked if it was possible for him to purchase land along this wondrous coastline?

"Wouldn't advise my worst enemy to buy land here," Len said. "Anyway, you gotta have at least five grand now. The locals are getting wise that ocean property is desirable see, even if only to foreign freaks, guess that's out a your ball park."

It sure seemed odd to him how Len could be so negative about his breath taking property, about his idealic lifestyle. But Len would say no more, he was put off by Tavo's question… he acted like he wanted to get rid of him.

But this was great news even though Len was a different story. He refused to answer anymore questions and made it clear that Tavo should keep his distance. He had no desire to renew any old acquaintances or be friends. There was no welcome mat. In fact, the sooner Tavo could make an exit, the better! And the biggest mistake Tavo could make in Negril was to ask questions! Still, Tavo was enthralled by the prospect of the availability of property. Then Len told him to get lost. Told him to go back to the Warf Club and drink his beer.

The next day Garth, Lens gardener, saw Tavo walking up the West End Road. He had stopped at a high cliff that jutted out into the ocean, and was gazing at the horizon. Garth ran up to him all excited, he'd eavesdropped, heard everything about Tavos interest in land. He knew of the perfect spot better than the land Tavo now stood on. He pulled on Tavos arm, said they had to hurry there were other hippies anxious to buy it. So they rushed up the road and he purchased two acres, sight unseen, from Clifton Harrot, Garth's friend, a local goat farmer and fisherman. The purchase was sight unseen because the jungle grew so thickly out of this coral outcropping that penetration into the land was impossible. Nevertheless, it had to be beautiful ocean front land as well--everything else in this place was. What the Hell! He wasn't going anywhere he was a fugitive from injustice. So he paid Clifton one thousand bucks as a down payment--the rest payable upon delivery of a registered title that Clifton would procure from Kingston. The deal was written and signed with Clifton's "X" on a piece of old brown paper bag and witnessed by Garth. "Dat de Jamaican way" said Garth, "lawyer dem cheat you."

He was now a land baron in paradise. He'd finally arrived; made a commitment. No longer homeless, country-less or purposeless although, his purpose was still rather ill defined. But he felt exhilarated felt almost delirious with joy, like a three-year-old waking up on Christmas morning. He'd made a beginning. He was realizing his father's dream. He'd made it happen! He'd live his own dream! And just think he'd only been in Jamaica a little over two weeks!

6

"People try to put us down
Just because we ge–ge–ge-get around
Talkin' 'bout my generation."

Peter Townsend
The Who
From the song *My Generation*

Garth had told him that he had an expatriate neighbor from the United States on the western border of his property. The guy's name was Nicholas Lebowitz—Nick—and he leased the next-door property from a Jamaican doctor. Tavo would soon get to know Nick more intimately, Garth predicted, he was getting married within the next two weeks, and would be throwing a wedding reception on his property. Nick might even be neighborly and invite Tavo.

But there was much more to be told about Nick, and what Garth and Clifton couldn't tell him because of the language barrier, he soon fond out first hand, by paying him a visit. Nicks leased property had also belonged to Clifton at one time. He sold it to a local Jamaican doctor who had the land cleared and built a three-bedroom villa with a swimming pool at the ocean's rock edge. The villa was now rundown; the yard overgrown with weeds, and the swimming pool so cracked it couldn't hold much water. All it held now were a few ducks the gardener raised, in a foot of slimy green water polluting the pool's bottom.

But what made this property so unique was that every night, you could stand on almost any spot and witness a nearly 300-degree, panorama of the Caribbean Sea as the sun set in a glorious, multi-colored western sky. Nick's leased property also had gorgeous coves studded with caves, as well as terraced sundecks and staircases built by the doctor's contractors, that led down to a vast crystalline sea. The water was deep and the cliffs steep, so you could step off the top into nothingness, then land with a tremendous splash in the refreshing emerald waters below.

Clifton claimed that Nick's coves were the very same ones where Calico Jack the pirate hid his boat while he took on fresh water hauled down over the cliff edge in barrels. A new pirate used the caves now, he confided in whispered Americanized patois, for hiding thousands of pounds of ganja waiting transfer to offshore smuggling boats.

As for Nick, he could usually be found floating on a rubber raft on the calm waters, snorkeling through the jagged coral reefs or tanning himself black on one of the many sundecks, a large ganja spliff dangling from his bronzed hand.

At one time, Nick was a copywriter for a large New York City Advertising Agency, but his venture among the working classes lasted only a week. He then turned to a more "appropriate career choice" of Rock and Roll concert promoter. He actually promoted a couple of Donovan concerts in the United States. Now he viewed himself as a modern Great Gatsby, but to his chagrin, without the great wealth. Nick was handsome, slim, with a perfect posture and a suspiciously effeminate sashay to his gate. He also felt a special affinity with the rich and famous, and that he was blessed with the debonair personality of a modern-day Humphrey Bogart. His diction and vocabulary were eloquent to the point of flamboyance, a partial result of a fine education at the best prep schools and prestigious colleges in the USA and Europe.

Now, his villa had developed into a crash pad for wandering Freaks, who popped in and stayed for the day, night, week, month or year. Some of the guest floppers and crashers were movie stars and major rock stars like Keith Richards and Mick Jagger. Less exalted crashers ran the gamut from heroin junkies, to Playboy bunnies from Hugh Heffner's playboy club in Ocho Rios, drug smugglers, schemers, scammers, to the occasional "guest" Rastafarian. Nick's hair was longish, but his clothes were always immaculate with a crisp starch and press. The villa's maids handled his patched Levi bell-bottoms with care like an Executive's three-piece suit.

When he chose to, he could be a real charmer, with a seductively devilish Cheshire Cat's grin. But he could turn hostile in an instant, usually over some minor disturbance from in his "normal" or daily routine. He had a deep reverence for wealth, especially for the well to do of the subculture, and he rarely displayed his dark side to them. Nick condescended, and scorned, all others who didn't live up to his inflated standards.

He turned on daily with huge ganja spliffs that he chain-smoked throughout the day and night, along with popping four to five Mandrex (British Quaaludes) daily. But this chemical cocktail never seem to produce the desired effect, since his main complaint when Tavo met him was a languorously despairing, "Oh, God, I never seem to get high anymore." His other big worry was growing old, and losing his looks. He worried over every tiny blemish and extra pound. To shore up his defense against these troubles, he ingested large quantities of royal jelly. If he thought that wasn't working and became depressed, he'd blast Eric Clapton's *Bell Bottom Blues, don't let me fade away* from his five-foot tall stereo speakers perched on the cliff's edge—his doomsday lament over his fate and of the Woodstock generation.

Nick had been living like this in his cliff villa for over a year. But, unlike Tavo, he was not alone in this new land of sun and fun. In addition to the wondering entourage, he had a house partner/friend/former rock and roll business associate who shared the expenses of his spaced out Gilligan's island lifestyle.

His partner, Norman Silverstein, was five-foot nine, thirty pounds overweight, with shoulder-length hair, a long unruly drooping Fu Manchu moustache and the eyes of a wild man. In contrast to Nick's somewhat controlled, smooth outward demeanor, Norman was extremely hyper and fidgety, continually pacing back and forth, mumbling to himself, or prattling in disjointed machine-gun bursts of trivia to anyone he could engage in a conversation. He often wrung his hands over some repressed worry and mumbled to himself like an old Hasidic Jew at the Wailing Wall. He was a time bomb, slowly ticking down.

Nick maintained a freewheeling control, dominating the ensemble of freaks that collected at his home regularly. But Norman was always in the background, pacing up and down nervously, wearing one of his loud, flower-printed shirts, smoking either an overly large tobacco cigar or a ten-inch ganja spliff.

Tavo was extremely curious about Nicks up coming wedding, but had still not received the invitation Garth had alluded to. So he walked over to Nick's to hint around, maybe Nick just forgot. When Norman saw him, he charged over to him, and attempted to throw him off the property. He screamed, "There's enough free-loading hippie schmucks hanging around eating and drinking us out of house and home!" But Nick intervened and informed Norman that Tavo was an old acquaintance of Len "Buddy" Stern's—considered by the expats to be the Wild West End's founder. So Norman mumbled a begrudged apology edged with paranoia and slunk away muttering obscenities to himself. But there was trouble brewing in paradise.

Though Nick was pissed off that Tavo had bought the property next door (Tavo was too low class and he had better use for it). He welcomed the opportunity to bounce his problems, concerns and scams off of a Psychologist from the subculture, as long as there was no "therapy crap" involved, he didn't need that shit! He didn't want to hear about Tavo's draft problems either. He was above that… his parents were loaded. They knew senators, congressmen, knew all the right strings to pull, who to pay off. He didn't have to worry about Nam… didn't have to give up his citizenship. His confessions must remain strictly one-sided! Anyway, he told Tavo that the Jamaican doctor, from whom they leased the property, had been busted in the US after landing his two-engine plane on a remote landing strip in the Florida Everglades. He was caught with five hundred pounds of high-grade ganja aboard. Forced to make a large payoff to the local redneck sheriff, the good doctor was forced to sell his cliff property and villa quick. He'd informed Nick that he had to have one hundred and twenty thousand dollars immediately or he would evict him and Norman. Nick was furious. Neither he nor Norman had anywhere near the kind of money to buy the land and eviction would terminate their cherished lifestyle. "My body is finally where my mind has always been," Nick pronounced with passion to Tavo. But he did have a plan. A long shot, but Nick saw it as a sure winner and pooh-poohed Tavo's cautionary warnings as asinine psychobabble.

His plan involved one of the many young wanderers through his crash pad. A young lady, Jane, with whom he'd, attended kindergarten and grade school in his hometown of Poughkeepsie, New York. She was the adopted daughter of a wealthy Jewish family, who just happened to be close friends with Nick's parents. The Jewish community was quite small and tight in Poughkeepsie.

The beauty of his plan was its simplicity. He boasted that he'd marry Jane, invite both sets of in-laws down to Jamaica for the romantic wedding, and hold an extravagant reception with the last of Norman and his money at the doctor's cliffside villa. Jamaican dignitaries, politicians, and high-rolling jetsetters would attend to impress and charm his and her parents. The Silver Chopsticks out of Kingston, the island's best Chinese restaurant, would cater the affair. Full-service bars would be set on the cliff's edge, staffed by waiters and bartenders resplendent in white-gloves and cummerbunds.

The soft Brazilian jazz of Jobim, played on his huge stereo would set a perfect, romantic, tasteful mood. The kicker was that Jane had been married before, to a heroin junkie from whom she was now divorced. She was also a junkie who kicked the habit from time to time by drinking enormous amounts of liquor and ingesting any other available drugs. She'd abandoned her two children to her parents' care, and they had promptly disowned her.

When Tavo met Jane at Nick's, he sensed trouble. She was six feet two and skinny, but not Vogue-model shapely. Her shoulders sagged under the weight of the world and her abdomen protruded like she had swallowed a bowling ball. Her hair was peroxide blond and straggly her face infested with pimples and boils. Her nose was broken almost flat across her face, making her look like she'd been hit by a waffle iron, although it was her former husband's fist. Jane was constantly scowling and complaining about the bad cards life had dealt her, which alienated everyone around her.

Jane's appearance and afflictions did not stir Nick's humanitarian spirit. This marriage was to be purely contractual, he explained to Tavo. In fact, he had a verbal contract with Jane that after the marriage, her parents would give them a million-dollar dowry. How could they possibly refuse? They were both rich, and she was marrying a nice Jewish, Poughkeepsie boy, who was not only well educated, refined, with great prospects, but also a personal friend of the family. What a step up from her former goy, junkie first husband!

Nick inserted the stipulation that as soon as the million dollars were safely secured, they would immediately divorce.

He'd care for her two children, as he was no schmuck, and provide the best possible boarding schools, at least until they reached eighteen years of age. For Jane's part, she could do anything she wanted; shoot junk to her heart's content, whatever, just as long as she left Negril for good and never bothered him again.

What could be more equitable? To Jane, this plot also sounded fantastic; she was penniless and in bad need of a fix. Five hundred thousand big ones with no strings attached, no commitments, no responsibilities, no fucking nagging parents, turned Nick into her Prince Charming.

Nick and Norman were ecstatic at the anticipated dowry. They smoked twice their usual portions of potent ganja and dropped acid. Norman spun off to a manic euphoria, like a Tasmanian devil on Methedrine.

Nick bragged that with his half of the loot, he would build a bar-restaurant, "a bistro such as the Caribbean has never seen before." The crash-pad house would be gutted and turned into a spacious indoor dining area in case of rain. The ducks would be kicked out of the dilapidated swimming pool on the cliff's edge and it would be built over to become the bar and gathering spot. Their bartenders would wear red fezzes like in Casablanca. They'd stand on a platform that would be constructed at the bottom of the pool and serve the patrons jockeying for seats around the bar at eye level. The food served would be the finest gourmet, five-star quality, prepared by master chefs. Only the best rock and roll, with occasional Bob Marley tunes, would play over the state-of-the-art house speaker system.

Nick and Norman were fed up with cheap rock stars, hippie deadbeats, and sneaky drug smugglers sponging off their gracious hospitality. Now they'd pay dearly for the prestige of being seen at the *ultimate worldwide jetsetter hangout.* And this splendid roadside attraction would be called NICK'S CAFE.

As Tavo rested from his day's labor, he was trying to clear a path through the thick jungle to the sea now; he contemplated the exciting events about to transpire next door. The cool evenings were perfect for reflection as he lay beneath his newly constructed lean-to with the trade winds fluttering the thatch fronds of his roof. Wouldn't it be great to live on land he owned next to a world-famous hot spot? He thought. While growing up in Detroit he lived next-door to a car wash operated by winos, and a greasy-broasted chicken joint. What a change, could this be the start of something humongus? His land would have more value but that didn't really matter to him. Maybe he could build a side business, a souvenir shop—sell seashells or something, who knew? But as he scrutinized the situation more an inner pessimism pervaded that only doom awaited anyone who became involved with Nick, Jane or Norman. Better keep some distance.

Nick confessed to him that he was in love, but not with Jane who he hated with a passion. His true love was a girl from South Carolina named Betty Lou. Betty Lou was everything Jane wasn't except for one thing: She was also a heroine junkie, but at least "in the process of kicking." She was gorgeous at five feet three with a *Sports Illustrated* swimsuit figure. Her mocha coloring with no tan lines complemented her long, straight, naturally blond-streaked chestnut hair and her large doe-like green (albeit bloodshot) eyes. Her lips were full and dripped a honeycombed southern-belle accent. At night, she could be found at the Yacht Club, a swinging bar that just opened in Negril during the last month and was owned by an American expatriate, Daniel Pough. It immediately became the nighttime hangout for locals and the few international freaks; it had to be hot. The only other spot was Willies. Betty Lou could be found there nightly in one of her clinging granny dresses with nothing underneath to conceal her exquisitely formed body. During the day, whether she was at the beach, on Nick's sundecks, or the Yatch Club's veranda, she wore nothing but a thin gold chain circling her slim waist. But every night, from nine PM until pass-out time, she hung on Daniel's arm as she slurped down eight-ounce beer mugs of straight tequila. She never slurred her words or showed any other effects of intoxication. Claimed liquor had no drastic impact on her after heroin. Around two o'clock in the morning she'd quietly slide off her bar stool, completely unconscious--the slate finally having been wiped clean--and be carried off to bed by Pough.

Nick was sure that after his cafe opened, he'd no longer have to share Betty. He'd supply her with his own personal tequila, as well as the sun and sea. He liked to say that he was passionately in love with her creamy, sun-tanned thighs.

Tavo attempted to assess these schemes, tried to make some sense out of it. But the cast of characters and scenes only reminded him of some spaced-out melodramatic Soap Opera, he never would have imagined taking place in an isolated fishing village he considered to be paradise, and right next to his land. The land that every inch of it he had come to love—not because he possessed it but because it had given him hope, hope of survival and sanctuary from that horrible war. Hope of a new beginning, a new life, a second chance.

He pondered if he should bother to make friends with Nick's group. They really didn't seem to want a genuine friendship, only a sounding board for their neuroses. The Jamaicans on the other hand, were starting to be more friendly, seemed to accept him openly and easily, although he wondered if this may only be on the surface. That easy warmth often masked a cultural difference as wide and difficult to bridge as the Grand Canyon.

There was the language barrier. Patois was a mish mash of English with African words and phrases thrown in and spoken in a singsong rhythm that made it indecipherable to his uncultured ear. Communication required repetitive laborious attempts and numerous hand and body language. But the language problems were minor compared to the rituals and belief systems that formed the basis of Jamaican rural society, whose deep African roots had not been diluted in any significant way by the modern western world, unlike its African American counterparts. But Tavo made a commitment that he would seize any and all opportunities to bond and to relate to the Jamaicans; after all it was their land he now called home. They were as curious about him and his ways as he was about theirs. Most were friendly and those he approached seemed to offer an unconditional friendship he'd seldom encountered in America or with his fellow expatriates. To bridge the gaps and become one of them would take time, understanding, and learning but he was prepared to succeed.

For the short term though, Nick's group offered some familiar conversation, and a semblance of fraternity, but it was a crazed and hedonistic one.

By the beginning of his third week in Negril, he felt the beginning of a transformation. He'd learned to use a machete, and with Clifton's help, had chopped and cleared about an eighth of an acre of jungle bush from his land. He now had a great view of the ocean. His lean-to, they constructed from bushwood poles. They cut, and lashed coconut palm fronds onto them to form a roof, and provide insulation from the torrential rains that hit from time to time. He cooked simple meals over a small fire at the entrance to this palm shack. But he continued to wander over to Nick's, to take a swim in the ocean and to wash with soap in one of the caves where Nick had installed a fresh-water shower, this was real luxury.

Since he wasn't fully accepted yet by the Negrilians and really didn't seek acceptance from the freaks, he felt alone, somewhat of an outcast. Thoughts of his past began to intrude. He dreamed and fantasized about Irene. Those memories made him remorseful, especially when his new Jamaican friends rattled off in Patois about obeah, a form of voodoo, or other mysterious rituals beyond his comprehension. What was she doing now? He guessed he probably hated her at first that is right after she dumped him and married shmuck face Rosenthal. But he didn't hate her anymore. Hate was an emotion he wanted no part of now, too destructive. He tried not to even hate Rosenthal though that was a tough one. But his bouts with grief were becoming less and less frequent; they didn't last as long because something or someone usually came around to distract him from self-pity. Also clearing his land foot by loving foot took up most of his time.

Strangely enough, he didn't miss much about the United States, like he had assumed he would. Negril was like a never-ending summer camp with day after day of perfect weather and glorious sunsets, that took place each night right over his cliffs, his own back a yard.

7

"Don't know if I'm up or down
'Scuse me while I kiss the sky"

Jimmy Hendrix

As the date for the wedding approached, arrangements were set in furious motion. Nick and Jane's parents were coming, and a Rabbi in Montego Bay would conduct the ceremony during the afternoon. The wedding party would consist of immediate family members only. Nick would wear a white tuxedo—like Bogart—and Jane a flowing white gown and veil. The wedding party would then journey to the Wild West End for the reception at Nick, and Norman's, which was set to begin at six o'clock in the evening.

On the day of the wedding, Tavo wandered over at around five o'clock dressed for the occasion in his best-flowered shirt, cut off corduroys and leather thongs. The long-promised invitation had arrived only that morning and he wanted a front row view of this grand occasion the likes of which Negril had never seen before. That's not to say that rural-country Jamaicans did not hold parties. They were veritable party animals. Yeah Mon! Almost any occasion translated into a festivity: weddings, births, deaths, Christmas, Easter, building a new house, birthdays, Independence Day, and almost anything else. Their parties tended to follow African traditions, with a ram goat sacrificed for the spirits or ancestors. Its blood split on the ground before it became the featured ingredient of a curry stew and its innards, head and testicles were boiled with green bananas and fiery peppers to make a soup called

Mannish Water—reputed to cure impotency in men and frigidity in women.

As he was sipping his first Red Stripe beer of the evening, awaiting the arrival of the wedding party, he observed a strange sight. The local Negril community began dribbling in; everyone from the seven-mile beach and the cliffs: six-months-old children to grandmas and grandpas in their nineties and every age in between. Some were in their best Sunday suits, the pants bottoms worn shiny from thirty years of church pew sitting. Some only wore old holy chinos and no shoes or socks. Rastafarians arrived, flashing dread locks down to their knees, laden with pound bales of Marijuana, coconut bongs, and beating on ancient goatskin drums. Farmers with worn and torn Panama hats came dragging bleating goats from ropes so they could offer a more traditional gift of sacrifice and respect, and because most of the locals were repelled by Chinese food, which they believed contained dog meat, a poor choice of fare for any celebration.

As he sat there, taking in the procession, to his astonishment he began to comprehend a little more about his new community's culture. Negril was such a small place that most of the inhabitants were related to one another in some manner—brothers, sisters, aunts, uncles, cousins, second cousins, third cousins, et cetera—so no one ever bothered to send invitations to parties. It was assumed that everyone was automatically invited. Written invitations would have been useless anyway, as most of them couldn't read or write. So, whenever there was a get together, anyone and everyone came.

Many of the older fishermen were already loaded on white overproof rum; they staggered through the gate, pushing and shoving one another, growling "blood claats" and "pussy claats" as they argued about the day's catch.

The local wandering freak subculture dropouts were also arriving and tuning up for the celebration. Tavo was seeing most of them for the first time, since he'd been completely occupied with the task of clearing his land and building his thatch hut. He noticed that not all of this group was as clean-cut as Nick or his drug smuggler pals. Some were dressed in pirate costumes reminiscent of Calico Jack, complete with black eye patches, skull and cross-bone hats, wild sashes, machete cutlasses, and gold rings dangling from pierced ears and noses. Others came adorned in the traditional Height-Asbury attire; ropes of love beads around necks, Indian head bands over lank, straggling hair, loin cloths, granny dresses, and tinkling Hindu finger cymbals.

Since these space cowboys and girls refused to be upstaged by either the farmers and their goats or by the Rastas and their ganja, they showed their respect for the occasion by bearing gifts of joyous psychedelics. They brought sunshine acid, pink purple Owsley acid, mescaline buttons, psilocybin mushrooms, along with the local mushroom tea, and immediately set about spiking the punch bowls with this potpourri of mind expansion.

Then something sinister caught Tavo's eye swinging on a hammock by the cliff's edge, not ten feet away was the nastiest looking freak he had ever seen, and the guy was glaring at him, really giving him the once over.

It was hard to tell how tall the guy was—laying down in the hammock, but what was apparent was all the scar tissue on his muscular frame. Looked like he had been in one hell of a motor cycle accident like Evil Kineval. He might have been good-looking at one time, even handsome, but now his face was disfigured and one eye was filmed over with an ugly cataract. He had long blond straight flowing hair—but even that was patchy like spots had been ripped out. But worst of all, the most horrifying, was a necklace he wore around his neck. It was a necklace of brown shriveled up dried apricots. At first he thought they were apricots, but the more he stared, and he couldn't stop staring, he realized what they were. Dried shriveled up human ears.

Now the guy was shooting something into his arm with a needle—ya he was shooting up—stretching a rubber belt tight on his arm—holding one end in his yellow teeth, making the veins bulge, banging it home and never taking his eye off of Tavo.

"What the fuck you looking at dip shit?" He snarled after letting the rubber belt snap out of his teeth.

Tavo didn't know what to say just continued to gape—never seen anyone shoot up before—never seen anyone look like this guy before—so mean, hardlooking—he looked right through you like he'd kill you— think no more about it than if he'd squished a dew worm.

"Get the fuck over here" he ordered "I know bout yous."

Tavo approached cautiously. Three feet from the guy now, that was close enough.

"You're the fucking coward draft dodger" he spit it out like putrid bile.

"See these" he pointed to the necklace "thirty gooks took ta make it, three tours a duty in Nam"

Tavo nodded lamely, still mute. "Got no use for cowards" he chided "Now get the fuck outta here, your God damn lucky ya know Len!"

Tavo backed up made a quick retreat—Shit! He thought that guy was scary as hell. That must be what Vietnam did to you—But he didn't want to think about that now or ever, so he grabbed a second beer and mingled with the hodge podge group, as the party entered the early stages of a genuine happening. He debated taking a hit of psilocybin passed to him by a local dread, but decided in favor of observing what was to come in a somewhat coherent fashion. By this time, at least three hundred people representing a full and widely varied spectrum of races, creeds, classes, cultures and subcultures and various degrees and modalities of inebriation were now undulating wildly together. This scene was surreal without any additional mind alterations.

Keith Richards showed up, looking like the devil but no more noticed than the local goat herder. Bob Marley made an appearance with some of the Wailers and was immediately absorbed into the gathering as well.

Someone axed the soothing Jobim jazz, it was the *Girl from Ipanema*, and cranked up the volume on Jimmy Hendrix's *Purple Haze*. It came screaming through Nick's five-foot tall stereo speakers, blasting across the calm Caribbean loud enough to shake Castro out of bed.

This was by far the best party he had ever been to, had ever hoped to attend, spoiled only slightly by that scary freak, and it was only seven o'clock at night. The bridal party hadn't even arrived, and the night was still young.

Tavo was handed a third beer by a starched bartender.

Gave into just one hit of mushroom tea, he'd forget that one-eyed guy and Vietnam now. He was beginning to feel no pain, the tea was working.. In fact, he felt himself spin with the music over the ocean and a warm cosmic love for everyone in attendance crept over him. But he glimpsed a shape taking form from his peripheral view that didn't harmonize with his warm, fuzzy state. It was Norman, appearing to be more anxiety-ridden, distraught, and out-of-control than ever. He was screaming "written invitation only, written invitation only!" at non-comprehending locals. Then Norman's attention was drawn to the buffet table and its array of delicious Chinese dishes. He had to redirect all his energy there, and waged a losing battle with a group of hippies suffering a ganja-induced munchies attack, who'd set upon the food like grizzly bears on a school of migrating salmon. Norman screamed, shouted, cursed, and attempted to physically pull them away from the buffet. But someone picked him up like a sack of potatoes, as his arms flailed like a drowning man's, and passed him around over the heads of the gathered group like a college freshman at a football game.

Everyone just dismissed Norman's temper tantrum as a minor bummer in light of the festive occasion's obvious success. Then the wedding party arrived, just as a pair of tall, muscular, and drunken locals stripped to the waist were hoisting a ram goat in the air by a rope over one end of the demolished buffet table. They slit its belly open with a razor-sharp machete, as it bleated its last bleat, and its bloody innards plopped onto the tablecloth with a loud "splat."

Tavo strained his neck to see the bridal parents' reaction to this event. Tried to imagine what his parents' reaction to this might have been. They were open-minded, but even they would have had reservations about this exotic ritual. He observed that Nick's and Jane's parents' reaction bordered on outright horror. After shrieking her lungs out, Jane's mother fainted flat on the ground, out stone cold. Tavo suspected that the party might not go as well from here on.

He pushed his way through the pulsating mass of wrecked humanity just in time to hear Jane's red-faced father ranting, as he threw his wife over his shoulder, that this was the most disgusting, degenerate scene he had ever witnessed. Further, he howled with fiery passion, Nicholas was a perverted swine. He'd never in a pig's ass receive a dime of his money.

Nick's father walked up to his son, slapped him across his face, spun on his heels and stormed out, dragging his wife by the hand as she berated her husband for not spending enough quality time with Nick when he was a boy. After the parent's exit, events kaleidoscoped in a blur. When Norman heard Jane's father's announcement of no dowry he picked up the buffet table and threw it over the forty-foot cliffs. The Chinese caterer hopped up and down mad as hell, hooted loudly in a strange tongue. Sounded like pots and pans clanging together.

Norman looked at him, insanely grabbed him by the seat of his pants and threw him over the cliff… you could hear his 'ping pang pongs' all the way down.

Next Norman went about systematically throwing over the cliff all the outdoor lounge furnishings, —the stereo speakers and sound system went next, followed by all the house furnishings.

Jane watched Norman in awe. Then took his lead, stripped off her wedding dress, and in all her naked unglory, threw it over the cliffs into the ocean, shouting drunken obscenities.

Rastas chanted down Babylon and Playboy bunnies followed Jane's lead, stripping gloriously naked and executed cheerleader cartwheels across the lawn.

Tavo struggled with his perception to take it all in at once but it happened too fast; layers upon layers; and truth be told, he'd have to admit that in his altered state he probably missed most of it. A Woodstock gone amok. Then Nick miraculously appeared, slumped next to him on the stone wall bordering the cliff's edge. He'd shed his wedding attire and was stripped down to bathing trunks, puffing from a mescaline-laced bong and exhaling streams of smoke like a Chinese dragon, and muttering over and over with each exhalation, "Oh, no. Oh, no. Oh, no." Then suddenly collapsed, nearly toppling over the edge of the cliff and onto the jagged rocks below. Tavo grabbed him by the seat of his trunks and held fast. Nick heaved his guts into empty space until there was nothing left in his stomach, his dry retching echoing into the night.

The party was definitely breaking up. There was no more music, food, liquor, or drugs. Everyone was hurrying to leave a rumor had sprung up that some of the Rolling Stones were going to jam with the Wailers at the Yacht Club. After making sure that Nick wouldn't kill himself—he'd passed out on the lawn and was snoring loudly—Tavo stumbled back across the street to his lean-to. Singing the lines from "Purple Haze" to himself, not knowing or caring if he was up or down, but certain this was the party to beat all parties. "Excuse me while I kiss the sky," he sung, then sniggered to himself, breaking up in a helpless fit of giggles.

The old adage that when things can't get worse they usually do held true for Nick. Tavo awoke the next morning, not sure whether last night had been a dream, to wails and screams that shook his palm thatch roof. Norman was screaming over and over, "BOOK ME, BOOK ME, BOOK ME, BOOK ME!" He stumbled out to the dirt road separating his property from Nick's to see Norman stark assed naked, with a regimental red and yellow striped tie knotted professionally around his neck, he was carrying a suitcase. Running up and down the dirt road, kicking up clouds of dust, in a frenzy to get somewhere. He'd stomp about twenty yards in one direction, then abruptly about face like a spinning top and march off in the opposite direction, his bugged-out eyes darting all over chanting his mad mantra, "BOOK ME, BOOK ME, BOOK ME!"

Trailing Norman was a mixed group of hippies and Jamaicans, some were attempting to talk to him, others yelled or tried to restrain him. But Norman's madness gave him superhuman strength, and anyone who came too close wound up on their ass. Norman was suffering from a schizophrenic break, Tavo figured, most likely brought on by the combination of excitement and drugs, coupled with the realization that his and Nick's scheme had back fired, and they weren't going to get any money.

Vaguely he recalled from his psychology training that Norman was probably beyond talk therapy's help; he needed a chemical restraint of some kind—a heavy dose of Thorazine should do the trick. So he continued on to Nick's to survey the damage from the night before, and see if anyone had access to a doctor armed with psychotropics. He found Nick slumped in a chair holding his head in both hands. Tavo approached him cautiously, and said. "Looks like Normans gone over the edge." Nick looked up at him, one of his eyes was blackened—he had a real shiner. "He's completely insane." He said.

"What's with the book me?" Tavo asked. "He wants to be booked right now on a plane back to the States." Nick said," but the son of a bitch won't put any clothes on, other than fucking striped tie—when I tried to dress him, the crazy ass smacked me in the eye."

"Looks like he needs help," said Tavo.

At this very moment, Nick moaned, Jesus-freak hippies and a weird Buddhist sect were attempting to convert Norman and bring him down with talk of the Lord and Krishna, while the Jamaicans were trying to stretch a pair of dirty underwear over his head. The underwear once belonged to a madwoman, and this was the Jamaican roots cure for insanity.

As he talked, Nick worked himself up into hysterics. Losing the million-dollar dowry and Norman's madness were the least of his problems, he blubbered with sweat pouring off his forehead. Jane, also freaked, and had fallen madly in love with him. She would no longer grant him a divorce. She'd actually moved all her clothes into his bedroom and was locked in there right now, refusing to leave or come out.

Shaking with panic and rage now, Nick grabbed Tavo by his T-shirt. "God damn it! Do something! He yelled. "You're supposed to be a fucking psychologist! Cure Norman! Talk Jane into her senses! Do something useful for a change!" Tavo stepped back; breaking Nicks grip on his shirt. This took more than a psychologist, he thought, it would take a wizard to straighten this mess out. Stymied, he crooned a little ditty to Nick, a tune that had calmed him in times of stress, times when he didn't know what else to do. "I wish I were an Oscar Meyer Wiener" he sang "For that is what I'd truly like to be/ For if I were an Oscar Meyer Wiener, / everyone would be in love with me."

Nick didn't get it and was about to punch him in the nose, when Tavo suggested they get to a phone and bring in a headshrinker equipped with Thorazine, fly him by helicopter if necessary.

It took a daylong car trip to Savanna La Mar, 20 miles away, to find a phone booth. A helicopter and psychiatrist were finally dispatched from Kingston. With the help of ten people holding Norman down, the good Doc administered enough Thorazine to subdue a racehorse. Then, they dressed him, loaded him on a plane, and shipped him back home and mom's loving care.

As for Jane, locked in Nick's bedroom, still shouting endearments to Nick. Tavo knew that love was often blind.

8

"Iye, Iye, Iye, Iye, Iye, Iye
You been huggin' up a big monkey man."

By Toots Herbert

As the aftershocks from Nick's wedding wore off, the Negril community settled back down to its quiet harmony with nature—the land and sea. Everything seemed the same again. The usual shouts and curses emanated from Nick's villa, although Tavo could not make out exactly what was happening. He could make a pretty good guess though. Nick wanted Jane out! In any event, Nick didn't approach him for any further advice or counsel, and that was fine by him. He found himself torn, needing counsel himself, some good one on one talk therapy. But there was no one to give it to him; he'd have to do it himself. Attaching himself to the more familiar hedonistic lifestyle of the expatriate subculture was not the way he wanted to go. Their only goal was smuggling ganja or getting stoned. They weren't too thrilled to get close to him either; something was different about him, especially his involvement with the Jamaicans.

But he worried that he had no set goal either. This was okay for a while but when he envisioned his future, he drew a blank. How would he function within this society over the long haul? He decided that for the time being, he'd flow with the rural Jamaican lifestyle, accept whatever this brought him.

Still, he obsessed over past choices, especially giving up his citizenship, his right to live in America. Maybe it would have been better to take his chances in the jungles of Vietnam or take Rosenthal's offer and sit behind a desk where he would have sent battle-stressed soldiers out to kill again and again. Was he a coward who took the easy way out by running away like that scary dude with the ears said? A coward 'cause he couldn't make a decision or stand up for his beliefs? Maybe he should have gone along like so many others and do his duty for God and country?

His self-therapy was starting to suck! He was sick of torturing himself with these thoughts, not being able to resolve his conflicting feelings; he tried to redirect himself into more productive tasks. His lean-to had begun to leak and soak his bed whenever it rained. Strange looking bugs crawled on him and inflicted their nasty bites during the night. It was time-consuming to build a bushwood fire every night to cook on, and next to impossible when the wood was wet. He was also tired of shitting in the bush and longed for a toilet. He knew he was lucky. After all, he had some money left and could construct a modest house to shelter himself from the elements and provide some comforts. Foot soldiers in Vietnam didn't have his option. Plus, being under constant bombardment from the Viet Cong they lived in continual fear of death from napalm or shrapnel raining from the sky. There it was again; even when he tried to think of something else that War hit him in the face.

While he was struggling with these weighty issues, and his guilt, Garth dropped by to see how he was doing.

Garth was close to his age, tall, slim, dark complexion, always in a pleasant mood, like he didn't have a care in the world. He wore an infectious ear-to-ear grin and was known by the locals as a "chatter box." He loved to talk the days away and was particularly fascinated with the new tribe of hippies that had descended on his community. The only reason he'd taken the job, as Len's gardener was to be near these strange aliens so he could observe their bizarre ways and pass on the gossip to his community.

Garth had been at Nick's wedding reception and was shaking with anticipation at the opportunity to rap with Tavo about the wild runnings at the party. He summoned up his best English for the occasion, so that Tavo might understand him perfectly not miss a word, and plopped himself down next to him, hunched on his heels Jamaican style on the red earth he began to chatter.

"Tavo, mon, me never seen tings like dat in all me natural born life! Hippie, dem a nasty bitch. Ah, oh! Gal hippie dem flash dem hairy pussy right in yo face. Big ugly, hairy ting. Me see it with me own two eyes, sir! Mon, Jamaican gal na do it. Jamaican gal cover dat ting in public. Me can't believe it. And de hippie mon; him 'na' care! Me hear dat hippie mon nyam de omon down dey! A true?"

"Ah, Yah Garth, it's true," Tavo said shyly, he wasn't expecting such an explicit outburst; "not only hippies. Most Americans do oral sex. It's not unnatural."

Garth was horrified at Tavo's casual response "Well master, me nuh know 'bout no oral sex," he scolded "All me knows is de hippie mon nyam de pussy and claim him love it too! Don' make no Jamaican in Negril know you nyam it. Dey nah eat nor drink with you again! An wha 'bout dem hippie mon? Me never see such foolishness. Dem a-take some drugs me never hear name of before. It turn dem fool-fool! Look pon Norman. Him walk up and down wid him cockie hanging like donkey. A mad mon dat!" Garth trembled, waved his arms wildly in disgust, continued heatedly "Me's a mon dat drink me Red Stripe, sometimes a dozen. Me drinks de rum, even drinks de blue stone waters. Me nah smoke de ganja though. Me is no fool! Ah! Oh!" He picked at his nose, rolled a booger into a ball and looked at it in contempt. Tavo didn't know what to say he sat silent, watching Garth roll the booger between his thumb and forefinger.

"Tavo mon, you is all right," Garth said as he flicked the booger off his finger into the bush. "You looks like dems with dem long hairs on you head, but you is not de same. Me can tell. You is Irie man. What makes dem other hippie carry on so?"

Tavo had been thinking along the same lines, took the opportunity to explain the "Hippie Psyche" to sort out his own mind set.

"Most of them aren't happy," he said, "America's been hard on em 'cause of the Vietnam War. They've been beaten and shot by the police, 'cause they protest the war."

Garth smacked a mosquito that had landed on Tavo's bicep, leaving a red smear of blood, and said "Me see dat, Mon, dem nuh happy. Some even have money like dirt. Me nuh have no money, but me is happy. Ah, oh! Me even been to America one time to pick de apple. Me nuh love it either! Go in a place wid big yella arch. Buy me de fish sandwich. Masta, me take one bite and spit it pon de floor." to emphasize his point he spat on the ground and said "America nuh have no natural food—sandwich nuh have nuh head nor tail on it. How dem can call dat fish? No wonder hippie no happy 'dere." Garth peered deeply into Tavo's eyes, seemed to be searching his soul. "An dem nuh love neaga in America either. Me hear seh dem hang him and burn big cross pon' him yard. Me nah go back dere, sah! Tell me, Mon, why dem hippie come a Jamaica? Dem feel seh Rasta an dem a brother?"

Tavo maintained his eye-lock with Garth felt Garth was trying to detect any racial prejudice he might harbor "Maybe, I don't know." he said "Rastas wear their hair long, smoke marijuana, wear beads and bright colors. Look, Bob Marley's music's outta sight! There's a common bond. Rastas preach peace and love; hippies are seeking peace and love. Another bond."

But Garth looked troubled. He pulled a limb off a nearby Papaya tree, he slapped it against his open palm and said, "Me nuh know 'bout no bonds, Mon. Me nuh love Rasta. Him dirty and nasty like mos' hippie mon. Him nuh work, sit down pon' him batty all day, puff pon' him spliff, get well red up. Hippie mon, him nuh work either, get red up pon spliffs same way an him tek whole heap a drugs. De' drugs make him brain soft. How can Nick's fader-in-law and madder-in-law love dat and give him dem money? Ah, oh! Me nah give me pickney nuh breads if dem tek drugs a tun fool like dat. Tavo, you nuh turn fool like dem others yet. Is best you stay far from dem! You is a mon jus' like me. We's men no matter what de color!" He looked at the blood smear on Tavo's arm where he'd smacked the mosquito and pointed to it "My blood red jus' like yours. Someone cut me; I bleeds jus' like you. I's a neaga; but in Jamaica, dat nuh matter. Me's a mon here. Me prefer be neaga dan hippie any day—ah Oh!" Garth threw the papaya branch on the ground, picked at his ragged shorts that had become wedged between his ass-cheeks stared off into the distance deep in thought. His face brightened he seemed to arrive at a decision and he turned to Tavo, excited now "We go to de Wharf Club tonight and drink de blue stone waters. Is best dat you become Jamaican now. Forget America wid all dem troubles. Dat place too heavy pon' your brain. You fire up de old Moke. We goin on a probe"

("The Moke" was an old Morris Minor car Tavo had bought in Sav-la-Mar fourth hand from an old Jamaican cane farmer. He had paid the princely sum of five hundred dollars for what looked like a flatbed miniature jeep with tiny wheels and a torn canvas top. It had to be push-started, and the gear stick lay flat on the floor where it was picked up by hand to shift in its two remaining gears. Every ten miles you had to stop, cool the car down and pour water into the radiator so it wouldn't blow up.)

Tavo was more than pleased, he was enthralled, felt he had passed Garth's test. He was being accepted. "Sure man," he said, "What the hell are blue stone waters?" Garth smiled mysteriously nodding his head up and down "You'll see me brother. You'll see. Pick me up at me yard tonight mon! Irie!" He slapped Tavo's hand in a soul shake and walked away whistling a calypso tune, not having a care in the world.

Tavo sat there, curious about the blue stone waters, but he was elated that Garth had considered him an equal and was including him in a night on the town. To him, this was a major breakthrough. He had to win acceptance here.

That evening he fired up the Moke—by pushing it down the dirt track road, running up and jumping in when it reached a high enough speed, then popping it into gear as it sputtered reluctantly alive. He pulled up to a stop about a mile down the road in front of Garth's shack letting the Moke idle, shouted for him to jump in for the mile and a half journey to the Wharf Club. Garth had heard the Moke's groaning long before its arrival and was ready. But he was not alone. A buxom young lady with light brown skin and shimmering blue eyes followed him.

Garth grinned with pride, puffed out his chest and introduced Tavo to his pretty companion. "Dis be Mona; him me gal frien'—some claim me common-law wife, me nuh know! But him give me seven pickney. Him have a nice fat pum-pum and me love him bad bad. Ah Oh!"

Mona blushed hotly and shouted, "Shut yuh mout mon, you chat too much."

Garth looked hurt he turned to her with sad blood hound eyes and said "Mona, me not a man wear two face under one hat. Me always speak me mind true. Tavo a come wid we to de Wharf Club. Him no trouble no one—him like me brother, bleeds same way. You stay outside and chat wid yuh frien' dem."

Mona folded her arms across her ample bosom in disgust, not looking at Tavo, "Shut you mout, mon. Me go in dat club if me choose to. Me nuh wan' have no business wid you and you nasty ass hippie frien' anyway!"

"Tavo nuh stay like other hippie mon!" Garth pleaded, "Me tell you dat already. Him no turn fool wid de funny drugs dem. Him nuh dat dirty! Him nuh even smell frozie."

Tavo tried to ignore this domestic dispute especially because it was over him. He gripped the Moke's steering wheel with both hands dodging the potholes in the road, and the ever-present goats, chickens, pigs, dogs, lizards, crabs, toads and pedestrians.

They were still arguing about him when the Moke reached the Wharf Club. He parked in front of the bar brushed the dust from his hair, and they headed for the bar just as the sun began to set behind the swaying palms. Mona remained outside sitting in the Moke, following Garth's directive with reluctance, clearly resentful. The midget, El Presidente was also outside the bar, and when he spied Mona alone in the Moke, he staggered over, swinging the half empty bottle of white rum that he'd been chugging on in one hand and brandishing an open ratchet knife in the other. El Presidente let loose with a string of his usual "Bumba claat, pussy claat and rass hole's" at Mona. Then fell to his knees in front of her and begged to nyam her pum pum. Apparently El Presidente had made an easy adjustment to American sexual practices.

Garth ignored them as he dragged Tavo into the bar after him. But Tavo was uneasy, hesitant. "Aren't you concerned with her safety, leaving her alone with that degenerate midget?" he said.

Garth frowned, looked at Tavo like he was an imbecile. "No, mon," he said, "Mona, him box his ears off if him get facetie. *El Presidente* him soon drunk pon de rum, soon fall asleep under de coconut tree. Him na trouble no one again till tomorrow. Ah! Oh!"

From inside the bar, Tavo watched the midget continue to harass Mona. Now he was attempting to grab her cantaloupe-like breasts. This finally roused her from her sulk, and she hauled off with a round-house punch so hard, it sent El

Presidente somersaulting end over end, until he landed smack on his ugly face under a coconut tree, out cold like a Popsicle. Down for the count.

Garth observed it all nonchalantly like it was an everyday occurrence. He ordered the bartender to bring on the blue stone waters. The bartender, also the owner, was William Macabee, a toothless, short, fat, balding, light brown guy, about forty years old. His sweat and food stained T-shirt and old khaki trousers were his sole attire.

William searched amongst the dusty liquor bottles and placed a fifth of vodka and a fifth of green crème de menthe on the sticky bar top. Fumbled around and found two empty half pint bottles Jamaicans called Q's and poured equal measures of half vodka, half crème de menthe into each one.

He fished out two mismatched jelly glasses from the back of the cupboard, and placed them, along with a large bowl of ice that he cracked into small pieces with a rusty ice pick, in front of them. Garth filled up the glasses by hand with ice and poured them full with the mixture from one of the Q's. When the liquid hit the ice in the glass it resembled sapphire like stones floating in a blue green sea, smoke boiled off the top from the heavy humidity and heat. Looked like a witch's brew.

Al Green lamented soulfully from the jukebox: "I ain't never never found me a girl. I ain't never never found me a girl to love me like you do" Memories stirred for his love Irene, and tears moistened his eyes. But he didn't want to spoil this important evening and held them in check, cheered somewhat by the blue stone waters which tasted like mint candy, the prospect of his long sought comradely and an evening of boozing. But the jukebox continued to haunt him with songs of lost loves by Jerry Butler, The Impressions, Major Lance, and the Three Degrees. Reggae tunes in between relieved the agony. He didn't fully comprehend the lyrics, but he managed to pick out phrases like "De bag of weed and de big black sow dem have fe run dem have fe run, when de soldier man a come, but dem nah run when de police mon a come"

The usual contingent of goats, chickens, and the odd pig sauntered in and out of the bar. Three rude boys with ratchet rings dangling out the back pockets of their jeans skanked to the beat in the back bar, while Garth joked with him and spun tall tales about his fishing, farming, and gathering abilities. The conversation and the blue stone waters began to lift him out of his funk. Then out of the corner of his eye he noticed a sight that made his blood run cold, cold as the blue stones. Skanking with the rude boys was that guy again; the Vietnam Vet who he'd met at Nick's wedding. He was wearing skintight black leather pants and grayish high healed snake skin boots.

He was shirtless and his scars throbbed red with the reggae beat—he'd at least shed the necklace of ears, and donned a gold marijuana leaf necklace instead. But the worst thing was he was purposely eyeballing Tavo. He picked his teeth with the sharp point of a ratchet knife.

Tavo tried to pretend he hadn't seen the guy and turned his full attention to Garth. "Look man" he said, "Whose that white guy back there? With the rude boys... I keep running into him... but don't look now okay!" Garth ignored his request and spun around staring openly at the guy... just like Tavo didn't want him to do... giving it all away.

He turned back to Tavo and shouted loud enough for the whole bar to hear "Dat Jamie Dice Mon! Him Len's muscle mon, don't trouble him... him dread fi true" Garth noticed Tavo's concern... his fear and consoled him "Mon jus' lef him alone him nah trouble you den!"

Tavo wondered what the guy was doing, how he was reacting but was too scared to turn around and look. Then Garth turned real serious and draping his arm over Tavo's shoulder whispered conspiratorially in his ear: "Tavo, mon, day some things in Jamaica you must know." He looked around the crowded bar to see if anyone was listening.

Satisfied that they had complete privacy he continued in a hushed tone. “Tings so dread me nuh even like to speak dem name! Ah, oh!”

Tavo was puzzled, he looked at Garth wide eyed, gullible “Like what?” he said, what could be worse than that dude Dice! Garth frowned, wrinkling his brow and strengthened his grasp on Tavo’s shoulder, protecting him. “Me nuh wan scare you mon, but you must know of de Rollin’ Calf! Him live right here in Negril. If you ever see him, mon, you fart fe true! Must run as fast as you can save yuh life!”

“Who the hell is Roland Calf?” Tavo shouted aggravated now by this mumbo jumbo.

Garth placed a finger on Tavo’s green-tinged lips “Shh… don’t talk so loud. Rollin’ Calf! Not a man! Him truly a beast from Hell! Him from Hell all right. Ah! Oh! Ah! Oh!” He was so shaken by speaking of this beast that he swallowed most of the remaining Q of “blue stone water” to calm himself down enough to explain this phenomenon. He grabbed Tavo by his biceps with both hands and shook him to drive home his point.

“Rollin Calf’s a large cow dat come out to roam in de midnight hours,” he whispered “ Him breathe pure green fire from him mouth and nose. When you sees one, Tavo, run mon. Never look back. Yuh hear me now?”

Garth was trembling and shaking now. He really believed what he was saying. Then he went outside to take a leak, leaving Tavo alone at the bar. He didn’t know how to react. He called William Macabee over to try to verify this new bit of cultural ho-ha, to find out if he was being put on. Plus he didn’t want to turn around and look at that Dice guy. He was the real beast!

“William, you ever see a Roland Calf?” he asked half jokingly winking at him, trying to be cool, afraid Dice would go into his coward routine again.

William looked at him fearfully, his eyes bugged from his head. He didn’t wink back at Tavo. He looked around the bar now, checking for eavesdroppers, then said "No, mon, me no see one, me see five!" He rushed away to the other end of the bar, muttering the Lords name crossing himself like a Catholic, like he was chased by some unspeakable horror beyond the understanding of a hippie outsider.

When Garth came back, he gazed at Tavo with genuine concern and hurt, shook his head in dismay, and said. "Me see you nuh believe in such tings, and is true dat since hippie mon come 'a Negril, Rollin' Calf not so frequent." Tavo looked befuddled. "Whys that", he said.

"Dat is because you hippie mon scare many of de brutes back in a' de' deep bush, but Rollin' Calf still travel around during de nights is best you beware!"

Tavo didn't know how to respond. He didn't want to offend Garth by questioning his beliefs. After all, Garth was fast becoming his first friend since leaving America. Maybe he should ask Garth for more information on these creatures. Pretend he believed. But then he felt a sharp strong tug on his T-shirt wheeled around and found himself eye to eye with a man who had the vacant look of a zombie grinning an idiotic grin at him. The man pushed his dirty, snot-dripping nose up against Tavo's neck and began to sniff him, grunting, gurgling like a wild animal.

He jumped back and grabbed hold of Garth for protection, pushed him in front of him used him as a shield. "What the hell is happening?" he yelled, hiding behind him. Garth roared with laughter and slapped the idiot good-naturedly on the back. "Is jus' Lloydie mon" he said. "Him nah trouble yuh. Him brain nuh strong like mine and yours and him nuh have no family. William let him sweep de club, and him sleep under de tables at night so him don't catch fresh cold. Everybody give him food when him hungry, treat him nice. Ah Oh! Him nice mon. Him brain too weak for him to talk but him nice mon." Garth looked at Tavo taking in his fears. "All him want mon is for you to buy him a Red Stripe, then him nah trouble you again."

Tavo stepped from behind Garth, inched closer to Lloydie, trying to regain his composure, trying to act brave now, like he hadn't really been scared "Oh, he's developmentally disabled?" he said.

"Me nuh know bout nuh disablement mon." Garth said, " Me already tell you, mon! Him brain soft. Must disable him don't it? But him good mon. Everyone in Negril treat him good. No one molest him and him don't trouble anybody. Him can't defend himself, so everyone give him food, beer… be kind to him." Tavo took a few crumpled Jamaican dollars out of his pocket shouted to William, ordered Lloydie a beer.

Garth shook his head pensively and looked at him puzzled; "You is strange mon! You no fears the real dangers of de Rollin' Calf but yuh fears nice Lloydie who wouldn't harm a hair pon yuh head. Me no understand oonou hippie at all."

Tavo was embarrassed… defensive, he stuttered "Ah, well I don't fear him anymore man," while handing Lloydie a cold beer. Lloydie grinned his thanks, stood at the bar drinking it, and pretended to join their conversation by moving his lips in mock-like speech.

Tavo pretended to be absorbed in a heart thumping reggae tune on the jukebox. He bobbed his head to the music, pondered this new cultural conundrum. America went to war, seeing devils everywhere in people who were different from its mainstream. Locked em away from sight, or shot, bombed, and otherwise got rid of them. Rural Jamaica on the other hand, understood from deep, ancient knowledge that the devil had been expelled from man long ago. The devil no longer inhabited humans; it roamed the night, causing terror.

He threw down more blue stone waters, not comfortable with this thought. Then Garth, thinking Tavo was smashed, ordered up a large plate of fried fish from the kitchen. "You eat these fish, mon" he coaxed. "Make you more sober than when you come in-a-here!" The fish were delicious, crisp on the outside and flaky white on the inside, with no fishy smell or taste. They were smothered with a sauce of vinegar, pimento, sliced scallion, onion, cho-cho, and fiery red hot peppers that caused tears to stream down his cheeks. He broke out in a heavy sweat and immediately felt cold sober. Well almost.

Garth nodded knowingly "Dem be country peppers on dem fishes" He said. "Dey come from Africa. Slave mon dem bring de seeds over pon de ships. You nuh feel red up again! Ah Oh!"

Tavo's head was clearer, although his mouth remained on fire. This called for more "blue stones" which they drank until both the Vodka and Creme de Menthe bottles were empty.

Tavo had only one recollection of actually leaving the Wharf Club. That was passing by Dice who sat on a Harley Davidson Chopper flicking his ratchet knife 'click-clack-click'. He thought he heard him call him a coward again. But when he cut through his fog, he found himself piloting the Moke up the West End Road. In the back seat, Garth boasted to a pouting Mona, "Da more me and Tavo drinks, de soberer we gets." Then he burst out singing to Mona that he was a killer ape—a big monkey man—he was ugly but he'd many fit and strong pickneys and she would soon be huggin' up a big monkey man. Ah! Oh!

9

"I feel so good in my neighborhood,
So here it is I will stay.

By Bob Marley
From the song *Kaya*

The morning after the "blue stones," Tavo awoke under his palm-thatched roof to the cheery songs of birds. The sun was already shining bright, he'd overslept. His tongue felt feathery like the metallic green Doctor Birds hovering suspended like helicopters around a hibiscus bush in front of his hut. Cling-Cling birds chattered excitedly in a nearby ackee tree laden with bright red fruit, causing his head to pound. But the smell of jasmine and exotic flowers permeating the airs fresh moisture from the night's dew helped clear his aching head. Small bright green lizards did push-ups and extended their ruby throats on the branches of nearby trees and bushes, staking out their territories. This was their home too!

Other than the rustling of the palm fronds and birdcalls, the morning seemed infinite and deep, it stilled his soul. If there was a God, this tropical paradise must be what he had in mind for His worship, he thought, surprised once again by his new spirituality. He could sit here for hours, undisturbed, melting into his Garden of Eden. And he felt secure that no supernatural being would expel him from this sacred place. It would take man to do that.

He tried to imagine what it would have been like to grow up here from childhood, knowing little of the outside world. Prior to 1960, when the road from Montego Bay was built, Negril had been cut off from civilization. To get there, you had to go by boat or donkey. Most Negrilians knew nothing of crowded, dirty, impersonal cities. Racial mistrust didn't exist here. Only the few who ventured out of Negril, like Garth, who left to pick apples in the States, had experienced racism, and they tended to leave that negative experience where they found it. Negril was truly devoid of the stresses and frustrations of his old daily life in the modern industrialized world, and he gave thanks for that.

The more he grew accustomed to this tranquil existence and formed friendships with the inhabitants, the less he missed his old life and the easier his adjustment became. At times, his past would drift away, like the fluffy white clouds over the Caribbean, leaving his mind cleansed by their passing. Except for Irene. No matter how deep his meditations were she still surfaced, reminding him of his hurt and longing. Vietnam also plagued him, even without that Dice guy reminding him. He felt a deep sadness for his peers still fighting and dying over there. Guilt for deserting them was his constant companion.

He was jolted out of his morning musings by the shrill ring-ring-ring of a bicycle bell. In front of his hut, was a Rasta man straddling an old bicycle. He'd met him a few times. A neighbor living a hundred yards down the road. His name was Herman, but everyone called him Heavy Higher. Heavy lived in a tree. He'd cut a path through the dense jungle to a large Banyan tree a hundred yards off the road and built a five by five-foot platform, twenty feet up its large trunk. It had a roof of thatch palm fronds open on the sides to catch the cool evening breeze. He'd nailed pieces of old boards to the tree trunk that formed a ladder for climbing access to his tree house.

Locals said that Heavy was a master thatch roofer. His craft passed down to the African-Jamaicans from the Arawak Indians, the original inhabitants of the island. When done correctly, these roofs could last up to twenty years without leaking. Heavy knew just the right way to lay the palm fronds bone side down, leaves pointing outward, and how to lash them to the wood poles with a jungle vine called a wisp, so even the strongest gale force winds couldn't blow them loose.

Heavy was the first Rastafarian he had met. At the time there weren't many of this sect living in Negril. Garth didn't like them; thought they were lazy, smoked too much herb. Most of the local community shared his attitude, although, like the hippies, Rastas were tolerated and left alone to practice their own thing.

Tavo knew little about them. Garth said that they believed in some sort of African religion that many of them wanted to return to Africa, there true home. He felt that Jamaica should "ship 'em all back if that's what they want, then they could bang dem drums, smoke de weed and run through de bush all day, jus' like de hippie mon." But Tavo didn't share his new friend's prejudice. He didn't know enough about them to feel one way or the other.

Heavy Higher was not called Heavy because he was overweight. He was extremely thin. His nickname derived from his habit of punctuating most of his comments with the word "heavy," which he'd picked up from the hippies who'd often comment "heavy," whenever he preached his spiritual philosophy.

'Heavy Higher' showed up today wearing a Harvard T-shirt, brown corduroy trousers, and Weejun loafers—an outfit that was either given or traded for marijuana by student travelers. From the neck down, he passed for a college man; but from the neck up, he looked more like a wise academic professor. His long dreadlocks fell to his waist in a tangle of knots that resembled cured ganja buds, and he had a long, scraggly, salt and pepper beard. If you looked closely, he resembled a skinny black Santa Claus or East Indian holy man, his eyes twinkling with delight and wonder and his mouth turned up in a warm existential smile to reveal two crooked teeth.

Attached to the front of his old bicycle was a rusted metal carrying basket filled to the top with radiant multi-colored hibiscus and bougainvillea blossoms. In the center of this shrine sat a tiny floppy-eared puppy whose shiny black coat was speckled with white patches. It yipped Tavo a raucous greeting, its pink tongue hanging out, flapping in the breeze.

Heavy leaned his rusted bicycle against a Cottonwood tree and handed Tavo the squirming puppy. "Here, my brother, praise Jah for this lovely morning! I've brought you this gift, a lovely puppy to keep you company to give you love. His name is Remus, Heavy! Heavy!" he said in a soft, hypnotically soothing voice, speaking proper King's English, although he could also speak the local patois.

Tavo was pleased he'd thought of him, but also disheartened. He scratched Remus behind the ears as the dog lapped at his hand. "Thanks man," he said "but I'm not sure if I can care for myself, much less a puppy." Worried that he still had no direction, no purpose in Jamaica.

But Heavy Higher would have none of it. "Oh, my brother, don't fret yourself" he said. "Jah will provide for you as He does all His children. This puppy is beautiful, he needs a home. He'll keep you company, protect you from harm in the night just as Jah himself would—give praise and thanks, Heavy! Heavy! Heavy!"

Tavo briefly reflected about his optimistic prophecy, but didn't look too sure, as Remus attempted to chew on his finger. He'd heard Heavy Higher was a true orthodox Rastafarian. Didn't eat meat—fish nor fowl, and shunned salt, living only on fruits, vegetables, and grains—most, of which he grew around his tree house. Like most Rastas, he also abstained from hard liquor. He smoked ganja, "the herbs of the land," with relish, and especially enjoyed large locally grown, handmade tobacco cigars. But the ganja herb was his holy sacrament to Jah, his direct link to the Almighty.

He sat down in front of Tavo's hut and placed the puppy in Tavo's lap, wanting him to warm up to Remus. Then noticed a half-full bottle of rum sitting in the corner of the lean-to. "Could I have a drink of rum", he asked, "the morning is warm."

"Wait Herman," Tavo said, "I thought Rastas didn't drink liquor."

He smiled benevolently, rolled his eyes to the heavens "Oh, brother Tavo, you don't understand! Jah is the only perfect one? All the rest of us are His children… we'll go astray from time to time. Jah in his Almighty wisdom is all forgiving of his earthly flock. He doesn't expect perfection from us, only praise to his name. It would be presumptuous of us to believe we could conduct ourselves in his supreme ways! We can only attempt, but never expect to achieve perfection. Irie brother. Heavy! Heavy!"

His wisdom made sense to Tavo, a hell of a lot more than Jimmy Swaggerts, so he handed over the bottle, and Heavy took a thirsty pull, smacking his lips and wiping them with the back of his hand. "Rasta is the lost tribe of Israel," he proselytized, waving his bony hand to the cosmos, "the first of the Jews who were born to the lands of Ethiopia in ancient Africa. Rasta is ruled by the true Jesus Christ, the exalted Emperor Haile Selassi I, Jah Rastafari! Nick Lebowitz, Norman Silverstein, Leonard Stern and their flock came way later than Rastafari. They don't follow the righteous path… wandered too far from their heritage, gone astray, but Jah loves them still and will bring them back into a one love flock in time. Praise Jah brother—the word is 'love.' Heavy! Heavy!"

This was news to Tavo. He wondered how Mrs Goldberg would feel if she knew she were a second-class Hebrew. Probably dismiss Heavy as some "crazy schvartza". "You see, brother," he continued, "Nick should never have married for money! Money is a curse to man… invented by man, not created by Jah! Jah Rastafari have no use for it. Jah has given man everything he needs for happiness and well-being right here on earth." He swept his emaciated arms in a wide circle to encompass all of Tavo's land. "Jah did not mean for the wicked to control his gifts and make others slaves in order to partake of them. But the wicked invented money and dole it out sparsely to control, manipulate, and dominate. That's what caused Nick to walk in misery. He must now do the righteous thing and love Jane, who Jah in his mighty wisdom has brought to him; money can't make him happy, only love, pure and simple love. Praise Jah Rastafari. Irie. Heavy! Heavy!"

Tavo considered this, tickled Remus' belly. He knew that Nick was miserable just as Heavy so eloquently described. Jane still refused to move out of his bedroom, while Nick ranted, raved, and cursed her and his misfortune daily. Their constant yelling, fighting and bickering broke the tranquility of the West End from sun-up to sunset.

But Tavo was reaching his doorstep to the righteous; his money was slowly disappearing. He'd never cared much for vegetables or greens; but if Heavy Higher could survive on em, he guessed he could too.

By this time Tavo had warmed to Remus. He tried to buy into Heavy's optimism and accepted his gift. Heavy Higher took another good belt of rum, and left, but he took Tavo's transient sense of security with him. The wind rustled the fruit on his ackee tree, sounding a faint tribal beat, seemed to signal new schemes brewing, new arrivals to Negril. But whatever changes would come, he still felt good here, and wanted to stay. This was his land now, his destiny for better or worse. His pilgrim ancestors didn't have it easy either, but they'd made it and he would too. To quote Heavy Higher.

"The word is love!"

10

"Cold ground was my bed last night,
And rock stone was my pillow too."

By Bob Marley
From the song *Cold Ground*

Negril and his life there had all been a dream. Drenched in sweat, he tried to run for his life. But he couldn't run. He was trapped to his waist in oozing stinking mud. Each effort to pump his legs only lodged him more firmly. Large horse flies buzzed around his head and bit him fiercely, painfully on his back and arms, but he couldn't swat them away because his hands clutched an M16 rifle. Sweat continued to pour off him in rivers as the tropical heat and humidity pressed in on him. Bombs exploded close by with ear-deafening thunder and more of the putrid muck rained on his face,. into his eyes. Men and boys screamed all around. John Curtis lay in the mud at his side face up, glassy eyed staring straight up! Forever dead. Five feet away and caught in the mud just like him was Manistoe Lowellen, III, and he was begging Tavo to shoot him. Manistoe's arm was blown off at the shoulder and his entire upper body was bloodied, he was slowly bleeding to death. He was pleading with Tavo to kill him, put him out of his misery. Machine-gun fire raked the slime within two feet of them, creating popping bubbles in the slimy gunk. The powerful scent of sulfur and harsh chemicals filled the air with death, threatening to choke them.

But he couldn't bring himself to shoot Manistoe; he was a coward and couldn't even kill the enemy when his life depended on it. But at least he had refused to counsel shell-shocked soldiers and send them back into battle.

Then Rosenthal's face materialized in front of him, it must be an acid flashback.... What a fucking time for that! Rosenthal looked just like he had at the draft board—a grinning yellow skull with its eye sockets oozing green glowing slime. HE or it was laughing hysterically... insanely. Then it spoke... no, it ranted that same echo-like voice, "See Gripps, you should have taken my therapy to heart... my career counseling. Ha! Ha! Ha! Taken that desk job in the rear Ha! Ha! Ha! One on one therapy would have been a lot easier than this, wouldn't it? Ha! Ha! Ha!

"Oh sweet psychopathology! All you would have done was hold a few cowards hands for a couple of minutes... stamp their forms saying, 'Fit for Combat'... Ha! Ha! Ha! Tough luck buddy now, your going to die... see what a conscience gets you Ha! Ha! Ha! But before you die I just thought I'd drop in and say goodbye... Let you know how Irene and I are getting along... Well we're doing just fine. I did get tired of fucking her pussy though. She almost liked tha.... so now I fuck her in the ass every night. Ha! Ha! Ha! Slam it to her dry! She hates that, says it hurts her, but it's oh so much fun to hear her beg me to stop. Ha! Ha! Ha!"

Tavo reached out tried to strangle him but he or it vanished like a puff of chordate smoke. Then the enemy, the Viet Cong, Charlie, as faceless as the back side of the moon, were gradually taking shape as they slipped over a mound of dirt and began bayoneting and shooting Tavo's comrades who were also lodged in the sticky rice paddy mud.

But there was one guy who wasn't lodged in the mud. He seemed to be able to walk right on top of the muck without sinking. It was Jamie Dice and he was firing a machine gun, sweating, his muscles bulging out from the strain of its weight and backfire. He was chuckling softly having a good time. The Viet Cong began to drop like flies.... bullets ripped into Dice, tearing pieces of his flesh away... but he continued to chuckle... giggling like he was being tickled. Charley had vanished now, either dead or retreated through the jungle. He'd saved them or some of them at least. But then he walked right up to Manistoe and blew his head away with a rapid burst of fire from the machine gun and shouted, "Sh shit! Ears blown to pieces, nobody count, nobody count!"

He proceeded to walk calmly up to the few remaining soldiers still left alive in Tavo's platoon and being careful now not to destroy the ears... let his machine gun blast away into their mid-sections strafing them, killing every last one... saving their ears except for Tavo. He threw his machine gun down and drew out a knife, a ratchet knife clicking the blade out 'click-clack-click'.

He was whistling now, humming a tune, it was the theme from Mash. He began to sing softly "Suicide is painless! Suicide is painless!" as he bent down and sliced the ears off of John Curtis.

Tavo watched in horror as he sliced the ears off of all his dead buddies. He was mumbling now, almost chanting... "Cowards! All a ya's cowards. It's all in the body count, body count, one little, two little, three little ears all strung in a row! Ha! Ha! Ha!

Tavo was screaming at him to stop shouting at him. Dice turned slowly towards him, he was stringing the ears now on a piece of monafilment.... grinning at him.

"I saved ya for last, dip shit!" he snarled, "You're the biggest coward... thought I'd slice your ears off while you're still alive! Ha! Ha! Ha!... Eni meani myni moe, catch a Tavo by the ear, Ha! Ha! Ha! If he hollers slice it off! Ha! Ha! Ha!"

This was crazy, insane. This whole war was crazy, made everyone insane.

His life flashed before his eyes, along with what he'd missed. He'd never live to have a family, to produce children. The Gripps name would end in Vietnam, where his remains would sink into a primeval swamp and nourish the rice paddies. His earless legacy. Fertilizer for Southeast Asia.

Suddenly, someone rose from the paddy. Dripping slime from his beard and dreadlocks was Heavy Higher. He bent his benevolent face toward Tavo and began gently washing the filth from his face with cooling spring water. He calmly spoke to him, "Tavo, my brother, is this the place where you would have sent your brothers to die when they came to you with their problems, when they could no longer tolerate the horrors of war? No, that is not the type of man you are. No brother, you were not meant for the fodder of cannons, for the wicked Babylon war machine. Your destiny is to have purpose and meaning before you meet Jah. It is not cowardly to refuse to fight or to die when you do not understand the reason why. It is brave. You are only a coward when you refuse to fight the wicked, knowing in your heart that they are evil. Evil in our time has many faces and deceives one more than ever with its masquerade. In ancient times, man easily recognized evil and good, and his decisions were easier. Today Jah tests men more and more—it is the brave man now who would question whether to kill his brother. Rasta knows that killing for political reasons is wrong, politics are but propaganda and shifts with the winds of man's folly. Tavo, stop troubling yourself with senseless worry. Stick by your decision to turn your back on that evil war. You and Jah know it to be the righteous one. Let no mortal man set doubt in you. Heavy! Heavy! Heavy!"

Tavo's surroundings gradually began transforming. He felt like he'd been shot… skewered on a bayonet like a shish kebab… his ears sliced off. But Heavy Higher was sponging away all the stinking ooze, and he was no longer sweating. A refreshing coolness crept over him. The stink of the bombs and nauseous chemicals disappeared so did the flies and the oppressive humidity. He felt a pleasant floating sensation. Heavy Higher spoke again in his calm reassuring manner.

"It's good to see you awake. You've been out with the dengue fever, for two days and nights. I used an old cure told to me by my granny. It broke your fever and drew the illness from your body." Tavo attempted to sit up mumbling dreamily, as Heavy continued to sponge him and said "I fetched some sulfur mud from the mineral spring at Little Bay and rubbed you all over with it to draw out the sickness. Then I make you drink a mixture of white rum with ganja herb soaked in it. It makes you sleep, dream and breaks the fever by causing the sweats. It's good to see you well again my brother, the dengue fever is bad!" They were both silent as Heavy washed the rest of the mud off. When he finished he counseled Tavo.

" You need to build a proper house. This old lean-to leaks bad, Clifton never understood the craft of the old thatch makers. You need insect screens, rub your body with the juice from the tobacco plant to repel the dengue mosquito. Chew the tobacco herb; rub its juice over your body! Mosquito is afraid of it!"

Tavo couldn't say what relieved him more: that he was not going to die in a rice paddy in Vietnam, or that the dream had washed away some of his haunting guilt tripping. Heavy showed him so much compassion, maybe even induced a healing dream. But before he could thank him, Heavy excused himself to go plant yams and give praise and thanks to Jah, leaving him alone, with time to reflect. Reflect on that part of the dream that wasn't healing… that part where Rosenthal sadistically sodomized Irene. God was that horrible, too horrible to even think about… And what about Dice! Really grotesque… could he have actually done those atrocities, well he probably didn't cut American soldiers ears off but he had chopped the ears off of Vietnamese's. He saw the proof of that.

Anyway it was only a dream, a bad nightmare caused by the dengue fever… dreams weren't real, they were only supposed to help you work through your problems in daily life. He just couldn't understand how the dream parts about Rosenthal and Dice had helped him. Better to forget those.

But Heavy Higher was right. He needed a decent house—nothing fancy but something that would shelter him from the elements and those damn dengue mosquitoes.

Len Stern, in a rare moment of friendliness, had told him that there was only one person in Negril with the skills to build a good house; Clyde Long. He'd built Len's and would likely be available for contracting anytime. Construction certainly wasn't booming in the area. Tavo had close to four thousand dollars left from his inheritance. Figured this should get him started, but he was totally ignorant of construction costs in the US, let alone Jamaica.

Len had recounted a weird story about this contractor. Len nicknamed Clyde, Gloom-and-Doom but wouldn't say why.

But did say that Clyde had shown up for work one morning, after half the work on his house was done, and thrust his right hand under Len's nose. Len screamed in disgust. The hand was infested with a mass of wiggling white worms that seemed to be boring right out of his flesh. It smelled just like a piece of putrid meat. A rival builder had thrown an obeah voodoo curse on him, Clyde said. Now his good working right hand had deteriorated to this sorry mess.

The rival contractor had gone to an Obeah man, a Mr Pingwee, and paid him a sum of money to disable his competition. Now Clyde had to go away for a few days to the nearby parish of Hanover to pay his own obeah man to reverse the curse so he could finish the house. Of course, he begged the money he needed from Len. When Tavo heard the story, he thought it amusing. Contractors here were like those in the

States: notorious weasels who stalled job completion with equally imaginative stories. At least Clyde had his wiggly worms for proof.

Len said he lived two months in his semi-completed house, until one day, without a word of explanation, Clyde showed up with his assistant and commenced nailing boards once again. Len pestered him to explain why he'd been gone so long, but Clyde was steadfastly mute. He merely thrust his hand once again under Len's nose. It was in perfect condition, without a sign of worms or scarring, and it smelled only of the Guinness Stout that he'd been drinking, and the Craven A's he'd been smoking since sun up.

Len warned Tavo not to pay Clyde all the contract money up front as he had, that could risk another obeah curse. Other than this one mishap, Len found no fault with him. He was a skilled worker and knowledgeable about building.

One morning, Clyde appeared out of nowhere at the opening of his lean-to, which was becoming more and more dilapidated and leaky by the day, as if he'd been summoned by telephone. The telephone that called him was the Negril version of jungle drums. Rumors about Tavo's plans to build had spread like wildfire over the small village. And he saw why Len had nicknamed Clyde Gloom-and-Doom. His face was scrunched into a massive frown but his coal black skin covered fine handsome Ethiopian features, he was as slim, strong and tall as Wilt Chamberlain.

Tavo crawled out of the hut and stood gazing up at him. Clyde looked down at him scornfully and said "Me hear seh you wan' built house. A true?" then punctuated this introduction by poking a long hard knuckled finger into Tavo's chest. "Me de bes' builder mon in Westmoreland." Poke. "Nottin' me cyan build." Poke, poke. "Garth, him mus' call me Uncle," poke, poke, poke. "Is me one build Len's house. Ah! Oh!" Poke, poke, poke.

Tavo urged him to sit down to discuss finances, but mostly he wanted to get out of the way of that bony poking finger. He figured that Clyde's hand had to be okay, from the prodding he'd just survived and asked him about it. Clyde refused to discuss details but claimed the hand had not troubled him for over a year. He thrust a finger adorned with a plastic ring holding a garish purple plastic stone that looked like it came out of a Cracker Jack box under Tavo's nose.

"See dat ring," he exclaimed proudly, "Me send away to faraway place a foreign an pay a big money. Dem call de place Chicago. Dat far away nuh true?" Tavo nodded an affirmation while rubbing his chest. "De most powerful obeah mon in de world live dere! Wid dis ring dat mon sends me, nothin' no harm me again. Dis ring here hab de most powerful obeah in it! Me is a mon now, a mon amongst mens! Ah Oh!"

Gloom and Doom sat down comfortably under a big fig tree and sucked on a Guinness Stout he had brought with him, staring at Tavo and continued his spiel with relish.

"Me knows you hippies are a funny tribe. You nuh understand and believe any ting true dat yuh caan see wid de naked eye! Ask Len 'bout me hand 'wid de worms 'pon it—him will make you know fe true. Ah! Oh!"

Tavo tried to steer the conversation back to the task at hand even though the worms interested him immensely. But by now Clyde had taken on an air of superiority and was stoically refusing to discuss financial matters. Tavo took the bull by the horns. "Clyde, let's talk about money for my house," he said firmly. "I believe you, about your hand and the ring, but we gotta discuss money! I don't want to give you the whole contract price up front that would break me. What I'd like is to pay you, you know, as we go along, okay? Cause I'm not sure I even have enough money to finish, see?"

With an especially ugly sneer, Clyde rose and delivered a spear-like poke to Tavo's chest it almost knocked him backwards. "All oonou hippie mon worry 'bout all de time is money!" he bellowed. "Weh wrong wid oonou? Fat Len him so rich him cyaan spend him money—yet money all him eber hab 'pon him brain." Clyde stood up, paced back and forth, kicking up red dust "Me is a mon nuh care wedder you hab all de money or no! Me is a mon who wi jus decide nuh fi work for you at all, if you no honor something first! Ah Oh! Me nah care if you hab money like dirt!"

"What kind of something?" Tavo asked sitting there staring at him bewildered. "I don't understand."

Clyde bent down and poked him soundly in the chest, "Ouch!" "Well, first off you must shed some blood."

"Oh, God, he wants me to kill somebody for him?" Tavo thought. "Hell no," he said shocked. "No way, man, I'm not killing anyone or cutting anyone. I've had enough troubles about war and death, that's why I am here in the first place. Why I left foreign! I ain't doin it!"

"T'cho, whey wrong wid you? Ha!" chuckled Clyde sarcastically and Tavo saw what could almost be called a smile pass over his face. "You hippie mon is a funny wild something fe true. Me nuh want yuh fi kill nobody. Me mean seh you must agree fi kill a ram goat same way as dem did do at Nick's wedding. When de blood drip 'pon de ground, de evil spirits keep away from de house, dats all." Clyde looked over his shoulder, sat back down and lowered his voice to a whisper "When Len was a build him house, him nuh kill no goat, him nuh shed no blood. Him nuh make de nice ram goat curry fi feed we. Dats why what happen to me han' happen. The spirits dem never happy! Ah Oh!"

Tavo thought he got it then remembered the ring. "Ok, I'll buy a goat and we'll curry it. No problem. But what about the ring? I thought.... Clyde impatiently interrupted him "De ring not dat powerful mon! But dat is not all. Yuh nuh say how big de goat is dat yuh goin buy. Yuh still have nuff problems mon!"

"Yah, but I don't know anything about different ram goat sizes".

Clyde's Gloom and Doom façade had almost vanished. He chuckled and a wicked grin cracked his face; "Tavo, you is a funny mon fe true. So what? Me must help you like you is a little pickney?" He turned stone serious in a flash again, and his gloom and doom was back. He wheeled on Tavo, shouting "Man yuh want de biggest ram goat! 'Bout forty-pound weight wid' de biggest seeds." And Clyde cupped his crotch with both hands to indicate the size of the proposed ram goat's scrotum. "See!"

"All right, man, okay, okay. I agree," Tavo stammered. "Now can we discuss the house? Like what size? Where it'll go? You know, how much materials we'll need? What'll it cost, stuff like that?"

"No, mon," replied Clyde disgustedly, chugging the last of the Guinness and flinging the empty bottle into the bush. "We nuh reach dat far yet. We have plenty more reason to reason. You must' also buy de rum. It mus' be de overproof white rum! You mus' buy beer, Red Stripe. You cyaan nyam de goat and nuh give libation to de ancestor spirits. Dat is wen you bring down de curses 'pon we fe true! De workmen dem nah go respect you, me nah go respect you, and everybody goin' be unhappy den! Mek de worms tek we."

"Okay man, Okay" said Tavo, his patience wearing thin. "I buy the rum and beer. Now let's talk ab—" but Clyde interrupted again with a poke to Tavo's chest before he could finish.

"Stop mon! You nah say how much of de liquor you will buy! Boy, you is really different from Jamaican mon fi true! I guess me have fi go-slow wid you, fi try make you understand! But boy, it hard!"

"All right, all right," Tavo agreed. Anything to pacify him and get on with the negotiations. "I'll buy a quart of overproof white rum and a dozen bottles of Red Stripe. Okay?"

Clyde became even more indignant. His patience was worn thin, as a Guinep leaf. “No mon! Dat not right. You tink one bottle of rum and twelve beer can do anything? No sah! You must buy two bottles of de rum and three dozen Red Stripe and me figet, me alone haffi get six Guinness Stout. Ah Oh!”

“Ok. Ok. Ok.” Tavo snapped.” “Now let’s talk about MY HOUSE, how much that’ll cost me, you know with material and….”

Again, Clyde cut him off, for the last time, with an imperious wave of his plastic bejeweled hand. “Me nah reason wid’ you nuh more for today. You wear me out mon. Besides we already reason out de biggest most important matters, so de rest is of little trouble.”

He abruptly turned around with remarkable grace, as if he was going to slam-dunk a basket. In a flash, all six foot, seven inches of him was striding down the dirt road in a cloud of red dust.

Tavo sat there with Remus, staring in wonderment after him, like he’d just beamed back up to the Starship Enterprise. Was this guy for real? In any case, no work would begin without first appeasing the spirits within and without.

Two days later, Clyde returned unannounced, much like before. This meeting went smoother. He said that he was pleased that Tavo had absorbed the wisdom from their first encounter. Claimed he really didn’t care when or how Tavo paid him as long as he had start-up pay for his workers and himself and materials on the site to start construction. No one had anything to do anyway; they may as well work. When Tavo had money he could pay them. After all, they all knew that white men could always find money somewhere. They were blessed.

Tavo designed a twenty-eight-foot diameter octagon with a palm-thatched roof. Clyde approved. Materials were ordered from Savanna La Mar the closest town, palm branches chopped down from the nearby swamp and cured, and cedar trees cut down from the forests and taken to the local mill. Clyde took Tavo around the countryside, negotiating for lumber growing on people's land, and making arrangements with the bushmen to do the cutting, gathering and chopping.

The day of the groundbreaking party, a motley, mixed bag of workers arrived. There were two shriveled carpenters who looked to be about ninety years old and a couple of young stone masons. One named Dragon had one blue eye and the build of George Foreman. Clyde told Tavo these guys could work from sun-up to sundown without breaking stride.

They followed the ancient rituals and everyone consumed goat curry with relish. The ram goat's testicles were roasted over an open fire and shared as a delicacy. The head and innards were made into soup. All were washed down with white rum mixed with a heavy, sickeningly sweet red syrup and drunk from calabash gourds. Everyone cracked numerous sweet jokes and slapped Tavo on the back for being an upright brother mon who did not wish to offend any of the ancestral spirits as Len had done, causing Clyde's hand to succumb to the worm curse.

Much talk and good spirited argument focused on island politics, particularly over the question of whether the Socialist Prime Minister, Michael Manley would help the poor of the country. Much ado was also made about the "christening" of the house, even though no work had started. From the workers' bantering, Tavo gathered that "christening" meant that he had to bed a "young gal" in the completed house to bring good luck. The workers also reminisced about other christenings of long ago. Evidently, it was the workers' prerogative to party outside the new dwelling and listen in on the good luck sexual activities taking place inside. They reenacted these past scenes of pleasure, imitating the screams and groans and comparing the various duration's of these sexual encounters.

Everybody wanted to know who the lady would be to christen the house with Tavo. So he told them with a dreamy, vapid look about his true love Irene, that she was probably now living a very different existence in Michigan. He briefly mentioned Donna, the nymphet in Key West, his other, fleeting diversion, in an effort to pacify their ribald curiosity. But when the workers realized he'd been celibate since coming to Jamaica, they grew extremely concerned. Everyone knew a niece, cousin, or sister that could expertly perform the christening task with him and they offered to bring them around. But gave due warning he must be prepared to take additional steps of commitment. Not necessarily marriage, but the christening gal would most likely want a live-in relationship. This was okay with everyone because Tavo would then have someone to cook his meals, clean house and give him many pickneys. During these discussions, it dawned on him that no gal over fourteen would be appropriate as they usually had a pickney and were spoken for already. The best age would be twelve, they concluded, at the most thirteen. There were no taboos regarding age as there were about oral sex. These guys considered robbing the cradle the norm. Though Tavo had to raise loud objections about courting of minors, the party was a huge success.

The spirits were appeased and he was hailed as a good sport even if he was a hippie with strange ways. Everybody left drunk, bellies filled, and content. Clyde took the goat skin to make a drum for the Quadrille Christmas dance that would take place in the hills behind Negril. Since the party was held on Friday, and no one worked on weekends, work on the house was not started until two days later.

Tavo was elated. He felt genuinely accepted by these guys. He'd found a home here: not with the hedonistic subculture, but with the real people of this strange and wonderful land. The door may have closed to the US, but another was opening, and cold ground would no longer be his bed at night. His land was taking shape; he would have a real house on land that he owned. Maybe, not a perfect island utopia like Huxley's but his utopia anyway. He slept the sleep of contentment, of one who knew he'd made the right choices on life's forked path. Except in his dream, Irene beckoned him as she swam half hidden in mist, under a Tropical waterfall, trying to swim away from a fierce crocodile. A crocodile with a hideous face that looked just like Harlen Rosenthal.

11

"I looked for her in Miami.
I looked for her in Negril."

By Bob Seeger
From the song *Sun Spot Baby*

Tavo's house was taking shape. All the time and effort gathering from the bush, negotiating for materials and throwing the party was paying off big time. The workers showed up every day at sunrise and worked sweat soaking hard to sunset. Clyde sometimes worked alongside of them, but most of the time he reveled in his role of contractor. He gave orders, drank Guinness Stout, smoked his Craven "A's" and bragged how good he was, underscoring his boasts, as always, with hard pokes to Tavo's chest. But he could care less; he was finally being productive; accomplishing something. He ignored Clyde's bony finger, too excited at seeing his house rise from his very own jungle paradise.

He was astounded at Clyde's workers, who hauled and mixed cement by hand all day under the sweltering tropical sun and tried to work alongside them, carrying sacks of cement or swinging a shovel to combine the gravel, sand and cement into a concrete mixture. But his efforts would peter out after an hour of toil, and he'd collapse under a coconut palm, sweat running from every pore nursing the numerous blisters that covered his hands.

It was during one of these recovery periods that he decided he'd been neglecting his American neighbor Nick. He was curious about the aftermath of his disastrous marriage and wondered what he was doing to cope. So he strolled over wiping sweat from his eyes and found Nick swinging reflectively back and forth in a hammock strung between two sea grape trees at the cliff's edge, next to the dilapidated and empty swimming pool. He was wearing a skimpy racing bathing suit; puffing mightily on a cigar-sized spliff.

"How ya doin, Nicholas," he said. "What's up?"

Nick took in Tavo's work-worn, dirty appearance, gave him a disgusted look.

"You're a sorry excuse for the human race," he said, "and don't address me as Nicholas." He did a lightning personality shift flashing his crafty Cheshire Cat grin then stared straight ahead, out to sea, ignoring him, waiting for him to respond.

"Who are you then?" Asked Tavo, perplexed.

"I'm Nick, you schmuck," he snarled turning his gaze back to Tavo spiteful now; back to his old self, "and your filthy construction worker feet are now standing on the world famous Nick's Cafe. Can't you see it? But I suppose you never could, lacking as you are in imagination, insight, or any type of progressive thought!"

Tavo looked over Nick's crash pad spread, rubbed the stubble on his chin and said, almost to himself, " Its gorgeous, I give ya that but I just don't see any cafe. All I see is a couple of naked freaks passed out on the lawn and a broken down villa. Anyways, what's going to happen when Dr Campbell kicks you out?"

Nick shook his head stared at him like he had the mental faculties of a turnip.

"You're such an asshole! Spend all your time prattling on with a bunch of crazed Jamaicans for what reason, no one knows. Then putter around in the dirt attempting to build a slum house, the likes of which a civilized person wouldn't set foot in." He blew a smoke ring of ganja smoke at Tavo contemptuously " I don't know why I attempt to enlighten you.

You can't comprehend the privilege you have to be living next door to what will soon be the garden paradise of the world, and I, Nick, will sit upon its throne." He re-lit his spliff that had gone out, took a greedy lung full, held it in then blew a large smoke cloud into Tavo's face. "Sell me your piece of land! Now! Before you fuck it up anymore... put some hillbilly trailer park on it. Maybe I can still salvage it with my creativity!"

Tavo squinted, coughed waved the smoke out of his face; he tried to match Nick's sarcasm and said, "Look, I love my land. I got nowhere to go. Anyway, you don't have the money to buy the doctor's property! Why you think you can buy mine?"

Nick feigned exasperation, and said in a condescending tone appropriate for conversation with a slow 3-year old, "The only reason I'm going to waste my time with you, is because I'm finally getting somewhat high. I'm at one with the world. My body is where my mind has always been. I dropped eight Mandrex and they've kicked in; I glow with ecstasy." He gazed over the ocean for a minute lost in his high then said "Anyway, since those two freaks passed out in the ozone on the lawn are beyond communication, I'm forced to tolerate you; seeing you're the only one present who's conscious."

Nick affected the posture of a demanding and critical British lord and ordered his sixty-year-old maid, Miss Opal, to prepare ackee and salt fish, for his lunch. Miss Opal scurried around catering to his demands shaking her head muttering under her breath, "Nick him a mad mon same way as Norman."

While he ate his lunch and between his screaming complaints that the food was too cold and too salty, he filled Tavo in on his new scam, bragging how his life would transform, ending his cursed miserable third world existence.

Since Jane refused to divorce him, he'd taken matters into his own hands. He got her loaded on Mandrex and conned her into flying to Haiti with him for a honeymoon. Once there, he threatened her, tried to get her to sign divorce papers. When that didn't work he scored some heroin and bribed her with a vial of stuff. That worked like a charm. "I've finally washed my hands clean of that miserable fucking junkie ugly cunt." Nick spat out. "That bitch is probably sucking all the black cocks of 'Port a Prince' right now—trying to come up with enough cash to score her next fix."

"That really low man" Tavo said.

"It's limbo time," said Nick. "How low can you go! Ha! Ha! Ha!"

But the best part happened on his return to Negril. He talked Len Stern, Jamie Dice and the other drug smugglers to come up with forty thousand dollars each to purchase the doctor's property and erect a bar/restaurant the likes of which the Caribbean had never seen. Of course, extravagant living quarters for Nick were part of his master plan. In return for their generosity, he'd give the drug runners lifetime membership to this luxury cafe, with unlimited free food and drinks.

However, this clandestine group of modern-day Calico Jacks demanded to be shareholders with profit sharing rights. They weren't dumb, casual free wheeling entrepreneurs. Desperate to hang onto his carefree existence, Nick agreed. "Besides" he said and winked conspiratorially to Tavo, "Those loser felons will all be busted by the DEA and locked away in the slammer, anyway, and I'll control everything! It'll be a Caribbean Casablanca; all my bartenders will wear red Moroccan fezzes. I'll swing in my hammock as the jet set, the rich and famous, the beautiful and the glamorous flock to Nick's Cafe. And Betty Lou with those smooth-as-silk sweet, tan thighs will leave that pencil-dick, faggot Daniel Pough at the Yatch Club and give me blowjobs 'round the clock. Or I'll have my pick of any princess in the crowd and she'll be honored to have the privilege to slurp the cum and lick the asshole of the internationally known Nick! The niggers on staff will be at my beck and call. Say, by the way, Tavo, how do you make a mint julep? I'm not much for drinking, prefer pharmaceuticals, but mint juleps fit my new image!"

"Uh I think its bourbon and mint," Tavo said, distractedly, thinking of another wedding nightmare, "maybe some sugar." Nick puffed away on his spliff, nodding smiling contentedly at his new prosperity, high as a kite now; the Ludes had kicked in.

Tavo looked at him and shook his head in disbelief. He suspected that his latest fantasy was already out of control spinning into another potential nightmare. Misunderstanding his look for one of self pity Nick said "Ya, ya, ya," I'll let you in occasionally… even let you drink one with me, but first sell me your land. I'll pay you five times what you paid for it. Moneys no problem now. It's a very generous offer. It wouldn't be worth spit if not for my efforts!" Tavo shook his head tried to speak but Nick cut him off. "Everything you touch turns to shit" Nick said. "Your land can serve as my parking lot for customers from the far corners of the world. Or maybe I'll turn it into a helicopter pad for the VIPs. Face facts, you're not cut out for a life of glamour and fame; you'd be much happier working on some papaya farm in Nicaragua."

While Nick prattled on, Tavo tried to maintain his cool, but the vision of his months of labor reduced to a concrete parking lot was too much, and a helicopter pad reminded him of Vietnam. He jumped up; no longer able contain himself. He smacked the table with his fist rattling the glasses, the silverware, and shouted, "I'm not selling! I love my place! This is where I'm making my stand. Forget it man!"

"Ah, fuck you and your melodramatic stand!" Nick yelled. "You're just a scum-sucking draft dodger. Stand my ass! I knew it was pointless trying to elevate your consciousness to a higher plane. Fuck you some more for wasting my precious time you low life bring down! Get the fuck out of my cafe, and don't come back!" He threw his plate of half-eaten ackee at Tavo it smashed into the wall barley missing his head.

Tavo headed for the door, a string of curses following him. Miss Opal cornered him on his way out the gate. "Don't feel no way, Tavo," she said, patting him on the back with a shaky hand. "Nick him speak to everybody like dat. Is only dem ganja smugglers him nuh facety wid. Him a mad mon fe true."

He didn't "feel no way." He just felt Nick was acting like a real asshole. If Nick lured drug dealers to save his property and develop it into a world-class cafe, more power to him. That might mean Negril would develop too. But he sure as hell wasn't going to give up his land to make it happen. All he could do now was wait and see—*qué será, será*. Maybe Negril would develop in a, positive way. Maybe all the Negrilians could share in its future prosperity. Maybe Jamaica's the new socialist government would act responsibly, enact laws to protect the environment, protect its splendor. Its beauty could be shared with the whole world. The rich, the famous, and the glamorous would flock here as Nick predicted. He sure didn't know any of them but there had to be some good people amongst them, like everybody else. Maybe some plain and ordinary folks would come too, share and learn from the locals as he had. That would be Irie!

12

*"If you not living good,
I beg you travel wide."*

By Bob Marley
From the song *Soul Rebel*

Until his rap with Nick he hadn't thought much about future changes in Negril. He'd been too preoccupied with his own changes—coming to terms with leaving everything familiar behind—his inner conflicts over Vietnam and Irene. Jamaica and her people had been good therapy so far, giving him a new positive frame of reference to view himself and that dreaded war.

It was easier to see mankind as a bunch of monkeys cutting up on island earth, not take life so seriously.

Even Nick's abuse rolled off his back easily now. He wrote him off as a spoiled rich kid jerk. What he did take seriously though was Negril's development. What direction would its growth take, he wondered? He began to agonize over it. Would the Jamaican government step in one day, take over and kick out all the free spirits the new-age buccaneers? Garth had told him the smugglers worried about this and paid off the local police, government officials and politicians, but they were still mistrustful. From what he knew—and his information was sketchy from Garth (Negril had no newspapers yet and he didn't have a radio)—the Jamaican government professed socialism. The space cadet, ganja pirates did not like those politics; any wealth they amassed could wind up being split up amongst the populace. They were all staunch Republicans, loved Richard Nixon.

Still, until that day when Nick through his lunch of ackee and salt fish at him, he'd always envisioned Negril as a simple peaceful fishing village populated by honest, hard working, sincere country folk who lived off a land and sea unspoiled by outside contamination. Its pristine waters had existed for millions of years and its reefs were teeming with life. Only a few naked children frolicking and splashing on its beach or a handful of fishermen rippled the sea's natural rhythms.

"You fool! We'll take paradise and put up a parking lot!" Nick had screamed at him, his parting shot that day he tried to buy his land. "And I'll be sitting on Boardwalk! Wake up asshole!"

Well, what could one man do to stop change? He'd been as effective at stopping the Vietnam War as a nat attacking an elephant. Already, more foreign outsiders, hippies, and jetsetters were discovering Negril and moving in. Most stayed for just a month or two, but more and more began to buy property and put down roots in much grander style.

The marijuana trade was also in full swing. With the smugglers vying against each other for the illicit crops, landing space on newly constructed air strips in the bush, and for prime hoarding caves and coves along the cliffs, where the green gold was stashed. Hidden until the mother ships picked it up and brought it to an insatiably hungry American market.

Accommodations were still scarce in Negril, so visitors usually crashed with local country people in sleeping bags on the cedar floorboards of their shacks, on the great open expanse of the seven-mile beach, or wherever they dropped after ingesting too much Mandrex, ganja, and white rum. Adventurous rock-and-roll stars still escaped to Negril to cool out after tours and avoid being hassled by fans. Most of them found their way to Nick's. Reggae music was also spreading worldwide, with the rise of its new prophet, Bob Marley. Something was definitely happening here.

To his surprise, Nick's Cafe was proceeding according to plan, well maybe not surprise it was fueled by an endless fund of ganja money. Anyway the ducks were kicked out and a floor was laid over the old, cracked swimming pool, a roof of cedar shingles covered its length and width. It became a large bar area. The sides were raised to create a waist-high sitting area and chairs were staggered all along it. The bartenders wore the red fezzes Nick bragged of, and the old house was gutted to form an inside dining area. Intimate tables and chair groupings were set out on the lawn overlooking the sea for outside dining. The old helpers' quarters were turned into a modern expansive kitchen, complete with industrialized hotel cooking equipment. No expense was spared on the construction of this lavish cafe; the ganja partners wanted to make back their investment quickly, given the uncertain nature of their business and the island's politics. But they did spare expenses when it came to the ultra plush living quarters Nick demanded. They gave him instead an eighteen-by-eighteen foot bungalow on the cliff edge with full view of the bar area so he could monitor pilfering. Now all those freeloading moochers would pay for the privilege of wining, dining, and getting stoned while taking in gorgeous sunsets through purple-hazed eyes.

Every night, during those spectacular sunsets Nick sashayed through the newly formed crowd wearing a bright Hawaiian shirt and his trademark razor-pressed, spotless, patched Levis. If a curious flower child asked if he were really Nick, he'd shrug his shoulders and reply, "Sometimes I am and sometimes I am not," then he'd mysteriously swish away as he rolled his eyes to the heavens a la Greta Garbo. You could almost hear him mutter, "I vant to be left alone."

Tavo often wandered over to Nick's Cafe at sunset to see Nick perform and take in the festivities; Nick's was the "in" place to be in Negril at that time of day. Go-go girls on location from around the world stood on the cut stone wall that surrounded the bar, undulating their hips and winding their waists to throbbing rock beats, the latest from the Doors, the Who, Cream, the Rolling Stones, The Isley Brothers and Bob Dylan. The bartenders whirled like dervishes as they frantically blended piña coladas and planter's punches, keeping time with the music as they appeased thirsty crowds. Rastafarians toked huge spliffs, then jumped off the forty-foot cliffs, melting into the blue-green sea below, emerging a few tense seconds later, shaking out their dreadlocks. Clothing was optional, bare breasted being the norm, and any drug could be ingested openly so long as it was shared and as long as it got you high enough to touch the sky. Nicks Cafe was no Willie's Discipline Club; each sunset party tried to achieve the bacchanal of his wedding. They always fell short, but no one ever complained as tomorrow offered another chance to try.

Just as Nick predicted, people were flocking to Negril and to his cafe from everywhere in the world. Many were card-carrying members of the notorious jet set. Most preferred to crash with the locals in informal, atmospheric mom and pop palm thatched shacks, although a few expensive, luxurious villas had recently sprung up along the beach.

The Negrilians continued to exercise complete acceptance of the strangers, no matter how bizarre and wild their behavior and how much it disrupted their quiet existence. Plus a few extra bucks in exchange for a floor to sleep on or a shared meal softened the blow, helped supplement a marginal existence of goat raising and fishing. As time went on and more and more dollars were stashed away under mattresses, the locals began developing business to cater to the needs of this growing transient group. Small bamboo restaurants serving local delicacies of fresh seafood along with coconut rice and peas sprung up on the beach. Others forsook their small goat and tobacco farms for cultivating a more lucrative product even more in demand, high-grade sensimillia marijuana. Farmers who had never seen more than a fifty or a hundred-dollar-a-year profit increased their earnings a hundred fold, simply by switching to a weed that was easier to grow than tobacco or yams. To these farmers, the hippies who coveted this herb were not much different than the Rastafarians who worshiped its mind-altering properties. Unlike the Rasta, though, the hippie was willing to pay top dollar for a smoke on the beach or to cart the weed home in planes and boats. They'd pay as much as ten American dollars a pound! Praise the Lord for the hippie mon! And praise be to Jah, as well, praise for Prime Minister Michael Manley, who turned a blind eye to laws against such commerce. Irie! Irie!

Nick was also cashing in, making money hand over fist from the high prices he charged customers for the right to watch his ritual sunset spectacle and down a few rum punches. He was soon able to buy out some of his more conservative partners. However, most of the smugglers weren't willing to part with their rights to a lifetime of wining and dining. They'd become as infamous as those pirates that were hung long ago on Rackham Key. And what good is notoriety unless you have a public showcase. Nick's Cafe, the Casablanca of the Caribbean, was the perfect spot to strut and preen. They were living a fairytale Peter Pan existence, complete with all the toys, and none of them ever expected to grow up. This Never Never Land offered more pleasure more excitement than Walt Disney World.

But the richer, the more famous Nick's grew, the greedier he became, and he coveted Tavo's land even more. One day, he threatened that if Tavo didn't sell his land for fifty thousand dollars (ten times what he paid for it) he would commit suicide by flinging himself out his bedroom window onto the jagged rocks below. His bones would bleach right there forever, reminding Tavo of his selfishness. The only reply Tavo came up with to his hyperdrama was that it had been nice knowing Nick. Any guilt over the bleached bones would last as long as it took for the next high wave to come along and wash em away.

Nick's next ploy was to send Betty Lou to him like an escort service to work him over with her powerful sexual charms… persuade him to sell. True to his prediction, Betty Lou had become a semi-permanent fixture at the Cafe, although she still divided her time between Nick's and the Yacht Club, which also continued to do a swinging business after Nick's sunset.

Betty Lou drenched Tavo in crocodile tears over Nick's imminent demise and couched her pleas in her sweet honey-suckled drawl. But he wouldn't budge. There was nowhere else in the world he wanted to be. His two-acre plot had become his personal piece of the universe, and, over the past few months, he'd become familiar with every rock, bush, tree, and plant—he even loved the ones bristling with vicious thorns that the Jamaicans called "macka jookers." He'd traveled far and wide and gone through hell for this piece of rock. It was the end of the line for him. He'd just begun the work that would transform it into his personal vision of paradise. Anyway he figured Nick would soon give up his efforts to get it away from him—he'd tried everything so far and failed.

But Tavo was no clairvoyant, had he been he would have realized that Nick's coveting his homestead was the least of his worries. At that very moment Len Stern, Jamie Dice, and boatman (no not Striker, the US government had stopped accepting Cuban immigrants with open arms and he was headed back to New Guinea to give the shrunken heads another try) were plotting their next smuggling operation right next door to him at Nick's bungalow.

They had kicked Nick out, no need for anyone more than necessary to be brought into their conspiracy to export drugs.

But Nick had made a quick sashay around the bar… make them think he'd left… then snuck back and put his ear to a small knot hole and eaves dropped… Dice was talking, he had the floor. "So listen up" he said, "we can't use Nick's caves no more to stash our herb… shit there's too many suckers all over the place now."

"We could go to Green Island," said Stern, "Buy a chunk of coastland, build a small fake resort you know—like a front, only store the weed in a cottage."

"That's bull shit," said Dice "Fuck that! Fuck putting more money in this fucked up island… shit it's going socialist… I ain't wastin no more bread here!"

"You got a point there." Stern said. "So what do we do? We gotta store it somewhere."

"Man it's right under your fucking nose" snarled Dice "We'll use the dip shits land next door"

"Ya, but what if he won't let us?" said Stern.

Dice reached into the back pocket of his black leather Levi's, pulled out his ratchet knife flicked it open 'click-clack-click'

"He ain't got no fucking choice," he said.

'Click-clack-click'

13

"One love, one heart.
Let's join together,
And I will feel all right."

By Bob Marley
From the song *One Love*

Five months after he started, Clyde finished Tavo's house and was putting on the finishing touches. Each of the bungalow's eight sides had a set of large, hand carved cedar shutter blinds through which tropical breezes blew and kept the interior cool. The thatched roof repelled the baking heat of the day, allowing whatever heat was there to rise and escape, while it kept rain and moisture out. Blue Mahoe, a native hardwood with a grain that held various hues of blue, green and white was used for the furnishings—a countertop with stools, table and chairs, a bed and closet. The cupboards and closet doors were made from Bambex, a basket weave of wooden bamboo strips that fishermen used on fish traps. The overall effect was completely Caribbean; old style building techniques applied to a modern design. Tavo used the last of his money to buy a two-burner propane stove and gas cylinder from a hardware store in Savanna La Mar. He also purchased two kerosene lanterns with Home Sweet Home written on their glass shades and a Coleman cooler. The ice truck rumbled up the road once a month and Clyde showed Tavo how to dig a hole under a large Guinep tree and line it with cedar shavings and sawdust. It would keep four to five blocks of ice for up to two weeks—even in the tropical heat.

He spent most of his days in his garden, a quarter-acre plot of land that surrounded the house. He planted exotic flowers that Garth brought him, along with banana, coconut, and papaya trees. Gardening turned out to be a great deal more difficult—like so many things in his life—than he first imagined. His "land" was actually eighty percent jagged limestone coral rock that had risen from the sea millions of years ago. The thick jungle that grew on it fought to send tendril-like roots into the rock in search for the occasional pocket of soil. Sharp pieces of broken ancient coral rock had to be laboriously removed by hand in order to find those pockets of dirt and plant. Then there were the ever-present weeds that seemed to sprout overnight on the bare rock after the previous day's work of prying them up. He hired an eighty-five-year-old local yam farmer, Jim Proud, to help part-time with the constant landscaping chores. But after an hour of work, he usually found Jim sleeping contentedly under a fig tree and he continued laboring solo. Beating back the ever-encroaching jungle left him at the end of the day scratched, cut, sore, and exhausted with oozing blisters on his hands and feet. But he was happy and content to be accomplishing something and the hard work kept his mind temporarily off of Irene.

One morning, after observing his futile attempts to arouse Jim from his nap, Clyde's stone mason called Tavo aside and suggested that he hire his younger brother Mannie as a gardener. Mannie was young, strong, and more than willing to put in a full good day's work. He readily agreed, and the next morning Mannie showed up for work wearing a clean white shirt, black tie, and black pressed slacks. Tavo was a little surprised at this get-up. It apparently was designed to make a good first impression, as Mannie immediately took off his dress clothes and donned a pair of rubberized boots, tattered corduroys, and set to the task of clearing, weeding, packing stone, building pathways and making well thought-out suggestions about what to plant where. He felt an instant communion between himself and Mannie. Although he usually talked in a rapid, machine-gun fire, heavy guttural patois, Mannie could also speak perfect English. He picked up his perfect diction and extensive vocabulary in only a few months work as a bartender at the Wharf club, where he held court, shooting the bull with rebellious college kids, imitated their dialect and figured out the meaning of unfamiliar words.

Mannie endeared himself to all he met. He had a quick good-humored laugh, endless charm, and crooned Caribbean folk songs as he labored under the hot sun. He was twenty years old, just four years younger than Tavo, but he harbored a fierce streak of self-sufficiency and independence. From the start, Mannie made Tavo aware that the most important reason he worked with him was to learn more about Americans and their ways. He believed the future of Negril would revolve around Americans and their relationships with Jamaicans, especially their ability to get along.

He told Tavo he'd previously held jobs as a Jamaican cowboy, driving a vast herd of bovines for a wealthy rancher. He'd also been a fisherman, stone mason, farmer, and thatch man. He stressed he did not smoke ganja or take strong drink, claiming these substances made one's brain soft.

Most of his jobs were short-lived he freely admitted. When he felt he'd learned all that he could, he'd leave. But he always set higher and higher goals for himself in order to become increasingly self-sufficient and knowledgeable. It was obvious to Tavo that Mannie was extremely intelligent, although he claimed never to have gone to school and couldn't read or write. He said his parents had died when he was only five, he'd been on his own from an early age. He lived with older brothers and sisters in the hills behind Negril and began to work his various jobs from age seven, in order to contribute to household expenses.

He was a lifesaver for Tavo; his vast knowledge of Jamaican bush life encompassed building, farming, cooking, fishing, gardening, and overall survival in a marginally primitive environment. He was six-foot three with light golden brown skin, a result of his mixed Scottish, East Indian, and African ancestry. The best of these races had come together to create fine handsome features, and every muscle of his body rippled like a body builder's. Negrilians claimed Mannie could carry two hundred-pound cement bags on his shoulders from sun up to sunset in the blistering tropical heat without breaking a sweat or tiring. Others spoke of him in awe as if he were the Jamaican version of Paul Bunion, Pecos Bill, and John Henry all rolled into one. Tales of his exploits achieved mythical proportions.

He could fish by himself out of a eighteen foot dugout canoe propelled by a forty horse power Evinrude engine and charge full force into a huge leaping school of tuna. As the boat flew through the air and slapped down with kidney jarring force on the white caps, he'd hook fish after fish with four lines. One wrapped around each hand and one around each large toe—all the while, maneuvering the boat. One wrong move, people would emphasize, like not setting the hook right or releasing the line at the precisely right moment, would mean the loss of an appendage.

Mannie could survive in the bush with no money, just living from the land. Tavo's funds were virtually gone by now, so he taught him how to spear fish from the coral reefs growing off the rocky cliffs that fronted his property, and how to dive for the spiny lobsters that inhabited crevices in the coral. Mannie could hold his breath up to five minutes while hunting this elusive prey. He also planted pumpkin squash, beans, yams and cho-cho between the rocky outcroppings to supplement a seafood diet. When times were very lean and fishing not so good, he would cook a concoction he called Monkey Stew, a soup-like porridge made from cornmeal and a small crustacean called Whelks. Whelks lived in the lime stone rock where it meets the sea, and had to be pried off with a sharp knife.

Since he had no home other than temporary stays with various siblings, Mannie moved in with Tavo, who welcomed his company along with the fraternity he longed for. Most evenings during the preparation of their evening meal and while they ate it, Mannie spun tales of bush folklore. One especially perked Tavos interest about River Mummas who enticed fishermen of the Morass wetlands. These River Mummas paralyzed their enthralled victims and captured their souls. He claimed they had the lower bodies of fish and the torsos and heads of beautiful women, and lived only in desolate parts of the rivers and swamps of Negril. Tavo tried to explain; educate him that these "Mummas" were really Manatees that early American sailors had called them Mermaids. But Mannie got annoyed, claiming that Jamaicans called the Manatee a Sea Cow… it wasn't the same thing as a River Mumma at all. Besides, if American sailors have a name for the River Mumma and call it a Mermaid that's sure proof they must exist! Or why name it?

Tavo didn't press his argument; he loved the stories too much and didn't want them to stop. Mannie also loved to spin tales about the Rollin' Calves who inhabited the dark bush and was especially fond of duppie ghost, stories. These sessions reminded Tavo of Boy Scout campers terrifying each other with deliciously scary stories told at night around a campfire. But to Mannie, like Garth, these devils were as real as the deep black nights in which they roamed. According to him, duppies could be captured by a living man, and then commanded to do devilishment against the wicked. The process for capture was fairly involved: one had to gather various herbs from the bush along with rat bat dung from a certain mountain cave, then sneak into a graveyard at the stroke of midnight. With the right incantations, one could then catch the duppie in a glass bottle and quickly put a stopper in it to prevent the duppy's escape.

Tavo never tired of hearing these tales. He found them fascinating, poetic and colorful. Mannie had a natural storytelling gift. Against the backdrop of a warm, star-studded Caribbean night lit by a blazing brushwood fire, his tales were better than a Steven King novel. So he took extreme care to never doubt Mannie again, as he had with the "Mumma" story.

Mannie was just as interested in Tavo and his tales of American life. As they shared cultures, a strong feeling of respect and mutual understanding formed between them. Tavo grew to consider Mannie the brother he never had, and Mannie looked for Tavo to be his link to the ever-increasing foreign changes that were taking place in his world, enacting their modern day version of Robinson Crusoe, but Tavo held no hopes of ever going home.

One sun-drenched morning, while they were preparing to spear fish off the cliff edge reef in front of his property, Mannie spotted a huge two hundred and fifty-pound sea turtle gliding ghost-like in the clear, still waters close to shore. He trembled with excitement and stammered, "I'll kill that mon. He'll feed us for a week... we sell some of the meat at the market! I'll carve jewelry out of him shell! Hippie mon an' woman love it! Yah mon, we make a money now!"

He pumped himself up with adrenaline for the kill, flexing his muscles and setting and resetting the spear sling as he prepared to leap from the cliff edge. But Tavo abruptly hit his arm, rudely knocking the spear gun from his grasp and the spear lodged deep in a nearby tree, vibrating. "Don't shoot it!" he shouted. "Turtles are endangered man! You keep killing em; they'll soon be gone. Come on man, let him go!"

Mannie shook with anger; this was the first dissension between them. "We're broke Mon!" he shouted and rocked the spear back and forth trying to dislodge it from the tree. "You've run out of money! I don't get a pay for three weeks.

If I don't kill that turtle, someone else will, see? It gonna die by someone's hand. Why not ours? Yuh talk foolishness man!"

"Maybe someone will kill it" Tavo said… "don't let it be us. Let it live. We'll eat Monkey Stew tonight. Come on man. Don't kill it. I mean it!"…. "Shit!"

Mannie waved his arms, beckoning Tavo to sit down with him on the cliff's edge. He'd calmed down some from his efforts to dislodge the spear. "We gotta reason Mon," he said. "This land's changing day by day since you hippies arrived. Where you see one or two turtles now, you used to see hundreds. Where you once walk the great beach for miles and not see a soul, now hippies lay pon it like dirt… turtles now afraid to walk there to lay them eggs! Me don't begrudge foreigners the beach. You tell I dey come from a cold, polluted, dying land. Your cliff land will one-day be worth a big money. Cliffs only run for three miles and nuff foreigners thirsty to enjoy them. I not like most Jamaicans, dem look at the hippie like some crazy white Rasta. Me know seh many of them study hard… work their brains at school. One day they'll become big mens… control countries and governments. They'll return, bring a bigger money to spend… bring all a we good fortune. Life will be easier for our children. But our land will be lost forever. Make we kill that turtle now man!"

Mannie jumped up, cocked his spear and prepared to leap into the sea. But by this time the turtle had swum far out, only a small dot on the horizon now.

"See, Tavo!" Mannie scolded, pointing out to sea in disgust. "You make us lose a good money… worrying yourself over problems you can't change!" He threw his spear to the ground, kicked it then paused a moment, the rest of his anger drained from his face. He looked at Tavo, nodding his head in thought then said; "Me nuh know, maybe it was in somebody's plan for that one turtle to survive, who knows?"

So they settled for a bucket of Whelks they pried off the cliffs and Tavo fantasized frying them in a garlic butter sauce served over rice instead of choking down another cornmeal Monkey Stew.

When they returned to the bungalow, that evening, they were startled to find three, overweight, slovenly freaks who greeted them with loud, boisterous drunken Southern hoops and hollers. "Hey, Man! We want to rent your house man." "We'll pay y'all twenty bucks a night," one said. "All we wants is a place to flop and plenty of sun, whisky, womens, drugs and relaxation! Haw! Haw! Haw!"

With no hesitation Mannie pumped their hands brimming over with hospitality, and said, "You've got a deal. Move right in make your selves at home! That's what Negril's for, enjoyment Mon! You got the right place, Tavo's place!"

Tavo pulled Mannie aside shook him. "Where the hell will we sleep?" he whispered.

Mannie looked like he could care less. "We sleep in de bush, we use to it!" he retorted. "Lean-to's still livable. All it needs is a few palm fronds. I'll take care of that! No problem Mon!"

To Tavo's amazement, he'd become a guest house operator in the span of a few seconds. He split the rent money with Mannie, pocketing $10 and giving him $10 to make up some of his back wages. Being homeless in Negril beat living in his cold, drafty Cass Corridor apartment in Detroit any day.

By the next morning, though, things were not quite cool runnings. The three paying houseguests were bitching. Really upset there was no water in the bungalow to flush the toilet or shower with.

Tavo hadn't overlooked these sanitary conveniences. He'd contracted the area's chief water commissioner, Lyle Letterman, to do the plumbing for the house. Actually, he'd bribed Lyle to connect his property to the government's main water line. Water was one convenience he did have… that is, occasionally, when it ran. His bribe was a bottle of white rum and the promise to give him the contract to run the pipes inside his house. Being a man of some honor, Lyle followed through with the first part and made the road connection so they had water flowing sporadically through a main pipe to bathe with and drink, but the indoor plumbing had never been connected. Lyle failed to show up for that part.

"You shouldn't give Lyle the plumbing job," Mannie reprimanded. "Him a rum head!" But they finally placated the cash-paying boarders, promising to have the situation under control in short order, and set off in the old Moke for the Wharf Club, the one place Lyle could always be found. It was mid-morning and Lyle was there all right. He was portly, slovenly, and light complected with a bulbous, misshapen bright red nose and squinty eyes. The Jamaican version of W.C. Fields, and he was loaded to the gills on rum, swaying on wobbly legs and holding onto the bar top with both hands as if he was trying to stop the rock-solid counter from moving.

Under abnormal circumstances—that is, when he was sober—Lyle was difficult to work with because he spoke patois like he had a mouth full of marbles. Tavo could never understand him and needed an interpreter. Stinking drunk, he was impossible and even the locals gave up on any form of dialogue, merely nodding their heads to the sounds that came from him, sounding like a bubbling pot of green pea soup.

Lyle had gotten his position as water commissioner for Negril only because his sister had married the head commissioner in Savanna La Mar. As there was sporadic water in Negril, he was given the job, figuring he couldn't fuck things up too badly.

Mannie was not about to allow Tavo to blow their chance to make some money. He instructed Tavo to let him persuade Lyle to connect the plumbing… he had a better chance of penetrating Lyle's alcoholic fog. But it was soon apparent to them that Lyle was not only drunk as a skunk, but obstinate as hell in his refusal to budge from his comfortable spot at the bar. He freed one hand from its clutch on the bar, almost falling on his ass, waved it around in the air, snapped his finger and ordered up more rum with a loud gurgling belch.

Mannie winked knowingly at Tavo. “Grab his feet when I grab his hands. We carry him out o’ here,” he whispered. “It’s the only way!” They latched hold of Lyle at the same time and proceeded to maneuver him out the door. Blinded by the light of day that he’d hoped not to see again until tomorrow, Lyle squealed burbling protests like a stuck pig. He fought and twisted like a three hundred-pound boa constrictor.

A small crowd of fishermen gathered to offer cheers and jokes as the two struggled to lift an enraged and flailing Lyle into the back of the Moke where Mannie tied his hands and feet together like a hog to keep him from injuring them or himself.

When they finally reached Tavo’s house, Mannie looked worried. He could understand enough of Lyle’s curses—which now sounded like the eruption of mud flats around Old Smokey—to realize that he was flatly refusing to do any work today.

“Let’s carry him into the bathroom, lock him in there,” Tavo said in a burst of inspiration. “Maybe he’ll have a change of heart. We got nothin’ to lose! Come on!”

They carried the wiggling, belching, farting Lyle past the three hippies seated on the porch… passing a king-sized joint back and forth as they stared wide-eyed at this spectacle. “FAR OUT, MAN!” they chorused.

Mannie threw Lyle’s plumbing tools in the bathroom after him, then shouted through the locked door, “You wi get out when de works done!”

Lyle cursed, wailed, moaned and pled in a cacophony that sounded like an explosion from a volcano. His rumblings went on for over an hour, but gradually began to diminish in strength. Even volcanoes run out of steam eventually. Finally, Lyle garbled in softer tones that he’d perform the task at hand if Tavo would only give him a cue of rum. He wondered aloud how civilized men could expect him to work under such coercion and unsympathetic conditions?

Tavo and Mannie were more than happy to honor his compromise. The rum was procured and he actually finished the job in fifteen minutes. He emerged from the bathroom all smiles, after a second jolt of rum for the job, and slapped Mannie and Tavo good-naturedly on the back, exclaiming what fine boys they were. Begging them a few more shillings in order to keep his appointments at the Wharf Club.

The three freaks were pleased to have their water, even chipped in a few bucks for Lyle's efforts, laughing hysterically. This morning's theater had been better than a Laurel and Hardy movie.

Wasn't it great when things came together? Tavo thought—one love!

14

"We don't need no more troubles
No more trouble
What we need is love"

Bob Marley
From the song *No More Troubles*

Wow! He was a businessman in his new home. If only his father was alive to see it. He actualized both their dreams. Sure, it was a small start, but the three Fabulous Freak brothers from Atlanta—or, as they pronounced it, "Hot Lanta"—stayed for a week and he was able to pay Mannie all his back wages, buy food staples, even sock a few bucks away under his mattress.

After the hippies left, he sat contentedly by his cliffside, witnessing yet another spectacular sunset reflecting with pride on how far he'd come. Just a few months ago, actually almost a year ago, he realized, he was a fugitive from the war, drifting and running. All that had changed. He owned his own land, ran a promising commercial endeavor. He wondered what Irene's parents, her family would think of him now. The dreamer had made his dreams come true. And yes, he could run a business. Maybe not in the traditional sense, but then Negril wasn't a traditional place, at least from a First World, conservative American point of view. He was finally filled with hope, filled with confidence, a sense of purpose now.

The foundation for his new life had been laid. He no longer felt scared, lonely or regretful about his past. Well, maybe a bit lonely. He still missed Irene, still thought of her constantly. But he wouldn't rob the Jamaican cradle, he promised himself he wouldn't get that desperate but there were few females who ventured to Negril for any length of time, living conditions were mostly Peace Corps primitive. The go-go girls and Playboy bunnies at Nick's typically came in for the day from Montego Bay or Ocho Rios and the few groupies in the area attached themselves to rock stars or drug smugglers.

Thinking about the smugglers, he felt that something was brewing among them. Dice and Len Stern were always huddled together at Nick's, deep in mysterious conversation, keeping their distance from the partying crowd. Then it really turned sour one day when Dice came slinking over to his property, decked out in his usual leathers, wearing motorcycle boots now, with that gold chain dangling a gold marijuana leaf decorating his naked chest. Without waiting for an invitation, he slumped into Tavos porch hammock and fixed his one blue, bloodshot eye on him in an ice-cold stare. He needed Tavo's land for his business, he stated flatly through a cloud of pot smoke. His rap went like this:

"Ya see man, we can't store our bales of pot in Nick's caves no more! Nick's our legitimate front now. Big crowds, makes too much money to close down for a week. Get the drift? We gotta keep rocking and rolling, see." He wasn't telling Tavo all this because he wanted to, but because he had to, had to let him know what was gonna happen, what his role was gonna be. "So, ya better keep your fucking trap shut," he snarled through clenched teeth. "We need your caves. Gotta go on with business. See? Anyways, you got no choice Fucker. Understand that from the start."

Tavo's caves were big enough to hold up to a ton of grass at a time and conceal it from view from air or sea. Dice considered himself no different from the other pirates of long ago. "We takes what we wants from whoever we wants," he boasted. "Them old time pirates hid their gold in them caves.

Same with our green gold." He pointed his half-smoked spliff at Tavo's chest, coughing and snickering; "Just be prepared for a truckload of dirt to show up on your ocean property. Only it ain't going to be all dirt, dickhead! Dirt's just going to cover the herb. Some niggers will scrape the dirt off, stash the sensimilla in your cave, see. At night they'll put it on canoes, transport it to our boat offshore. You ain't gotta do nothing 'cept keep quiet. See? 'Cause dip shit, there's two ways you can leave this Island. On a nice cool, safe, air-conditioned jet plane or in a plastic body bag just like in 'Nam. Got it?!"

Dice waved away Tavo's attempts to reply with the 'click-clack-click' of his ratchet knife. He hacked up a lung full of greenish pot residue and projected it squarely between Tavo's feet. "Look, I ain't askin' you. I'm tellin' ya!" he snapped, "You'll even get a couple yards of free topsoil outta the deal to plant your fucking bananas in."

He got out of the hammock, strode over, and shoved Tavo on the shoulder, knocking him back against the window shutters. Then swaggered like a Mafia wise guy back to Nick's where he spent the rest of the day drinking Red Stripe and bragging to the syndicate about what a chump and pushover Tavo had been. "Piece a cake, no challenge man! Just a fuckin coward!"

Tavo sat there utterly dejected, with Remus, who at least had got off a snarl and a nip at Dice's hard motorcycle boot before making a retreat under a banana sucker. Had he come this far, he agonized, experienced this much, to be shoved around by some sleazy punk? His life had always been plagued by institutions and jerks pushin' him around—that is, until he reached these shores. Now it seemed it would start all over again. And there was the real possibility that he'd be implicated in the operations of an international drug smuggling ring in exchange for a handful of dirt. If he said or did nothing, his land would become their base of operation. It was like giving his okay. He'd stepped deep in shit again. Anyway he didn't want any part of pot distribution, sale or marketing, let alone be implicated a felon.

It looked like he would be stymied again by pricks trying to bend him to their way. This avoidance-avoidance game was getting old. Was his new home really any safer than Vietnam? Had a new colonialist subculture conquered Negril? At least there was no Agent Orange or napalm here, yet.

As he worried over this latest turn of events, Mannie returned from the hills where he'd been searching for wild orchids to decorate a rubber tree shading Tavo's house. He scrutinized Tavo, who was lost in thought, his brow wrinkled, looked like he was in mental pain; "Why you wearing a screw face on such a fine morning?" Mannie said, " Look like duppie walk on your sleep last night!"

Tavo swallowed hard and said. "No, worse man, Jamie Dice is gonna use my caves to store his herb!"

Mannie's eyes lit up. What? Another financial opportunity. "So, mon." he said, That's not so dread. How much bread he's giving you for that privilege?"

"No, listen man. I don't want any of his money. Besides, all he's giving is a couple yards of top soil!"

Now Mannie screwed up his face. "That's not right, dem rogues have money like dirt. He must give you some!"

Tavo shook his head "Listen, that's not the point. I don't want to be involved, don't want to get busted. I'd go to jail, be deported… lose my land, everything."

"Not to fret yourself, man," Mannie interjected. "Everyone involved in dis here drug business! Jamie and Len be well connected. Them pays off the police, the army, the politician man, have big-time lawyer for protection too. Len have judges in the USA in him back pocket! You can't get busted. You fret too much man."

Tavo picked up a rock in frustration pitched it at a land crab that was nibbling on one of his banana suckers, missing him wide. "Look, maybe it's safe or maybe it isn't. Maybe there are

D.E.A. agents in Jamaica. Maybe they infiltrate dope rings, and make busts! You don't know!"

"I never hears of them DEA," Mannie said as he grabbed a stick and smacked the crab's shell wide open with a loud crack. "Why they want to stick them nose in Jamaica's business?" He give the crab another sound whack as its legs jerked a spasmodically last jerk. "Is America that want the ganja. DEA must be a real sneaky bitch. One thing me know, it's not proper for another man to tell you what to do with your own lands; lands that you pay for… work hard on. Jamie be pushing you around, riding your back. Not right man!" He kicked the dead crab into the bush like a soccer ball.

"Listen Mannie. America wants to stop you from growing herb. Don't you see?"

"No mon, that be foolish, mon. If them never want it, Jamaica wouldn't grow it for them. Sometimes it be difficult to understand you people!"

"I know, I know," said Tavo. "It's topsy-turvy. That's not the issue. Don't you see? If I don't go along with Dice, he'll break my legs if I'm lucky… toss me to the sharks if I'm not!"

Mannie spread his legs and grabbed his crotch with one hand, cupped his balls, "Ah, now me sees, you have your same old worries again and again! You scared. That no way to live your life, mon. You tell me every day how you love this land. Only way to prove it is stand up for it. You truly love it… must be willing to die for it." Mannie began to pace furiously, taking long strides, looking for another land crab to crack, hitting his open palm with the stick, and thinking. He finally said, "Tavo, me could go over to Nick's, box that Dice's ears. Him maybe tough, but him not tougher than me. I don't think that make you feel no better though. Me think you tougher than them bossie bossie bunch of smugglers. Tougher than you think. You give them guys too much power mon. Them can't have power over you… you don't give it to em! I won't always be by yuh side, but I know one thing, I going prosper just like

Negril. Obeah woman tell me so. She say, one day I'll be a big man with a resort and a farm. Check your visions. Know your destiny. Each man must do that!"

Tavo looked at him sharply, he wasn't convinced didn't know if he understood what Mannie was even getting at. "Come on" he said, "a vision is just a vision. I'm just one person alone against all that power… all that wealth. What chance I got? I am fucked!"

Mannie stood tall and cupped his balls with his one hand again "I've said all me going say. Now is up to you. I'm leaving for a week, go back to the hills… look 'bout me sister cows. But me leave you with one ting. Me hear story bout a man long ago who box a big giant down with a likkle rock stone. Him only use a likkle sling-shot. Dat man check for him vision." Tavo looked at him like he was nuts. "Come on man" he said exasperated "That's just some old Bible story"

Mannie said no more, broke the crab stick across his knee tossed the pieces into the bush and purposely went about hanging the colorful orchids on the rubber tree humming some calypso tune, it sounded like Day O. Tavo stood there and watched him forlornly and thought of another old parable, the one about the ant and the rubber tree. "Give me a break" he mumbled under his breath. No one really believed that crap about an ant moving a rubber tree plant.

15

"I am a rebel
Soul rebel
Lord have mercy
I am a capturer
Soul adventurer"

Bob Marley
From the song *Soul Rebel*

Before Mannie left for the hills he'd given Tavo a sort of reprieve telling him that the smugglers would probably not use his land for a long time. What they usually did was scout the countryside for months, testing, buying up small plots of the high-grade sensimilla. Then it had to mature be harvested, cured like tobacco, baled, then put into large tight drums and stored in limestone caves in the cockpit country. Dice and Len wouldn't even move it off the island then. They'd wait for a time when grass was in short supply in the United States when the price was driven to its highest. Only then would they smuggle the weed out by boat. This process could take up to six months. Depending on their greed or the market, it might even take a year.

It at least gave him room to maneuver, gave him some time to come up with some David and Goliath intervention. But he doubted he could ever move that rubber tree.

In the meantime, he did make it a point not to hide from Dice… show him the fear he felt inside. He could attempt to do that much. Fear was a state of mind; he tried to convince himself. If he didn't succumb to it, maybe it would go away. Ya, sure get real, Dice was a monster! A killer!

So he continued to show up almost every other evening at Nick's to drink a Red Stripe or two and watch the nightly carnival. He wasn't going to hide from Dice. His cottage was continually rented out now, and he was able to afford beers at Nicks while still saving money and paying Mannie his weekly wage.

Dice and the boys never acknowledged him beyond a surly grunt if he happened to pass by them at the bar. Once though, as he was digging the nightly scene at the bar, Dice approached him flicking his ratchet knife 'click-clack-click-clack'.

"Nick wants you in his private bungalow," he snarled. "Ya better not keep him waiting!" 'click-clack-click-clack' "Ya know what's good for ya!"

Remember he prodded himself, show no fear. Ya sure, easy ta say. But he looked him square in that one eye, and said "Ya, I heard ya" and slowly walked away hoping that knife wouldn't end up in his back… slice his ears off.

When he reached Nick's cottage, Nick was swaying in his hammock as usual, completely naked, smoking a zucchini-sized spliff and casually observing the goings on at his packed, rocking hedonistic bar. Ginger Baker's drums pounded out the rhythm for 'Cross Roads' through his speakers in the background. People were packed in now, three deep at the bar, shouting at bartenders to slam the colada blenders into fifth gear. Shapely babes strutted around naked as the day they were born—maybe wearing a gold chain around their waist or an Indian feather in their hair. Spliffs were rolled, lit up and passed around like it was Amsterdam. Mandrex was shared and swallowed like M&Ms.

Woodstock wasn't the final fling, the last goodbye. Nick kept it alive for those who couldn't turn out the light and say good night. Betty Lou was stretched out naked beside Nick on a chaise lounge, soaking up the last rays of the sun, sipping on her usual mug of Tequila taking in the bar scene with him. Her bronzed skin made a stunning contrast with the shimmering emerald ocean and blue sky, and tiny beads of sweat sparkled on her peach fuzz that ran from her navel to her downy crotch.

Nick's dreams had come to fruition, he thought. When Nick saw him he grinned a wider-than-ever Cheshire Cat grin, "God, you're a sorry looking ass" he said. "Have you finally come to your senses? You know, sell your land to me? But wait, I've changed my offer. I'll only give you ten grand for it now." He tried to protest but Nick cut him off "Oh, don't think for a minute that I don't know what goes on in this town. I know that pack of felonious animals want to smuggle their dope from your caves. What a shame. Ha! Ha! Ha! What a turn of fate," he smirked, and winked at Betty Lou, while rubbing pungent coconut oil on her bronzed naked ass. She giggled seductively.

"Better sign your land over to me quick before you become one of the bones Dice tosses to the DEA to keep 'em off his back," he said, faking mock concern.

Tavo looked out to sea visibly upset, trying not to show it. Shit! He knew the whole story. But he didn't respond, didn't know what to say. Nick took his silence for consent "You see, Tavo, they'd never toss me away, I'm much too valuable to those drug dealing pigs. They need me as their front. Their egos are so over enlarged they couldn't go a day without being seen in my world-famous cafe! Put simply, I'm useful to them and they know it. I've got the chutzpa to play in the big time. You, on the other hand, are nothing but a pimple on the fickle ass of fate, just waiting to be squeezed!" He was on a roll, certain now he had Tavo by the short hairs.

"Face facts," he went on, "what have you done in Jamaica in a year's time anyway? Put up a lousy thatched hut fit for red necks? Big deal! Then wallow in low class cultural muck with jungle bunnies playing an idiotic game of Robinson Crusoe!" He thumped his chest with his fist. "Look at me! I've accomplished something with my life. I've developed a world class business. Do you realize the Sheraton Hotel chain wants to franchise my ideas… pay me huge consulting fees? Hollywood producers are lining up at my door for the rights to my story." Tavo tried to interject; he was coming out of his daze, wanted to put a stop to Nicks pontificating wanted to get a word in edge wise. Nick just flicked his wrist at him cut him off breezily "Oh, I know I haven't written my manuscript yet, but I'll soon take a sabbatical to Morocco, you know, for inspiration… compile my memoirs while smoking kief under a Banyan tree." Nick became distracted for a few seconds as he absently massaged one of Betty Lou's large, luscious breasts with more coconut oil then yawned with exaggerated boredom. Tavo gaped at them, but mostly at her, mesmerized by the sweet smell of the oil and the sensual jiggling of her breasts. She made a low purring sigh. Jesus! It had been along time since he touched one of those. He was jolted out of his brief reverie by Nick's voice, louder now, bragging "Do you know, I can't walk the streets of Manhattan or Paris without being recognized? It's all becoming so mundane. I need a new drug. Wish someone would invent one so I could get high once more. Tell you what," he shouted, remembering his original train of thought. "I'm in a generous mood. Betty Lou just gave me a deep smacking, slurpy slow blowjob… I feel just fabulous."

"Oh, Nick," she said, feigning embarrassment. "Ah don't know what you all is talking about. Ah just don't get it!" she drawled fluttering of her long eyelashes.

"Ah, shut the fuck up cunt," Nick snapped, and turned back to Tavo aggravated now that he hadn't snapped up his offer. "Okay, okay, I'll pay you fifteen thousand big ones. Go buy a recreational vehicle, drink beer to your hearts content in a trailer park. You're out of your league here. You're not made for high-class living. Come on, you know that. You're a meat and potatoes kinda guy. Get real. You can't wheel and deal in the fast lane. Do yourself and everyone a favor, accept my offer. Let the big boys run the show! Go throw a Frisbee in the park. Marry a fat air headed greenie, tree hugger slut; have a dozen screaming crumb-crushers. No, wait! Find yourself a lice-infested commune for losers, I could care less! Ha! Ha! Ha!" Betty Lou smirked, then stuck her pink tongue out at Tavo.

But he stood his ground, pointed a finger at Nick's zinc covered nose, spoke deliberately, forcefully "Forget it man! How many times I gotta tell you? I ain't selling! That's final, finished. Comprende, amigo?"

Nick shook with fury, hurled his glowing spliff at him, barely missing his head, sparks singed his hair. His sudden movement jolted Betty Lou off her lounge chair and she landed with a thump on the board decking. She shrieked a piercing squeal of agony as three large splinters lodged in her plush posterior. Nick ignored her; his anger focused directly on Tavo. "You scum!" he screamed. "You prick! Fuck you, you little worm! You'll come crawling to me! I won't even spit on you! Go back and live like a savage in the jungle! You'll get busted with all that grass in your cave… thrown in the slammer. You'll beg me for bail money then ass hole, and I won't even spit on you!

Tavo took the hint. Time to retreat to his peaceful refuge; forget Nick's onslaught of garbage. He walked casually away; oblivious to the curses Nick hurled at his back. But on the way out under Nick's stone archway stood Dice, blocking his way, sticking his foot out like he was going to trip him.

"Where ya going, dick head?" he said. "Time ta plant your bananas?"

"Gonna mellow out okay," said Tavo, trying to step around his motorcycle boot, trying to look him in his one eye. Scared as hell! Sure he was, but he was trying his best not to show it. Was he pulling it off?

"Ya you do that" said Dice, "but don't forget ta keep your trap shut, got a feeling the DEA might be snooping around, see… you blow our cover man, you're dead. 'Click-clack-click' went his ratchet knife.

Jamaican nights usually helped to wash away the troubles of Tavos day. But tonight he was really shaken, after his run in with Dice. Man this guy wasn't fooling around. Now the DEA was getting interested, sounded like they were in Jamaica. That's all he needed. He'd probably get the gas chamber, nothing they'd like better than to burn a 'scum sucking pinko hippie draft dodging drug smuggler'. Maybe he should sell his land to Nick, look for another boat and flee to some other island. He lay in a hammock and watched a brown spotted night gecko pluck a moth from the kerosene lantern. He pictured himself like that helpless bug. Tonight no calmness overtook him. He fretted, sweated, tossed and turned but finally drifted off to a restless sleep. By morning, he still had no concrete plan. His fitful sleep had produced no solutions but there had to be a solution for Dice, a way to save his land.

Later that day, Mannie returned from visiting his sister in a state of elation. Christmas season was approaching and the traditional Quadrille dance was this very evening. The ceremony that Clyde had spoken of when he'd taken the sacrificial goatskin from the house party. Mannie insisted that Tavo attend. It would help him forget his troubles. He'd be the first white man invited to the festival, but Mannie had also invited another white guy so Tavo wouldn't feel out of place, not feel no way.

The other white man was none other than John Curtis. His crazy buddy with the duck. Mannie had met him at the Wharf Club where he'd been inquiring about Tavo's whereabouts. The perfect occasion to spring this surprise, and help him get his mind off of Dice. John had rented a tree house on the beach from Mannie's cousin, Brother Pum. A five-foot by five-foot thatched structure, very similar to Heavy Higher's tree house. John had rented it to "Cool out, to do his art work." He'd also rented a Honda 90 motorcycle and Mannie insisted he pick Tavo up, knowing the old Moke would never make it up the washed-out roads to Orange Hill, deep in the mountainous interior where the dance would be held.

Tavo was elated, excited not only of seeing a familiar face from home but also about the dance. More than a welcome distraction from his dilemma with Dice. Man was he sick of worrying about that guy.

John arrived right before the setting sun, his long hair in a single braid hanging past his waist. Down the length of his braid, he had substituted multicolored flowers for the Viet Cong flag he had worn at the induction center. They gave the appearance of a Hawaiian lei attached to the back of his head. Other than that, all he wore was a pair of white painter's bib overalls so splotched with paints of different hues that hardly any of the original white showed. He couldn't even be bothered with shoes or socks; a lone tattoo that read "John" adorned his scrawny bicep.

When he saw Tavo he jumped off his bike letting it fall to the ground, ran over and hugged him. They embraced slapped high fives, shook each other in a freak fraternity dance of friendship and camaraderie then fell to the ground mock wrestling, laughing and tickling each other. After they caught their breath John pulled a spliff from his braid, and fired it up. Tavo immediately started peppering him with questions. "How'd you know I was in Negril? What happened with you at the Draft board? Thought you'd be in Nam man."

John took a drag on his spliff; inhaled deeply and let the smoke out slowly, he sighed pleasurably. "Word's out man. Best dope in the world's comin' outta Negril… Heard through one of my connections that you were here… had to look you up."

Tavo looked surprised, he had no idea anyone knew where he was. "No kidding?" He said. "Thought I was forgotten about… but what about Vietnam? What happened with you?" John coughed and laughed at the same time, passed the spliff to him. "Man, I was labeled crazy as a loon…me and my duck. Walked inta that shrink Rosenthal's office and the duck hopped right up on his desk. Shit a green glob right on a stack a his papers."

Tavo choked on a stream of ganja smoke, and they broke up in a fit of uncontrolled giggles. John fought back his giggles and continued his story. "Wait, wait…That was just the beginning" He said. "That asshole Rosenthal broke out in a sweat, coughing and wheezing and turned beet red. Couldn't catch his breath… almost sucked an inhaler down his throat trying to clear his air passage. He musta been allergic to birds or somethin. What a trip! So he stamps my papers UNFIT TO SERVE, mumbles a bunch of psycho mumbo-jumbo and pushed me and the duck out the door."

They were really stoned on the spliff now, slapped high fives and rolled on the ground, tears streaming down their faces, overcome now with hysterical laughter. It took them a few minutes to regain control then John looked at him seriously. "Say man, that reminds me… I almost forgot I got something for ya!"

He reached into his pocket, fumbled around for a few seconds and pulled out a dirty crumpled cocktail napkin.

"What's that?" Tavo asked

"Man, right before I came down I saw Rosenthal again and Irene at Alvin's Finer Bar… Paul Butterfield was playin, really blowing the harp man"

"What about Irene?" Tavo shouted… "she gave you that?"

"Let me explain man. They just stopped in the bar for a second, Rosenthal hated the blues, wanted to leave right away."

"So what the hell happened, what's that napkin?" He said he was shaking with anticipation. "Well I went over to em, wanted to ask Rosenthal, he seen any migrating mallards lately. Ha! Ha!

"So go on man, what did Irene say… she ask bout me, mention me?"

"Nah, nothing like that, but I told her I was gonna visit ya…. Rosenthal wanted to know where you were but I wouldn't tell him… what a prick, figured he might turn the law on you!"

"So what's the paper ya got then?" Tavo asked anxiously.

"Well Irene got up went to the john, walked by my table on the way out and dropped it next ta my beer. Think she said give it to Tavo, or something bout you, couldn't hear good… Butterfield was really wailing, playing 'Hoochie Coochie Man' ya know… anyways here it is."

Tavo snatched it up… almost took John's hand off, unfolded it, look at it, turned it around in his hands.

"There's something written on it man but it's so smeared, blurred, I can't read a thing. What the hell you do wash with it?"

"I told ya man she dropped it by my beer, shit, tables all wet, covered with beer, ya know. Sorry man. Can't understand what she sees in that jerk Rosenthal anyways." Tavo was pissed, what a bummer, what could she have tried to communicate? Probably nothing, John was most likely shit faced, got everything mixed up. Anyway Mannie was waiting for them at the Quadrille. This wasn't the time to get in a funk. So he changed the subject suggested they not waste time, only about an hour of daylight left, best to reach Orange Hill soon. After dark it'd be impossible to find. They split, with Tavo riding on the back of John's rattling motorbike acting as guide into the same area where he'd roamed with Clyde during the months they hunted for cedar trees to build his house. But first he stuffed the napkin into his shorts. Didn't want to lose that, maybe he could still decipher it later, hold it up to a light or something.

If Negril was wild in terms of lack of development and amenities, the area they headed off for was downright desolate. As the Honda jerked and bucked up the red-clay, bauxite-rich dirt road, the jungle on each side of them became thicker and thicker. Innumerable swamps spread out under steep outcroppings of pocketed limestone cliffs. In some spots the oozing water, muck and morass swallowed up the road, forced them to dismount and carry the bike on their shoulders, wading through this mess. When they could ride the bike, vines and branches reached out to grab them, scratching their faces and bodies.

This was Mannie's home ground, it was easy to see why he believed in Duppies and Rollin' Calves. As the approaching nighttime lengthened their shadows, Tavo could almost see those devils lurking in the bush. Every mile or so, rising up out of nowhere, there appeared an old clapboard shack that sold the typical staples. The shacks were lit by flickering kerosene torches and cast an eerie glow through the pitch-black night, let them know they had not been completely swallowed up by an uninhabited land. Cows, goats, donkeys and pigs ambled into their path, just as startled, as they were to see another living creature. When the road climbed at a fifty-degree incline, it took on the shape and texture of a washed-out streambed, and, again, they were forced to dismount and push the bike over the boulder-strewn surface, as they slapped hungry mosquitoes that buzzed, dive-bombed and stung them.

Orange Hill was about five miles from Negril's West End and it was pitch black when they arrived. They knew they had found the right place. Music echoed off cockpit cliffs, like the soundtrack from a *National Geographic* special, set within the deepest part of sub-Sahara Africa, drowning out the serenade of crickets and tree frogs.

As they drew closer, they saw that the music originated from a large enclosure of eight-foot tall bamboo fencing. Made it impossible to observe the musicians inside. Next door to this enclosure was a shack looked like it served as a bar for the Quadrille festivities. About twenty villagers of all ages and sexes mingled around it, drinking beer and stout. It was here they wandered first, the ride had worked up a powerful thirst. They leaft the bike leaning up against a nearby cottonwood tree.

They never noticed, in fact, no one at the dance noticed the stranger. He was a white guy like them, only he head not been invited, he was tall, thin, in his twenties, with long hair just like them hippies. He stood silently behind the shack, hiding in the dense bush invisible to the partiers… and he watched Tavo's and John's every move. Never took his eyes off them.

Oblivious, like everyone else to this guy, they walked up to the shack where an old rickety table was lit up by kerosene bottle torch. Mannie was sitting around the table with two youths about eighteen years old and a middle-aged Rastafarian. They walked over, noticed that the men were engaged in a kind of card game. Mannie shook their hands, invited them to sit in and play a few hands. John took up the offer immediately. Tavo headed for the shack bar, and bought the table a round of beers. Then he pulled up an old tree stump, sat back, and sipped on his beer. All he wanted to do was groove on the drums that continued to beat an insane rhythm, gaze up at the dark sky with its winking constellations, just level with the vibes.

All the village of Orange Hill had turned out to take part in this fun. Small children stood around, peeping through the bamboo slits of the enclosure, village elders congregated around a blazing fire drinking rum and beer, some smoked large cornhusk spliffs. The oldest men and women smoked large hand-rolled tobacco cigars. Curried goat and fried fish were served out of large kerosene cans from the back of the bar. These sights, sounds, and smells came together to recreate in Tavos mind a vision of a long forgotten wild and mysterious Congo basin. The chorus of drums of divergent resonance boomed out a frantic rhythm, high-pitched flutes screeched like banshees. Fireflies called ‘Peenie Wallies’, twinkled and glowed like stars from the bush. Logwood smoke intermingled with the smell of night jasmine blossoms, to produce exotic, almost sexual aromas.

Then Tavo happened to focus back on the card game. He became confused. Thought they were playing Stud Poker. But this was unlike any stud poker he knew. The first thing that struck him was that the group of gamblers used marbles and bottle caps for poker chips. He noticed that some of the cards were turned up at random, exposing the player’s hole card. Then John got a hole card dealt face up and demanded why his bluff card was shown to everyone. Peals of laughter rang out from the other players. Mannie grinned, and said “John, cool man! Card deck is the only one we have in the village. From wear and tear, some cards ‘mark’ man, we all know de face value a dem. Since we don’t want cheat you dealer just turn em face-up so you see them.”

John took it in stride laughed good-naturedly and said. “My man, better not apply for a job as a dealer in Vegas! The Pit Boss would have you wearing cement shoes you expose the ‘marked cards’ to the marks!”

Mannie scratched his head, didn’t understand what ‘cement shoes’, ‘pit Boss’ meant, even where Vegas’ was, and changed the subject. “Hey Tavo, John,” he said pointing at the bamboo enclosure “ dat de real Quadrille dance behind dat fence over there. Cost fifty cents to enter for dat you get to dance the celebration and one shot of white rum! Try it mon!”

John’s eyes rolled when he heard the magic “rum” word, he was on his feet immediately, yelling over the drumming, “Let’s go in, man! The whole hometown is shouting!”

After paying their fifty cents to a smiling grandma, puffing on a huge cigar, stationed at the old rusted zinc door, they entered and took in a sight that blew them away! The closest description for what they saw was an African version of a western square dance, but that description fell far short.

In one corner of the bamboo corral, an eight-man band played. The musicians were spry, elderly "youngsters" who ranged in age from early eighties to late nineties. They were seated on tree stumps, naked from the waist up! The music they wailed out was primitive and deafening, it vibrated Tavo and John's souls with ancient messages.

Five of the musical "youngsters" kept the beat with syncopated frenzy, pounding on goatskin-covered drums of varying sizes, as sweat flew off their naked arms and chests. The other three blew on bamboo flutes. They produced an ancient African beat, a rhythmic screeching tune that captivated and hypnotized them.

In the center of the enclosure were six "younger" women, aged sixty to eighty, dressed in white frocks and dancing with male partners. They gyrated, shook, and twirled with lightning undulations that made the two dizzy just watching it. The women lifted their heavy, muscled male partners off their feet and swung them around through the air without missing a beat, bump, or grind, weaving in and out in a beautifully choreographed circle.

After fifteen minutes, the men either dropped or were thrown one by one on the earthen floor, dripping with sweat, completely exhausted. The drums and flutes stopped abruptly, signaling the end of that dance, and the men were helped to their feet by onlookers and administered a shot of white rum to bring them back to life. To John and Tavo's amazement, the women were as fresh and crisp, in their starched whites, as ever. The women laughed until tears ran down their radiant faces, and the crowd joined them, except for the male dancers.

They were still slumped on the ground and being ministered to with shots of rum.

Then Clyde Long—Gloom and Doom, entered the dance, he put his arms around Tavo and John and ushered them aside. He led them to a dark corner in the back. Poking them both soundly in the chest, using both his hands at once, he told them that Quadrille was an ancient ritual woman's dance from Africa. On this special night the omen were possessed by supernatural powers that transformed them into physically superior beings. Prior to the dance, all the omen of the village assemble for secret meetings no mens could attend. They conjured up powerful spiritual forces.

Clyde slyly urged them to join the next set of dancing. It would be rude not to take part, could cause offense, he warned them. Gave them his old supernatural rap. Despite his reputation as a good dancer, Tavo was hesitant, but John was anxious to plunge right in. He pulled Tavo aside, literally shaking with excitement. He shouted over the drumming that was beginning to rev up again "Far out man. Sure as hell's better than them tourist traps in Montego Bay, where they dress Jamaicans up like clowns in a circus. You know, make 'em spit fire, twist themselves up like faggots into pretzels, for over-the-knee-socked tourists! Man, this is real Jamaica! Let's get it on! Let's boogie!"

John shoved Tavo into the circle of women, knocking him off balance and a well-built gal with radiant honey-brown skin instantly grabbed him. She looked to be in her sixties, but her face was as fresh as a young girl's. She threw her arms around his neck and ground her pelvis into his in a suggestive circular pump and grind motion. The drums picked up their sensual thumping rhythm and the flutes blew a piercing wail.

Tavo was swept off his feet and twirled through the air like a rag doll, the dance hall spun around him. The kerosene lanterns transformed into balls of twirling disco lights. He struggled with all his might to brace his feet on the floor for balance, tried a few dance steps, but his effort was futile. He couldn't even get a toehold, his exertion only tired him. He was forced to yield, and was passed, thrown, and tossed from woman to woman, like a sack of grain. Each one humping her pelvis into his. At first it was arousing, but he was far too dizzy and exhausted to stay turned on. It felt like a ride on the Wild Mouse at the carnival, and all he wished for was the ordeal to end so he could come back to solid earth, regain his balance and throw up. After one final futile effort to keep his balance, and hold onto dear earth, he felt himself tossed like a Frisbee across the room, where he came to a spinning stop soaked in sweat. Mannie rushed over to him, grabbed him under his armpits and hauled him to his feet. He poured a blast of nerve jangling white rum down his throat, and Tavo coughed and hacked as the 180 Proof hit his gullet and set it on fire. Then he heard the ladies chant. They were cackling, and laughing, "Hippie mon, hippie mon, dem no stand up to Jamaican omon. Ah! Oh! Ha! Ha! Ha! Hee! Hee!"

John had fared no better. Clyde was sloshing him with the rum too and he was getting his chest poked to hamburger to boot. They tried to stagger out, weaving, bumping into the laughing women, attempting to hold one another up. When they finally found their way out, into the star-studded night, John shouted to the heavens, "Man that was better than Woodstock! Far out! Tavo, you got it made. Them Africans put a Doors concert to shame!"

The rest of the evening was nonstop merriment and dancing. John became shit-faced drunk, stoned. He partook of every goodie offered him in huge quantities; spliffs, rum, cigars and more rum. Tavo watched him stumbling walking into a tree, then falling on his ass as he attempted to climb on the back of a donkey backwards. He figured it was about time they begin their trek back down the hill to Negril. Man was John wasted! But John put up a fight, no way man did he want this party to end. Slurring his words now he pleaded with Tavo "Wait, man, wait, wait," he said. "I wanna top off this happening... a light show! Ya, man, that's theys need a... a... a... grand finale! How bout thaaaat man!" Tavo had no idea what the hell he was rambling about, but mumbled "ya, sure!" anything to pacifying him, get him out of here.

John dug deep into his overalls, fumbled and fished around for awhile, then brought out three plastic cylinder tubes about six inches long, they looked to be a half inch in diameter. After some stoned scrutiny, he wasn't exactly sober either, it dawned on Tavo that these were tubes kids carried by back in America on Halloween. When they were bent, the chemicals inside flowed together to produce an eerie green glow. They looked like large 'Peenie Wallies', helped motorists see the kids better. Before he could say anything like this might not be to cool, John staggered over to the shack bar and bent one of the tubes, releasing its eerie glow into the black night. Frightened, awed, "ooohs" and "aaahs" rose up from the startled crowd of merry makers.

Encouraged by the response, which he mistook in his inebriation to be expressions of approval, John took a pocketknife from his leather hip holster and slit the tube open at one end. He waved the tube unsteadily like a spastic tennis player giving a serve and splashed the green glowing fluid from inside the tube onto the board wall of the bar shack. It glowed wherever he splashed it, like the shack was full of holes. It pulsated, looked like some cosmic being had come alive from inside. "LOVE" he shouted. The crowd's cries escalated, they became roars of utter terror, but John was oblivious, too shit faced. He slit another tube open and painted his face with the ghost-like glow. His face looked like a floating skull bobbing in the night breeze. Panic reigned supreme. The villagers ran like gazelles for the bush, they screamed, shouted, cursed "Obeah mon, Obeah mon, Comin' like de Rollin Calf. Run, Run, Run fe yuh life! Holy Jesus! De devil deh pon we! Run! Run!"

Tavo stood stone still like he was in shock, it all happened so fast. He had no time to react and his mouth gaped open at this bizarre spectacle. Finally he came to and grabbed John, shook him, yelled, "You really fucked up man! You scared the shit out of these people! We gotta split, man!" He pulled John over to the Honda and struggled to kick it over, but his foot kept slipping off the starter peg. It finally caught and sputtered to life, after repeated attempts.

They beat a hasty retreat back down the hills through the night. John's head glowing through the night like a headless horseman, causing panic and terror at every shack and hamlet they passed. John kept mumbling, "Sorry man, sorry man. Didn't know, didn't know. Who'da thought they'd get so uptight!"

The next morning, Mannie showed up at Tavo's, where they were still recovering, and hung over bad. He was bubbling, excited, waving his arms, hopping up and down, thrilled to be bearing the news. The Orange Hill people believed John to be a powerful Obeah man, who'd conjured up a Rollin' Calf. But Tavo was pissed. He showed Mannie one of John's tubes, and explained how it worked. He told Mannie to go back to the hills, tell the villagers what really happened. Mannie rubbed his chin, thinking, nodded sagely "That's alright" he said. "Might not be so bad to be known as a friend of a powerful Obeah man. Dem men get great respect, men of science. Me nah mek them know the secret of the powers."

Tavo looked surprised, "You mean the hill people don't hate us?" he said. "I was sure John had screwed up my chance for friendship with them."

Mannie chuckled "No mon, dem no hate you. Dem only believe seh you in council with a great Obeah man from foreign."

John grinned from ear to ear, slapped Tavo on the back. “See, man, everything’s cool. Just got elected King Obeah Hippie Mon! Heavy man!”

Tavo didn’t have to put with Johns bragging for long, although he wouldn’t have minded. John had to split for Detroit that very day. His stay was up, and Tavo would really miss him. Damn! He was a reminder of home and a friend. But before he left, he gave Tavo two glow tubes, and said “Take these man, you never know when some obeah might come in handy. He stuck his fingers into his mouth, pulled his cheeks wide apart, distorting his face like a monster and said. “Obee Doobee Dooo!”

16

"The whole hometown is shouting"

By anonymous
Afro-American blues artist

In the weeks following John's departure, more and more members of the sub culture began to show up at Tavo's front door, looking for a place to rent. Back in America, word of mouth, the underground grapevine, was the only medium other than the underground press and Rock and Roll that carried credibility. And as word of "Tavo's Negril Pad" or "Tavo's Negril Digs" spread, his business grew. This was no joke anymore, he was really developing a resort. Making it happen!

Mannie asked him why he didn't give his place a name. "You sketching out plans for a second house" he said. "You makin this into a real resort business. You haffi have a name man. Wha bout "Tavo's Resort" like how Nick him name his place after himself?"

Tavo was peeling a banana. Getting ready to eat it. He tapped his foot, took a bite of the banana, thinking he's right, you gotta have a name, just never thought about it before. "I'll name it Banana Shout or maybe Mellow Yellow Shout!" he said, looking at the half-eaten banana "No Banana Shout. Yah that's good, it'll stick in peoples' minds more original."

Mannie frowned, widening his nostrils trying to understand it's meaning, "You name it "Banana" 'cause you plant banana suckers. Den you name it "Shout" cause we Jamaicans say "shout someone" when you calls they names? Den many will calls on you. Right, Tavo?"

"Close," he said smiling, "but no cigar. I was thinking of a story John told me, a true story about something that happened to him in Detroit. The "Shout" part is in his honor."

Mannie smiled. "Me think me understand now. John's a powerful obeah man; him can bring you luck. But me don't understand the "Shout" how that honoring him?

Silence hung in the air. Tavo scraped his toe in the dirt pondering his explanation. "It's a long story, you wanna hear it?"

"Sure mon, we got nothing but time!"

"Okay, here goes. In John's hometown Detroit, he's known as an artist not an obeah man. He told me that a big bank hired him to make a fifty-foot tall bronze sculpture for their front entrance. Paid him big money to do it too! I think he said they paid him something like a hundred thousand bucks. But John's not a money manager. So he hired some Detroit autoworkers, who'd lost their jobs—you know laid off—'cause these guys had helped put Detroit on the map as the auto manufacturing capital of the world. John said they didn't deserve to be unemployed, see their families go hungry. Anyways, the project took him almost two years to complete. He ended up not makin' a cent 'cause all the money went to pay the workers, even though he designed the sculpture, supervised its building. But he didn't give a shit, you know. See Detroit's made up of mostly Black Americans, John also wanted to pay his respects to their heritage. You know, honor their contribution to the development of the city. So he named the sculpture *Home Town Shout* from an old Black American blues song. "Me likes this story already," Mannie said, "forward star!"

"Anyways, he explained the significance of the name to the mayor and the bank president, two straight white guys. Man, they got pissed off. The Mayor screamed at John… they hadn't given him a fortune to build a work of art so he could give it some ridiculous jigaboo name. The Mayor renamed it *A Visualization of Form in the Abstract*. Man, John was really hurt, cause the Mayor trampled on his artistic, his social sensibilities. So on the day of the lavish unveiling ceremony put on by the bank for the City fathers, the local establishment press and the national media, John chugged a fifth of whiskey, got so stinking drunk he could hardly talk." Tavo began giggling in spasms and had to stop talking as tears ran down his cheeks. Mannie took hold of Tavos shoulders shook him impatiently, "Go on wid de story mon! Me want fe know de ending…wha happen? Tell me mon!"

He had to wipe the tears from his eyes regain his composure then went on "So the mayor introduced John to the Press, all the big shots, passed him a drawstring to pull the covering off the sculpture. With all eyes on him, John blew lunch all over the Mayor, in full view of all of America tuned to the six o'clock news on TV." Tavo shook with sidesplitting laughter. "See Mannie, I think it's a great way to honor him."

Mannie sat in thought, then smiled at Tavo. "You hippies got a strange way of looking at things. Not sure I'll ever understand your ways. But me do understand dat it not right to hurt a man's pride. Me thinks John him might really be one obia mon fe true! Banana Shout be a fine name! Yeh mon, that Irie!"

17

"Oh, let the power fall on I
For I
Let the power fall on I"

Derrick Laurel
From the song
Let the Power Fall on I
Michael Manley's
Political theme song

By the beginning of Tavo's second year in Negril, he noticed major changes were transforming his peaceful fishing village's face; really corrupting its soul. Sometimes these changes distracted him from worrying about his upcoming date with Jaime Dice, but he was still reminded, of his soon to be felonious fate, every time he saw him at Nick's. Witch was just about every time he went over there. Like the other night. He had been peacefully sipping a Red Stripe at the bar watching the sun set, listening to Santana soulfully wail 'Vive La Vida' from Nicks speakers, watching an amazingly beautiful playboy bunny—down for her day off from Hugh Hefners Playboy Club in Ocho Rios. She was sensually swaying to the beat, undulating on the stone wall to Carlo's reverberating guitar, taking all of her clothes off. Actually just stepping out of her bikini bottoms, that's all she had on, when Dice walked up to him, stood between him and the beautiful chick, blocking his view of the spectacular sunset, blocking his view of that gorgeous naked the bunny.

"Listen dip shit" he said. "I think you're a weak link."

"What do you mean?" said Tavo. Dice reached over, pinched the bunny on her shapely butt, she screamed, gave them a dirty look and quickly danced away from them.

"You heard what I said fucker!"

"Ya, so?" Tavo said, trying to brave it out. Stand up, show him no fear.

Dice pulled out his ratchet knife twirled it by its ring around his finger like an old cowboy six shooter.

"I just got it from Stern, one a his paid off politicians says the DEA and CIA are thick as shit here now, see!"

"I don't know nothin about them," said Tavo his legs shaking now. He put his hands on his knees tried to keep them still.

Dice scowled at him, put a finger to his cracked lips, then slashed his hand across his throat in a knife cutting motion. "Just don't be a weak link" he said, "keep your fucking trap shut!" He spit over the stone wall, slithered away, flipping his ratchet knife open and closed, open and closed. "Click, clack, click, click, clack, click"

Christ on a crutch thought Tavo, *that dudes a full-blown psychopath!* But Dices mention of Stern brought to his mind, his questionable 'mentor'. Mannie said he'd just sold his land to a multi-millionaire Italian playboy jet setter for over a hundred times the purchase price he'd forked over only a few years before. But Len didn't leave the island. He purchased that concealed bay near Green Island, the closest town to Negril, and set up business from a less high profile base. But he didn't forget about Tavo's caves as Dice had so rudely reminded him. He didn't want to use his land for smuggling, why run the risk? Then there was the Italian, who bought Sterns land. Flew in his own personal construction crew from Italy to build a major hotel, complete with restaurant and bar. Man were the locals pissed, didn't benefit from jobs on the construction site. Those Italian workers couldn't speak

English. Jamaicans found their fast-talking hand waving jabbering annoying. Fist fights and screaming matches broke out all over town, especially in the bars, or anywhere else these cultures collided. Man Negril was really going through some changes he thought.

The Jamaican government even began to take notice of his sanctuary and its growing popularity with his counter-culture. In order to accommodate the fast-paced influx, a local Member of Parliament obtained government funds to pave and widen the road from Willies Wharf Club roundabout to Nick's Cafe. Most of the property along this stretch was soon bought in a gold rush of speculation, Ya Mon! Height Asbury ain't dead just moved!

Two fast-talking wheeler/dealer freaks from New York City purchased five acres of cliff property set on a natural cove with huge caves, a mile down the road from him, and built a thatched roofed African condominium village they dubbed AweeMaway. But these guys were the used-car salesmen of the subculture and they launched a pyramid marketing scam to soak the trusting peace and love generation. They needed large sums of cash to buy their valuable cliff land now, so they tantalized an architect with promises of villa ownership, got him to draw up plans of their projected development. The design featured five groupings of ten lavish, thatched A-frame bungalows, separated by winding, lushly landscaped pathways decorated by huge African Tiki-style mahogany woodcarvings. Each grouping would have its own pool, a large centralized bar and restaurant would cater to these guys and their guests all-inclusive style.

With the plans drawn up, they set out on a high pressure selling spree, rapping to visitors, and tourists, persuading them to cough up twenty thousand bucks in exchange for a lifetime ownership in their own tropical isle paradise fantasy. But what wasn't mentioned was the small fact that the money from the first thirty units would have to go towards the purchase of the cliff land. So what if they even did sell all fifty units, they'd never raise enough money to build all of em. Most investors would never see ownership of their dream bungalows. But it was "brotherly love... everything's groovy," the deals were consummated by a mere handshake. These con artists secured the land and built three huts, which satisfied the first few investors. No Problem Mon! Problems didn't arise until later on, when more than three groups of suckers arrived simultaneously. But these dudes knew their game and managed to keep the con alive by pleading business problems with builders—"What can we do. Jamaicans are slow workers. Soon come!"

Tavo saw that they weren't the only crooks to land on his dream shores. Down near the roundabout, just two hundred yards from Willie's was an abandoned, dilapidated cut stone structure with a leaky, caved-in, cedar shingle roof. A man reportedly owned it from Kingston, but he hadn't been seen there for as long as anyone could remember, nor could anyone recall what the building's original purpose had been. But it was fairly large—sixty by seventy feet, and had been taken over by a hippie from Oregon, nick named Jerry the Pirate. The Pirate swept the place out. He hung a skull and crossbones flag over a make-shift bar built out of old bamboo, set out a few kerosene lanterns for light and spun s rock and roll tunes from a battery operated record player full blast. He named it The Pirate's Den. After dark, the bar took on a funky, crypt-like atmosphere. You could picture Calico Jack or the Bluebeards of old in this den of iniquity, downing a few rum punches, and bragging about their exploits on the bounding main. From behind the bar, the Pirate would size up likely-looking prey—trust fund babies and the like—then lay the bait: fifty-fifty partnership in his thriving enterprise for a mere ten thousand dollar investment. Together, he'd urge, they'd "turn the place around take it to a higher level than either Nick's Cafe or the Yacht Club. Hell, we'll put 'em both outta business". He'd say,

That was the hook! He was able to sell the Den's fifty-percent non-existent ownership continuously.

After successfully bilking an unsuspecting dupe, the Pirate would celebrate by swallowing a handful Mandrex, and drink a bottle of rum while chain smoking spliffs. When good and smashed he'd dress up just like a pirate of yore, complete with boots, eye patch, pirate's hat and bandanna, and two machetes to serve as cutlasses. He'd ramble up and down the West End road in his get-up, ranting, raving and wielding his cutlasses, pretending he was wallowing in the gore, like it was his final binge before heading out to sea again. He'd never forget to stop at Nick's, where he'd attempt to buy out the bar, before he either ran out o money or was thrown out for menacing behavior, too threatening even for the no-holds barred crowd. He'd then stumble back in the direction of his Den. Jamaicans who lived on the road found his spectacle entertaining, great sport! They'd follow en masse in his path and bring the pickneys out to cheer him on and play pirate with him. Eventually, he'd pass out on the roadside, where some kinder spectator would pick him up and carry him home to sleep it off, until he felt well enough to go fishing again for his next victim.

Tavo watched the scams of these hustlers with sadness and foreboding. Negril's swift-paced course of development scared him. It was a free for all. What was worse, he felt, was he had played a part in it. Maybe not a major part but he missed the unspoiled paradise that he'd first washed up on, and he agonized over these scoundrels. That's why they took his mind off of Dice. They gave him something less threatening to worry about. He couldn't help but think that their behavior was not the way to prosperity. They were bound screw over Negril, give it a bad name. But maybe all those dots on the map that became boom towns overnight had their share of rip-off artists too, he tried to rationalize. Certainly the Old West was full of scammers, so was Alaska, same with the banks of the

Mississippi River in Mark Twain's day. From what he'd seen in Negril, most of his generation he'd thought were different, thought were enlightened, were exactly the same as the establishment they claimed to loath. The only difference was the mask. He was glad he'd got here early and thrown in with the locals. "Dem na where two face under one hat!"

He noticed that wealthy Jamaicans started to arrive too. Jerome Bennett, a futuristic thinker from Kingston, had African style bungalows prefabricated in Kingston and carted to Negril on semi trucks. They were erected in uniform rows on a large cliff, overlooking the sea. He called his claim on paradise Rock Village Resort. While local workmen didn't exactly applaud the idea of prefabricated huts, at least builders like Clyde got jobs nailing the sides together and thatching the roofs. Bennett was more welcome than the Italians. His resort sprang up overnight and was immediately swarmed with yuppies paying inflated rents. With his village's instant success, Jerome was soon breaking ground for a large hotel on the beach called Coconuts.

But Tavo saw that some of these wheeler-dealers out foxed themselves. A Black American cocaine dealer, who'd fled the US one step ahead of the DEA, bought an acre of land on the West End Road and built a huge geodesic dome sixty feet in diameter and three stories high, which he covered with fiberglass and named "Pachyderm Something." But electrical lines hadn't been run to the West End yet, so his dream dome wasn't air conditioned, and the tropical sun baked the interior to over a hundred and fifty degrees Fahrenheit during the day and it never cooled off at night. The coke man abandoned his piece of paradise, split for parts unknown, one step ahead of the law, never to be heard from again.

As his peaceful lazy fishing village disappeared bit by bit, the biggest force for change crashed ashore in a tidal wave… cocaine. Maybe it landed with the coke man. No one really knew for sure. Perhaps it was because of the vast amounts of expendable money made on the ganja trade. Or maybe the subculture was changing just as quickly as his Jamaican outpost.

Anyway he sixties were over. Vietnam was drawing to a close. The ideals that once held his generation together to fight for change disappeared, creating a vacuum. Some drifted back to the establishment; others adopted more radical approaches to dropping out with drugs, or heavy identity groups like cults.

In any case, he watched in dismay as more potent drugs became the norm in Negril, and Sam Smart, known loyally as Crazy Sam, took on the role of distributor. Sam was an emaciated six-foot tall dude who blew in from Louisiana. He wore long kinky knotted hair, was covered with dirt and grime and always wired to the gills. He served as his own mule, smuggling coke strapped to his body from Columbia to Kingston. He had bullet wound scars on his legs that he'd proudly display to anyone coked up enough to follow his hyperactive rap. He'd been shot numerous times while awaiting delivery of his product in a hotel room in Bogota, trapped in the midst of a revolutionary gun battle.

Sam would transport his nose candy to the new Hotels and Resorts up and down the Beach and the West End Road in a custom-made 1969 Ford Escort that looked like one of the old rusted spaceships Han Solo rode through the universe in "Star Wars." He'd welded all the doors shut so that the only way to get in it was by climbing in or out of the windows. He'd also removed all the seats in the car except for the driver's bucket seat, and had bolted two three-foot tall stereo speakers to the floor in the back. From these he belted out demonic heavy metal rock, making his bizarre vehicle shake and tremble as it roared up and down Negril's only thoroughfare delivering his marching powder to depraved jetsetters, and freaks who cold afford it. He got rich quick but didn't know what to do with it. To fucked up, cause he consumed mason jars of rum and coke and snorted grams of his product, during his daily runs. Thought he was Hans Solo crusin the galaxy.

He'd never been busted though and was stopped only once by the local police. He didn't bear the name Smart for nothin'. He'd strewn the interior of his space ship with every conceivable type of trash and dirt, from old grease cans and their contents to broken bottles, rusty tin cans, even human excrement. When that lone Jamaican police stopped him and ordered a search, Sam leaped out the window, chattering a mile a minute and invited the immaculately pressed and starched cop to knock himself out. "Take your time, Officer!" he said, and stepped back, dancing from foot to foot, jumping up and down in an excited adrenaline rush to watch. Before the cop had made a dent in his search of the cars interior, he looked and smelled like a sewer worker after a day's toil. He climbed outta that car window like he'd seen a Rollin' Calf, nauseous, sick to his stomach. Since Police were personally responsible for the care and upkeep of their uniforms, word quickly spread among the constabulary that busting this crazed hippie for some stupid white powder "Don't worth it!"

Negril was becoming a modern-day sanctuary for pirates, just like Port Royal Jamaica in its heyday when it was considered "the wickedest city in the world." He feared guilt by association, since these guys all looked just like him. Come on! Jamaicans probably figured they were all the same. If they got a bad name, he'd get one too!

Mannie told him that ever since Jamaica's Independence a strong desire to cast away the old signs of slavery's shackles arose, and created a solidarity to forge the people's own direction for the future. "We forget dem days of slavery mon!" He proudly proclaimed. Now ministers in the socialist government refused to wear the traditional suit and tie and donned instead the more casual bush jacket, favored by African leaders. These changes were more than a facelift. Tavo now listened to the JBC news most nights, on his newly purchased battery-operated transistor radio and began to realize more fundamental changes were afoot. Jamaica earned most of its foreign exchange through bauxite, an ore that America coveted and converted into aluminum. Some earnings came from the newly expanding tourism industry and smaller amounts came from bananas and sugar. But his island homes greatest income was from rich bauxite mines in its interior, near Mandeville. The British had leased this bauxite land on a long-term basis for a song to American companies like Kaiser and Alcoa. Jamaica's new Prime Minister, Michael Manley, was pissed off that these companies were ripping off his country. So his first major policy change, upon taking office, was to declare that the vast revenues earned by US companies from the peoples mines would be taxed. He'd educate, feed and give health care to the downtrodden masses in Kingston's slums and shantytowns. "Ya Mon!" And the Jamaicans loved him for it. But Tavo guessed America wouldn't love him, at least the big boys wouldn't, and it would cost them a few profit sharing points. Americans might even have to recycle their beer and soda cans for a while. Jamaica was exerting its newfound independence on a global scale. Looked like they'd bump heads with powerful forces big time. What did it all mean for him? Would he be caught in the middle of another war? Another international political battle like Nam? Or a drug war? A pawn again? Was that his role in life? He couldn't seem to escape it. This war was going on all over the planet; there was no escape!

In any event, international politics diverted the Jamaican government's attention away from Negril's runaway development, 'round the clock skullduggery, and non-stop partying. But he felt it was only a matter of time until someone in power would take notice. He just hoped that when they did, he could salvage a little peace, love, and justice for himself. And he knew it was essential now more than ever to find a way to stop Dice from converting his land into a drug smuggling base. Sooner or latter the shit would hit the fan. Sometimes it felt like there was a solution trying to break through, break through into his consciousness. It was just to damn subliminal. It just lay there hidden under layers of his brain tissue. He wished he could peel those layers like an artichoke—get to the core—stop that thug once and for all. He had to hang on to his dream…. He was sick of running anyway; there was no where left to run to.

18

"All my love, all my kissin'
You don't know what you've been a-missin'

Buddy Holly

"You better stop doggin' me around
If you don't stop
I'm gonna put you down"

Alonzo Tucker

Jamie Dice could sure spin him out on a tangent. Get him to thinking about all kinds of turmoil, just to stop him from worrying about his most pressing concern. So he meditated even more now on sleepy little Jamaica. Like how she was finally waking up and demanding by what right could anyone push her around. It reminded him of his protests against Vietnam and his civil rights marches, although issues of racism were refreshingly absent here. He just hoped no soldier man would smack Jamaica up side the head the way he had been. Anyway even if Britain had taken the shirt off the Jamaican people's backs and given it to America, they allowed black people to take part in Jamaica's mainstream, ever since freedom from slavery. They'd always held major political office, even though they were often forbidden to go against the King's or Queen's wishes. Jamaicans were doctors; lawyers, accountants, and teachers never denied opportunity because of skin color.

Mannie and the other Jamaicans he knew had no feelings of inferiority. They fished, lived off the land, worked construction, met and conquered any challenge they encountered in their environment. Mannie had no concept of what it was to live in a country where he couldn't go to certain places or achieve his goals because of his color. Tavo was ashamed when he would have to explain how things were over in his country and hedge with comments like "Things are finally changing there." Deeply embarrassed.

Although he didn't use these exact words Mannie said people of color in America must live a life of bitterness, blame, and have lower expectations for themselves. He sensed that Black people in the US must be deeply wounded, psychologically damaged. Even if things changed for them right now, he'd say, it might take them years to get on their feet and hold their heads high. Freedom, he knew entailed more than removing chains; it also meant freedom from social, political, and mental oppression.

So even though his new homeland was experiencing growing pains, Tavo felt optimistic to be living in a country that treated men as equals. He grew even more determined to become part of Jamaica. Part of its successful development. He wanted to contribute to its independence, its future, in whatever way he could. So far, he'd only built a house, but at least he employed some people in the process and was earning foreign exchange. He was even stashing some bucks away saving to build again. In fact, he was about to summon Clyde and begin the tedious chest pounding construction process.

Mannie insisted his new bungalow should be 'a whole heap bigger' than his first. "Tavo, you gotta consider the future more, mon!" he said. "You needs a house with more bedrooms. When you takes a 'oman an have a bunch a pickney, must have four bedrooms, maybe more!"

The mention of pickney was a stab of pain in his heart, felt like a crack had opened. He almost cried out for Irene. But wistfully said, " I don't know if that'll happen. I can't get used to marrying a baby and everyone over sixteen already has a bunch of pickney."

"Me nah say no more mon, life always brings changes dat you can't see. Who knows? Maybe one day a 'omen will come from foreign and meets your strange age requirement."

In any event, he was turning away prospective renters daily. Negril was a major happening. So he went with Mannies suggestion. He designed a two-story, two bathrooms, four-bedroom house, with a large covered porch area and a separate kitchen area made out of bamboo. Of course, it would have a palm-thatched roof for coolness and all the bedrooms had to have wide cedar shuttered windows for ventilation. This house would be able to hold a bunch of partying hippies or a 'oman and a bunch of pickney. Irie Mon!

Clyde approved the design. He agreed with Mannie, it was time for Tavo to get down to pickney making. Tavo squirmed. He tried to divert Clyds interest in his love life, along with his finger poking. His chest couldn't take it anymore. This time they struck a quicker ceremonial contract. He was learning the Jamaican ways, adapting to the culture. Although Clyde did convinced him to agree to a bigger ram goat and more booze. "Ya Mon! Dis house be much larger dan de las." Construction proceeded at a good pace, Jamaican style, and after four months, it was half-completed, with its thatched roof in place and a leaky water hookup courtesy of Lyle. Once again, for the time being at least, Tavo and Mannie had drier, more comfortable shelter in paradise.

During final construction, when Clyde was putting on the finishing touches and Tavo was carrying cedar boards from the front of his property, to the house, he was startled by a shrill feminine cry: "Hey, Tavo!" That voice, sounded familiar. Where had he heard it before? He dropped the cedar boards he was carrying and ran to the front of his property. A shapely young gal was standing at the front of Nick's driveway. She looked familiar too, short, cute, with long, frizzed-out brownish hair. Then she started to run towards him waving her arms, shouting his name again. As she got closer, he spotted her T-shirt, a black silhouette of Che Gueverra on white and it him right between the eyes. Bullseye! Donna! His almost fling over two years ago, his almost night of balling, that cute fox from Sloppy Joe's Bar in Key West.

"Donna!" he shouted, emotion swelling along with another part of his anatomy. "What're you doing here?" he said lamely, as she charged over and threw her arms around him. She showered him with sisterly kisses. She was panting breathlessly, then said, "I'm on vacation! Never thought I'd find ya again. Anyways I asked around, found out you bolted out the door with that chauvinistic monster after he ripped off the bar. Someone said he was headed for Negril."

"Actually, I passed out and he bolted… shanghaied me."

"Far out," she said, smiling up at him sexily. "What a trip ta find you!"

"Ya" said Tavo, "I can't believe you came here looking for me."

"Well I had to split Key West anyway. Too small a place; everyone knew everyone else's business. 'Sides, it was filling up with narks and creeps. I crash in LA now… guess what? I'm gonna produce movies!" She threw her arms around him again and gave him another hug this one seemed a little too motherly for his liking. "I'm just a grip right now." she said and seemed to distance herself just a little. "But that's the first step! Isn't that the coolest?" She looked at him dreamily. He didn't know what to do; she was giving him a hard on. He stuck his hand in his pants pocket tried to force it between his legs. "You never told me what you're doing here?" she said, "Whats with all the lumber?"

"This is my home now… I'm building some cottages to rent out" he said turning side ways now trying to hide that boner, but beamed with pride. She gazed admiringly into his eyes

"That's the grooviest. A real Caribbean land developer." "Yeah. Well I guess you could call me that," he stammered, loving the attention but embarrassed by his pesky woody.

Donna lifted up a cedar board, slung it right over her shoulder "Here, let me help you carry some wood. I wanna see all you've done. Lead the way!"

He could think of only one wood he wanted her to haul but grabbed the board from her and said, "Wait a minute! You're on vacation, you don't wanna carry lumber." But she refused to be dissuaded. "No, no, I really want to do this." She said, "It's the only way to really get into something. You gotta experience it first-hand. That's what my guru says. Throw yourself in there completely… your whole being… only way to get the most out of it."

Armed with her cosmic wisdom, they schlepped lumber back and forth to Clyde and his industrious crew. But when the Jamaicans saw him and his young lady hard at work, sweating happily together, laughing, kidding around, having a good time, they went wild! They cracked HARD CORE, sexual jokes about her potential as a house-christening mate, and hooted and hollered. To his relief, their rank patois chat went over her head. She begged for a translation, and he mumbled their banter had something to do with the weather, local politics, stuff like that. But his fidgeting and hedging only added to the further amusement of the gang.

At the end of the day, he invited her to stay for the night in his nearly complete new home. When she accepted, he almost collapsed on the spot… tried to maintain his cool. This was great! But first, he suggested they take a cooling swim, wash off their grime, better not push to fast. Don't blow it now.

Tavo and Mannie had sledgehammered rough steps down the limestone cliff, to the ocean's edge. From this spot, a large cave opened up onto the ocean where you could sit, virtually unobserved from anywhere on the property, and look out from its cool shady interior onto the bright shimmering ice blue-green sea. Yeah, this was the very cave Dice wanted for his weed hideout. It was here that he led her holding her hand now.

As they reached the edge of the sea, she casually removed her T-shirt, cut-off shorts and sandals. She leapt completely naked into the calm clear sea yelling, "Last one in is Richard Nixon." This was just what he had hoped for. He hurriedly shed his grimy shorts and plunged in headfirst. They frolicked for over an hour like happy porpoises, splashing and ducking one another, floating lazily on their backs, submerging into the depths and playing with the frisky fish that swarmed around them. Strange naked mammals indeed!

Then Donna pulled herself up onto the rocks, climbed into the farthest recess of the cave and beckoned him to join her. She found a large, smooth, flat rock, twisted herself into a full lotus yoga sitting posture and focused her eyes steadily on the horizon. He clambered unsteadily after her, attempting with embarrassment to hide his enormous throbbing erection. She observed his condition with dreamy blue eyes; her well-formed breasts stood out and swung back and forth like dew-topped mountain peaks beaded glistening with drops of water. She looked him in the eyes, pouting playfully "Sit down in front of me, cross your legs just like mine. It's a perfect spot to meditate! Don't let animal nature ruin this precious moment. Let me lead you in a mantra that Guru, Swami Rama Dama Rama, taught me."

He tried everything in his power to will his purplish engorged prong to stop its one-eyed gaping at this luscious naked girl. He squatted, tried to follow her instructions. After a minute or two, he was able to twist his legs over each other in a painful approximation of her position, but his boner still stood straight up, pointing accusingly at his chin. He felt embarrassed and foolish as his cock executed a rhythmic bobbing dance in time to the pounding of the surf. Donna giggled, and softly teased him "My guru says we gotta strive to reach a higher plane of reality. He says earthly things like money; drugs and sex must be left behind so we ascend to more advanced levels. You know, base cravings like you're now experiencing come from lower chakras. To get rid of 'em, you gotta let your emotions wash over you, not hold onto negatives. You gotta visualize the higher chakras that resides between your eyes, you know, your third eye."

But the only third eye he was aware of was the one staring at her from between his legs. She persisted. "You gotta release your body's desires to reach Nirvana." she said "Like me. I've been celibate for over a year. Given up all drugs, alcohol, and red meat. Sri Rama Dama Rama knows! Says these desires encapsulate the soul, keeps us from transcending our mortal plane. If we don't, we're doomed to reincarnate over and over again to this earthly entrapment."

With her words "celibate for a year", Tavo's stare rose from her budding clitoris, to her shining blue eyes and his "third eye" gradually collapsed to a forty-five degree angle, aimed now at her lovely navel. She stared at his shriveling member, saying nothing until it had completed its southward trek and lay limply on his leg like a stale cocktail weenie. "See, it's working" she said. "I knew when I first met you that you were different, sensed you were deeper… more advanced spiritually than the typical male that only had getting laid on his mind!" She grabbed both of his hands in hers, beaming widely and instructed: "Now let's just hold hands. Concentrate on your third eye… I'll repeat my mantra. We'll join together on a heavenly plane of bliss that'll far surpasses any sexual encounter." She closed her eyes and began chanting some strange words that sounded like sliding vowels, he tried to repeat them with her, but felt as deflated as a punctured blimp.

His embarrassment was retreating along with his hard-on. What a bummer! His first real opportunity for sex had been swept away by some demented East Indian thousands of miles away. This wasn't the stuff romance was made of! He should be wooing and wining the fair damsel here in paradise. Just look at the natural beauty around them! Just look at her natural beauty! What could be more conducive to passionate lovemaking? Here they were two tanned young bodies, naked, free as the day they were born, like Adam and Eve in Eden. These thoughts crowded out any transcendental mantra, kept up a persistent thunder in his mind, although he still kept trying to mimic the gibberish she was mumbling.

One thing was working though. His cock had shriveled to the size of a wilted, day-old blintz; her asexual resolve deflated his horniness like a rusty nail in an inner tube. After a while, he couldn't take it any more. Looking at her now, like a wet hound dog, hoping for a long shot, he said "Donna don't you think Swami Rama Dama would understand our natural urges just this once? It'd be a good stepping stone you know, if we fulfilled those urges yeah… that's right… and then went on to higher planes. Wouldn't have to look back regretfully on what we missed?"

She broke from her trance, cast him a disgusted, parental look, like he'd just broken grandmas prized vase. "Oh man! You miss the whole point! Don't you see? We just had the most beautiful sex ever! You know, I felt myself having multiple mental orgasms with you while we chanted together. Wasn't it just as good for you?"

"Ah… yes, guess so" he lied, " Felt like… like I came! Like the Milky Way."

Donna hugged him "Oh Tavo, you say the nicest things. Let's get something to eat. Sex always makes me famished!" She planted a platonic kiss on his forehead, stepped into her shorts, and covered her lovely jiggling breasts with Che's stoic bearded face. He never imagined that he could experience jealousy for a dead revolutionary.

They ate at the Hungry Lion, a local vegetarian restaurant that had opened recently and spent the night together in one of the bedrooms of his new house. But he wasn't able to broach the subject of real flesh-slapping sex again, for fear of really pissing her off and ruining the only friendship he'd managed with a member of the opposite sex since setting foot in the tropics. In any event, Donna said she had to leave the next morning to catch a flight to Hollywood. She was starting a new job on a black and white horror film about zombies, or about something dead in the night. He sure didn't sleep soundly. The only thing dead in his night was his dick.

They woke the next morning to the sounds of Clyde and the workers shouting out salutes—singing at the top of their voices calypso songs about "the big bamboo and stiff stalks of sugar cane." She gave him a motherly peck on the cheek to bid him a parting goodbye. It would have made Swami what's-his-name proud. "Life's like a circular flowing ocean," she said as they stood outside his door. "One never knows when its currents may wash us together again." Easy for you to say, he thought and heard an echo in his mind—a line from a blues song— "Got my mojo working, just won't work on you!"

After her departure, Clyde stalked around the property, sulking and pouting, scolding him. Poking him in the chest, harder than ever. "You shoulda tell me bout de house christening mon! Dat way, me and de boys coulda gather outside de window an listen to de celebration! You spoil de t'ing, mon." Tavo bought him a couple of Dragon Stouts, to calm him down, he tried to explain: "Americans, even hippies, treasure certain private moments." He said. Clyde nodded his head knowingly; he agreed, even some Jamaican women were like that. Some of the ones he'd known must muffle their screaming orgasms he so professionally induced for fear of disturbing the neighbors.

When Tavo and Clyde had gone into the hill country to negotiate for thatch or cedar logs; Clyde would often disappear, leaving him alone with some ancient granny and a bunch of naked, bug-eyed pickneys staring at him. He'd return after an hour or two, a rare grin breaking his gloom and doom expression. He'd poke Tavo soundly in the chest, then boast and brag for the rest of the day about the sexual romps he'd just had with one of his many lovers. Although he lived with his common-law wife, an extremely obese three hundred and fifty pounder named Claudia, and they had ten children. Clyde loved to swell up his chest with pride over the thirty or so additional pickneys he had by dozens of women living in the back bush, all unknown to Claudia.

On this particular day after Donna's sexual teasing, Tavo was in no mood for Clyde's incessant chest poking, or sexual boasts. He had a bad case of the blue balls. Was sick of hearing about how Clyde outfoxed the Obeah men, what a great builder, cocksman, and all around talented fellow he was. When he got into his macho rap, he'd go on for hours, leaving Tavo's chest feeling like a piece of raw hamburger leaving his ego just as ground-up. He was about to grab Clyde's bony finger, give it a knuckle-cracking wrench. To hell with finishing the house. A guy could only take so much! But before he could follow through, the ground under their feet began rumbling and shaking like a 4.5 earthquake, on the Richter Scale. They looked at the same time towards the direction of the quaking to see Clyde's wife Claudia charging towards the work site like a wild elephant gone mad, her blubber bouncing and rolling with each giantess stride. In a matter of seconds, she was on top of them. They stood stock-still, staring at her, mouths open, Clyde's poking finger still frozen on Tavo's chest from his latest boast.

With one massive sweep of her humongous arm, Claudia snatched up Clyde's finger in her meaty paw and bent it backwards until it touched his wrist. Clyde shrieked in agony, sank to his knees, as she held on to his bent finger with one hand and twisted his nose with the forefinger of her other, screaming the rankest patois curses Tavo had ever heard. He didn't understand all of the words, but gleaned they related to his infidelities. Then she let go of his nose, grabbed a two-by-four lying nearby, turned Clyde over her knee like a naughty little boy and whaled on his ass in traditional woodshed style. He howled like a screech owl. But she wasn't finished. She shoved and kicked him down the road in front of the entire neighborhood, stopping every few yards to give his backside a well-placed crack with the two-by-four, keeping up her stream of "bumba claat" curses.

Tavo, Mannie and all the workers went into shock seeing Clyde's comedown, but soon came out of it and slapped high fives. They roared with laughter until tears fell down their cheeks. Poetic justice described in song and fables rarely occurred in real life, but when it did it, boy, was it ever sweet! He rubbed his sore chest for the last time. If only something like this could happen to Jamie Dice.

Fat chance! he thought.

19

"This morning I woke up in a curfew
Strange faces standing over me—"

—Bob Marley

Tavo was now approaching his third year in Paradise and his ten thousand dollars was gone, but he'd turned it into a two-acre, two-house, one lean-to resort business that showed no signs of slowing down. With money flowing in on a regular basis, there was no reason not to keep expanding. Well there was one reason, Dice—Shit! He could lose it all! Still what else could he do—nothing else to do with his money. He had no passport, couldn't travel anywhere, nothing to spend it on in Negril anyway, and building was a productive activity. It kept his mind active, kept him thinking he had a goal, kept him from agonizing over Dice. So he kept on trucking, hoping he'd come up with a plan for those smugglers in time.

He refused to overbuild or use concrete on his resort though; careful to preserve his property's primal beauty. This was the land of his dreams, his father's drams and even his father's, father's, father's, his destiny.

The gardens he continued to plant radiated with a rainbow of bold, tropical color. Banana trees grew everywhere, providing a constant supply of fruit, cooling shade, and the dense exotic look of a rain forest. He wanted each of his cottages to give the feeling of a private Garden of Eden, with each bungalow out of the view of the others. That's what Negril was really all about, he thought. People came here to get away from ugly, dirty concrete structures—impersonal cities. Besides, using the natural foliage and local building materials was far more cost effective. Clyde was more comfortable working with them, and construction proceeded with cool runnings. But his MrNatural concept did not win admirers from the international jet set or from a lot of locals, either. They were hell bent on turning Negril into a garish, Miami Beach-style concrete jungle. What slowed down this runaway development was the government's law against buildings over three stories. Although there were hundreds of other restrictions on the books, this was the only one they chose to enforce. He wasn't about to repeat what he hated about North America in Jamaica, even if most believed the way to civilization and a tourist boom was to mimic the self-destructive Promised Land. Now that he was more established, he began sending postcards to some old friends back home, letting em know he was okay, and inviting them down for a visit. Just brief, typical messages: "Having a wonderful time; wish you were here!" He wanted to send one to Irene but didn't have the balls, she probably wasn't interested—didn't care—maybe Harlen would intercept it, try and extradite him—better off not knowing. He should try and forget about her.

His second house was rented out most of the time now, and he was planning a third. Occasionally he and Mannie spent a night in one of the cottages, and Mannie would bring one of his numerous girlfriends over. But he never boasted of his sexual prowess like Clyde, didn't have to. Women literally chased after the Moke like groupies when Mannie was a passenger. But a meaningful relationship continued to elude him. Occasionally, there was a one-night stand with some spaced-out hippie chick, but these encounters gave only sporadic relief, not the soul mate he yearned for. Anyway, most female visitors stayed for only a week or two, and they were more interested in the Rastas who were drifting to Negril to take part in the free love philosophy. Heavy Higher warned him that these new arrivals were "just dreadlocks men! Fake Rastafarians who only grow locks to attract white pussy. They don't believe in the doctrine and spirituality of His Imperial Majesty—not a drop of righteous in their bones. The big bamboo was their only god!"

More rock stars were also coming to Negril. He heard on the JBC news that the lead guitarist of a prominent band who was recording a record at a Kingston studio overdosed on Mandrex and was carted off to a local hospital for detox. The doctors discovered he'd been popping fifteen Mandrex Quaaludes per day and inforced a strict program of withdrawal, knocking down his daily dosage by one each day. After two weeks they figured they'd have him detoxed, cleaned up, send him home. But, when they did a pre-release blood test, they found he was even more toxic than he'd been upon admission—found him lying in his bed grinning like an idiot loaded to the gills! They learned from an orderly he'd been getting out of bed, walking out of the hospital, and heading across the street where there was a pharmacy. There, the pharmacist said he purchased bottles full of Mandrex, no big deal you didn't need a prescription. He'd upped his dosage to twenty per day never wanted to leave Jamaica! The Manley government didn't think these runnings were too cool—made an island-wide check on where else this drug was being sold. To their astonishment, the sleepy little fishing village of Green Island was ordering cases on a weekly basis [this town had the closest pharmacy to Negril] and selling as many bottles as the hippies wanted. The result was a pile of knocked out visitors littering the roadsides, from the beach to the West End. Some stoned out zombies even wound up in the ocean, having driven rental cars or motorcycles off a hairpin curve on the West End Road—which earned the nickname "Mandrex corner". "Back to back belly to belly I don't give a damn cause it don't matter really. Almost every dawn brought the vision of psycho-hypnotized drivers and their passengers sitting in their vehicles or clinging to motorcycles in the shallow sea waters that bordered the curve. Miraculously, hardly anyone was ever injured; their bodies were as loose as putty from the 'ludes—they bounced like beach balls off any hard objects they encountered.

The government did give a damn; they didn't appreciate this zombie jamboree being acted out. They came down with a get-tough policy, making it illegal to obtain Mandrex without a prescription. As soon as word got out, there was a massive run on the local pharmacies in the bordering villages. Hippies stood in lines that extended for blocks, to get their one bottle per customer ration, until the stocks went dry. But the authorities had been alerted and decided to send a strong message to the displaced Height-Asbury community that was quickly transplanting on their peaceful western shores. After all, big international money was finally taking an interest in Negril. It wouldn't do to have straight-laced investment bankers and financiers driving through and seeing scruffy dropouts passed out along the roadsides or copulating openly on the beaches. Even Michael Manley's socialist government could take an up-against-the-wall tact when the "Yankee dollar" flashed in its powerful face.

The only one to hear of the massive raid the government planed for Negril, was Stern still well connected to government officials involved in his pot smuggling. These officials didn't want to kill their golden goose, so they warned Stern not to be in the wrong place at the wrong time. He knew when the raid by the Jamaican Army would take place. He made like Paul Revere, hopping on his Suzuki dirt bike riding up and down the West End, crying, "Raid by the Army! Hide your stashes! Raid by the Army! Clean up for the day!" He didn't want Nicks customers busted, he was part owner after all, he didn't want Negril to get a rep as a police state.

Tavo was glad for the warning but he didn't have much to worry about. He didn't fool with Mandrex and rarely smoked weed any more. It was so readily available and widely accepted here, it lost its rebel for him appeal. He only wished that Dice wouldn't get the warning, then get deported, but knew that was wishful thinking. Shit! He was Stern's right hand man. He suspected Mannie kept weed in his room to sell to guests, albeit without his blessings.

Mannie had approached him, just the week before asking if he could sell a bag to one of the guests. An argument ensued. "If me don't sell the ganja to the tourist, someone else will," he said, reasoning along the same old lines he took for the sea turtle debate. "Why not let me make a money, mon? Anyway, no local police nah lock me up fe such a petty ting." Marshalling his ultimate gem of logic, he said, "the fine for a spliff only a dollar US, Michael Manley himself, let all de ganja man dem out of jail after him election!" They had argued back and forth with no resolution, same as before, only this time nothing swam away and escaped over the horizon. Ganja was on land and going nowhere. It sure wasn't endangered, and thrived in ever-increasing large plots in the hills.

Tavo tried to make his point. He made it clear to Mannie he didn't want ganja sold at his resort. Told him to sell it somewhere else. No problem! That is, until a dude from Chicago, who was renting one of his houses, stumbled up to him in a state of agitated paranoia, stuttering a mile a minute. "Hey, ma-ma-ma-man, w-w-what da fuck you tryin' to do t-to me?" he stammered. "Set me u-u-u-up for ba-ba-bust?"

Tavo looked confused "What are you talking about, buddy?" he said. "No one here wants any trouble."

"Oh, yeah! W-w-w-well what about that Jamaican pa-pa-pa-pa-pal a yours? Asked him to sell me a bag of pa-pa-pa-pot… twenty bucks worth. Gave me a fuckin three-pound sack, ma-ma-ma-man! How in hell can I s-s-s-smoke three pounds in a week? M-m-m-man. Back home th-th-thats a major felony. I could get life imprisonment!"

"Christ on a pole!" Tavo yelled. Mannie had charged the guy the going price for ganja what smugglers paid the farmers.

Instead of giving the guy his expected ounce, he'd given him a three-pound weight. He couldn't conceive of paying as much money for only one-ounce.

Tavo dissected the cultural; the legal niceties of ganja selling in Jamaica for his guest, calmed him down a little. Then took most of the weed from him, leaving the guy with just enough smoke for the rest of his stay. But he confronted Mannie soon after, pissed at his blatant role as house pusher. A major rift exploded between them about the pot, the pushing, those same culturally divergent values, looked like they'd never be bridged. Somehow they managed to remain friends, their bond was too strong, but Tavo could see the writing on the wall—knew that Mannie's independence, his ambition would continue to lead him on his self-directed path. Anyway the day before the big raid, he warned Mannie to clean out any ganja in his room. The stuttering guest had left the day before and a hippie Dead Head couple, Ken and Debbie, from Colorado had moved in. He made sure to warn them about the raid, he knew they had to be holding.

The Raid came the next day, a much more extravagant show of force than he'd ever imagined. He'd envisioned couple of Army Jeeps carrying, at the most, maybe a half dozen troops. But the dawn brought huge armored tanks, equipped with long, menacing cannons chewing up the tiny West End Road, trailed by five Bedford truck paddy wagons and a force of over one hundred soldiers! He almost shit his pants! Serious business; these guys weren't playing, armed to the teeth. They brandished M-16s or sub-machine guns.

Before he could compose himself, try and act cool, so the guests wouldn't freak out, at least twenty soldiers were marching towards one of his cottages. The one where Mr and Mrs DeadHead were sleeping. They quickly surrounded it, and five of the meanest-looking ones kicked open the front door like a SWAT team on a crack raid. The startled couple fell out of bed, terrorized by the brutal faces that woke them out of their numbed slumber. The soldiers, five bayonets were pointing right at their throats. After a thorough search, they didn't even find a twig of herb. They'd smoked it all the night before. But the soldiers did find cold Red Stripes in Ken's ice chest and helped themselves, passing them to their buddies, popping the tops, drinking every last brew. Then they departed without so much as an apology, not even a "thank you." "Weren't as nasty as the National Guard at Kent State," Ken said to Debbie laconically, more than grateful not to be dead. "Shit! We could a been shot!"

Meanwhile, Tavo frantically hunted Mannie down—make sure he didn't have any traces of pot lying around, even seeds or stems. He found him weeding in the garden paying no attention to the raid, like it was an every day occurrence. Then his heart sank when Mannie told him no worries: he'd taken his twenty-pound stash out of his room and put it in the zinc tool shed they'd recently built. At least he had the decency to look a little shame-faced and whispered "Maybe they don't bother look in there!"

Tavo gritted his teeth gnashed his molars, summoned up his entire resolve -to stop him from taking a swing at Mannie. No matter how hard he tried to stay clean, he still got those buckets of shit dumped on him. Couldn't he be lucky this time; have someone waiting with a roll of toilet paper to wipe it off. There was. But not a person; it was Remus. His dog had mutated away from the prototypical skinny—mangy island mutt to a three-foot, ninety-pound canine menace. He sensed the soldiers meant trouble and responded to this threat to his happy life in typical doggy style. He bared his lips exposed an exquisitely dangerous-looking set of sharpened fangs, and released a low, rumbling, and wonderfully vicious growl. It seemed to originate from some deep instinctual, wild part of him. One soldier pointed his machinegun at Remus; "Get dat raas claat dog outa here before me blast him blood seed." He shouted.

Mannie snatched up Remus still growling, snapping, and kicking his legs now and threw him in the tool shed. He swiftly locked him in, along with the twenty pounds of green budding trouble. The sour faced armed forces made a thorough search of his house excluding, of course, the shed; didn't want any part a dat bad dog mon!

Needless to say they found nothing and left to make easier busts along with West End and the seven-mile-beach where hippie's proudly advertised "better living through chemistry" vacations. There Hippies were rousted and tossed into Bedfords, in scenes reminiscent of mass arrests at protest sit-ins at Army recruitment centers and on University campuses. Most of the detained were not jailed for any length of time; Jamaican's really had a soft spot in their hearts for hippies; but they were escorted onto any plane headed north, with less of a tan than they expected.

"Mon, you worry too much," Mannie had the nerve to say after it was all over. "I've protection mon! I tell you dat already. Big things in store for me. Remember seh me tell you dat! Anyways, one a de soldier dem was me cousin. Even if dem did find de weed, dem wouldn't trouble we."

But the Dead Heads, Ken and Debbie were still shaken up. Even so, they said it was their best vacation ever, shouldn't let the "Man" bring you down! They couldn't wait to return to Negril next year. Everything was still groovy in paradise!

But un-noticed by Tavo; Jamie Dice at that very same time, all during the raid, was driving a four-wheel drive jeep through the hilly countryside, over those same rough roads to Orange Hill where he and John had attended the Quadrille. Stopping ever so often at one of the huge ganja plantations rolling a spliff from one of the plants, smoking, testing the THC content, rubbing the buds between his fingers, checking for hash, negotiating, buying up only the choicest fields. 'Click-clack-click' 'click-clack-click'

20

"I wish I had some knowledge
Of this foreign policy
Beating—Beating—Beating around the bush"

Hugh Masekela
From the song *Beating Around the Bush*

The army raid was an eye opener; it forced him to take a closer look at the shores he'd washed up on. What the heck was happening on this Island he loved, called home... developed a resort on, made his last stand on? Mannie could explain politics, the runnings, to a degree; but typically, he chose not to become concerned with those matters or to examine them in depth. He figured that government was better left to the big guys in Kingston. All he needed to do was to keep on truckin' in his steady, forward-looking direction—he'd easily sidestep any stumbling block tossed in his way, he always had. But Tavo felt different—he was a foreigner, a hippie draft dodger, and a fugitive from injustice, with no visa—about to become a drug smuggler. He needed to know everything he could if he was going to survive here, not get busted, and sent back to America, where he'd get the double whammy.

Mannie claimed a visa was no big deal, he had yet another relative, this one in immigration, who'd push the paperwork through. No problem mon! Things were sure easy when you lived in a bureaucracy where everyone was related to everyone else! But still, he worried about the big picture. What the hell was all this socialism about?

He'd recently become kind of friendly with a dude from Kingston, Barrington Simmons, the one who owned the Hungry Lion Restaurant down the road where he had eaten with Donna during that ball aching night. Garth, the master gossip, informed him that although Barrington was a Jamaican, he was very different from the typical Negrilian or hill person that Tavo knew. According to him Barrington was raised in Kingston in "upper-class"! He picked up from Garth's respect mingled with contempt that there might be some prejudice on the island after all. One based not on color but status. "Him educated inna college a England. Him have every advantage weh de majority of poor people will nevah have," Garth said, his awe warring with resentment. "But Barrington rebel 'gainst dis privilege! "Him only Jamaican I know who turn foolish hippie just like dose from foreign!"

Barrington looked more like a British mod rocker, a cross between Bob Marley and Jimmy Hendrix to Tavo. Of Portuguese descent, he was thin, sharp featured, with very light skin. "Him brush" Garth had said. He wore his hair shoulder-length in curly dread locks. He dressed like Hendrix too even in the hot tropics, with high-heeled boots, ruffled shirts and flared satin bell-bottoms.

He'd arrived in Negril right after Tavo, fed up with the uptight, conservative Kingstonian lifestyle. A true crusader for his generation in Jamaica. Few members of the tight family groups of wealth rebelled against traditional ways. He was the first to tune in, turn on, and drop out. And he had brought to Negril with him his gorgeous wife, Gabriella, and their two small children. Barrington had purchased two acres of land close to his on the West End and built a couple of thatched roof cottages, along with his vegetarian or Ital restaurant, as the Rastas called it.

He felt a kinship with Barrington the first time they met. His attitude was upbeat; he had a quick wit, endearing laugh and a stubborn spirit that refused to be absorbed by a mundane, suburban, straight-laced, and class-conscious Kingstonian existence. He figured Barrington must have the inner scoop on changes taking place with the government, figured he could enlighten him. Help him get over and survive here. So he walked down the road to the Hungry Lion to pick his brain. See what he could learn about these current nefarious runnings.

When he reached the stone archway entrance of the restaurant, Barrington was busily packing his English Land Rover. He flashed a friendly grin in greeting and gave him the two finger peace salute, "Hail, Star!" He said. "Peace" said Tavo giving him the peace sign back. "What's up?" "Just getting ready to trip into Kingston, drop these wheels off for some repairs." "Far out" Tavo said, "Never been there, what's it like?" "Come along for the ride man—keep me company! After I drop the Rover off we'll pick up a loaner from my brother. Be back in Negril in a couple a days. Yah man! Spend the night at a really far-out place in the Blue Mountains."

Tavo smiled, walked over to the Rover, nodding his agreement. Timing couldn't have been better. He was coming down with Island Fever anyway; a great opportunity to get out of Negril, get to know Barrington better, get answers to his questions, and see Kingston at the same time. Maybe even find a way to get Dice off his back. Stop his operation. Barrington might have some ideas.

Barrington gave last minute instructions for the restaurant, said his good-byes to his family, and after swinging back to Banana Shout so he could pick-up a pair of cut-offs and a fresh T-shirt, they set off on what he anticipated to be, hoped to be a thrilling new adventure. A quest for truth—maybe even his salvation.

By the time they left, the sun was just setting in the west, but they were on Jamaican time, and not to worry, mon "Soon

Come." The approaching night soon swallowed them up as quickly as a gecko lizard swallows an anancy spider, and they bumped their way in the dark over jarring, pot-holed roads headed toward the great metropolis of Kingston.

Thirty minutes into their ride, they'd just crossed over Big Bridge and were approaching the dense, ripening sweet-smelling sugar cane fields of Savanna La Mar. Barrington pulled out two Black Beauty amphetamines from his breast pocket, popped one, handed the other to Tavo, and fired up a large spliff. "Take it man!" he prompted. Tavo looked at the pill uncertain. "I don't know man" he said, "How strong is it?" "Go wan, take it its just speed, it'll smooth out the potholes... focus our concentration. Yah man, lessen the road dangers!" Not wanting to be a bring down Tavo dry swallowed the speed and took a healthy pull of the weed. After a few more miles, the combination kicked in; his drooping eyelids sprung open and his brain began to race on overdrive. His inhibitions lifted, he started chattering like a magpie.

"Hey, Barrington, what's happening here, man? What's the government up to? How far is Kingston? What're people like there? How come you left it?" His questions exploded like roman candles. "Where are we now? Why're cows all over the road? When will we get there? How tall are the Blue Mountains? What's Michael Manley like? What does the patois words Kaya and Bongo Nyah mean? Yeah, yeah, what does Jamaica mean? What da ya think is our purpose in the cosmos anyway?"

Barrington took his eyes off the road for a moment, stared at him in disbelief—annoyed. "Whoa man, slow down." He said. "Stop goofing around! We're in serious times of change in Jamaica." "What do you mean?" said Tavo. "Your government is really fucking us over." he said and smacked the steering wheel with his fist. "Don't ya know what Nixon's up to?" pounding the dashboard with his fist now. "After Michael claimed all the bauxite mines for the people, that snake threatened to ruin our tourist business in retaliation!" He took a huge lungful of smoke from the spliff, and passed it to Tavo then continued to speak while holding the toke in his lungs, talking in a squeaky voice "This very minute, the island is crawling with CIA and DEA agents. They're thick as thieves with the opposition scum here who oppose Manley. They're all over the place—those motherfuckers!" Barrington exhaled a cloud of ganja smoke and its intense odor enveloped the entire cabin of the Rover. He waved the spliff threateningly at Tavo. "They arm poor Jamaican youths, give 'em a pile of money, order 'em to hold up and rob American tourist, so the news will reach the international media networks, scare tourists away!"

Tavo sat there not knowing what to say, but not liking this conversation not liking the implied blame. Barrington grew increasingly agitated, more passionate and spit out the window in contempt. "Montego Bay, Ocho Rios are like ghost towns," he said. "No middle-class tourists are coming here any more. Negril's the only place that's doing business. The crowd we cater to knows not to trust establishment bullshit, but most hippies don't have big money to spend." Barrington suddenly swerved the Rover to miss a meandering cow and hit a two-foot deep pothole, banging Tavo's head against the roof of the car really smacking his melon. But Barrington was oblivious to his discomfort, shouting now. "Jamaican people in those north coast towns depend on camera-slinging-Bermuda shorts wearing tourists to feed their families, to send their pickney to school. Fuck man! Nixon sent Bush here to issue threats of reprisal to Michael. Yah man! If we don't cave into his demands to rape us of our bauxite." "You're putting me on." said Tavo. "I kid you not! Then Michael called Bush a bloody asshole right to his face! Right on, motherfucker! But Michael's days might be numbered. You Americans don't fool around. You've even threatened to assassinate Bob Marley if he continues to sing. No bullshitting. Bob's a prophet man. His messages reach all over the world, a real threat to the power structure."

Barrington abruptly swerved to avoid an old man riding a rusty bicycle without lights. A tree branch struck Tavo across the face as the car careened into the bush. "Sorry man!" Barrington said. "But oppressed people all over the globe will unite behind his music, throw off that colonialists' domination bullshit, that's what has them scared!" Now he was glaring at Tavo shaking his finger at him. "My only problem with you, is this, your place is back in your country."

Tavo was taken aback by his last comment, but after his initial barrage of speed induced rambling questions, it was impossible to get a word in edgewise. So he sat there listening, rubbing his head, wiping blood from his face where the branch had scratched him, shacking his foot like Thumper Rabbit and grinding his molars flat. At least Barrington knew the score.

Pointing an accusing finger at him, he continued his tirade "Ya see man, you should a joined the weathermen, or the SLA. Your place is over there, fight force with force. Michael's not going to be pushed around. I know man. He'll fight fire with fire. We're not alone in the Caribbean. Come on! Castro's our brother! We've opened up full diplomatic relations with him. Ya man! We know how your people hate his guts, fear him." Insanely, Barrington pulled the Rover completely off the road, ramming into a ditch as a speeding 10-ton semi truck bared down on them from around a hidden bend, once again thumping Tavo's skull off the roof like a pumpkin. " Sorry sport, just a blind spot" he said and jerked the steering wheel forcing the Rover back on track. "But what the Hell has Castro ever done? Educate his people? Give'em all proper health care? Eradicate crime? Give back his peoples' dignity?" "You got a point." Said Tavo, still rubbing his head and becoming increasingly paranoid by the picture Barrington was painting. "When Tricky Dickey or Lonesome George find out we're on Castros course, watch out man!" He Pointed his finger at Tavo again, staring him down not watching the road again and shouted “That’s why I say you should have stayed over there, fight for the liberation of your own fucking country keep those bastards away from us!”

“Listen man” he said rubbing his head looking hurt, feeling a mixture now of paranoia and agitation. “Look what happened to anyone who was ever successful at fighting them—like King, Malcolm X, Kent State students even Kennedy. The military industrial complex, it’s too powerful. If I gotta fight, I’ll do my fighting here. I’m not running any more. If the battle is worldwide, I’ll make my last stand in Jamaica. Negril’s West End that’s the fucking edge of the rock for me!” Barrington mumbled something sounded like fuck it Tavo couldn’t tell, then he stared straight ahead into the night, silent.

But his professed courage was short-lived it invoked the specter of his encounters with Jamie Dice and his gang of smugglers. He sat silent now also, hurt more emotionally than from the physical road banging. Hurt by his self-loathing. He didn’t even have the balls to stand up to Dice. He was all mouth, easy to brag to Barrington while he was safe in a Land Rover, stoned once again on drugs with Irish hippie courage. Barrington noticed his funk, took on a more a sympathetic air. “Tavo, you’re a good guy.” He said “People in power know what’s going on in Negril, what the scene’s all about. Island’s too small for everyone not to know the runnings. You’re accepted man, didn’t mean to come down so hard on you. Just ease back, smoke, enjoy the spliff. You’re welcome to fight here! Irie, man!”

The rest of the journey went allot mellower. Barrington focused his attention more as they wound their way slowly up the hairpin turns to the refreshingly cool town of Mandeville. Then as the sun broke the horizon with an eerie glow, competing for a few moments with the millions of stars twinkling in the fleeting darkness, the Easy Riders of the tropics approached the wide valley below the Blue Mountains that is Kingston, Jamaica's capital city.

The roads were bare of traffic, as the city's morning bumper to bumper car jam was still a few hours away. They zoomed through the outskirts of the city, and Tavo gaped at a panorama of the worst poverty and living conditions he could ever imagine. Miles and miles of board tin and cardboard shacks nailed and held together by the sheer force of will to survive stretched before him. Rubbish and piles of garbage were strewn everywhere, creating the only landscaping. A heavy putrid smell of rot, death and despair filled the Rover. A few early risers were staggering about, rubbing their eyes, and looking like zombies coming to half-life but this was no jamboree. They were passing through Trench Town, Barrington told him, where over one million people lived, stressing this was not a place to dally. "But Trench Town is probably the most soulful spot in the world," he added. "Rhythm and blues, soca, calypso, ska, reggae and jazz throb twenty-four hours from radios blasting from each and every home, betting shop, rum bar and grocery shack."

Tavo took note of the rhythms they pounded out from every where, but the abject poverty turned his stomach, and saddened him. Forlornly he took it all in with disgust. Then the ghetto gradually gave way to small stucco and cement block houses in various shades of pastels fronted by small yards that bloomed with flowers and fruit trees. This wasn't so bad reminded him of more of his old neighborhood in Detroit. They then began a slow ascent into the hills surrounding Kingston; the vista gave way to larger dwellings, then finally to huge mansions with beautifully landscaped grounds that looked like botanical gardens. "Grown up as a child here," Barrington said, "attended prep school here prior to college in England. "This is the old Kingston establishment, man." "This is amassing said Tavo. "Iv never seen so much wealth!" "Ya but they're still trying to pretend they're Englishmen around here. Said

Barrington. "But they're just a bunch of god damn piggies. Michael'll soon give their backsides a good whacking! He'll tear down those slums we just came through, build some decent housing, educate the youth, then they'll know their true heritage, not what some fucking Limey told 'em. Let Jah light shine in Irie full sky wide coverage!"

A monumental task, Tavo thought. But more power to any man who could make a dent in that vision of horrid poverty that still burned in his brain. After a few more miles of winding road, Barrington turned into one of the mansion's wide driveways ablaze in the morning's sunshine and bordered by dazzling pink and white surprise bougainvillea as pure as a virgin's breath. What a contrast to that slum horror that had come before he thought! This was Barrington's older brother Peter's house. Peter had swallowed all that Barrington scorned, and was a chief accountant for a huge, multi-national cigarette company, with a branch located in downtown Kingston.

Peter was just opening the door to his sparkling brand new Mercedes Benz, ready to fight the morning rush hour traffic suburban stylie spiffed up like a lord in a dark three-piece suit and tie; carrying a gleaming leather briefcase. Barrington brought the Rover to a screeching halt, jarring Tavo out of his semi-hungover, comedown haze. He sat in the Rover too spaced out to move, as Barrington catapulted out and gave Peter a brotherly embrace. They talked for several minutes, seemed to be in serious conversation, but were too far up the driveway for him to overhear what they were saying. From time to time, Peter would glance back at the Rover and shake his head with a grim look of consternation. When Barrington returned he looked pleased, "Peter's cool, man. He'll loan me his Jeep to drive back to Negril. No problem."

Tavo felt funny, ill at ease. "He sure gave me a strange look." He said.

"Don't mind that man. He never saw a real hippie in the flesh before. Peter's all right. He'll eventually come around.

Just hasn't become a man of vision—a man of destiny—like me. But let's not bring ourselves down any more by hanging around here. Jump into the Jeep man. We're heading out of Babylon."

They transferred their few belongings to Peter's Jeep, and Barrington floored the accelerator, racing out of the driveway. A few minutes later he turned onto Constance Spring Road, a main thoroughfare, and expertly piloted the four-wheeler through the long backed up lines of morning rush hour, weaving and darting in and out of traffic, squealing around corners on two wheels. Most of the commuters were headed for their concrete office towers in the modern part of town known as New Kingston the banking center. At the end of Hope Road, leading out of town, where it made an abrupt halt, cut off by a deep gorge, they made a sharp left and began a slow ascent up into the Blue Mountains. The cars, diesel spewing buses, and trucks seemed to vanish. And as they climbed higher into the mountain, the road itself all but disappeared, leaving a curving dirt pathway wide enough for only one car at a time to pass in either direction.

They continued to climb at a forty-five degree angle through a dense, lush rain forest; looked like it could have been part of the Amazon basin. At times, the road's edge seemed to drop into space, down to green valleys carved out by rushing streams thousands of feet below. Wild birds whistled piercing cries that echoed off the gorge walls and seemed to signal their approach as they hairpinned their way steadily upward. Red gingers, multi-colored haliconias, giant Paleozoic ferns, and wild orchids grew everywhere, clinging to the steep mountain's edge, creating a tropical Eden. Just a short hour before, they'd been engulfed in poverty, dust, dirt and carbon monoxide fumes! Jamaica was nothing if not a land of contrasts! Tavo thought.

After another hour or so of this awe-inspiring landscape Barrington pulled abruptly to the left, onto a hidden driveway cut through the dense jungle. Tavo figured they had to be at least four thousand feet high. The air was laden with the morning's dew and felt cool and refreshing. The driveway slowly meandered into lush gardens ablaze with hibiscus, anthurium, bougainvillea, hybrid orchids, and numerous other flowers of every possible hue and fragrance. Hundreds of fruit trees dotted the flowered landscape, bearing oranges, mangoes, star apples, ackee, custard fruit, sour sop, neaseberry, papaya, jack fruit and more. Finally, the vista opened onto a great lawn of manicured, brilliantly green grass, big as a football field. Set like the crown jewel in the center was a plantation great house. Looked like it was built in the seventeen hundreds. It was covered with gingerbread, but it had been completely renovated and modernized. It gleamed in pristine white splendor, a man-made centerpiece for heaven on earth. The air here was twenty degrees cooler than the stifling furnace heat of Kingston and lavishly perfumed with the sweet bouquet of those thousands of blossoming flowers.

Kingston looked like a child's erector set town, from up here, as unreal and distant as if it were on the moon. Barrington acted right at home, puffed out his chest and made a wide sweep with his arms. "What do you think, man? Not bad, huh? My old prep schoolmate bought this place couple years ago." Tavo, mesmerized by the spectacular view, said, "What is it? Where are we?"

"Strawberry Hill man. Where the old British colonial rulers used to have tea, watch their subjects in Kingston suffer!" Barrington said. Tavo rubbed his eyes like he was awaking from a dream. "Your friend—he's rich, huh?"

"Sure" Barrington said, "he formed a record company in England. Produces some enlightened English Rock groups, Jamaican reggae, African groups too. Right on! This old place of slavery now belongs to someone who's spreading the word of truth, the word of liberation." He slapped Tavo on the back, and they entered the house, too exhausted to fully appreciate the splendid view, but still too wired from the uppers for sleep. Barrington whipped out a couple of Mandrex, handed one to Tavo, he wanted to ensure they'd get some rest, in preparation for the drive back to Negril the following morning. Stumbling through the old mansion, trying to find his way to one of the plush and spacious guest bedrooms, Tavo swallowed it. Through his poly drug abused eyes he noticed that the house's interior had been restored to its former days of glory, complete with original antique furniture upholstered in crushed satiny-smooth velvet of all colors. The King and Queen of England wouldn't have felt out of place here.

The Mandrex did the trick, he dropped off to sleep as soon as he found the bedroom and his head hit the pillow, still dressed in his cutoffs and T-shirt, nestled comfortably on a huge king-sized, hand-carved mahogany pedestal bed, draped with gold satin fringe. If any dreams came to him in his REM-deprived sleep, they couldn't match the one he had just been in.

But dream he did, if only for a minute. He dreamt he was opening up that cocktail napkin John had given him and in clean clear bright beautiful handwriting, Irene's handwriting, was a note. It read that she was leaving Harlen and his brutish sexual deviation, she couldn't take it any more, couldn't take his depraved sadism, and she was coming to Jamaica… she still loved him, wanted him more than ever. But then Dice appeared in his dream and he was fighting with Irene. He pinned her down, was crushing her, raping her… she screamed, screamed for Tavo to stop him. Dice was ginning, grunting, slamming it to her, laughing, heckling Tavo, egging him on to stop him—calling him a coward. But he was powerless, still afraid, a coward, he couldn't move, just stood there and cried, watched him rape her… cried like a baby. He thought he'd lose his mind he couldn't take it—wished he were dead!

A deafening banging jarred him wide-awake. He'd no idea what time it was or how long he'd slept, dreamt that horrible nightmare. But it was light out now, and an uncharacteristic gray gloom penetrated the massive shutters of his room. What's more, the shutters pounded and flapped against the sides of the house with a force that threatened to tear them off their hinges. Outside, a wind howled, grating the splitting nerve endings in his chemically nightmare tortured brain.

He rubbed his bloodshot eyes and peered through the window to see distant trees bent almost in half from the winds that whistled like mortar bombs. Making his way through the dark corridors of the house by touch, he finally found his way to the main living room. He saw Barrington relaxing in a high-backed loveseat, boots propped up on a table, and grooving on a blues tune that he blew out of a harmonica in time with the thundering sounds of nature all around them. Sounded like he was playing 'I am A Man' just like Muddy Waters' and he was cool, calm and collected just like Muddy. "A hurricane hit while we crashed," he shouted over the cacophony of wind, rain, lightning, and thunder. "Electricity's down, got a portable radio, runs on batteries. Tuned in some weather information. It's offshore to the west of us, bout a hundred miles from the coast of Negril."

Still scared by the dream and now this, Tavo yelled, "BUMBA CLOD!" But Barrington maintained his air of confidence. "Not to worry man" he said, "it's going to settle down in eight hours or so. We're safe here. This house is like a fortress, don't know if there'll be any heavy damage to Negril though. One big problem—just picked it up on JBC—the road up to Strawberry Hill and Newcastle has been washed out. Won't be fixed for at least six months."

Tavo strained to see outside the banging shutters "Oh, no! We're fucked now!" he said. But Barrington appeared not the least bit concerned, and picked at his ear distractedly thinking. "Let's have some food, always think best on a full stomach."

Tavo looked on in amazement, as Barrington snapped his fingers and an old wrinkled lady dressed in a starched British maid's uniform appeared out of no where. She rang a small silver bell set on a golden tray. A butler materialized—seemed melt out of the woodwork and announced in perfect English, over the pounding winds of the hurricane, "Mr Simmons, Mr Gripps, brunch is served!"

He led the two misfits to an adjoining bowling alley sized dining room as if nothing was out of the ordinary. In the center of this room, under enormous crystal chandeliers, they saw a fifty-foot solid oak table. At each end, two place settings had been laid, complete with sterling silverware, fine English bone china, crystal glasses and decanters of wine. A candelabrum glowed amidst colorful flower arrangements on the table. Tavo felt alien, weird, out of place. This was too bizarre for Christsakes! Barrington on the other hand was completely at home. He slouched in a hand-carved dining chair and cocked his foot up onto the polished table, as he grabbed a decanter of wine and took a generous slug. Some of the wine trickled down his chin and onto the white linen tablecloth. He wiped his mouth with the back of his hand, and passed the grape to Tavo.

Five servants scurried about, ferrying from the kitchen to the dining room freshly baked breads, more wine, cheeses, trays of tropical fruits, steamed fish, lobster mornay, escargots, more wine, fresh linens, topped off by piping hot Blue Mountain coffee, key lime pie, ice cream, sixty-year-old French brandy and Havana cigars. They feasted like aristos.

Not able to pack any more in, Barrington belched and rubbed his stomach "Not bad, aye Tavo?" He sighed. "What a life! After the revolution, some traditions should remain. Don't you think?"

Tavo looked around uneasily, confused, "I don't know, man" he said. "This is great, but don't you think it's a bit much? These people who work here, well they just seem I don't know… pretty subservient!"

Barrington sprang from his seat knocking over the wine, spilling it across the table and snapped "So what man! Some people will always be like that. Nothing you can do about it, man! Forget it." Wanting to change the subject now—not digging that Tavo had picked up on his real roots, he said. "I got a plan, tomorrow morning this storm'll be outta here, and we're history. Down the mountain we go! Got my wife and children to think about now! I'll leave Peter's Jeep here. He can pick it up when they repair the roads. Borrow some other wheels in town. We gotta get to Negril soon as possible!"

Tavo was not so sure, not so confidant, he tapped his foot and replied uneasily "How in the hell do we get down this mountain? The road's gone man. Didn't you say landslides are covering it!" Barrington waved his concern away with a flick of his wrist "We walk, brother. We walk. No problem."

With that said, Barrington popped a Mandrex, polished off another goblet of wine, lit a spliff and proceeded to wail on his blues harp like Willie Dixon now, playing 'Mellow Down Easy', while the turbulent storm swirled all around them.

When they awoke the next morning, and except for a few scattered tree branches and the odd uprooted tree, it was as if there had been no storm at all. The sky was a perfect pristine blue, and the sun shone bright. The wind had calmed to a refreshing light breeze. Birds chirped excitedly at this renewal. But the road into the estate was completely washed out; many parts submerged under three to four feet deep heaps of mud.

After a hearty breakfast of ackee and salt fish, fried plantains, boiled green bananas, johnny cakes, callaloo, mango jelly and fresh fruits and juices, served with all the ceremony of the day before, it was time to down a good jolt of piping hot Blue Mountain coffee and split. 'What the Hell.'

But Tavo fretted "How are we gonna get down man?" he said. "It's all jungle out there, slopes at least seventy degrees all the way down, more than four thousand feet! Muddier than Woodstock!"

Barrington blew a couple of notes on his harmonica, they sounded sour now, scratched a spot on his nose; thought a moment, then said "We get down the same bloody way we got up here except without the car—hike it. I'm not staying up here for months! Don't know what might happen to my family!"

Barrington pulled off his high-heeled Beatles boots that completed his costume of tight leather pants and billowing shirt, and pried off the heels with his ratchet knife, leaving exposed nails on the soles to act as cleats. Tavo at least was wearing Timberland moccasins they seemed fairly appropriate for this venture. They headed out, with Tavo looking like a first time skydiver, and started their downward trek.

But it was all they could do to stay on their feet, impossible to stay up right. They slipped, slid, fell, tumbled and stumbled. After the first three minutes, they were covered head to toe with mud. The reddish goop oozed between their fingers as they grabbed the mud banks for support, their fingers clawing for ferns or tree branches to cling to. Tiny waterfalls appeared out of nowhere to offer a welcome cleansing, but moments later, they were completely covered in mud again. Branches, prickly vines, and rock outcroppings scratched their skin and ripped at their clothes, insects buzzed them and biting ants feasted on their sores. Barrington laughed throughout it all to keep their spirits up—to egg them onward—although the sharp downward angle gave them a momentum of their own. Never mind going back now it was much too steep and slippery.

Tavo had to hug on to a tree to stop from falling off a ledge that plunged a thousand feet straight down. Barrington wasn't so lucky, he slipped over the edge, his fall halted only by an old crooked tree, its roots precariously growing on to the side of the cliff. He dangled by a branch, shouting, screaming for help, his legs flailing in midair. Tavo grabbed a wisp vine hanging from a nearby tree. Looked like the ones Heavy Higher used for thatching—they grew prolific here—and cut off a twenty foot length with his Swiss army knife, tied a slip knot noose, like he'd seen Heavy do, and secured the other end around a rock. He lowered the noose to Barrington who struggled to secure it around his waist with one hand. Tavo pulled him up onto the muddy bank, his feet still kicking for a toehold even when he reached solid ground.

Barrington looked scared shitless, any pretext of self-composure had vanished, but then he cracked a smiled as he gasped for breath and said. "Thanks man! You saved my ass. For a moment there, I was sure I was dead! Started paying my respects to Jah!" Tavo lay on his back in the mud, also panting for breath, but managed to smirk at Barrington. "Think General Westmoreland will give me the Medal of Honor?" he said. Barrington laughed, hugged him "Nah man, not if he knew it was a guy like me you saved. Think he'd rather cut your balls off! Let's get the hell outta here! Give thanks, it isn't Vietnam!"

After another three hours making their way halfway down, they fell to a stop at a small encampment of poor rural folk. A cook fire blazed in front of their small shack carved into the mountain face. There were ten or so naked pickney who immediately hid in the bush and peered at them from behind huge ferns and cocoa leaves, startled by this pair of monstrous clay people. But the elders realized quickly that they had nothing to fear, and offered them hot coffee and pieces of roasted yam to restore their energy. After resting awhile they continued on. Another hour and a half later, after a treacherous sliding descent, they finally rolled into the upper-class suburb Stony Hill and walked into the backyard of a six-bedroom villa complete with swimming pool and tennis court.

Typically, Barrington knew the owners, a young, professional British couple left over from Colonial days, and Tavo sighed with relief as they were welcomed into the home with open arms, despite their muddy condition and

Barrington's revolutionary persuasions. They'd made it back to civilization and safety. After washing the mud off and doctoring their cuts and bruises, the friendly couple drove them to Peter's house to pick up another transport, just as the sun began its descent over Kingston Harbor. Tavo marveled how Barrington's friends, his family had helped him out, despite his political leanings. Before he could ask about this, Barrington focused all his energy like a sharpshooter on returning to Negril that very night. Tavo pleaded for a good night's sleep, but Barrington wouldn't here of it. He prodded Tavo's tired sorry ass into an old pickup truck parked in the back of Peter's garage. Soon, they were cruising through the traffic of downtown Kingston. Barrington swallowed another Black Beauty, shoved one into Tavo's mouth, and fired up his trusty spliff. The one hundred and ten miles ride back to Negril required a degree of stamina that they had already exhausted tenfold. The towns of Old Harbor, May Pen, Mandeville, Santa Cruz, New Market and Blue Fields whizzed by through the night like comets from the heavens.

But after Ferris, the final little village before Negril, Barrington slammed on the brakes, and the pickup came to a sliding halt in front of two yellow sawhorses blocking the main road. A red stripe policeman walked up to the pick up and announced with bureaucratic elaborateness "All roads to Negril block with flood waters. Be weeks before de waters receded nuf to make dem passable again. You haffi turn around back to Kingston or wait it out in a Black River."

Barrington spun the truck around; told Tavo they could make it to Negril by country roads that wound through Grange Hill. "Man, it's worth a try" he said. "No guest houses or places to sleep around here and I'm not back-tracking all the way to Black River, gotta see if my family's okay."

They made it as far as Grange Hill, a sleepy little sugar cane town twenty miles from Negril, with no trouble. Now they had to traverse the ten miles of low-lying sugar cane fields that surrounded Savanna La Mar, and, hopefully, hit the more elevated main road of Sheffield, just outside of Negril. But it was the cane fields, not the roads that proved to be the major obstacle. Cane grew everywhere like tall grass, topping off at a height of over twelve feet. And the roads in this vast expanse of standing sucrose were a rat's maze. Every quarter mile or so, the mud and dirt road they were traveling either came to a dead end or hit a four-way crossroad. No way to tell which direction was which, the sky was cloud-covered, providing no stars for guidance, and there were no signs, houses, trees or landmarks for reference points. They could be going in the wrong direction or traveling in circles, for all they knew. Tavo felt like they were a pair of bugs, trapped in the vast expanse a golf course green, trying to find the cup.

After traveling like this for hours, he spotted a faint light down one of the cane rows, pointed it out and Barrington headed for it. Sure enough, it was a house, standing out there amidst the expansive cane fields, all by its lonesome self. Barrington smacked the dash soundly with his open palm. "That's the overseer's house. Gotta roust him out of bed. He'll know the way out!"

No time for standing on ceremony. They could meander through this maze for days without finding their way out. So they yelled, hollered, beeped the horn until an old white man, in striped Pajamas and a night cap, looking like a casting reject from *Deliverance*, staggered out the front door. He was rubbing the sleep from his eyes, cradling a shotgun on his arm. He stared at them as if they were crazy deciding whether or not he should shoot them. But when he deciphered their story, the old geezer headed haltingly for his Land Rover and agreed to show them the way out, provided they promise never to come his way again, wake him up again!

In a matter of minutes he led them directly to the main road back to Negril. It turned out that they were only about seven miles from home. Barrington let loose a rebel hoot, smashed his foot down on the accelerator screeching the tires. The old dude shouted something Tavo couldn't make out; they left him in a cloud of exhaust fumes.

The next instant, before they had gone an eighth of a mile, they came to a splashing halt, submerged up to the door frames in a slow-moving stream that covered the road as far as the headlights revealed.

Barrington banged his head on the steering wheel screaming "We're fucked now!" But, just then, lights appeared out of nowhere from behind them. Knowing what lay ahead, the old man had followed them. He shouted they were bloody daffy, but hooked the pick up on chains and pulled them through a mile or more of flood waters. Luckily the engine started after he gave them a few jump-starts.

So with luck, stupidity, the blind assurance of youth, amphetamines, herb, and, of course, the old dude's aid, they made it back to Negril. It turned out; they were the only ones who did. Floodwaters covered all roads into town for over two weeks. And no one else was fortunate enough to encounter the sweet old sugar cane man.

After their exploit, word spread throughout the Negril community, the Easy Riders possessed strange powers, were men of science. They used powerful obeah—harnessed spirits—bid duppies to carry them through flood waters, and who knew what else?

21

"Oh ma-ma, ma-ma"
You've got me livin on The Front Line"

Eddie Grant

Tavo felt as if he had been away from Negril for a year instead of four hectic days. The trip had engraved a lasting impression. Saving Barringtons life boosted his self-confidence. Surviving the hurricane, fighting his way through the jungle made him feel strong, made him feel like a survivor, like he could survive anything now. Well almost, in his mind Dice was still more powerful than a hurricane, and he had forgot to mention his dilemma to Barrington. But he figured Barrington probably didn't have any solutions anyway. He was beginning to see it as his problem, his problem alone to solve. Yea sure, fat chance; you had some hope when you matched wits with nature; hoods and wise guys never gave you a break. And what good was it to have the rep of an obeah man? A guy who could slice the ears off of dead people would just laugh at that mumbo-jumbo. But rapping with Barrington gave him a clearer understanding of the Jamaican condition, although now that he knew more, he was even more confused, had more questions. Like, how could America and England rob Jamaica and her people of their land, natural resources, their cultural and their belief systems, their very lives? Leave them with no past or future? Then those same villains spread lies, propaganda, claimed they were lazy, shiftless, and inferior. England did it in slavery days, the colonial era, but this bauxite bull shit proved those evils had not gone away. Like Malcolm X, Michael Manley wanted economic independence; to control what was rightfully Jamaica's so her people could determine their own destiny. This wasn't just a case of racism. It was a struggle of poor, oppressed peoples, and racism was a tool—propaganda to keep the downtrodden masses from unifying. If that didn't work, bring on the CIA, the DEA; bring them to their knees. Neocolonial powers feared Manley, feared charismatic leaders who understood, who could debunk their manipulations that could lead people toward a common goal of self-realization that challenged the status quo. Negril's hedonism merely masked the core of a land that cried out for real independence. Looked to Tavo like Jamaica had as much chance for that as he did in thwarting Dice. David and Goliath—Ants and rubber tree stories never happened in real life sorry to say.

But he took solace for the short term that luckily; the storm's damage to his Banana Shout was minimal. Mannie had battened down the hatches and Clyde's solid construction had withstood the winds. Mannie also reported that Nick had been over to see him, three times during his absence. Strange indeed he seldom left the bar and never visited him before. What's more, he'd even braved the storm once to look for him. He decided to pay him a visit, see what was up. This had to be serious. He probably just wanted his property though. He never gave up. Probably had some new scam, some new trick up his sleeve. But he felt protected now by an ever-expanding psychic armor against Nick's insults, so he walked confidently onto his wood-decked patio at the cliff's edge, where he found Nick wielding a razor blade, he was busy chopping something, it looked like brown powdered sugar. He was totally oblivious to Tavo's presence. Then he slowly looked up as if he were leisurely scanning the distant horizon but he was having trouble focusing. His eyes were like pinpoints. He appeared to be completely transformed, like he'd finally achieved that elusive sense of inner peace he'd always sought, always talked about. His sly Cheshire Cat grin was replaced by a soft smile of benevolent content. He looked like a new Nick, mellow and at peace.

Nick finally waved a languid slow-motion welcome with his outstretched arm and said, almost crooning "Oh come, sit down, please make yourself comfortable, my old friend."

He looked around to see who Nick could be talking to, realized there was nobody else there, it had to be him. So he pulled up a wicker chair and said, "What's happenin? Where sure in a good mood today."

"Yes, yes. Right on the mark Tavo. Everything's just fabulous with me! I've finally arrived! Found the ultimate trip, perfect sensations! I've gotten high, really high, for the first time, the only time, after so many wasted years of trying!" He sighed a sigh of total relief. "Here, old pal. You must try some of my discovery. It's the greatest. Come, join me in total ecstasy!"

"What the hell is it?" Tavo asked.

Nick looked at him through glazed, unfocused eyes, he looked amused by his lameness "Persian heroin" he said. "Not as good as China White, but it'll do till I can score the good stuff. Snort a line or smoke a puff, poof, you're there. The perfect drug of choice. Far superior to insipid cocaine, a drug for jabbering idiots and fools. Yes, yes Smack's my clipper ship to sail me over the oceans of my mind to nirvanas bliss." Nick's head bobbed up and down in slow motion like a plastic clown's on a string. He appeared to fall asleep then awoke as if from a dream. "Only down side," he said like they'd still been conversing all along "It costs a fortune… almost unheard of in Jamaica. Niggers don't have the class for it, but the French are starting to bring it in. It's really a high-status drug, you know! Anyway, my tastes have always been expensive… I can afford them!"

Tavo looked at Nick sternly, grabbed his shoulders, and shook him trying to get his attention "Look man that makes no sense! What about those poor people in the ghettoes who're strung out on heroin. Try tellin' them about status! You know it's addictive as hell!"

"Tavo, you really are bourgeois. Petty, petty, petty! Should know better than to expect you'd comprehend the good life. Anyway, I'm only chipping—just snorting. I can't get addicted. I can handle it" And he went into another nod. Tavo stood there tapping his foot waiting for him to rejoin the living. Thinking of leaving. Then all of a sudden Nick was back. "Never mind." He said, oblivious to his lost time "I want to speak with you about other matters, my old friend." This second use of the word "friend" made Tavo squirm suspiciously, but he sat down anyway and said, "I'm listening, but make it quick" Figuring it was another of his land schemes. Nick began to slur his words now, barely managed to get out "Got a proposition that'll make you money, my pal… upgrade your lovely resort!"

What a transformation! He'd never considered Banana Shout more than a rat-invested hovel. Now he's calling it a lovely resort. A complete personality change.

"What do you say?" he persisted. "Come on! Get high with me. Might not always be in a generous mood, you know!"

"Don't think so! Smack's not my bag. Just got back from Kingston with Barrington, gotta cool out. Got a lot on my mind. What's with this proposition?"

Nick waved an unsteady limp hand to dismiss him "Barrington! Ha!" he laughed, "what a fucking ball of confusion; loves to play the pampered revolutionary."

"So what's with this proposition?" Tavo asked, trying to get him back on track, growing impatient.

It took all Nicks concentration, the smack was really in control, hitting him hard, but he finally told Tavo that he'd decided it was time to record his memoirs for posterity. He was primed, wanted to cash in on his fame, become even more well known, to say nothing of the big bucks his story would bring. The only problem was, he couldn't concentrate in the fun house-mad house atmosphere of the Cafe. He still hadn't given up on getting a hold of Tavo's land… he'd just put it on the back burner for now. He knew the time was quickly approaching when Dice would start to use Banana Shout as a smuggling base. Time was on his side; eventually Tavo would be busted along with the rest of the riff raff.

The smack was really in over-drive now and he struggled for words. "Worst part's hassle of managing this place." He mumbled. "Niggers driving me nuts. Stupid blunderings. Always correcting, reprimanding. Need well-deserved rest—constant stream of hassles. Morocco beckons, Casablanca. Gotta go there get inspiration. Gotta go!"

His plan was to relate his life story into a tape recorder so some renowned publishing house would assign a flunky to transcribe it. Set it in book form. He didn't have a publisher yet, but he was confident. As soon as word got out that he had a tape, they'd all line up at his door for the rights. All he'd have to do was pick the most prestigious house—the one to offer the most dough. Might take him two months to get in the groove and complete his project. And here was the kicker. He needed someone to manage Nick's Cafe in his absence. He'd decided to bestow this honor on none other than Tavo Gripps, especially since none of his smuggler partners would ever consider work of that sort.

Though it took him hours to get it all out, he proposed that Tavo lease the Cafe for a mere three thousand bucks a month; he could net double that amount with no problem. He ran a well-oiled machine, he boasted, even though the retards and oafs that worked for him got on his nerves drove him crazy. "You on the other hand, shouldn't have any trouble with them since you seem to actually enjoy their insipid company" he said. "Besides, I've taught these ignorant bush savages gourmet cooking skills, and my bartenders can compete with those at any bar in New York or Paris when it comes to mixology. As for the waiters, they're polished enough to serve royalty. All you really have to do is lie in my hammock, make your presence felt marginally, not get in the way or screw anything up, and collect a profit of three thousand bucks a month. What could be easier?"

Nick had hired Tavo's friend Garth as general manager. Garth intervened when Nick lost it and pissed off the staff with his raging tantrums. Garth could calm everyone down so they wouldn't take him apart. He usually did this by convincing the workers that Nick was mad, just like Norman. Hurting crazy people was a Jamaican taboo. And Garth's uncle was the local judge, who decided whether or not the Cafe would get a permanent liquor license. Garth was necessary for cool legal runnings. But Nick felt Tavo should be present to greet dignitaries, famous personae, though, of course, not with Nick's inimitable flare. But at least he had a little more couth than Garth. That dumb nose picker!

He knew Tavo didn't have enough money for the lease up front, but never mind. He could pay him from the profits upon his return. Tavo could use the dough, his land tax and water bill was due and he'd spent all his money on constructing his last cottage. So the deal was consummated with a handshake, and Nick immediately set about packing and making arrangements for his rendezvous in the fictional haunt of his alter ego, Humphrey Bogart.

Mannie's response to news of his venture was weighted with caution.

"Me think that might not be a good plan," he warned. "Nick, him not well-loved by the staff and Garth don't really know how to run that place. But as long as you don't have to pay him no money up front, give it a try. All you gonna lose is your time—you gain by experience!"

With those tentative words of encouragement, he threw himself into the job of taking inventory alongside Nick of the food and liquor stores. Nick showed him how to run the generator and acquainted him with the staff's work schedules and pay scales. He also gave him a list of the various Jamaicans who delivered the wholesale stock items, from fresh native lobsters, fish, fruits and vegetables, to importers who brought New York steaks, smoked salmon and bagels.

When all the last minute instructions were in place, Nick shut his suitcase and donned a sharp white tuxedo jacket, white shirt and a black bow tie. No more patched bellbottom jeans for him now, it was Bogart style all the way. He topped it off with a good strong hit of Persian Brown, mellow as he could be, and took off for the Montego Bay Airport without a glance backwards, not a care in the world, except for his next score.

The first couple of weeks at Nick's went smoothly enough. Business was booming, especially at sunset when all of Negril's tourist population would arrive to swill down gallons of banana daiquiris and piña coladas, marked up two hundred percent. But no one complained. There was always the rumor that a rock and roll superstar was going to show up, plus the sunsets were the best in the west, and often culminated in a splash of brilliant green. The famous but rare Green Splash!

Tavo now had a ring side seat and everyday beginning at four o'clock Rastas began setting up huge coconut and bamboo bongs through out the café, stuffing them from pound sacks of senseimilia, blasting them a fire and casting the bar in a cloud of ganja smoke. Babes wandered up to the bar naked as the day they were born, glistening with coconut oil and ordered rum punches nonchalantly. Sam Smart laid out foot long lines of coke for them on the bar counter and they snorted them up hungrily. The Rastas laced their bongs with Sam's coke now. Jah was not on their minds any longer—then they'd leap from the forty-foot cliffs, dreadlocks streaming in the breeze splashing like happy zonked hairy marlins in the ocean below.

The police never showed up to wreck the fun. Actually there was only one police in Negril. Dalton Bell known as Ding-Dong and he could care less how the hippie mon amused himself. Ding-Dong was growing his own plot of marijuana in the hills hoping his would be a good crop—with a good strong THC count and Dice would buy it from him. The Jamaican army had long since departed no longer a threat. They had bigger fish to fry. They had Prime Minister Michael Manley to protect. Manley feared with good reason, the CIA planned his assassination and had called his troops in for support… set up road blocks, and tried to stop the guns the CIA was now flooding the island with.

Towards the end of his third week as resident manager, a tall, well groomed, longhaired, handsome guy in his late twenties began showing up for every sunset. Tavo thought he had seen him before, but couldn't quite place him. He wasn't that much different from the rest of the crowd, the thing that made him stand out was at every setting sun, he'd reach deep down into his corduroy jeans and come up with two or three crisp one hundred dollar US greenbacks. He'd smack 'em onto the bar with a flourish and shout, drinks were on him. This produced an even bigger cheer of approval than the sunset. Almost as big as Sam's coke.

He was always a welcome sight, especially to Tavo; the bar's business began to slacken towards the end of April. One afternoon just before sunset, one of the bartenders didn't show up for work and Tavo had to jump behind the bar to serve the thirsty stoned gathering. The tall slim guy was there as usual. He approached Tavo, slapped his big bills down soundly in front of him and roared, "Drinks all around!" After the crowd had dispersed to eat dinner at more reasonably priced local spots on the cliffs, the flush dude approached him, offered to buy him a drink, introduced himself as Dee Williams. Tavo acknowledged his greeting, shook his hand, then busied himself loading empties in cases and taking inventory of empty rum bottles. He didn't have time for chitchat. But Williams made it clear, he wanted to sit down later "to talk some serious business." What that meant Tavo had no idea, but not wanting to offend this high roller, he told him to meet him at Banana Shout after closing time.

He usually closed the bar at about eleven thirty, after most of the customers were either completely blottoed or had wandered down to dig one of the open-air reggae concerts that were starting to proliferate on the beach. Then he'd lock up the remaining liquor stock, in the storage area, under the floor of the swimming pool bar, and count the cash for the day.

Business on this day was definitely not good. As May approached, Negril's business was slackening. Most hippies came to escape the cold in North America and went elsewhere like Telluride to summer. Nick never mentioned this and Tavo never considered the possibility. But the day's receipts brought home the grim reality. He was just about breaking even, maybe even losing money, shit!

When he reached his house that evening, depressed, worried over this downturn, he found Dee lying in the hammock under his thatched front porch, smoking a giant spliff, looking like the lord of manor. "Hi ya buddy, have a hit of some primo sensei, man!" he called out.

Tavo was in no mood to party, plus he didn't relish getting loaded with a stranger, acting like his best friend. He refused the offered spliff and Dee looked offended "What's the matter man? Take a toke. Great for the head, 'specially after sweating in that bar all night!"

"No thanks, I'll pass." Tavo said moodily still distracted by the bar's downturn. "Cold beer's fine for me. You smoke. Feel free!"

"Hey man, something wrong? You paranoid? Thought everyone smoked grass nowadays!"

"Don't know about anybody else, just don't do it much. You go ahead… do your own thing."

Dee looked him up and down giving him the once over, then became serious like he could sense Tavo was in no mood for small talk "Okay man. I'll get right to the point" he said. "I can see you're busy, got a hip club to run, I can get next to that… own three Friday's franchises in the States." Tavo rolled his eyes. What was his point? Get to it or leave. "Not rich are ya?" he said, somewhat sarcastically.

"Ya. Born rich. The old man owned and raised racehorses for the Kentucky Derby. Once you got money just seems to attract more! C'mon man, take a hit."

Tavo pushed the outstretched spliff away "No thanks." He said, he just wished this guy would leave, get the hell out of his hammock so he could have some peace.

"Ya, ya. You don't smoke, big deal." he said, like he was offended.

"Listen man," Tavo said, and tried to remain patient, "I just don't feel like it, okay. I'll have a beer." He fished a frosty Red Stripe from his Coleman cooler and popped the top on the side opener, suds oozed out of its top. He looked around searching for an exit, hoping this guy would get the hint, get to his point. Dee had lit another spliff, looked like he was really getting comfortable, had no intentions of splitting. "Yeah! So! You're a rich guy, what about it?" he said, maybe he would have to get rude with him.

"That's right man." He said, ignoring Tavos sarcasm. "Bored to tears too. America's not where it's at any more, not for me anyway. But you got it made man, owning Nick's Cafe and Banana Shout Resort. Nothing but fun and sun, screwing all those cute hippie chicks." He grinned lecherously, nodded his head, gave Tavo a knowing wink. "That's me all the way man. That's where I'm at too," and thrust the spliff under Tavo's nose again. Tavo pushed it away.

"No man." He said, visibly annoyed now by this pest. "Listen, I don't own Nick's, just leasing it for a couple of months." God, why wouldn't this guy take a hint and leave!

"Is that right?" Dee said. Seemed to give that answer more than a passing thought. "Well, who owns Nick's?"

Tavo shifted his weight from foot to foot, uncomfortable with the mention of Nick, reminding him of the money he would owe him for the lease. "Uh, Nick." He said "But he ain't here."

"Here, take a drag." He prompted. "Oh, right. Keep forgetting you aren't getting' high tonight." He silently puffed on the spliff, actually a fat roach now roach, he appeared to be deep in thought, either that or stoned, it was hard to tell. Tavo was about to ask him to get out of his hammock, he'd had enough of this dick dance, when the guy said, "Listen. I'm not beating around the bush any more. I'm a businessman. I want to buy Nick's Cafe and Banana Shout!"

Tavo was stunned! "You what!"

He smiled, "That's right friend," and a little bell went off in Tavo's head, he immediately went on the defensive. Whenever he heard the words 'friend' or 'pal' lately he felt the need to put a protective hand over his wallet.

"I want both properties." The guy said, "I assume you own Banana Shout, right?"

"Ya, sure. Free and clear," he said, seeing no harm in this disclosure.

"Okay, I'll lay my cards right on the table. We all know Negril is going to be big time. It's already booming. So I'm going to offer you and Nick an even larger deal! Say, what's Nicks his full name anyway?"

"Lebowitz." Tavo said.

"Nicholas Lebowitz," he repeated slowly, like he was engraving it on his memory. "What kinda deal you talkin about" Tavo asked, figured he'd play along for a few more minutes, see what he was up to. "You see, I am prepared to trade you guys one of my Friday's franchises—the best one in Columbus, Ohio—nets, let me emphasize *nets*, well over a million a year."

"You gotta be kidding me!" Tavo yelped, he looked paralyzed.

Dee frowned, nodded knowingly "Okay. Okay, man. You drive a hard bargain," mistaking Tavo's cry of astonishment for a "no deal." "I'll throw in a million bucks cash up front. Sweeten the pot. Just gotta get out of America man. It's a real bring-down. You guys got it made here, dreams come true, the envy of everyone. I've been after that all my life. Shit, you two made it happen. How about it? With all that money you guys can start over again, do even better!"

"Holy Moley!" Tavo thought, doing some quick math. Was this guy for real? That was a lot a bread to be waving around. Nick definitely stood to gain the most. But even if he wound up with a quarter or less of the total from this deal, it was still two hundred and fifty thousand cash, plus a quarter ownership in a Friday's, which meant another two hundred and fifty thou every year. This was big time! But he'd have to be partners with Nick. And that was surely the down side. Maybe he could sell his share to Nick! On second thought, where would he be then? Dee was right. He did have it made! He cherished his life in Negril and his property was increasing in value every day. Anyway, he couldn't ever go back to the States, and he wasn't sure he wanted to endure the hassles of starting over someplace else, not even with a lot of cash. He absolutely loved his place, his last stand, his destiny. No, definitely not. This was not right for him. This was his dream to live, not Dee's. A quote from Robinson Crusoe popped into his mind: "All the good things of this world are of no further good to us than they are for our use." He'd all he wanted to use, and more right here.

But He didn't want to poison this deal for Nick or offend this high roller. Nick might feel differently about selling his Cafe. Maybe he should check around and find out if this dude was on the level. People floated in and out of Negril daily, bearing tall tales that usually turned out to be bullcrap.

Dee interrupted his silent ruminations "Well, pal, are you going to say something, or just stand there with your mouth open, catching bugs?"

Tavo was jolted back. "Just thinking is all," he said, sure didn't seem like this guy was kidding around. "It's a big step… sounds like a good deal you know for everybody. Tell me more about your bar in Ohio!" He was trying hard now to act cool, act like he knew what he was doing.

"Oh, I got it, man," Dee said, looking at him now like a sly fox. "Don't think I am on the level, right? Not to worry, I'll come over tomorrow night and bring a floor plan of the bar, complete with a flow chart, hierarchy of management, the whole shebang. We finalize this deal; I'll bring a million in cash to Jamaica. Show you I'm on the up and up. Deposit it in the Cayman Islands. I'm sure you guys are slick. Won't turn it into worthless Jamaican currency."

Tavo fidgeted, twirled the cafe's keys on his finger. Nick might be interested; he didn't want to blow the deal for him. "Sounds smooth to me" he said, sure seemed like this guy was on the level.

Dee looked him square in the eyes, trying to see if he was getting through, then said "Sure man, smooth as silk. But I got a couple of questions for you. You gotta understand, I don't just go throwing money around. This is serious business."

"Sure," Tavo said, feeling a little more confident now about his own abilities to wheel and deal, not minding his new role in the world of high finance. "Fire away."

"First of all, I gotta know where you got your money to build your resort." He held up his hand to stop Tavo's reply "No, listen man, I don't care if it came from smuggling pot, already figure it did. Shit, no one can connect me with you after I'm the owner. It's just my business policy to know the complete backgrounds of the individuals I'm involved with. You know, more for my own personal satisfaction, I get kicks doing business with tough guys." Tavo attempted to speak, but Dee cut him off again "Listen man, I love my smoke. You smugglers are performing a great service for America shipping out primo stuff, turning everyone on. Just like Johnny Appleseeds!"

"Hey, fella!" Tavo finally cut in, not pleased with the direction his rap had taken. "Get your kicks somewhere else! I'm no smuggler man. Never even sold an ounce a grass. Just came down here to get my head straight, see? Land was cheap then. Sweated my damn balls off to make it work too!"

Dee winked at him conspiratorially, chuckled "Sure, sure, man," he said. "Cut the Swiss Family Robinson crap. You can open up with me; I been straight with you man. For Christ's sake! I told ya this won't have no adverse effect on our deal!" He finally got out of the hammock, he didn't appear high now, and draped his arm around Tavo's shoulder in genuine friendship. "Only reason I asked to begin with is I get a vicarious thrill knowing I've bought a resort from a notorious drug runner. You know, a real rush. Come on, mellow out man, puff de weed brother. Ha ha. I love de way Jamaicans talk… so melodious."

Tavo shrugged his arm off his shoulder, had to make him understand "Listen, you don't get it. I'm not gonna make up some story for your cheap thrills!"

Dee threw the roach to the floor, ground it out with his boot. "Okay man. Don't get so hot. Just drop it. I believe you." Sincerity oozed from him and he shook Tavo's hand. "Listen man, our deal still stands okay. Tell Nick though, pronto. He's not gonna want to pass this up. I'll even fly my personal attorney in. Proof of my commitment! You guys can deposit the cash offshore—no taxes. Nobody the wiser! Tomorrow night I'll bring over all the paperwork on Friday's to show you. You'll see I'm no bullshit artist. This is real man!"

Without further comment, Dee split, headed for his bungalow on the beach or some reggae show, wherever he hung out—probably the Yacht Club, Tavo thought. It stayed open most of the night and still drew the late night crowd.

He stretched out in his hammock, as he sipped another cold Red Stripe and replayed the conversation. Something was wrong, but he couldn't put his finger on it. Just a feeling, his sixth sense warned that something about this guy was fishy. He certainly had all the right answers. Maybe that was it: he was just a little too pat, almost rehearsed, like he had anticipated all of his doubts before he even formulated them. But who was he to judge. He'd very little contact with the well to do. For all he knew, they were all as polished as Dee, got their jollies off by living through other's adventures. There was no need for concern, especially for Nick. These guys were the only kind he hung out with. If anybody could spot a scam artist, Nick could. Anyway, he figured he'd done right. He hadn't opened his mouth to him about Nick's business, nor had he killed any potential deal. He'd left the door wide open for Nick. If he wasn't interested, he'd stay put right where he was—in Africa. Not to worry. He'd just tell Nick about these new runnings. He's a big boy. Let him decide what he wanted to do. Besides, if he didn't tell him and Nick was interested, there would be hell to pay! Tomorrow figured to be one hectic, headachy day. Not only did he have to spend twelve hours trying to run the Cafe, now he had to get to Savanna La Mar and make a call to Nick in Africa. What a pain! At least Nick had given him the name and number of the hotel he would be staying at—just in case he really screwed things up and needed his expert consultation. That was a laugh! Not that he wasn't capable of screwing things up—anyway, things had a way of screwing up on their own. But there was just not enough business, and that wasn't his fault. Not much consolation! Nick would really be pissed off. Shit! He couldn't even pay him the lease!

22

De higher de monkey climb
De more him expose him ass

—Old Jamaican Folk Saying

Savanna La Mar wasn't his favorite place. He dreaded going there even more than walking into Nick's, now that the profit margin had all but disappeared. The only times he ventured to this crazy town was when he had to pay his land taxes and water bill, it was the closest designated city to Negril.

It took him about an hour and a half in the Moke to get there, twice the usual time because of the car's broken radiator. As usual, traffic was backed up all along the main road, Great Saint George Street. Goats, fat stinking sows, and mean-tempered donkeys wandered in and out of smoking diesel trucks, mini buses, bicycles, motorcycles and pushcarts carrying everything from coconuts to fertilizer and bales of fabric. To make matters worse the heat seemed to be the most oppressive of anywhere on the island. There were very few trees or anything else to cast a shade. Two and three story dirty cement block buildings crowded out every living thing that tried to send down roots. The people here seemed as reluctant to be there as he did. Everyone yelled, shouted and cursed at one another, and the drivers constantly laid on their blaring horns, as if that would control the meandering mob of animals and pedestrians.

Ear-splitting decibels of reggae music blasted from gigantic speakers in front of most shops, for no better reason than to add to the annoyance and chaos. The usually enjoyable Reggae music took on a completely different feeling here than when heard under a star-studded sky on a cool evening at Negril's beach. Here, drum and bass pounded a warning to get out of Dodge as fast as possible. Ragged schizophrenic beggars were the only ones who grooved on the vibe; they twirled to the rhythm on most of "Sav's" street corners, private parts waving in the wind through their tattered rags. The only ones at home in psycho Savanna La Mar.

But "Sav" offered the modern convenience of a public telephone. All he had to do was wait in line in the blazing sun and dodge pigs and beggars for two hours or so, until it was his turn. By the time he reached the phone he was drenched in sweat, as if he'd spent the day on a Mississippi chain gang. But he was nothing if not lucky, sometimes anyway. It must have been sundown in Africa when he called; Nick was at the hotel and had just snorted a few lines of top-grade heroin. Over the crackling connection, Tavo shouted a concise summary of Dee's deal. Nick was elated.

"Why, that's fantastic, my dear friend," he crooned sweetly. "I was getting bored with Jamaica anyway. It's time to cast my fate to the winds again. With that money those winds will blow me to even bigger and better shores." The line went silent for a few seconds. "Keep that fish on the hook Tavo. Don't fuck anything up until my return." Even over the transatlantic phone lines, he could hear the excitement in Nick's voice. "In fact, don't speak to him at all. You're apt to insult him somehow, mess things up. You don't know how to handle class like his! Just tell him I'll be there in two days, got it. Then, back off!"

"Ya, okay" Tavo said. "But I'm not in on this… want no part of it. I haven't told him yet, but I'm not selling my resort!"

"Fuck you! You're a dreamer. You don't have a resort. You've got a flop house for losers from the 60's… just don't mess up my deal… you're a real ass! This is your perfect chance to get out… get out before you're busted with those smugglers and lose everything! Don't know why I waste my time trying to help you… just remember don't do anything to screw up my deal, got it?"

He promised not to interfere and hung up, figuring he'd done his part. Let Nick do what he wanted. But he'd forgotten to mention the sliding profits! What the hell. There was nothing he could do about it. And although he hated to agree with Nick about anything, he'd been right about one thing: he wasn't cut out to wheel and deal. So what! He didn't want to. He was content to plod along like the proverbial tortoise, enjoy what he'd been lucky enough to achieve so far. Guys like Nick were born knowing how to operate. It wasn't something you could learn in school.

Suddenly, he remembered something he'd put on the back burner. Mike Dorfman, a friend from home, was arriving today. Mike had sent him a postcard informing him of his arrival date and time.

He was excited whenever a friend from America paid a visit. Gave him a chance to catch up on happenings in the States, renew old friendships. He'd met Mike in Chicago at the Democratic Convention right before his aborted army physical. Mike was a recent graduate in philosophy from the University of Wisconsin. He'd crashed in his north side Chicago apartment when the police became nasty at the convention and began cracking bones and heads. They'd written each other occasionally during his exile, and Mike had been lucky enough to find a job teaching in one of Chicago's ghettos; deferred him from military service. Evidently, the government figured this occupation was just as dangerous as Nam. Great! Mike would fill him in on what was up back home, take his mind off the money he owed Nick.

When he pulled the puttering, sputtering, steaming Moke into his yard, Dorfman had arrived and was swinging in his hammock, cooling out with a spliff and a tall tropical drink of some kind. Mike rolled out of the hammock and clasped him in a bear hug. "Man, you really got it made—gone native all the way… a grass shack resort in paradise. You're one lucky dude. Escape from Nam; find a dream come true! Turned shit into gold!"

Tavo smiled "Yeah, can't complain," then reconsidered. "Although right now it feels like the gold's turning back to shit." Mike looked confused and Tavo seized the opportunity to unburden his troubles—talk it out. "I leased Nick's Cafe next door but business ain't so good and Nick's coming back day after tomorrow" he said. "I really haven't kept too good a track of the profit and loss sheet. You know finances were never my strong suit. Fact is I can't even hang out with you now. Gotta do some overdue accounting, figure out where I'm at!"

Mike patted him on the back "No worries, man, I'll help ya. We'll finish twice as fast. Point me at them numbers."

"Thanks man." Tavo said. "Wait man, before we get started, let me lay on you what's been happening with me, okay. Just started my own travel business right outta my apartment. What a trip! Called this charter airline company, gave them a fast-talking line of bullshit. Convinced 'em I was a real travel agent and they gave me the okay to book flights to Jamaica. Shit, man. I can keep your cottages full and make some cash too. Only charge you twenty percent!"

"Yeah! Sounds great," Tavo said, twenty percent seemed steep though. "Sure you'll do a dynamite job. Right now, I can't concentrate on anything 'til I sort out the figures and deal with this Cafe's business!"

He brought out a suitcase full of receipts and bankbooks, and the two spent the remainder of the afternoon pouring over cash paid out for staff salaries, lobsters, mangoes, pineapples, liquor, etc., etc., etc. and more. After five hours of tedium, using a hand calculator, they figured out that Tavo owed Nick just over two thousand dollars.

Mike chewed on a pencil, "Jeez, what a pisser. Looks like you got fucked. But look man, Nick'll understand. He's one of us, ain't he? He's a hippie right!"

"Ya right, as understanding as Mayor Daley would be to Black Panthers holding a benefit barbecue on his front lawn!" Tavo said.

"Gee man, that's tough. How did it happen? The losses that is?" Mike asked.

Tavo wrinkled his brow in thought. "Business fell off, so Garth invited all his buddies in to make the place look more crowded. But I think he just gave them drinks on the house. Nobody paid for anything. Damn, if it weren't for Dee I'd be in a bigger hole!"

"Who the hell are Dee and Garth?" Mike asked.

"Garth's an old Jamaican friend of mine and Dee's this American dude who wants to buy Banana Shout and Nick's Café. Rich guy, born with the silver spoon, you know."

"Ya, know the kind." Mike sighed. "Listen, I hope you're not considering selling him your place. Like I told you man, I'm gonna build my business around your resort! I've already lined up enough people I know to keep you filled for the next year. Don't wanna start dealing with somebody I don't know. Shit, he could fuck the place up. Build some Holiday Inn on it."

"Ya, well I got other problems too, maybe I should sell, don't know if I can hold on to this place. You wouldn't believe what goes on here behind the scenes. Let me tell you about this Dice guy. He's…."

But Mike slapped Tavo soundly on the back. "Fuck it!" he said "Don't sell man, my plan's for a small office on Webster and Halsted. Market and promote Negril, the real Jamaica." Mike walked off the porch, picked a hibiscus flower, pulled its petals off, pondering. "Say man," he said, "you know, there's this Georgia peanut farmer Jimmy Carter. May run for the

White House. If he gets in I think he's gonna grant amnesty to all draft dodgers. Means you can come home again!"

Tavo looked shocked "You think he could really pull that off?"

"Sure, man. Why not, if he's the Pres.?"

But even that couldn't pull him out of his funk. He was still trying to figure out how he was going to break the news to Nick. About the money he couldn't repay him. He had to pass on hanging with Mike, who took off to splash in the sea, sun himself like a beached whale on the cliffs, puff cigar-spliffs like a smokestack, drop a few Mandrex, gorge himself on three pound lobster, all that figuring about food had made him hungry. Oh ya and those naked nymphs hanging around Nick's bar had perked Mikes other hunger.

When the day of reckoning arrived, the sun shone as brightly as ever despite the cloud of doom following Tavo like a hovering John Crow.

But Nick's return was not near as fearsome as he anticipated. Before he could get there to tell him the bad news, Dee showed up so Tavo escorted him to Nick's bungalow and made a quick introduction. When Dee sat down, Tavo quickly informed Nick of the two thousand dollar short fall, stammering that he'd do his best to pay him back some of the money, but he thought Nick had overcharged him on the lease, knowing that business would slump. He felt he should cut him some slack. His timing was on target. Nick was at his most charming for those he considered VIP, and Dee was certainly in that category.

Instead of tearing into him, Nick dismissed him with a flick of his wrist and a brief look of disdain, like he were a serf worrying the king with some trivial matter. "Oh, don't bother me with your sniveling problems," he said "I could care less about a mere two thousand. Typical! Trust you to fuck up a moneymaking business. I expected it. Par for the course. Now leave us alone. We've important business to discuss."

"But what about the money?" Tavo pressured. He needed closure for his peace of mind.

"Will you PLEASE stop pestering me!" Nick shouted, he didn't want any mention of sliding profits in front of Dee. "Forget it! You don't owe me a cent. Stop your sniveling.

"Sure you won't reconsider going in on this deal?" said Dee. "I'd really like to combine the two properties."

"Don't waste your time with him" Nick said. "You'll eventually get his land anyway… I'll explain it all to you later—how he's fucked royally! Now leave us alone Gripps. Get Out NOW!"

He needed no further prodding. Let off the hook, for the lease, and in front of a witness to boot, he exited quickly, while the getting was good. At least his long hours of work hadn't put him in debt. It was a break-even deal, could have been much worse. He recalled yet another quote from Robinson Crusoe: "I saw, though too late, the folly of beginning a work before we count the cost, and before we judge rightly of our own strength to go through with it." He'd take that to heart in the future.

Two days later just after Mike returned to Chicago, Tavo heard the sound of a bicycle bell, not Heavy Higher's, this bell signaled the arrival of a telegram delivered from Negril's postal clerk. It was from Mike and all it said was, "Extremely Urgent. Call Me Immediately!" Shit! What was this all about? What could be so urgent? Mike wasn't usually given to hysterics, he figured it must be something important. Maybe a VIP booking for his Resort. He'd better find out what was up. So he found himself making another dreaded trip to Savanna La Mar.

Sav was just as blisteringly hot and insane. The stench of decaying garbage and animal waste assaulted his nostrils, but he only had to stand in line for one hour this time, and he stepped in only one pile of pig shit during the wait for the phone. Mike answered on the first ring with an aggressive, businesslike, "Island Hotline."

He had to shout in the phone to be heard over the singing static "Mike, this better be good! Calling from here makes Calcutta look first world. What the hell's so urgent?"

Mike's voice echoed and crackled over the poor connection "Oh, man, I'm glad you called! You're in some deep shit. Hang on to the phone booth, brace yourself man." "What are you talking about." Shouted Tavo." "When I left, got to Miami Airport, to connect with a Chicago flight, shit man, I was strip-searched. I'm talking body cavity search. Really humiliating man. The old rubber finger."

Tavo wiped sweat from his eyes and interrupted Mike's rambling "That's what you dragged me to Sav for, you idiot! You could a written me 'bout that!"

"No man. Wait. That isn't it at all. It's when I get out of Customs after being poked and prodded—I see this gal Dorothy way over in the distance, up against this supporting column. You know, the chick I met over at Nick's—always real out of it—screwed up on Mandrex—I was never able to get laid, she was seein' double all the time!"

"That's great, Mike. Just what I wanna hear about; the blue balls of your love life. Jesus Christ! I can't believe you!"

"Wait, man! Quit interrupting and just listen! That chick's trip was to strap a couple of bottles of Mandrex to her crotch, throw a granny dress on, smuggle 'em back to Miami. That's how she financed her trips back and forth to Negril. She told me all about it when I was trying to ball her. Anyways, I see her in the airport, talking to these three dudes. I figure after the hassle I'd been through I'd slide over, score me a few 'ludes for my trip back to Chicago 'fore she unloads 'em all. So I casually stroll over but as I get close, I see that two of those dudes are wearing three piece suits. Real strange man, can't figure no big time business man wasting his time with a piddly shit couple bottles of 'ludes."

Exasperated now, Tavo slammed his fist into the door of the booth "Okay, man. Get to the point. This long distance is costing a fortune."

"Ya, I know, kid. Hang in there. Gotta give you the background first. Anyways, I get closer still and sees one of the dudes is a long hair. "What's goin' on here?' I'm wondering, so I sneaks up real close, hid on the other side of the big pillar to listen, peep around the corner. Shit. It was that Dee guy man. The guy you pointed out to me at Nick's—the one you said wants to buy your property and the Cafe. Now I am really curious, see. Can't figure out why some big shot space cowboy is messing around with someone like her; never gave that chick a second look at Nick's. I slide a little closer, my back to the column—just outta sight and listen real close. Man, Dorothy is weeping hysterically. All three guys, even Dee are shaking her down. Like they're threatening her with ten to twenty years in prison if she don't cooperate, lay a dime on who she's smuggling for!" Tavos legs started to tremble. "Man, I didn't know what to do. I'm still pissed off at being shaken down in Customs myself, so I back way up, maybe ten yards, pretend to be wandering casual like through the airport, looking for my plane connection. Walk right up to 'em and say, 'Hey, Dee! What's happenin' man?' Know what? He immediately jumps over to Dorothy, wraps his arm around her, comforts her, and smooth as silk says that the two suits are DEA agents, just busted her for smuggling, and he's only lending her a hand, hiring a couple of lawyers to take her case. Tells me 'Not to worry' he'll have her released in a coupla hours. Poor Dorothy is so stoned, confused, scared, she doesn't say a thing, just keeps crying, actually puts her head on his shoulder. Looks real convincing. Only, I'd heard what went down before. Man, that guy coulda won an Oscar for his performance. Then he turns to me, says, 'If you talk to Nick tell him everything's okay,' I played dumb. 'Sure thing,' I tells him, 'Good luck,' something lame like that. Anyways, that's why I telegrammed you. Keep away from him man. He's a DEA agent for sure!"

Tavo slumped down and sat on the bottom of the phone booth, said nothing for a few seconds just let the phone dangle there, then realized that Mike was still on the line picked it up. "What a bummer! Thanks for the warning man. I don't think I've got anything to sweat though. But things make sense now. He sure tried to pry information outta me. Even tried to get me to smoke a spliff with him. Good thing I'm clean."

"Better warn Nick," Mike said.

Tavo had the same thoughts, and said, "I'm sure Nick saw right through him." But why would he mention a meeting for next week? Would have thought Nick would've blown him off!

"Yeah, well you better make sure he knows the score," Mike said.

"Yeah, right. No problem," Tavo said. "Thanks again for the info." Mike hung up. He stood there staring at a pregnant goat nosing through a pile of garbage at his feet. The dead phone buzzing in his hand, until a fat, sweating mama poked him in the side with her umbrella. Prodded him to move his bumba claat aside so she could call her pickney in Brooklyn.

On the way back to Negril, it really sunk in. Dee had tried to set him up with a well-planned out sham. An undercover DEA agent trolling the waters for information and victims! And to think of the taxpayers' money he was blowing every night at Nicks to set up his cover! Nick was probably really furious at him by now. He had to have seen through the guy's bullcrap immediately, tore into him and laughed in his face. By now, Nick probably wanted his lease money he'd so graciously let slide. But why had he set up another meeting? Maybe he was going to string the guy along and then burst his bubble, screw around with him… play the fish, give him more rope to hang himself with. Anyway, he figured he might as well face the music with Nick sooner rather than later. Neither one of them was going anywhere now, and he might just as well try to set a payment schedule that wouldn't kill him, then get on with his own life. At least his ass wasn't exposed.

23

Jamaican mon a trouble
Y-O
Nigga mon a trouble
Nigga mon a break ya bones

Traditional Jamaican Calypso

Tavo walked into Nick's that evening, stiffening his resolve to withstand the abuse and tantrums he expected. The usual assembly of Rastas and freaks were free jumping off the cliffs without a care and the sun was executing its slow, graceful dive behind enormous cumulus clouds, creating a brilliant burst of colorful firework displays against the horizon.

Sam was doing a brisk business selling grams of coke at the bar. The line of buyers almost as long as those waiting to buy the iced smoothie blended tropical drinks.

Jamie Dice lounged against a coconut tree, arm around a gorgeous blond—her naked tits stood out like ripe grapefruits. Dice cupped one and leered an evil grin at him; he had a black patch over his cataract eye now. Made him look just like a degenerate murderous pirate. He pointed at him now, said something to the blond that he couldn't hear over the blasting music. They both broke up in laughter.

He walked away, ignored them, found Nick trying to oversee his main event, swinging in his hammock, stoned on "the good stuff". His head bobbed on his chest and his eyelids drooped like he was on the verge of sleep. "Well-l-l, my friend

Tavo," he garbled his words like he'd just woken from a deep sleep, "bang up with me, join my ascent to Nirvana."

Nick's arm dangled limply. A punctured wound stood out on a blue vein; a needle lay on the wooden deck below him with a red outline of blood in its glass vile. Tavo kicked it away, shook the hammock, forcing him to make eye contact "Listen man, snap out of it! We gotta talk. I'm sure you saw through Dee, so I just want to say I'm sorry for dragging you back from Africa for his phony scheme. I'd no idea it was a trap 'til I talked to Dorfman."

Even in his smack-induced fog certain words began to penetrate, "Settle down…" he said imperiously. "What are you rambling about? My business dealings with that lovely man are really no concern of yours. In a few weeks… " Tavo waited a few seconds while he nodded off into a deep sleep, then he sprung back from wherever he'd retreated and continued, as if no interruption had occurred. "In a few weeks, I'll be on my worldwide journey in pursuit of the best beaches—the most beautiful people life has to offer. I'll go to Bali, Thailand, Katmandu, Java, Martinique, wherever the winds blow me, wherever the opium poppy blooms year 'round. Jamaica's become a middle class nightmare; very low class. The movie is over; leave your seat; exit the rear."

"This ain't no movie man! Don't tell me you made a deal with him?" Tavo shouted incredulously, shaking Nick's hammock again, trying to get through to him.

"Stop rocking my hammock" he said, peering at Tavo through dilated pupils, having trouble seeing him. "Not that it's any of your business, but I'm conducting, uh financial discussions with him. He's obsessed with thoughts of owning Nick's and Banana Shout. Real impulsive… stupid enough to offer me a fortune for the rights to reign supreme on this decaying paradise, ha, ha, ha. Fuck him! That's his problem. What do I care if he doesn't have the, um foresight to see the downward spiral of Negril… long as I have his money!"

Tavo couldn't believe his ears "Man, don't tell me you made a deal with him! He's a fake, a fraud!"

"What are you prattling about, Tavo?" he cut in. "Try main line, mellow yourself out… your hyperactivity… making me nervous, really bringing me down. You're such a fucking pest!"

"Look man," Tavo cried grabbing the hammock again, shaking even harder. "Don't you get it! Dee's a DEA agent. He's trying to build a case; obtain information on whoever he can. I just hope you didn't open up about Len or Dice or the rest of 'em, cause if you did, your ass is grass."

That was enough to penetrate even Nick's numbed consciousness. He flew out of the hammock like he'd been seared by hot iron. Clutching Tavo's T-shirt with both hands, he shook him, demanded to know why he would say such vicious lies. But the sweat that poured from his forehead, armpits and the palms of his hands made it plain he knew all too well Tavo wasn't putting him on.

He recounted in detail his phone conversation with Dorfman. Nick quivered and shook, actually cried. He'd swallowed Dee's charade like a hungry bass goes after a wiggling night crawler. And, what's more, he'd bragged about every intricate detail: the financing of Nick's Cafe with drug-smuggling monies; the names of those who invested in the enterprise and the intricate machinations of Len's and Dice's export company. He was in some deep shit. All the China White or Persian Brown heroin couldn't blot him out of this one, unless he overdosed, which, by now, he was seriously contemplating.

Nick wobbled back and forth on his shaking feet, so stoned on smack; he almost fell flat on his face. He grabbed a hold of Tavo's T-shirt with both hands to stop his fall, steady himself. He tried to shake him, but he was so out of it there was no power, no force in his hands. All he could really do was hang on to him, tears streamed down his cheeks, his face contorted in a fearful grimace. "You have to do something!" he wailed. "This is all your fault, oh God they'll kill me! Cut my dick off… shove it down my throat! You're the one, its all your fault, you scum!"

Tavo pushed him away, shoved him back down into his hammock. It wasn't hard; he had no strength left in him—cause of the smack—cause of the news. He started to go into another nod. He was mumbling now, blabbering like a baby. "All Tavo's fault… should never married Jane, all her fault…. Parents didn't give me money…. Norman's fault… let party get out of hand… oh God, oh God gotta get out of town… score more smack… go to Mexico… no, no, too close, the dopes too weak… Nigeria's better…. Maybe Iran… oh no, oh no, I shouldn't have mooned the Rabbi at my Bar Mitzvah, pissed dad off… oh shit! I'm a dead man, dead man…. Tell them its all Tavo's fault, his fault.

Tavo knew Nick would do just that, push as much blame as he could on him. He was in deep trouble. Nick not only disclosed the details of his Café financing and Len and Dice's smuggling operations to Dee; he'd also bragged of their plans to use Tavo's caves to store their weed. He boasted that to get Tavo's land, all Dee had to do was jus wait for Tavo to be busted, then give him a pittance for the land, just enough to make bail. He'd have it all then!

Tavo felt as low as a wingless fly on a cowflop in Death Valley. His predicament was partially his own fault for having been taken in by Dee, like Nick said, and he knew that Dice would thoroughly agree; would hold him responsible too. Nick would try and worm out of it, lay it on him. This looked like the end; caught right between the DEA and a murderous drug smuggler… the best he could hope for was live imprisonment. His dreams of paradise up in a cloud of ganja smoke.

Mannie found him later that day outside his lean-to, slumped over, head in his hands, staring at a group of industrious ants who were burrowing out a new colony with bureaucratic precision, plagued by none of the hassles man creates to impede his own progress.

"Why you look so screw face, mon?" he asked. "You resemble porpoise with him mouth upside down!"

Tavo gave him a mournful look, shaking his head "I'm in big trouble, me and Nick. Man, I don't know how I always wind up in the thick of things. All I do is try to mind my own business."

"Dats the way life go sometime mon! What happen? Tings not so bad if you reason it out."

So he told him the entire story about Dee, Nick's disastrous disclosures, the sham million bucks and the franchise trade. But Mannie showed little empathy for his plight. In fact, he was downright pleased. "Mon, me never trust dat Dee," he said with a sly smirk. "Him informer, na true? Him a bring million US dollars a Jamaica fe buy Nick's? But dat no problem for you. Dat more a problem fe Dee… good fortune fe we."

Tavo smacked his forehead with the palm of his hand, exacerbated, frustrated with Mannies reasoning and said, "Man, don't you get it? He's a DEA for Christ sake! He's just going to show that money to Nick to keep up his front. He's setting up a bust for Stern and Dice and me too! When they find out who brought the heat down on 'em it'll be all hell to pay for me." Tavo rose to his feet, paced around the ant colony, furiously smacking his forehead as if that might drive a solution into his brain.

Mannie kicked at the anthill, scattering ants in all directions. "Calm down mon!" he said. "Mek we reason dis ting out. Maybe dere's a solution. You say you don't want Dice use your lands for smuggling. Now, if him get a bust him can't use it again. So dat take care a dat" He rung his hands in a washing motion to emphasize his solution like he'd cleared the matter up.

Tavo poked at the scurrying ants with a stick shook his head and said, "Yeah, but Dice will get busted after he uses my land then I'll get busted too. Don't you see? I'm still fucked!" But Mannie would not be swayed or didn't understand. "Forget bout that for now man." He said, "Me want to know more 'bout that big money Dee gonna bring. My mother always used to say dat a fool an him money easy fe separate, and me don't have no problem separating that rass-hole from him money. No problem mon! I just wan know when him bring it!"

Tavo looked at him as if he had lost his mind, he couldn't believe what he was hearing, and shouted. " You can't rob the DEA! What are you, crazy? Besides, when Dice uses my property for smuggling and gets cracked, he'll implicate me. Rat me out. Don't you see? I got no way outa this mess!"

"Me no say anything 'bout rob, me no tief!" Mannie said wrinkling his brow in deep thought. "A plan just come to me brain. You never hear 'bout Robin Hood?"

"Yea, sure. Rob the rich and give to the poor. So what! What's your point?"

"Yes man, dat da point, brother. And nobody never say Robin Hood a wicked thief. Him only take from the wicked rich people who make all the evil law to tax de poor. So him no really tief, only get even. All the common peoples love him. Is same way here. Jamaicans no invite DEA here to fool 'round… cause worries in our land. Him is just like dat bad sheriff. We no want fe him foreign laws 'bout the herb here. We no business wid dat! Him need fe learn a rass lesson. Play with puppy, puppy lick you face. Ah oh!"

Mannie sat Tavo on the ground and sketched out a plan in the dirt with his stick, destroying the rest of the ant colony but leaving an ugly ant lion's lair nearby greedily sucking up scurrying ants. What he proposed was uncomplicated enough, but involved components that Tavo thought could lead to an international war! And hairs on the back of his neck stood on end.

Mannie said he'd engage the help of the local Negril constabulary. No problem mon! Negril had only the two policemen and Mannie knew them both well, they grew up together in Orange Hill, hell, one was his cousin. All he had to do to cement their cooperation was share the loot. After all, they were poor too. Tavo would join in, he was needed to find out the time and date of Dee's arrival and not let on to anyone else, not even Dice or Stern, that he knew Dee's true identity.

Mannie would coordinate with his cousin, Constable Dalton "Ding-Dong" Bell, the head of the Negril station, to set up a roadblock just outside of town. Road blocks were no big deal, remember Prime Minister Michael Manley feared that the CIA was actively engaged in smuggling weapons into the island for a coup d'etat. So these road checks happened all the time searching for guns, and all vehicles were stopped. If drugs were found and you didn't have the right family relationships, say la vie. Sometimes the searches included the passengers' persons, and no one was exempt from this hassle, not even foreign tourists. But buying the arresting officer a couple of cold beers could usually settle the matter. Large quantities plus a million American dollars was a different matter. Under Jamaica's stringent currency laws to protect the export of foreign currency, persons found with more than a few hundred US dollars had better have a damn good explanation or face immediate arrest, prosecution and stiff jail sentences.

Mannie was so excited he was jumping up and down like a Zulu warrior, stuttering a rapid stream of patois, Tavo could hardly understand him. "Ding-Dong him personally, search Dee's taxi and seize de money! We be rich mon!" Tavo grabbed his shoulders with both hands, shook him, and looked him straight in the eye. "Listen man," he yelled. "Stop hoppin up an down for gods sakes down! We'll all get busted man!

You can't rob the DEA. That's like robbing the American government!"

Mannie tried to collect himself but his eyes darted around like a wild mans. "Listen, mon." he said "Ding-Dong will plant five pound of ganja in the car. He'll bust Dee for dealing in herb… dealing in black market currency! The judge send him away for three—four years and we take all de monies!"

"You're insane." Tavo said. "America's not going to let you get away with throwing one of their agents in the slammer… then walk with all that cash! Get real!"

"You na no know nufin mon! George Bush really piss off Michael Manley. When your country nuh pay we for our bauxite, Michael invite Castro here. Castro say not to worry. Him wi build our hospitals, schools, even bring doctors here to treat de people dem for free! Say all exploited people must stick together, help one another! Castro him nother Robin Hood! Den America do some foolishness wid de World Bank, stop all loan and credit to we. Nixon behind dat one. Rice, flour and salt fish so short, poor people a starve. Me hears it all on de JBC. Michael him vex bad bad. Him na have no love fe no CIA, FBI, or DEA mon. Him nah talk to America no more… him na mind Dee spend a few years a bruck rock stone a General Penitentiary. Ah oh! Make him think twice to romp wid neaga mon again! Dis be REVOLUTION!"

Tavo couldn't believe his ears. Son of a bitch! Another Vietnam! No escaping this time. "Yeah, well I'm screwed either way," he groaned. "I'm sure Dee reported everything about Nick, Stern… Dice and me to his higher-ups in the DEA. I'm American, not Jamaican, and a draft dodger and a drug smuggler, caught right in the middle."

Mannie was still too excited to take him seriously, to let any of his worries sink in. He had dollar signs in his eyes "Me nuh know mon," he said "You cyaan change dat… too bad your country so sneaky. But me put dat money to good use build me own resort, develop big cattle ranch and peanut farm! Send me five pickney to secondary school, even university."

"Don't you get it?" Tavo wailed. "This could cause a war!"

"War? Me no business with war! America start war pon we aready. All we do a defend we country. Poor people wi dead fe hungry, we nuh grow herb, own we bauxite. If America so 'fraid fe ganja, dem people shouldn't smoke it. Dice just giving your people what dem like. Dee shoulda stay a him own yard, spend time dealin' wid it over dere! A nuh fi we problem." Mannie broke his ant poking stick across his knee in anger, it made a nasty crack. He had worked himself up into a rage forgetting about the money now. Americas covert meddling really offended him.

"Look," Tavo said, trying to calm him down now. "This is going to result in serious trouble." But Mannie wasn't listening. All worked up now about the injustices, indignant as hell, he pounded his fist in his open palm. "So what Uncle Sam gon do? Drop a big bomb pon we?"

"I wouldn't put it past him" Tavo said, "Not one big bomb but a lot of little ones, just like Vietnam! Shit! I woulda been better off there!"

"You worry too much mon! Jamaican people love you. You is a man of honor, Tavo. You no wear two face under one hat. This be your home now, for better or worse. Stop fret mon! We all going get rich! Irie Brother!"

24

"And hey—hey, Mr cop
Ain't' got no birth cerv-atificate on me now
Road Block"

Bob Marley

Tavo needed space to think, time to think—about where he'd been… where he was heading. He just couldn't get a handle on any of it; it just got worse day by day!

Negril's seven miles beach provided the space, the solitude. He wandered along its powdery, palm-lined sands as the sea licked at his feet. The same beach he'd washed up on with Striker just three short years ago. He searched his head for solutions. But all that came was, his land of sanctuary would soon become another war zone. Napalm would burn the lush jungles and melt the beach into a hunk of hardened glass. The six foot high mounds of discarded pink conch shells that gleamed in the sun gave no hint to his dilemma, any more than the fishermen's children frolicking in the waves. They were as oblivious as fish swimming in the sea to what was taking place around them, until they were hooked and yanked from the depths.

Why couldn't his life be as clear as the crystalline waters alongside him? Might as well go along with Mannie's plan. Six of one, half a dozen of the other. If Dee could be stopped, he'd at least some chance of averting certain disaster from Dice for the short term. If he got a little revenge in the bargain, well that's just the icing on the cake.

He headed straight to Nick's, armed with Mannie's proposal. But when Nick spotted him standing over his hammock, he flinched, burying his face in his hands, trembling.

"Oh God," he said; "what kind of fuckery are you going to lay on me today? I can't take it any more. Oh please God! Leave me alone! Leave me alone! It's all your fault!"

"Cut the my fault crap, this ain't no fuckery," Tavo said with more assurance than he felt. " We might have a way out!"

"What did you bring, a loaded gun, a change of identity… the Federal Protection Program?"

Tavo laid out Mannie's whole plan, leaving out no details, stressing the possibly that maybe the DEA wouldn't risk more men or further involvement and just drop everything… snoop somewhere less risky.

"That just might work," Nick said, recovering some composure, pondering the possibilities, then said with just a crack of his old Cheshire Cat grin, "I've got nothing to lose. With that lying scum bag rotting away in some Jamaican jail, I never have to let on that you made me let the cat out of the bag." Widening his grin just a little more now. "Hey, maybe we can even pick up on some of that money. What do you say?… old pal! Why, we can con those dumb niggers out of our fair share of the money—you know, for our cooperation!"

"No way!" Tavo said. "Just feel lucky if this saves your ass man!"

"You're a sanctimonious fucking hypocrite," Nick shouted. "They couldn't pull it off without us! Where do you think you're coming from, you beer guzzling hillbilly?"

"Fuck you!" Tavo snapped, fed up with Nick's insults. "Just keep Dee on the hook. Don't let on that his cover's blown. If you screw this up, you're on your own! You try and get any of that money, you'll wind up playing Superman ten thousand feet in the air, out the door of Jaime Dice's ganja plane."

"Take a flying fuck at a rolling doughnut, you Pollack," Nick screamed.

"Just stay out of it" Tavo warned "and let me know what flight Dee's on or your ass is grass, and you fucking well know it!"

Nick simmered, his face turned red in frustration, he wanted that dough. "Yeah, yeah. You'll know." He finally said, "Now get out! Leave me alone. If I never see your ass again it will be too soon! This whole mess is all your fault anyway, Dr Fraud Psychologist. You couldn't even tell the difference between real wealth and a scum sucking DEA agent! You make me want to puke! I hate your guts! Hate you! You fraud!"

Tavo went straight to his yard and saw Mannie jumping up and down again, like that Zulu again, under a coconut palm, waving his arms like a windmill, sputtering and stammering, agitated. Circling him were a group of eight men and women. As he got closer, he realized they were his newly arrived guests from California. Some were crying.

"What's going on here?" he demanded. "What happened with Ding Dong? Why are these guests crying?"

"Ding Dong soon come. Him love it!" Mannie said with a grin.

"So what's with the guests man? What's wrong? Plumbing break? Water lock off again?"

"No, man. I just talking to dem. Dese hippies, cho man! …the weirdest ones me see so far… say dem come from some East tribe."

"That's EST—an encounter group," shouted a bearded guy proudly, the most collected of the group. "Your yardman is crude… rude, but also enlightening! I'm sorry to say!"

"I don't get it!" said Tavo "What's the problem?"

Mannie pointed his finger at the group shaking it "Tavo, dese peoples loves to be upset. Dem tell me seh dem pay thousands of dollars to sit round inna a circle den insult one another. Dem do it for days. So me tell dem seh me wi insult dem fe much less. Me call them rass hole and bumba claat—everyt'ing me think of. But dem no pay me yet!"

"Yes, yes," said the bearded guy. "He's absolutely right. Having others point out our faults and weaknesses we come to understand ourselves, and…."

Mannie interrupted, looking like he finally understood, "I gets it!" he said, "You pay a money to somebody to call you a dumb shit! But me specs you must already know you is one."

A rat faced, skinny woman broke into tears again, "Now see here, my good fellow," she blubbered "you're taking this a bit far. That's not the point at all."

"This therapy has gone far enough for one day," Tavo interjected. "Why don't you break up now, chill out, take a swim!"

The group agreed. They'd taken this session to the limit, but they invited Mannie to attend an encounter the following morning on the beach. Claimed they would break through his cultural stereotyping, and, at the same time, free themselves of their own prejudices. Mannie absolutely refused. If any of them called him an asshole, he'd punch them in the nose.

When they left, Mannie put his arm around Tavo confided in him, he hoped Dee was a member of the East tribe too, that way, jail wouldn't be so hard on him. But he knew that Jamaicans in the slammer would do more than call him an asshole—they'd tear him a new one.

"That bothers me a lot, " Tavo said. "How long you think he'll be in jail for?"

"Who can say? America been seizing Air Jamaica planes. Dem say dem find weed 'pon dem, but never let Jamaican authorities see de herb. When de judge see Dee a transport plenty ganja, he not go so easy. It payback time! And don't forget," he said rubbing his thumb and forefinger together, "de judge have piece of the action too"

That didn't set well with Tavo. He wasn't sure Dee's punishment fit his crime. He's probably just a recent college graduate trying to do his job, following orders. His chances for survival in a Jamaican jail were slim to none—hard labor on a diet of rice and peas. If that didn't kill him, his ass-banging buddies would!

Just then drumming sounded from a newly formed Rastafarian camp that had taken up residence on Heavy Higher's land. A brother dread from Kingston, Jawa had recently moved there with his dreadlocke flock. Now African drumming echoed from there through the days. Usually it took on a soothing, heartbeat rhythm, but today, it sounded a warning. Tavo wished the drumming would take him back in time too, to a jungle where the enemy was clearly defined; easily understood. His favorite cartoon character, Pogo Possum, popped into his mind for some strange reason. "We've met the enemy and the enemy is us." Pogo shouted. Good grief he thought, he must be losing his mind. As he contemplated his sanity, Mannie shook him back to the hear and now, and said, "Dee arriving today—must pedal me bicycle down de road to police station! Check it out!" Jawa's drums suddenly went silent. For once, the stillness seemed oppressive. But Tavo's heart beat louder than any drum. Then he heard the shrill cry of a cling-cling bird. The bush was listening; waiting to learn its fate, waiting to respond.

25

"I'm gonna rescue you
For I'm courageous

—Larry Duncan
From the song *Rescue You*
On Air Freight
Black Market Reggae Band

Tavo's palms sweated; his heart raced. He'd made up his mind to try and help Dee. He had to. He couldn't let the guy rot; die in jail even if he was a schmuck. All he really tried to do was dig up info on him and there wasn't anything on him yet to discover… hell he didn't deserve to die for that, he was just a young guy like himself.

Everyday there were stories in the Gleaner newspaper of Jamaicans dying in jail. They stuffed prisoners in twenty or more to a ten by ten foot cell and they dropped dead like flies, succumbing to heat exhaustion, suffocation, and dehydration. If tough locals who were used to this heat and deprivation couldn't make it, Dee didn't have a chance.

The sun was setting, and it would soon be dark. Maybe a good night's sleep would help him to see things clearer, formulate a plan. He popped the cap on an iced Red Stripe and wandered down to his cliff-front to catch the evening breeze and the sun set, he had to think had to calm himself. Just as he was sitting down on the cliff edge, trying to force his legs into a lotus position like Donna, meditate on the horizon, the shit hit the fan from every direction.

A huge dump truck rambled down his drive, coughing and spewing black diesel fumes, groaning under its load. It stopped on the small rise just behind one of his bungalows. Jamie Dice jumped out of the passenger's side, dressed in all black leather looking more menacing than ever. He began shouting orders to a crew of six Jamaicans who sat on top of what looked like a load of topsoil.

"Get your asses in gear motherfuckers," he yelled through clenched teeth, biting down hard on a cigar-shaped spliff, sounding like a viscous slave driver; all he lacked was a bloody whip. "Shovel that dirt off! Move those bales into that goddamn cave! I want this shit stored away now!" The time had arrived to set his smuggling operation into motion. It was time to follow through with his threats. Tavo was fucked!

Dice slowly swaggered over to him, curled his lip back over his spliff, and fixed him with a menacing one-eyed stare that read 'Don't even think of messing with me'. He pulled out a silver plated colt 45, it almost looked like a toy, but it wasn't. He fired a round off into the air, over Tavos head, then pointed it at his chest. But before he could say anything, or issue any verbal threats someone yelled from his front gate—the one the truck had just pulled through, the one Dice had padlocked shut. The voice sounded like a young woman's. "Gotta check whose here." he mumbled. "Yeah? Go-wan," Dice said. "Just don't bring no one snooping around… get rid 'o the bitch … ya know what's good for ya!" To drive home his point, he waved the 45's barrel under Tavo's nose, smacking his nose with it, causing it to bleed.

Tavo staggered to his gate trying to rub the blood from his nose. He was hurt more mentally than physically. When the day of reckoning arrived he'd wimped out once again. But as he walked closer to the gate he couldn't believe his eyes. His knees trembled. They threatened to buckle under him. Standing there and smiling that unforgotten smile was Irene, her eyes sparkling green and hazel in the sun set—more amazing to him than any Green Splash. It was all he could do to walk the few feet between them; he had to grab hold of some pusstail flowers that lined the drive for support. They broke off, so when he was finally face to face with her, he was clutching handfuls of the long, fuzzy, red flowers, he must have looked odd indeed, like his hands were sprouting red dread locks. Irene giggled and threw her arms around him over the gate, giving him a hug he'd never stopped dreaming about.

"Oh, Tavo," she cried. "I've missed you so much." Tears flowed down her cheeks. Tavo wouldn't let her go. Kept right on hugging her over the gate, the pusstails still clutched in his trembling hands. All his fears about Dice vanished. Irene finally broke their embrace and stood there, looking at him, laughing and crying at the same time. "Well, aren't you going to invite me in?" she asked. "Or are you just going to stand there holding those weird flowers?"

Tavo threw the puss tails down, fumbled with the lock on the gate and his mouth; he had to pick the lock with his penknife. He finally got both to work.

"Irene," he finally gasped. "What are you doing here?"

"I'm here on vacation with Harlen," she said and his hopes collapsed along with his heart. She could see his disappointment. Impossible for him to hide it.

"Forgot." Was all he said, sounding as dumb as he felt.

Irene hugged him again "Please Tavo, don't talk about him… I'm just glad—real glad—that you still care. Come on; show me your place. I don't have a lot of time."

Tavo started to lead her down the pathway to the sea dejected now then remembered Dice and the ganja. "Go this way instead," he said, actually he was shouting, and pushed her to his first cottage just out of sight of the marijuana truck, where Dices workmen were busy unloading the huge bales.

"Tavo, why are you pushing me?" she protested. He realized that he was actually shoving her down the garden pathway.

"I'm sorry," he said. "It's just that I'm so flabbergasted—overwhelmed—seeing you again. How did you ever find me?" She turned to him gazing into his eyes; she held his hand and squeezed it. He thought he saw something in her look, a flicker of old feelings, maybe even of love.

"Your old friends know where you are," she said "I run into them sometimes… they brag about you all the time. They miss you too." She squeezed his hand again, making certain that he was still there. "But you," he asked "Why? I mean I'm glad, but how did you…." Irene cut him off "I convinced Harlen to take a vacation here. He's too pious to be jealous, so he agreed and here I am" and smiled the smile he loved, had always dreamed of.

When they reached his cottage his hands were trembling so much, he couldn't get the door open. He dropped the key at least five times. He finally forced the key into the hole using both hands to steady his shaking and led Irene inside. He burned his fingers while trying to light a kerosene lantern. Then Irene started telling him about her marriage. Things didn't sound too great and his hopes rose. Harlen, she said, was a complete sweat sock, thinking only of his work, his practice, and his office, where he spent most of his waking hours. And life in Bloomfield Hills, Michigan was a complete bore. Harlen figured her place was in the home, arranging flowers and fluffing throw pillows, catering to his every need. As for sex, she started to explain and Tavo shuddered, leaned forward, wanting to know but at the same time dreading to hear. But before she had a chance to say anything the front door flew open with a bang, almost dropping off its hinges. Mannie stood in the doorway silhouetted in the lamplight with two bulging one hundred pound flour sacks slung over his shoulders. He was dripping sweat. He dumped the sack's contents on the floor at Irene's feet. It was Jamaican currency; a pile of twenty dollar bound bills towering four feet high, looked like over a million JA dollars.

"Jesus Christ!" Tavo shouted, his eyes bugged out, so did Irene's. "What's going on here?" she said, "Who's he? What's that?"

Before Mannie could answer or Tavo make up an excuse, another figure cast a long dark shadow across the light—none other than Harlen Rosenthal. He stood there, hands on his hips, oozing pompous disgust and contempt. He looked more evil than he had at the draft board. He sneered at Tavo. "I'll tell you what's going on, Irene." He said "When our table at Nicks was ready and you weren't back, I walked over to look for you. I proceeded down to the cliff front—even though you know I don't like heights—thinking maybe you were watching the sunset. Well, I saw it all," and he shook his fist at Tavo. "I always told you he was a sociopath, with a severely deviant personality disorder. Now I have the proof. This little worm's a marijuana smuggler. I saw a group of Negroes stacking huge bales of it in some God-awful cave. I just barely made it out of there with my life. Those savages looked like they would have cut my throat. Want proof?" And he gave a wicked ugly laugh and thrust a pointing bony finger at the money. "Just look at that stack of illegal currency lying at your feet." Then he crossed his arms tightly over his chest to emphasize his point. Irene looked at Tavo then at the money then at Harlen and back at the money. Mannie seemed oblivious to it all. He just sat there on his haunches staring at his cash. "Come, Irene" Harlen ordered. "Our table is ready. I warned you that seeing him again would only upset you. You know, dear, you really can't take this kind of excitement." Harlen began to tug at her arm; he tried to pull her out the door. Irene wiggled out of his grasp, stomped her foot.

"Harlen, I am not excited… not the way you think." She turned and faced Tavo. "Is this true what he said?" She looked up at him, her green eyes pleading for him to deny it.

"No. No. I swear. It's rather complicated; but I'm not involved in any of it. Honest to God!"

"So now he's got another label right from the books" Harlen snorted "pathological liar. Come Irene, before you regress into hysterics."

"Wait! Give him a chance to explain…. And don't tell me what to do!"

"Calm yourself Irene. I'll give him a chance. If only to show you once and for all… how fortunate you are to have terminated your relationship with that psychopath" he said and puffed himself up with self-important piety. "I'll even buy him dinner tomorrow and he can explain all he wants then. That's how much above this little melodrama I am. Have him join us tomorrow night at Nick's Café. I really hate to do this—take him apart in front of you. It won't be pretty, but the time has come, Irene, for you to let go of any old misshapen fantasies you may still be clinging to."

Reluctantly, Irene started to leave, but when they reached the door, she turned and said, "See you tomorrow Tavo. Don't forget. You have to come."

Tavo stood there stunned by it all. He hadn't been able to say a word, to confused by everything, the money, Dices pistol waving, the smuggling, Rosenthal, Irene, everything hitting him at once! Sensory overload! Mannie ignored it all, too busy counting five-inch stacks of the money into three-foot piles. Not paying the least bit of attention to what had just happened. Tavo tried to shake his trance and stepped in front of Mannie. "What's happening" he asked more for just something to say to help break his trance. He figured he knew all to well already.

"Dee, him taken care of now." Mannie said "Ding-Dong have him in lockup. Dis my share—half a million dollars US but me change it into Jamaican monies on de black market, worth more den!" Mannie smiled up at Tavo with the self-assured smile of a rich man. But there was something else in his smile. "Mon! Me see de way dat gal look pon you, see you loves her—loves her bad," he said and winked at Tavo. "Now you and she can live here together. Me leff. Is time. I gonna build my own resort now. You knows everything you need to know 'bout Jamaica. You learns to walk good in our land. We's always brothers in spirit. Ah-O!"

For about the hundredth time in this crazy mixed up day, he didn't know what to say. There were tears in his eyes. He hugged Mannie. Asked him to stay but knew he wouldn't. Mannie told him to live with his gal now, have pickneys now. Tavo told him he doubted if Irene would ever live with him—she was married to that tall guy she just left with. Mannie looked at him like he was a fool. "Me see de way she look pon you," he said again. "A you she love mon. She no love dat deh tall nasty stone face man. Him look like him drop in a pool a cement—stiffen him up. Dat mon no have no love in him to give anyone. Ah oh!"

"I don't know," Tavo said.

"Yes mon! You go after dat gal, mon! It no matter she married. Don't bother yourself 'bout dat business. Dat only laws, not de heart!"

"Listen, I feel like I'm being drawn and quartered… pulled in a hundred directions. I can't even think straight. What's gonna happen to Dee? Look what Dice's up to! He's got ten tons of dope in my cave for Christ sake!"

Mannie just laughed, shook Tavo's hand and said, "Don't worry bout Dee, Ding Dong plant de herb on him. Him tek a quarter of de money. De other quarter him give to him brother de judge. Dee not any trouble again. Him well take care of. Only leave Jamie Dice and de gal you gots to be concern 'bout. As for de gal, me thinks dats a sure bet if you nuh mek dat stiff man follie 'round with you. For Dice, me nuh know. Is time you stand up to him. Run him off… make him give you a money. Him not so tough. Dere always be bullies mon, but dem no bully you, you nuh let dem!"

"Easier said than done." Said Tavo. Mannie just shook his head and looked at all the cash lying at his feet. "Time me leff. You is on your own now. But you really always was. Jus' nuh know it. Me have no worries 'bout you. You walk good!" He started to stuff the cash back into the sacks it took him awhile. Tavo watched him, forlorn, wishing he was as sure of Irene as Mannie. When Mannie finished he slung the sacks over his broad shoulders and disappeared into the pitch-black night.

Tavo sat alone. He tried to prioritize, but it everything seemed equally pressing. At least some things, like his meeting with Irene, were put off 'till tomorrow. Yes, he still loved her more than ever. And Dice wasn't scheduled to set sail until tomorrow night either, according to Mannie that's when his smuggling boat would arrive. That pushed the matter of Dee to priority number one. He felt like the guy who spun plates on poles for "The Ed Sullivan Show;" the guy who ran back and forth from one to the next, trying to keep them all rotating, until the spinning reached a crescendo and they all came crashing down.

He fired up the old Moke and drove down to the police station, not knowing what he'd do when he arrived, but figuring he had to at least check on Dee. The police station was no more than an old two-room clapboard shack, equipped with a rotting desk held up by a slanting wooden floor. Attached to it was a 1950 aluminum house trailer about thirty feet long and partitioned into eight tiny cells by old plywood boards, where selected prisoners waited until they could be sent to the Savanna La Mar lock-up.

As Tavo neared the jail screams, he heard shouts and cursing echoing loudly from the trailer's tin walls. When he entered the office he saw Ding-Dong Bell seated behind his old desk, feet propped up, his pressed red striped shirt unbuttoned to the waist, a new gold chain adorned his neck. He was smoking a cigar and sharing a case of beer with another officer. Reggae music blared from a small portable radio to drown out the clamor from the holding pens.

Ding Dong rose unsteadily to his feet and grabbed Tavo's hand, pumping it furiously "Tavo, mon, you one good

American! Come in mon! Pull up a chair, grab a beer. Dey ice cold and me have plenty more out back!"

"Thanks," he said. "But I need to have a serious talk with you. Right now!"

"No problem, mon. Drink a Red Stripe. Drink as many as you likes, make we reason de res' of de night!"

The iced beer froze Tavo's pipes all the way down; cleared some of the haze from his head. But Bell was excitedly making plans for how he would spend his share of the captured money. He wouldn't shut up for a minute.

"Tavo mon, dis some of me last days in dis here uniform" he said proudly thumping his chest with his fist. "Me bound for Hollywood. Dat in California, don't it? Well, me going there anyway. Me a go star inna movies mon. Yes mon! Cowboy movies. Shoot me Colt 45 just like de Lone Ranger and dat Outlaw Jose Wales. Me look better dan dat Sidney Portier. Ah oh! Him star inna one cowboy movie me see... if him can do it, me do it too. Ah oh!"

"Yeah, that's great," Tavo said marveling at Bells optimism. "Wish you luck. You got Dee locked up, right?"

"Yeah, mon. Him lock up safe and sound. Me put him in a cell with old Moses."

Moses was a harmless, old, deaf mute beggar who wandered into the jail each night for a place to sleep, not unlike Otis of Mayberry. "Me no put him in with any of de other criminals." Bell said. "Dem would eat him alive fe true! Me feel sorry for him when him go a Kingston. Him nah last a week in dere. Dem goin fuck him like cow. Beat him too!"

"That's what I want to reason about," Tavo said. "Doesn't seem right for him to be treated that severe."

"Me agree. Never arrest no hippie mon fe ganja before. But dis one interfere wid our herb business and dat no right. We all make a little money from dat and me here seh dis man is really a informer de CIA dem sen come fe arrest de good hippie smuggler. Dat nuh right. Smuggler help we, buy we ganja.

Now dis mon want stop dat good life. Dat foolishness mon!" Bell popped the cap off another Red Stripe and chugged it down in one swallow, belched and wiped his mouth. "Tavo, you is alright. You deliver dis man and him breads right to we. Make we look good to de Kingston bosses; like we doing we jobs, catch a big time drug mon! Now him a sacrifice, just like de ram goat. Smuggling, de herb business, wi go on same way. You one national hero, mon!" Ding-Dong smacked him soundly on the back and pushed another beer at him.

Tavo looked at the beer frowned, picked it up and took a sip. "Look, man the American government might not be real pleased about this." He said, worry lines wrinkling his brow.

Ding Dong tried to ignore his concern, brushed some imaginary lint from his pressed trousers "Me no business wid dat. Me soon gone a foreign. Soon be another John Wayne. You will see!"

"What if he were to escape?" Tavo wondered out loud, it just came to him, then he said, "You know, like break out or something. You got the money man! Why not let him off? He's learned a damn good lesson! He's not gonna trouble anyone again."

Bell was silent for a while, watching a lizard crawl across his desk. He rolled up newspaper smacked the lizard and chuckled as its eyes popped out of its head. "Me nuh know and me nuh care one way or de other." he said. "Me soon gone, and de judge, him soon gone to someplace call Las Vagus. Say him can triple him money on de gambling tables. So me no business wid dat hippie mon again. Me wi leave it up to you, mon. Whatever you want do wid him is okay by me!"

"Let me see him, Bell."

"No problem. Give him a cold beer. Dat cell well hot and Moses him smell frowzy bad fe true!"

"But I want to talk to him alone. Okay?"

"Ya, mon. Me gone look 'bout some fry fish. Maybe kill a goat, drink some mannish water. We gonna party all night. Bring out the hippie mon," he shouted to his corporal partner.

Dee was led out, looking disheveled and in need of a good delousing. But most of all, he looked terrified. His eyes blinked rapidly and darted all over the place, finally fixing with horror on the dead lizard, belly up on Ding-Dong's desk. The corporal sat him down firmly in a chair in front of Tavo and stepped outside to stand guard with his M16. As soon as he stepped outside, Dee latched on to Tavo, tugging and twisting his shirtfront. "Oh shit man. I can't believe what's happened man!"

"Yeah, looks like your ass is in a sling," Tavo casually agreed.

"Worse than that man. They're talking about years in a Kingston jail on some phony charge of conspiracy to export grass! I can't deal with that man! I can't even stand to spend another minute in this sweatbox! They got me locked up with some crazy man, a real psychopath. Won't say a word, just stares off into space. He'll probably strangle me in my sleep!"

"That's just old Moses. He's harmless, just a deaf mute beggar is all."

"Yeah? Easy for you to say. He smells like a dead fish. Listen, they won't even allow me a phone call. You gotta let the US Embassy know I'm here man. Only tell 'em Jack Williamson is being detained here. Got that? Jack Williamson."

"What the hell are you talking about Dee?"

"Just tell 'em!" he said "Trust me?" Tavo sneered and looked him in the eyes. "Trust You?" he said, "I don't even know who you are! Anyways, you can't make a call cause Negril doesn't have a phone. Besides, the US pulled their embassy staff out yesterday to protest Jamaica's new relations with Cuba." He looked hard at Dee. "If you want me to help, you better level with me!" He said.

Dee looked away, looked out the door "I have leveled with you man," he lied.

"I'm outta here man." Tavo said. "You're on your own. Can't say I didn't try to help you." He reached as far as the door, it quickly hit Dee that he was really leaving. "Wait!" he yelled. "If I tell you the truth, do you swear ta get me outta here?"

"If it's the truth! I might be able to work something out. But only if I believe you. Jerk me around, I walk outta here, and you're on your own."

"All right man. Okay." Dee whispered. "I'm an agent, just an agent that's all."

"Oh ya an agent?" Tavo acted surprised. "What kind a agent—CIA, DEA?"

Dee looked around nervously, put his fingers to his lips whispered, "DEA man. But I'm only a scout, just gathering intelligence that's all. Honest to God!"

"That's all!" Tavo said, pissed now at the nerve of this guy's minimizing attitude. "So. Go on. What did you find out? What did you tell them? You didn't implicate me in anything, did ya?"

"Look man, you seem clean to me. I can't help it if you're under suspicion just because of where you're at and all the activity going on around you. For Christ's sake give me a break!"

"Go on." Tavo said, "you aren't tellin me everything."

"You're okay so far, honest! Nobody's got anything on you. I swear."

"Come on, Dee or Jack, whatever the hell your name is. Give me the whole picture or you're on your own. What about Nick and his partners?"

"Well, that's a different story. First move they make to get another load off this island, they've had it. An interceptor boat's waiting offshore right now."

Tavo pounded the wall with his fist. "Shit. I'm fucked."

"So, you're not mixed up with them" Dee said. "I never said that."

"You tell me. They store their weed in one of my caves. But I didn't give them permission. They threatened me… just moved it in. What the hell could I do? They weren't giving me any money, not paying me anything. So I'm okay right?"

"Sure that's right." Dee agreed a little bit too quickly. Tavo could see he was being had. "Come on man" he said "Your yankin my chain." And he started to walk away.

"Wait!" Dee shouted. "I'll level with ya! If I'm honest, you'll remember your promise, get me out okay?"

"You heard me," said Tavo, "I keep my word long as you don't con me!"

"Okay, okay," he said, "Once busted, these guys sing like birds, you know that. They point the finger at everyone, even their grandmothers! I can't help that; you know how things are. Nothin I can do about it. Anyone mentioned by two others in connection with a crime and that means even just knowing about it can be arrested too. Its called "misprision of a felony."
"And I suppose there ain't no statute of limitations on drugs!" Tavo said. Dee sat silent. His silence was answer enough. How the hell did he get into this mess? "Look, they can't extradite me." Tavo said trying to convince himself, "There's not even an embassy here any more. Come on man, I got a feeling you're not telling me everything, this is your last chance!"

"Okay, okay. This is the truth man! Manley has maybe another year in power, if he's lucky. You see the way he can't even supply his people with rice any more. The CIA don't even have to kill him; they just cut off his aid money make sure he's got no money to operate. The people'll vote him out themselves. Hey man, that's democracy. What can I do?"

"Then what happens?" Tavo asked.

"We got the guy from the other party right in our back pockets. He'll do whatever we want, that means you'll probably be sent home, extradited. I'm sorry man, I didn't tell ya ta come here get involved with those guys. Shit! I'm just doing my job. What do you want from me?"

"God! I'm truly fucked." Tavo groaned.

Thinking Tavo might do something crazy from sheer desperation and not about to let his only hope of help get away, he grabbed a hold of his shirt again. "Look man, I'm really sorry, but I came clean with you. You gotta help me outta here, you promised remember? I'll pull some weight for you, you know get your sentence reduced. You help me; maybe I can get you two to five that ain't too bad. Shit! You woulda got life."

"I'm a draft dodger too. They'll double hang me." Tavo said. "I'll lose my resort, just like Nick said!"

"Just pray McGovern or someone like him gets elected! Come on man, I've told you everything. I promise I'll do what I can for you."

"Ya right, two to five, but I'm a man of my word, I'll see what I can do. Bells started celebrating. It should go on for a couple of days at least, he'll be stinking drunk. I'll get some tin snips… cut you outta here while he's partying."

"Great, man. Do it! Get going. Hurry!"

"Wait! That's the easy part. You can't just walk outta here and expect to calmly board a minibus, pass through immigration and jump on a plane for Miami. They got a mug shot of you. They'll be looking for you on the roads… especially the airports. What you need is a disguise. You know, change your appearance."

"Oh? Yeah right. What'll I do?" he asked.

"Give me a minute. I'm thinking!" Tavo said and took his time before answering, make the guy sweat some like he was… "They'll be looking for a twenty-year old, white, thin, long-haired male. We'll dress you up just the opposite—like a fat Jamaican higgler lady! Yeah, that's it! No one's looking for a fat Jamaican mama!"

"You're outta you're fucking mind man! I can't be no Jamaican woman!"

"Look, no one would ever suspect. That's the only way I see it'll work. My ass is on the line here, too you know." At least he could have some fun with this, considering that everything else was going down the tubes. Why not at least go down laughing?

"Take it or leave it, man," he said. "I'm not going to risk you getting caught making your escape, then finger me for aiding and abetting. I gotta live here man, at least until I 'm extradited. Sure don't want to share a jail cell with you and Moses!"

"Alright, alright." Dee said ready to agree to anything that would get him out of jail. "Go ahead. I got no choice. Just get me outta here!"

Tavo was enjoying himself now, if only for the moment. "It'll take a little time to get your getup together. Just hang tight and don't worry about Moses. He's just a poor old beggar!"

Tavo called for Bell, and Dee/Jack was led back into his cell while Moses was brought out temporarily to kill a goat that Ding-Dong had bought for the celebration.

"Tavo mon, what you plan for dat boy?" Bell asked eyeing him suspiciously.

"Only a lesson in humility. He's going to experience what it's like to be black like you for a while."

Bell looked offended and said, "Me no black mon; me is brown!"

"Just an expression, man. Don't be so touchy!" he said then told him of the escape plan with the tin snips and the disguise.

Ding-Dong roared with laughter "You is a real jokester mon! Dis gonna be de sport of de year, liven up de party fe true!"

"The only thing I need from you, Ding Dong, aside from your cooperation, is a blank immigration landing card, so we can give him a feminine identity to go with his costume."

"No problem mon. Me brother-in-law is de immigration officer. Him will get one, soon come!"

Tavo got Bell to push the Moke to a coughing start and headed back up the West End Road with at least one problem somewhat under control. But before he'd even reached Mandrex curve, something snapped in his head. It sounded like a brittle tree branch breaking off in the wind with a sharp crack. He hoped it wasn't an acid flashback. Then all the events in his past flooded his consciousness, threatened to drive him insane. Like being betrayed by Irene's mother. Losing Irene to Harlen. The humiliation at the induction center. Insulted and abused by Beulah and Crinkles. Being pushed around by Jamie Dice. Insulted by Nick. Set up by Dee/Jack. They all melted together, but instead of making him crazy they energized him. Oddly they emerged into the lyrics of an old Motown song; it exploded in his brain. "You're driving me crazy," the lyrics boomed, but he wasn't crazy. Angry, sure, pissed off like never before, but he knew he wasn't crazy. "You broke my heart cause I couldn't dance," the song echoed on. Did that mean he'd never stood up for himself, faced his problems squarely? "You didn't even want me around," it blasted. And why should Irene want him around if he had no guts? He thought. But now, the song belted words of encouragement: "And now I'm back, to let you know I can really shake 'em down!" Yeah! That was how he felt! He was going to shake Dice, screw him up good. No more Mr Nice Guy pushed all over the place. "I can really move," the lyrics shouted. "I'm in the groove." Yeah! That was more like it! He could move! He was in the groove! His feverish, stressed out brain was forming a plan to stop that load of dope, stop that sick son of a bitch pirate Dice for good. He had to save his ass too, no one else would! Then it came to him on the song's melody, the reverberations of the song's lyrics that wouldn't stop. "I can mash potatoes; I can do the twist. /Now tell me, baby. /Do you like it like this?" Yes, he liked it. Loved it! He'd show that Rosenthal too. What did he have to lose, after losing everything already? “Tell me! /Tell me! /Just work, work and don’t get lazy. / Watch me now,” the song egged him on, pushed him on. All he had to do was work out the details, fine-tune everything. Maybe, just maybe, he’d come out of this smelling like a rose yet. If he stayed up all night, worked out his plan over and over again. He’d have to keep those plates spinning in the air with great skill: timing would be everything and his whole hometown would be shouting.

As soon as the first light streaked the dawn’s sky, he headed straight for Garth’s. Luckily, Mona was not there. He talked Garth into letting him borrow an old dress of hers, even her Sunday wig, claiming they were for some carnival festivity at the police station—not a total lie. When he arrived at the station, not much had changed. Bell was really plastered but in good spirits and Tavo set about cutting a small hole in the side of the tin trailer. But this was more difficult than he first imagined. To begin with, he had to first drill a small hole to get the snips to take a first bite. All he had was the tiny drill on his Swiss army knife. But after about an hour he succeeded. In another hour’s time, he’d cut an opening about the size of his fist—enough to see Dee and Moses, just large enough to pass the costume through. Dee poked out his nose. He was covered with sweat he looked terrified. “Jesus Christ, man,” he whispered. “What took you so long? I thought I was going to be murdered. When those cops brought Moses back in here late last night he had blood all over him, right up to his armpits. He must have murdered a dozen people!”

“Sorry man” Tavo said. “Thought he was harmless, guess even an old beggar’s got his limit! Listen, I got a can of black shoe polish. Strip down and cover yourself with it. Then tie one of those old pillows around your waist with a torn bed sheet. Better tie Moses’ pillow on your ass too. Then put this dress on and this wig. I even brought lipstick—make it look good! But before you get all dolled up, better spend some time enlarging that hole with these snips, so's you can crawl out. It's slow going and I'm not cutting any more. Tins stronger than I thought."

Tavo left and joined Bell for a couple of cold ones as Jack/Dee worked feverishly away on the trailer.

Bell didn't want to miss seeing Dee jump out of that cell looking like a Jamaican mama. So the two sat hiding behind a Banyan tree, quietly sipping their brews no more than a few feet away.

The afternoon wore on, and Dee managed to get a fair-sized hole cut so they could partially see into the cell. They watched with amusement as he stripped down and began smearing the polish all over himself. But they weren't the only two interested. Moses was not amused he was enthralled. He watched in wonder as Dee transformed from an ugly caterpillar into a beautiful, albeit portly, butterfly. Then to Tavo and Bell's amazement a magnificent, throbbing erection standing straight up at least two feet, poked up like a base ball bat from Moses's torn trousers! What he lacked in vocal abilities, he more than made up for in sexual equipment. Moses began uttering the first sounds anyone in Negril had ever heard him make. It was like a soft, low moaning, an almost joyful whimpering. At the same time, he grasped his huge woodrow in both hands and began rubbing it up and down furiously, really flogging the Bishop. His eyes bugged out wide like a wild animal and a dribble of spit hung in a long strand from his quivering chin.

"I'm getting outta here, man!" Dee shouted, forgetting where he was. "This guy's nuts!" He began crawling headfirst through the opening. But when his head and torso emerged into freedom, he got stuck—and the expression on his face changed from relief to extreme horror. His head and upper body jolted back and forth like a piston, as if someone were pulling and pushing him from behind. Moses had mounted him and was humping Dee's pillowed backside with the fury of a sex starved Harry Reems.

Tavo rushed over and ordered him to be quiet, grasped him by the shoulders and gradually eased him all the way out so that Moses was forced to relinquish his powerful love grip. But as soon as Dee was upright, Moses shot out of that hole like a cannonball, his purple pulsating prong grasped tightly in his fist, holding it like a spear. He made a ferocious leap for Dee, wrapped his arms and legs tightly around his right thigh, and humped it like a horny bloodhound. Dee shook his leg like he'd stepped into a hornet's nest and tried to pry Moses's head back with both hands, but to no avail. Moses hung on like a snapping turtle to a stick. The love dance was soon over though, and, with a final moan of pleasure, Moses shot his load onto his shoe-polished leg then fell to the ground trembling, his eyes rolled back into his head. He then crawled slowly back to the cell's opening and passively climbed inside, looking embarrassed because of his amorous display.

"Well, old buddy," said Tavo, suppressing a belly laugh. "Looks like the disguise works. It sure fooled old Moses. All you gotta do now is re-polish your leg where he squirted you. I even got you a blank landing card!"

"Good God!" Dee gasped trying to wipe Moses' cum off with a corner of his dress. "That crazy fucker was strong as a bull! Get me outta here!"

"Hold on," Tavo said, not wanting to end the fun so soon. "Hide behind that fig tree over there. Let me scout the way first—make sure no one's watching." When Dee crouched behind the tree, Tavo walked back to the station to say so long to Bell, and found him rolling on the floor with a piece of masking tape plastered over his mouth to muffle the bellows of his laughter, looking like he was about to explode. He ripped the tape free when he saw Tavo. "Mon, dat is de funniest thing me eber see," he exulted. "Me have to block me mouth to stop de laughter. Old Moses get himself one fine piece a pussy! What a time! Me not only get rich, but me have de time of me life too. Oh, mon! Me love you hippies! Fe true!"

The scene put a shine on his day as well, but it was far from over. Much was left to do, and a lot of luck and timing would be needed to bring it off. As for Dee, he should be home free—just hop on a minivan and head for the Sangster Airport in Mo-Bay. Tavo presented him with a bunch of bright pink anthurium flowers to add to his disguise; wished him luck then asked if Dice was captured, would he, Tavo, be in any hot water? Dee/Jack didn't think so, unless Dice were to use his land to store the marijuana first and then get caught with it. The pressure would be off him, if he could somehow abort Dice's drug run and any and all future smuggling attempts from his property. But that was a big if!

26

"I am going to be
Your number one"

John Holt & the Paragons

"If you a bull bucker
I man a duppie conqueror"

Peter Tosh

"I'm in the groove; I can really move; I can really shake 'em down." That same old song, the one by the Contours, from Motown was still assaulting his brain, it wouldn't quit. It encapsulated all that he would no longer tolerate it gave him strength gave him resolve. Nick's movie may be over, but his was just beginning. He dressed in his best-flowered shirt and corduroy Levi's and headed for the Cafe and his date with Irene. Too bad Rosenthal had to be there.

But neither one was there when he arrived, so he pulled a chair up to the pool bar, which was packed as usual with the "in crowd". He was a little early; the sun had another half-hour before it set and lit up the sky with its brilliant colors. He didn't have to wait long, minutes later; he watched Irene and Harlen enter through the canopy-covered archway at the front entrance.

Irene was as gorgeous as ever, and Harlen just as stiff, like he was about to receive a rectal exam. Tavo walked over. Sure, he was nervous, but he also felt centered confidant now. He pulled that caper off with Dee "no problem mon", and that Contours melody still swirled around in his head. It had become his mantra now. Not given to him by some East Indian but arising spontaneously out of his Motown roots, from the Buddha of SOUL. It gave him transcendence, made him feel almost invincible. He was in the groove! When he walked up to Harlen and Irene softly whistling 'Do You Love Me' Harlen made no pretence of civility, no handshake and that was fine with Tavo. But before Irene could say anything Harlen sprang to stiff attention, insisted that they get a table right away, his asthma was acting up, triggered, he thought, by allergies to either plant pollen or birds. He was very allergic to birds. Remembering John's duck, Tavo didn't even try to suppress his chuckle, and Harlen glared at him through watery eyes, wiping his nose on a monogrammed handkerchief. A waiter showed them to an outdoor table at the edge of the cliff with an excellent view of the sea and a distant view of Tavo's property.

As soon as they were seated and had ordered cocktails, Rosenthal laid into him. His only reprieve was when a hummingbird hovered over their flower arrangement on the table, causing Harlen to interrupt himself, take repeated sucks on his pocket respirator inhaler and wave his arms like windmill, trying to shoo the hummer away. Through his gasps, wheezes and arm waving he managed to spit out, "I'm waiting for that explanation regarding those illicit activities I observed taking place on your land yesterday"—cough, hack, sputter. "By now I'm sure you had time to invent some wild tale! Let's hear it so we can get this over with. Irene needs to see for herself what a psychopathic liar you really are." Wheeze, sneeze, spasm.

Just as Tavo started to speak up in his defense, he was diverted by something taking place on the sea right below the horizon. Something he had not expected to happen until well after dark. But here it was. A small fleet of dugout cotton wood canoes had gathered straight out to sea from Nick's—and from

Banana Shout. For all practical purposes, they were a group of fishermen putting out to sea. Each small boat had a kerosene lantern, as if they were doing nothing more than getting ready for a night of bottom fishing for grouper. But Tavo knew better. Soon one light at a time would go out. Then they would paddle quietly in to shore under the cover of darkness, head straight to his cave where they'd load the bales of green gold and transfer them to Jamie Dice, waiting in his mother ship just out of sight over the horizon. The Coast Guard would bust Dice, along with Tavo for sure now!

Irene broke his concentration she was tugging at arm he hadn't realized he hadn't said a word just sat there humming 'Do You Love Me' "Well, we're waiting to listen to your feeble excuses." Harlan said, "Then I've got every intention of turning you in to the authorities!"

"Harlen, do you have to be so pushy?" Irene said. "Tavo will explain everything. I'm sure of it" But she didn't look too sure, she couldn't figure why Tavo was just sitting there in a trance, just humming and whistling some old Motown song.

Then Harlen let out another wheezing gasp and swatted at a night bat buzz-bombing his head, it plucked an insect out of the air inches from his face. He sucked harder than ever on his inhaler almost swallowing it.

Tavo jumped up knocking over their drinks, surprising everyone. Harlens fruit punch landed in his lap. Tavo started shouting to a Ska song playing on Nick's loud speakers. "Not everyone can cha-cha-cha. Not all can do the twist. But everybody, and especially me, can do the Jamaica Ska! Watch me now! I'm in the groove," he yelled.

Harlen stopped sucking on his inhaler tried to wipe the smoothie off his starched bermudas with the tablecloth. His face was contorting, he started to look like that evil skull again, the one Tavo had hallucinated at the induction center. He shook an accusing finger at him, he was spitting anger, white froth bubbled at the corners of his mouth. "You see, Irene." He shouted, "He's certifiably insane. All those drugs he takes have turned his mind to mush. All he can do is babble in schizophrenic parody! He's the biggest character disorder I've ever encountered! We're getting out of here!"

"No wait," Tavo shouted. "I've got business to take care of for an hour or so. Please don't leave. I'll join you for desert. Something real important just came up. I gotta go, but please don't leave till I get back. I promise I'll set everything straight!" Harlen started to say something but Irene cut him off. "We'll wait," she cried out, as Tavo bolted from the table like a madman and charged out of the café. He headed straight for Banana Shout. This was his only chance, and he had to work quickly. Had to make it work! "Just work, work, work, and don't get lazy. Watch me now," he sang out.

When he reached the door of his house he charged through, stripped all his clothes off and proceeded to do just as Dee/Jack had done: smear dark shoe polish all over his body, all but his face, until he was as black as the night outside. He reached under his bed and retrieved one of the Halloween glow sticks John had left him. He held it in his hands he stroked it like a pet animal and grinned "I am in the groove now," he sang softly, insanely, and crept silently to his cave, naked, invisible in the night. He strained his neck to peer over the cliff and into the cave, where all the canoes were lined up at its mouth. Three Jamaicans were carefully loading them with bales of marijuana. When they were all filled, they'd paddle out in a group to keep watch on one another—making sure no one got greedy and took off with a load. "Watch me now," Tavo sang under his breath, as he carefully slit the glow tube with his Swiss army knife. He drenched his head with the glowing green chemical and smeared the remainder on his hands.

He looked like a disembodied glowing head and hands, floating ghostlike, duppy like, in the night breeze. He crept over to the cave's entrance. He was no more than a few feet from the canoes, hidden from view by a large coral rock. He could smell the sweat of the workers. He crouched down low tightening the muscles in his calves then sprung up with all the force he had in his rubbery knees and landed smack dab in the middle of the loading activities. He screamed a string of curses at the top of his lungs: "RASSHOLE!! BUMBA CLAAT!!" "I CAN MASH POTATOES!!!" "I CAN DO DE TWIST!! NOW TELL ME RASSHOLES, DO YOU LIKE IT LIKE THIS!!"

The loaders and canoe paddlers went into total shock completely terrorized. Their eyes bugged out like saucers and their hair stood on end, they looked like cartoon characters with their fingers stuck in electric sockets. In their haste to escape this demonic duppy Rollin calf, they overturned the wobbly canoes, spilling all the dope in the ocean. It was like a hand grenade had been dropped in that cave. The loaders plunged into the water and swam with the speed of Mark Spitz to the bobbing boats, righting them again, and paddling away like forty-five horsepower engines powered them. Their paddles churned the sea like the blades of an electric fan on high speed.

Some of the men clung to the sides of the canoes, not being able to scramble on board fast enough. They forgot about the ganja completely and it floated slowly out to sea, carried in every direction by the currents and tides. There were three or four bales left in the cave and Tavo kicked them into the ocean, as he flapped about doing the mash potato and rotating his hips to the twist, jumping up high in the air and landing finally in a James Brown split. He screamed at the top of his lungs now screamed to the heavens "I can do the monkey; I can do the twist; Come on everybody watch me now do the Banana Shout! This is my land, Dice you sleazy punk!"

Jamie Dice's mother ship wouldn't set sail tonight loaded down with pot for the Coast Guard to intercept, and he was sure that Dice's days of moving dope off his land were finished. If he knew Jamaicans as well as he thought he did, they'd never set foot on his property again and risk another encounter with that "Green Winnie Rollin Calf Duppie!" It had taken over half-hour to foil Dice. Just barely enough time left to meet Irene. All he had to do was wash off the glow and shoe polish. Then he'd show that Rosenthal too. "I can really move. I'm in the groove," he sang with gusto "The whole town is Banana shouting!"

But the green glow on his face and hands wouldn't wash off. Then, he remembered John saying, "It glows until the chemical reaction is finished, can't be wiped off." Shit! As for the shoe polish, all he managed to do was smear it around—maybe lighten it up a bit. He still had the skin color of a dark African. But he had no options now. Didn't even know where Irene and Harlen were staying, so he couldn't meet up with her later. She could be leaving any time now; he had to hurry! He put on a long-sleeved shirt and long pants thinking he could at least disguise the shoe polish. Now only his glowing head and hands showed—and he made straight for Nick's. "Now tell me, baby, do you like it like this?" he sang, "Here comes the Big Banana!"

He entered Nick's to a reception identical to the one in the cave. When the bartenders saw his head, glowing like a green jack-o-lantern, they hopped over the bar, leaving their red fezzes behind and leaped off the forty-foot cliff into the sea below. The waiters, cooks and cashiers followed, leaving only stoned bewildered customers and bar patrons. But they soon grooved on his hippie voodoo. They applauded and cheered the appearance of this headless horseman wonder of the counterculture. But not Rosenthal. When Tavo walked over to their table, he was forcefully pulling on Irene's arm, demanding that they get out of this madhouse. Looked like he was hurting her.

"Sec what that psychopath has done now, Irene," he tried to yell but was too hoarse now from his allergic bird reactions to do more than squeak. "He's played upon these poor Negroes' superstitions scared them to death. It's his idea of some sick joke!"

Tavo's heart was beating double time. He was pumped up with adrenaline like Sam Smart on an ounce of coke free-base. He was so pissed off at seeing Harlen hurting Irene he was seeing triple. "Now I am back to let you know I can really shake 'em down," he shouted right into Harlens face.

Harlen turned red like a devil sputtering now trying to catch his breath he tried to berate Irene forever having gone out with Tavo, let alone considering marrying him. But his voice had just about failed him. He sounded like worn out sandpaper. Irene was trying to defend herself from his ramblings the best she could. But she looked uncertain herself. Who could blame her given that Tavo was green, glowing, and possibly even slimy? To say nothing about that song he kept singing continuously.

"I've had it," Tavo shouted. "If you hurt Irene I'm gonna lose it!"

Harlen grinned like a creepy skull and shook his finger in Tavo's face "As if you haven't already lost it!" he rasped "And now you're threatening me? You sadistic, felonious little draft dodger." He turned and faced Irene. "I've been patient enough with your regressive infantile behavior. We're leaving!" Harlen grabbed her around the waist and tried to pull her away. She let loose a screech. "Stop! Stop! Ouch! You're hurting me!"

That catapulted Tavo over his limit. "And now I am back to let you know I can really shake 'em down," he yelled out.

He picked up the first thing handy, a slice of gooey, cream-covered banana cream cake that was sitting untouched on a table next to them, and mashed it dead center into Rosenthal's scowling ugly stone face.

Harlen let go of Irene and just stood there, the sticky goop running down his face. He mumbled something about suing Tavo about litigation in court, reporting him to the authorities. He was fuming and muttering psycho-babble, he ordered Irene to follow him, to leave immediately, persevering now-hysterical "I'm the doctor! I'm the doctor! I'm the doctor" He mumbled, but didn't sound so sure himself anymore.

Just then, they heard a noisy furious quacking "Quack! Quack! Quack!" The pair of ducks from Nick's old swimming pool waddled over to them, curious about all the commotion and hungry for the pieces of cake on the ground by Harlen's feet. One nipped Harlen's shin to make him move from his guard over the banana cake and the other rapidly flapped its wings in a warning confirmation of his partner's nip. Harlen shrieked in terror, looked as scared as those ganja loaders in the cave. He fumbled for his inhaler and ran out of Nicks, sucking on the respirator bumping into customers still breathlessly trying to order Irene to follow but he only sounded like stale air rushing out of a punctured inner tube.

To Tavo's surprise, Irene remained. He wouldn't blame her for leaving, he had to look crazy, he was acting insane, but she didn't leave with Harlen. Instead she embraced him and planted a passionate kiss square on those green lit-up lips, while the two ducks contentedly gobbled up the cake crumbs at their feet. Tavo kissed her back, a kiss he wanted to last forever, but they finally stopped and gazed into each other's eyes. Then he pulled out that old crumpled napkin from his corduroys; the one John gave him, the one Irene gave to John at Alvin's Finer Bar. "Just want to know," he said, "what you wrote on this? I've kept it all this time!"

"I still love you!" she said.

EPILOGUE

Irene divorced Harlen and married Tavo, and they stayed on in Jamaica, and continued to develop Banana Shout Resort. Besides Banana Shout they developed two blond, blue-eyed pickney—a girl for him and a boy for her. Dee/Jack was never heard of or seen again, although he was reported have quit the DEA. He was teased too much, really embarrassed, so he joined a Christian religious cult in Waco Texas.

Jamie Dice never attempted to use Tavo's land for smuggling again. He was later apprehended while waiting for a small freighter to unload tons of pot in a Mississippi swamp, chased by coon dogs, he was run up a Cyprus tree. He's now serving twenty years after ratting out his partners.

Len Stern disappeared completely from the Jamaican scene after the green glowing duppy incident in Tavos cave, and after being rated out by Dice. Thems that know where he is don't say.

Michael Manley was voted out of office by a starving majority, and, with the financial help of Ronald Reagan and George Bush, the newly elected Prime Minister, Edward Seaga, led an aggressive campaign to eradicate ganja fields and blow up clandestine air strips all over the island. Although this stopped most of the flow of pot to the States, grass was replaced in Jamaica by a far more profitable and dangerous commodity—cocaine. Like Prohibition days why smuggle beer when there was whisky?

Nick was no longer capable of running the cafe, too strung out addicted to his good stuff, and so with a spike in his now golden arm, he sold the Cafe to two young enterprising Americans. It took a lot of cash now to stay even with his habit. He is said to be wandering to this day, still in search of the perfect high.

Mannie built his resort down the road from Banana Shout Resort and had enough left over for his cattle farm. He sent all his pickney to secondary school. One is attending Cambridge University in England. Some good came from all those tax payers money after all.

Ding-Dong Bell went to Hollywood but never made it into the movies. His accent was too thick, and there wasn't much demand for Jamaican actors. Instead he wound up on an LAPD SWAT team raiding crack dens. But when the mood strikes him he's known to point his thirty eight at crack dealers and say "Go on rass hole make me day!"

Heavy Higher still lives in his tree and sells his carvings to tourists. He's also developed a nice side business of selling roots cures and herbal medicine.

Garth runs a restaurant called Rocky Bell with his brother-in-law. And once a year on the full harvest moon he and Tavo venture to the Warf Club to drink "De Blue Stone Waters." But Tavo never ever questions his beliefs in the 'Rollin Calf'. He knows how real that green devil mon can be!

Barrington continues to run his successful veggie restaurant, the Hungry Lion. He claims that even though Jamaica lost the revolution the powers in control can't keep his people down forever. "Don't romp with nigga mon! Nigga mon broke ya bones!"

Mike Dorfman built his small travel business, Island Hotline, into the biggest Caribbean travel agency in the United States and received a gold plaque from the Jamaican Tourist Board. He still charges Tavo twenty percent commission on his bookings. His revolution died when Mayor Daly's cops busted heads in Lincoln Park.

Clyde is still a building contractor but no longer strays from home. He sometimes consults with Tavo when he thinks the worms might take his hand again. After all Tavo was able to summon a Green Duppy on his resort. Not bad for a hippie mon.

Donna produces blockbuster movies in Hollywood. She possessed the perseverance and drive to succeed when most give up. Maybe there is something to that Swami meditation. Every Halloween she sends Tavo a greeting card with a jack-o-lantern on it.

Striker continues to smuggle shrunken heads from Borneo, now that the heat was turned up on smuggling pot and America no longer welcomes Cuban immigrants.

Jane, Nick's ex-wife, made her way back to Jamaica from Haiti. She swore off all drugs and married the Chinese caterer who Norman threw into the ocean at the wedding, took responsibility for her children, and turned out to be a fine mom. She helps manage the Golden Chopsticks Restaurant in Kingston.

After spending two years in the Betty Ford Clinic, Betty Lou also is clean from drugs. She now counsels others with similar problems.

Manistoe Lowellen the third joined the Air Force as a Career Officer after the Vietnam War was over, paying for his oversized uniform. He was the first Officer to come out of the closet and demand equal rights for gays in the military.

Norman Silverstein, after recuperating in a private sanitarium, went to Colombia, South America to smuggle emeralds.

Harlen Rosenthal also spent a short stay in a mental institution to recuperate from his trip to Jamaica. He closed his private practice and is now a paid hack doing only Forensic Psychiatry, testifying for criminal defense attorneys using the insanity plea. He almost had one claim to national fame but the defense decided to go with "If it doesn't fit you must acquit" rather than an insanity plea.

Beulah and Crinkles were arrested for burning down an African American church in Key Largo, and sentenced to long jail terms.

Sam Smart now hangs out in his bar The Pirate's Cave on Negril's West End. His cocaine dealing days came to an abrupt end when the new Jamaican political leaders ordered him to back off. They considered it far too lucrative a business to have a spaced out freak in control. The political dons could do a much better job, and ensure that the higher ups got their fair share.

John Curtis' duck 'Fuzzy' died of old age. He buried him on the front lawn of his small suburban house in Southfield Michigan. As a memorial he built a large thirty-foot iron sculpture of a black fist clutching a large yellow banana over his pet's grave. He named it HOME TOWN BANANA SHOUT. Every Halloween he paints KING OBEAH HIPPIE MON in green glow on the sculpture's thumb.

Mrs Goldberg took a little convincing after Tavo and Irene got married, but came around completely when their pickneys were born. She now visits them in Jamaica every year, and boasts to all and sundry of her "daughter and son-in-law and their resort paradise in the Caribbean."

The peanut farmer, Jimmy Carter, was elected to office and granted amnesty to all draft evaders—evaders sounded better than dodgers—so Tavo could go home again. But he chose not to do so. Jamaica was his home. It wasn't until 1994, when his children were in their teens, that he made a trip to Washington, DC, with the family. The first place they visited was the huge, black wall of stone carved with the names of the Vietnam War dead. His children wanted the whole story. Why was Tavo crying? Why were other people crying? Why were they taking pictures and rubbing paper against the wall to capture impressions of a name? He could give them no explanation that could make that war understandable. A distant wail of a saxophone blowing in the wind somewhere with hurt offered a lament. But nothing could ever make that war all right… make it understandable.

9 781928 704737